# Sadie June, Who Were You?

Taylor Ashely

Taylor Ashely

ISBN: 9798995453802



Cover created on Canva by the author.
Follow on Instagram: @taylor.ashely.author

Taylor Ashely

# Prologue

## Jimmy

♪♪♪

The sun is coming up as I brew some coffee. I look out the window while waiting for my coffee. My eyes are looking outside, but my brain isn't processing anything that they are seeing.

Last night is still reeling through my mind. My baby sister, Sadie, invited me to go to a movie with her and Gen, her best friend. It was an indie chick flick from a local director who prides himself on having a John Hughes vibe.

*The female lead was completely oblivious to the fact that her best male friend was head-over-heels for her. It was one of those stories that you can find all over the YA section of the library. He sits back, watching her crush on other guys while he stays in the friend zone. He hopes that if he waits long enough that she will realize how perfect they are for one another and fall in love with him. Unfortunately, she ends up falling for the wrong guy. The guy that she falls for is pretty much his polar opposite. He has to watch the girl he loves get her heart broken by a total jerk. It was very* Sixteen Candles*.*

*Throughout the movie, I found myself turning to watch Gen instead of the film on the screen. Her whole body lights up when she laughs. The light from the screen kept cascading upon her face and enhancing her natural beauty. Seeing her in the dim light from the screen brought up so many memories of our movie marathons over the years.*

*At the end of the night, Sadie fell asleep in the car. I drove Gen home and walked her to her front door. I held myself back from kissing her. As I've done hundreds, if not thousands, of times before. I kept kicking my own ass the whole drive home for not making a move.*

*I decided last night though, for the first time ever, that I am no longer going to hold back. I'm going to discuss it this morning with Sadie before I go to work. She is the only reason that I have waited for so long. I love her so much and I don't want her to hate me for being in love with her best friend. I want to make a move, but not without having Sadie's blessing first. I've waited long enough. Plus, if she knows, maybe she can give me some sort of idea of Gen's feelings towards me. She flirts with me pretty often, but for all I know, she might flirt with everyone. It could even be some long drawn-out inside joke between her and Sadie. I wouldn't put it past the two of them. They are always causing trouble together.*

I'm pouring my coffee when Sadie comes into the kitchen. She is in her stretchy pink athletic jacket and black leggings. Her auburn hair is pulled tightly into a ponytail at the top of her head

*She looks awfully peppy for someone who just woke up. If I didn't think she would hit me, I would call her out for looking like a cheerleader. She hates cheerleaders!*

"Hey, Sade, can we talk for a minute? There is something I need to talk to you about."

I glance at the clock on the oven. It's five-thirty.

"When I get back, okay? I am going for my morning run. I'll be right back." Sadie kisses my cheek. "Love you."

*She runs every morning on the trails behind our house. This is her daily regimen, pre-coffee. I have no idea how she functions enough to run without some sort of caffeine in her system. I can barely form sentences prior to my first cup.*

"Uh, yeah, okay. I'll see you when you get back, I guess." I try not to let her see my disappointment.

*I've waited almost seven years. I guess I can wait a few minutes longer.*

Sadie grabs her water bottle and goes out the door, jogging toward the trail in the woods.

*What am I even going to say to her? 'Hey, by the way, I am crazy in love with your best friend and have been since I was fourteen.' Yeah, that would go over well. Not!*

I stare out the window and it starts snowing big fluffy flakes. This is the first snowfall of the season.

*It feels like a fresh start. It is fitting for today, I think. After I tell Sadie, I am going to invite her and Gen to go check out some new albums with me today after work. Then, depending on Sadie's reaction, I am going to make a move. Honestly, I may need to just bite the bullet and make a move whether Sadie is mad or not. Something inside me is urging me to act on these impulses as soon as possible. I feel like our relationship is coming to a metaphorical head. If I don't do something soon, I feel like it might be too late.*

I am contemplating different ways today could work out: *A*, Sadie and Gen could both hate me for it; *B*, Sadie could hate me while Gen loves me; *C*, Sadie could laugh in my face and Gen could think I'm an idiot, etc.

I am tapping my fingers on the table incessantly.

*Where the hell is Sadie? It seems like it has been forever.*

I look over at the oven to check the time. It's been an hour since Sadie left. Something in the pit of my stomach tightens.

*She is never gone this long on a run and definitely not without a jacket. It's snowing and she loathes the cold.*

I decide to go find her. I walk outside, heading straight for the path that she disappeared down. The snow is making the ground slick beneath my feet. I grip tree trunks as I go to keep from slipping.

"Sadie! Sadie! Sadie June, where are you?" I am yelling her name like I am calling a wandering dog back home. The sound is reverberating off the bare trees. I stop to listen. I don't hear her footsteps in any direction. She is nowhere to be found, so far.

I keep advancing into the woods. I turn the corner of the trail and spot the pink of her jacket on the ground. I run toward it and realize Sadie is sprawled on the ground. Her auburn hair is caked with blood. I just start screaming her name, willing her to respond in some way. She doesn't move at all. I stop dead in my tracks to watch for breathing. She isn't moving. Not a single muscle.

"*No, no, no, no!* No! *Sadie!*" I am sobbing in an instant. Everything in front of me is turning to blurred colors. I scoop Sadie into my arms. My amazing little sister and best friend lay lifeless in my arms. "I love you so much, Sadie. Please. Please don't go. I need you. Gen needs you. Mom and Dad need you. Please. Please, God. *Sadie!*"

*It hurts to breathe. This is the hardest thing I have ever done.*

I keep walking, zombie-like toward the house.

*I have to get her inside to where it's warm.*

I'm holding her tight to me and rocking her like I used to do when we were small and she would get hurt or cry.

I'm almost back to the house when I see the back door open and hear Mom let out a terrible guttural scream. She is sobbing as I walk into the kitchen and lay Sadie on the floor lightly.

"My baby. My poor, poor baby. Sadie, sweetie, please. Wake up. Talk to me. Please wake up. Please. *Please.*" Mom is hysterical and hugging Sadie to her chest.

Dad walks into the kitchen, drawn by the commotion. He is immediately broken by the sight of his precious daughter lying lifeless on the floor. He collapses to his knees and screams.

*911. I need to call 911. Sadie needs help.*

I pull my phone from my pocket and dial.

"911. What's your emergency?"

"There's been an accident. My, my baby sister is dead. She is *so* bloody and she isn't breathing." I am crying so hard and trembling. I'm not sure how easily understood I am at this moment, but I can't calm my tears.

"I need you to try and calm down a bit. What's your address?"

"850 Juniper Way." At this point, I am only a moment shy of hyperventilating.

"I have an ambulance on their way. How old is she?"

"Nineteen. She is only nineteen." My voice is shaking as much as my body is. The tears are still streaming down my face.

*This can't be real. This cannot be happening.*

The ambulance took an excruciating six minutes and fifty-seven seconds to get to our house. My parents are both crying and holding onto Sadie's hands. I can't stop pacing and trembling.

Three paramedics come through the door. Two are carrying a stretcher. The other has a defibrillator. They try CPR first. When that is unsuccessful, they cut open Sadie's shirt and place the defibrillator paddles on her chest. They try to revive her for a full ten minutes. When they stop trying, we all know that it is officially over.

"Time of death, six fifty-seven. Mark it down." One of the paramedics said this as if he was stating the weather or what he had for breakfast instead of world-shattering news. He looks up at the three of us with sympathetic eyes. The other paramedics load Sadie's lifeless corpse onto the stretcher and take her away.

I'm sobbing uncontrollably now, as I watch the ambulance drive away with lights, but no sirens. That's when it hits me.

*Someone has to tell Gen. My parents are in no condition to speak to Gen. I guess it's left up to me.*

I reluctantly take my phone back out of my pocket and dial Gen's number. It rings three times before she answers.

"Hello? Jimmy? Why are you calling me?" She sounds like she just woke up due to my call.

I am still sobbing and can barely speak. "Sadie died."

Gen lets out an atrocious scream that I never want to hear again in my life and then hangs up.

*I just had to break the heart of the girl I love while my heart is breaking too. How am I supposed to go on without Sadie?*

# Chapter One

## Genevieve

The freezing rain is drizzling down my window pane when I open my eyes. This is the first Saturday since everything changed.

*A week ago, I woke up to Sadie dancing around my room while raiding my closet. That was something that I had grown accustomed to: her auburn locks flipping side-to-side with the beat of music from the 1980s while tossing around my clothes. I am really going to miss that, along with a million other little things that Sadie had forced me to love. At first, I had found Sadie's love for the 80's beyond annoying, but now I find myself in tears wishing that David Bowie was playing quietly on my radio like it had last week.*

I drag myself out from beneath my heavy comforter and prepare myself for my least favorite activity: human interaction. I know my mother will attempt to talk to me. I would just stay in my room all day, but I need coffee. My feet lightly press against the cold hardwood.

*I hate my feet being cold. This is going to be an extremely long winter. It is only the second week of November and it's already been in the 20's every day for the past week.*

I throw on my gray Hamstead High hoodie and slowly open my door.

As I step into the hall, I can hear Mom in the kitchen. She must be making breakfast. She is humming a tune that sounds vaguely familiar, but I can't quite place it. I make my descent to Hell. The bottom stair squeaks as I step on it. I cringe, hoping that Mom didn't hear. As I slowly slink into the kitchen, Mom stops humming and looks at me with sadness in her eyes.

*Normally, we are very close, but this past week has been awful. I don't want to talk about it, but she does. She cannot accept the fact that sometimes I just want to shut out the entire world until I feel better.*

"Gen, honey, how are you holding up?"

"Mom. Don't. *Please.*"

I don't even try to hide my exasperated sigh.

"You need to talk about this eventually."

"Yeah, maybe I do, but not today."

*Even I could hear the snarkiness in my voice. Later, I will feel bad about acting this way. I know I will. I can't help it though.*

I grab my favorite mug: teal with orange and green polka dots painted on the porcelain.

*Sadie bought this mug at a thrift store in Charleston three summers ago. I have used this mug daily since then and I will continue to use it for the rest of my life.*

I fill the mug with dark coffee and inhale the aroma.

*This is the only unchanging thing in my life right now. I need some sort of stability to keep me grounded so that I don't fall down the rabbit hole of depression.*

"Genevieve, I know that this is going to be difficult. I just want you to know that I am here for you whenever you're ready to talk."

"I know, Mom. Thank you."

*She is trying so hard, but I am* so *not ready to talk about Sadie. It has only been eighty-seven hours and twenty-three minutes without her in my life.*

*Sadie and I met eight years ago when we were eleven. She had just moved into the area from the other side of the country. Most people ignored her because she was the new kid. They treated her like tainted meat. I, on the other hand, gravitated toward her. She was vastly different from anyone that I had ever met. Sadie was completely obsessed with pop culture from the decade that her parents met and fell in love. She was spunky and confident. Even when everyone else was stumbling awkwardly through puberty, she managed to love her wavy auburn hair and the fact that she was easily half a foot shorter than a majority of our classmates. We quickly became inseparable. In the eight years of our friendship, we were only apart for seven days when she went to Florida to see her grandmother. Tuesday morning, that all changed. We became separated forever. Tuesday morning was the day that my best friend died. How is life ever going to be okay again?*

Mom is staring at me as if I might crumble if she even dares to breathe too loudly. I glance in her direction and let out a sigh as I sip at my coffee.

*I wish she would just leave me alone and go shopping or something. Unfortunately, she is scared that something might happen to me if she leaves. I guess that is partially my own fault.*

"Baby girl, we need to get you something to wear tomorrow. Why don't you go shower and get ready? Then, we can go shopping for something."

"I already have something to wear. I want to wear something that I know Sadie liked. She loved my green jumpsuit. She always said it made me look eclectic."

"You're supposed to wear black to a funeral, Gen."

"Black is to show people that you feel bad for *their* loss. I am utterly heartbroken over *my* loss! I'm wearing what Sadie would have wanted."

*Here I go.*

The tears are starting up again.

*Three. Two. One.*

I am crying so hard that I am drooling and can't breathe. My heart is breaking all over again. I'm choking on this terrible lump in my throat.

*Sadie,* my *Sadie, is gone forever.*

Mom has her arms wrapped tightly around me and she is shushing me like an inconsolable infant. I just fold myself into her body and continue to sob. Mom breaks at this point and starts crying too. We drop to the floor, a tangle of grief that cannot be tamed. We stay like this for what feels like hours. When we finally begin to compose ourselves, Mom pulls away just enough to look me in the eye. She just stares at me silently for five or ten minutes.

*This quiet moment with Mom is one that I think I will cherish for the rest of my days.*

"I loved her too, kiddo. She was like a second daughter to me. You know that. We were the Three Amigas." Mom lets out a light chuckle. She still has tears in her hazel eyes. "I know that it doesn't seem like it now, but it will get easier to handle with time. Being without her won't get easier, but getting through the day without tears will eventually."

"How am I supposed to do anything without tears? Everything I do and everywhere I go makes me think of her. We did everything together for almost a decade." I can feel my heart crumbling into pieces.

"It's going to be really hard, but we *will* get through this *together*."

*Sadie did not deserve to die. This is so unfair. Why did such a beautiful soul have to depart this life at only nineteen? I will never understand this. She was beautiful and tenacious and incredible. She had so much ahead of her still. Tomorrow, I will have to face all of these people who will be saying their condolences. All of our friends and classmates will be a sobbing mess and I'm sure I can handle most of them, but there is one who I am dreading seeing: Sadie's brother, Jimmy. It was his voice that broke the news to me that we had both lost our precious Sadie. Normally, he is one of my favorite people though. The thought of seeing him ties my stomach into tight knots.*

My coffee is turning ice cold in my hands. The flavor is bitter in my mouth right now. The knots in my stomach are making me nauseous. I just keep replaying moments shared with Sadie in my head. I am unaware of how much time is passing as I stare off into the abyss. My eyes are completely out of focus and everything in front of me is blurred.

"Gen, are you hungry?" Mom's voice makes me jump and snap out of my own grieving world.

"Hungry? No, not really."

*The truth is: I have only eaten four crackers since I heard the news. Then I proceeded to cry so hard that I threw them all up. My stomach keeps turning into all of these little knots every few minutes or so. It seems like whenever I think that they are finally going to cease for a while, they start right back up. I truly feel like I could go months without eating and would be perfectly fine. The only thing that is going to lead to my demise is living day-to-day without her in my life. Note to self: remember to research if you can actually die from a broken heart.*

Mom is watching me very closely. If I blink for a second too long, she might begin to panic. I know that this is hurting her too. I feel like breaking down again.

*I refuse to let her see me crack against the pressure of grief. She is already trying to coddle me. If I let myself give in, she might threaten to send me back to Dr. Malkowitz.*

*Dr. Leanna Malkowitz is one of the best therapists in the state. I went to therapy with her weekly for two years after Dad died. She wasn't terrible of her own accord. There are only so many times that you can sit there and tell someone that you are upset because you're grieving and going through puberty simultaneously. At one point, about six months after Dad succumbed to his cancer, I had an eating disorder and then about a year later, a suicide attempt. Those were both when I was pulled deep into the thralls of my depression. If it weren't for Sadie and Dr. Malkowitz, I would have never made it through. I don't want to go through therapy again. It was exhausting. Learning to live without someone who has been such a huge part of my daily life is going to be nearly impossible. I don't think spending hundreds of dollars for someone to guide me through it is going to help.*

"I think I am going to go lay back down." I remove myself from my seat at the kitchen table.

"I really wish you wouldn't, Gen. You know that's how it all starts."

"How what starts, Mom? Depression? Newsflash, that has been happening for a while now. Don't worry. I won't let myself go down that horrible road again. I have better coping skills now."

*Am I trying to convince her or myself?*

*After Dad died, I spent the first few weeks in my bed without showering or brushing my hair. When Mom had finally coaxed me out of my room, she helped me shampoo my hair and doused it in a conditioner that smelled of coconuts. Even with the copious amounts of conditioner, my mother had to brush furiously at snarled bunches of hair while I cried out in pain. In the end, we had to cut four inches off of my hair. During those weeks that I stayed in my room, Sadie would call and we would spend silent hours on the phone just listening to one another breathe. She understood that I wanted to be alone, but she didn't want to leave me completely isolated. At that point, we had only been friends for about a year. If anything positive came out of my father's demise, it had to have been the strengthening of my bond with Sadie. Now she is gone, too. What am I left with this time? Absolutely nothing.*

Mom is just staring at me with bewilderment in her eyes.

*She always likes to pretend that I wasn't scarred with a mental illness since the young age of twelve. This just cements my loathing of human interaction.*

Without another word, I turn from the kitchen and head for the solace of my bedroom where I spent hundreds of nights with Sadie watching One Tree Hill, Gossip Girl or some other teen drama.

*If I just stay in the place where the memories are mine and hers alone, I might manage to get through the day a little easier.*

I reach my bedroom door and pause to look at the tiny initials carved in the wood near the handle.

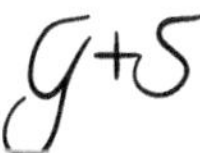

*Sadie etched that in the oak door during the summer between junior high and freshman year. It was a promise that we were a package deal. One never left without the other. Not until Tuesday, that is. That was the summer that we wore tie-dyed everything and lived in the sun-drenched grass behind my house. Both of us had tanned skin by the time school came around. We were giddy with the prospects of the high school years to come when we returned to school that September linked arm-in-arm.*

I open the door and collapse onto my bed, letting the tears fall from my burning eyes. As I lay surrounded by the comfort of my own bed, I feel my phone vibrating. I instinctively reach for it tangled in my blankets. It's a text from Jimmy.

Gen, I need to hear your voice.
Can you call me? Please?

*The last thing I want to do right now is talk to Jimmy. He is an undeniable part of my life, but one that I am not ready to face. If I talk to him, it will undoubtedly turn my mind to that phone call on Tuesday morning. The one that changed everything.*

I'm not ready to talk yet.

Maybe later. Sorry.

*Perhaps sleeping would make it easier to face him. I highly doubt that though.*

I close my eyes and lay in silence. If I lay utterly still, I know that I will drift into sleep eventually. My eyes are wet and burning still. Closing them offers a brief moment of relief. I take a deep breath through my nose and sink further into my pillow.

*I'm with Sadie. We are laughing at ourselves while we pose ridiculously in the mirror. Our smiles are lined with black lips. Our eyes are doused in colorful eyeshadow. Morrisey is blaring from my speaker. Skirts made of tattered tulle and cut band tees are hugging our bodies tightly. Atop our heads are messes of crimped and teased hair. Most people would only dress like this for Halloween or a themed party, not us. This was a random Wednesday last November. We had nothing better to do than to just enjoy each other's company and do something that we loved. This isn't a dream. It's a memory that I will cherish forever.*

A sudden knock at my door startles me out of my memory-filled slumber. Groggily, I sit up and wipe my eyes with the heels of my hands. It takes a moment for my eyes to adjust. It's dark outside now. The only light is coming from the crack beneath my door.

"I'm up. Come in." Mom comes in with a plate of pizza. It smells wonderful and I begin to realize how hungry my body truly is. I take the plate wordlessly and begin scarfing down the pizza.

"I am so happy that you're eating something. I don't want to seem pushy, or like I'm prying into your personal life, but I think you should really call Jimmy. He has called me four times to check on you and he even stopped by earlier. He needs you. I think you really need him too."

"I'll think about it."

"Eat and then you should probably shower. It will help, you know."

I hand my mom the crumb and grease-stained plate, signaling that it was time for her to retreat back downstairs and leave me alone. She looks at me with worry creasing her brows. She lightly brushes my hair from my face with her free hand. I look up at her with my bloodshot eyes. She looks pretty much the same as always, but a bit more worn-down than normal. Grief does that to people.

"Okay. I'll shower first and then I will call Jimmy." I drag myself out of bed.

*I really could use a shower. It will probably help wake me up and make me feel a bit better. Plus, I'm starting to smell like I've been running all day.*

Once in the bathroom, I stare at myself in the mirror.

*I look ragged and like I have been doing hard drugs. Sadie would hate me looking like this. That's it! I'm going to start taking care of myself and make sure that I'm living the way Sadie would want me to.*

The warmth of the shower is soothing the hurt inside me. The shower is normally my favorite place to cry because no one can decipher tears from the running water hitting my face. Right now, no tears are coming though. The sadness is still very much here, but the water won't well up in my eyes. I am thankful for this when I start shampooing my hair and the bathroom air swarms with the scent of green apples.

*Sadie had bought me this shampoo a few weeks ago. She had stopped at the store for snacks on her way to my house for a movie marathon and spotted the colorful bottle on an end cap. She said that when she sniffed it, she was immediately transported back to when I pilfered all of the green apple Jolly Ranchers out of her mom's candy cabinet at their house.*

*Clip. Clop. Clip. Clop.*

Mom's slippers are slapping their way down the hall to her bedroom, signaling that she is turning in for the night. That's when it hits me that I have no idea what time it is. I had never looked at the clock on my phone when I got out of bed. All I know is that I slept the day away uninterrupted.

Once I am all clean, I step from the shower as steam envelopes me. I towel off and wrap my favorite fluffy towel around me, toga-style. I locate my phone in my room and see that I have five unopened text messages from Jimmy.

Gen. This is hard for both of us.
We need each other.

Sadie wouldn't want us to lose
each other too.

Call me, please.

I'm here whenever you're ready to talk.

Gen, I hope you're okay.
You're starting to freak me out.

I open my closet door and see an oversized Rush tee crumpled in a pile on the floor. I quickly pick it up and hold it to my face. I inhale deeply. It still smells like Sadie. This was her favorite shirt. Her poppy perfume is comforting me and making me smile for the first time since I got the news. I quickly throw it over my head and hug myself tightly.

*This shirt used to belong to Sadie's dad, Henry. He bought it at a Rush concert when he was first dating Maryann. At an early age, Sadie claimed stake to this shirt and cherished it like a precious heirloom.*

With her shirt on to help me feel close to her again, I climb onto my bed and take a deep breath.

*I have to call him. I can't continue ignoring his existence. I couldn't even if I wanted to. Who am I kidding?*

I hit his name and press the phone icon. It only rings once before he answers.

"Gen! Thank God! I was beginning to worry about you!"

"Sorry, I fell asleep earlier. Mom said you stopped by?"

"Yeah, I did. I needed to see.... No. I *need* to see you." He corrected himself, immediately aware of the obvious lie that he had just told.

*Truth be told, I really need to see him too.*

"Well, I guess you could come over if you want. I slept all day, so I probably won't be getting much sleep tonight.

*I secretly hope that he will decline the invitation and use needing sleep for tomorrow as an excuse.*

"Really? I would love that. I will be there in ten minutes or less."

# Jimmy

*I hadn't heard Gen's voice since Tuesday morning until she just called me. I have been trying to get a hold of her again since Tuesday. Not having her around has made this week even tougher than it would have been anyway. I am still ready to let her know how I feel, but I don't want to do it now when we are both still so raw from Sadie. She finally agreed to see me. That's at least a step in the right direction. When I stopped at her house earlier today, Darcy told me that she was not handling it well and needed her rest. Then, Darcy hugged me tight and we both silently cried. She told me that she would talk to Gen for me.*

As soon as I hang up from talking to Gen, I grab my jacket and keys. I rush out the door and get in my car. I know all of the routes in town so well that I just drive there without noticing anything I'm passing. All I can think about right now is getting to Gen's house to make sure that she is okay.

*I worry about her a lot because of her past. Back when her and Sadie weren't quite fourteen, she attempted suicide. That was actually shortly after I realized that I had feelings for her. Seeing her with the bandages on her wrists killed me. Sadie and I wouldn't let her out of our sight for a long time after that. We started to learn her warning signs and when she would start to slip, we would do anything possible to cheer her up. Sadie was her rock through all of it. Without Sadie, I am deathly afraid of what might happen to her.*

I pull up to Gen's house and take a deep breath before I walk to the door. I knock twice and slip my hands into my jean pockets. Gen opens the door and all I can do is stare at her. Her hair is damp and wavy. Her eyes look raw around the edges. The girl that I am in love with looks so vulnerable, but yet so beautiful.

## Genevieve

Like a prompt pizza delivery driver, Jimmy knocks on the front door after eight minutes.

*He must have run out the door once I offered to see him.*

I open the door, bracing myself, unsure if I am ready to see him. He is standing there in his distressed denim jacket and a black tee. His red hair is disheveled like he has been running his hands through it repeatedly. His skin is paler than normal. His blue eyes are lined with red and circled by dark half-moons.

We just stare at each other for a moment and then he wraps me up in his arms. I don't fight any of the emotions spilling out of me. I let go and all of the tears that I thought had finally dried up start to spew out of me once again. Jimmy is sobbing hard and his chest is heaving rapidly with his staggered breathing. We stay there for a while, just holding onto one another while we release all of our messy emotions. Finally, he backs away a step or two and notices what shirt I'm wearing.

*I'm suddenly aware of how much of a difference the three inches between Sadie and I actually makes. On her, this shirt hit her mid-thigh. On me, it hits me just below my underwear in the front and barely covers my ass in the back.*

"This was just in my closet..." I stammer, trying to explain what I am doing wearing his sister's shirt.

"She would want you to have it anyway. Plus, it looks good on you." I involuntarily blush.

"Let's sit on the couch. It's a little drafty right here." My legs are covered in goosebumps from the nighttime breeze coming in the still-open front door. I run my hands over my bare forearms to warm them up.

He lets a small chuckle escape from him. Jimmy and I shyly look to the floor, the wall, the ceiling, anywhere but at each other.

*It was as if we both thought that if we were able to laugh that we would somehow dismiss our mutual loss. This is the first time that we have seen each other since that call, which had been very short. That call consisted of Jimmy trying to speak through stifled sobs and me letting out a horrendous scream that sent my mother flying into my room. I didn't ask anymore then. All I had to know at that point was that I had lost her. I had hung the phone up, completely numb. Now, I don't know what to say first.*

We have been sitting in awkward silence for a few moments. The only noise is our occasional sniffles.

*I can't take the rigidity anymore. I have to break the silence.*

"I just can't believe that she is gone. I didn't even ask how she died. I feel horrible. I haven't really stopped crying at all. I just miss her so much." As I ramble, I am starting to feel like I will never stop crying.

"I don't know where to start." He put his hands through his hair, pausing to squeeze handfuls of his hair.

*This must be what messed up his hair tonight.*

"Neither do I. I can't think straight. I'm sorry that I've been so distant since you called me the other day. I've been afraid of hearing your voice or seeing your face. I was afraid that seeing you, without her, would make everything seem more real, more permanent." I keep stealing quick glances at him, but I am mostly talking to the couch cushion between us.

"I found her, you know. It was *me*." Jimmy looks like he is going to fall apart all over again, reliving it while telling me what transpired on Tuesday morning. I just sit silently, waiting for him to go on. I'm not really sure what to say to that anyway. "She got up and said she was going for her morning run. She kissed me on the cheek at five-thirty, grabbed her water and went out the door. I watched her jog to the trail behind the house."

He pauses again, trying to maintain his composure. "I kept waiting for her to come back. It had started to snow a few minutes after she went out the door. I figured she wouldn't be gone long. I was going to invite you guys to hit the record store with me. They had gotten some new releases over the weekend. When she wasn't back by six-thirty, I decided to go looking for her. She was only wearing her light athletic jacket. There was no way that she would be out there longer than half an hour."

Another moment to compose himself as he is sobbing profusely right now. "I went into the woods and followed the trail. I made it to the second bend, you know the one with the fallen tree, before I saw her sprawled out on the ground. There was some snow on her back and blood in her hair. A lot of blood." Great heaving sobs are coming now.

"She must have slipped on the new snow when she jumped over the trunk. You know how much she loved that leap of hers. She smashed her head on that huge boulder. I called her name, over and over, louder and louder, until I was screaming so loud that my voice hurt. She wasn't moving at all. I knew. I didn't want to believe it, but I *knew*. I was crying and could barely see anymore, but I scooped her up in my arms and carried her home." He is burying his face in his hands now, guttural sounds escaping from his throat.

"Oh, Jimmy..." Before I know what I am doing, I am pulling him into my arms and comforting him. I'm petting his hair and telling him that it's okay, but we both know that it's not and never will be again.

"I just kept whispering to her that I loved her so much and that I needed her to be okay. I was rocking her in my arms like a baby when we were walking back to the house. My baby sister." He is breaking even more and squeezing me as tightly as he can. His voice is thick and croaky with tears. "I wasn't quite at the door when Mom saw us. She was screaming and crying, crying and screaming. Dad heard the commotion and came running in. He collapsed to the ground sobbing. I had to call 911. I had to tell them that there had been an accident and that my sister had died." At last, he seems to be at a stopping point.

"Jimmy. She loved you so much. You know that, right?"

I am squeezing him so tightly to my body that Sadie's Rush shirt is now caught on one of the buttons of his jacket and my midriff is now bare. I can't care about anything right now other than holding onto my last living and breathing piece of Sadie.

*Jimmy is only fifteen months older than Sadie. They were always together, except for the first year or two of our friendship that were spent at my house in order to avoid Jimmy's annoying friends and their boyish ways. That ended around July of our thirteenth year. He was the cooler older brother that invited us to hang out with him and his friends.*

*He threw a bonfire and invited us to come. We gladly attended. Sadie had a crush on one of his friends, David. He was a bit of a rebel and wore tees for illusive bands that we had never heard of. She hung all over him that night. I sat alone on a blanket by the fire all night. That was the first time that I felt more like a sidekick than a partner-in-crime. The boys all played practical jokes on one another and drank beers pilfered from their parents. I spent most of the night in solitude until Jimmy noticed me alone. He quickly ambled over and sat beside me.*

*"Sup, Gen? Where's Sade?" I pointed to the edge of the woods where she had just been standing with David, but she was gone and so was he. My jaw dropped a bit as I noticed her absence. Jimmy quickly looked around. "Shit! Gen, where did she go?" I just shook my head, scared because I didn't have an answer for him. "Who was she talking to over there?"*

*"David. Who else?" I said with unintended venom in my voice. He looked at me with eyes full of pure terror. I didn't understand what the big deal was about her talking to him. He was Jimmy's friend, after all. Wasn't he? The look on Jimmy's face told me otherwise and then he bolted into the darkness of the woods, on the very trail where he would find his sister dead six years later. I stood in anticipation, waiting to see where Jimmy had gone and why he was so upset. We all heard some yelling over the stereo, but it wasn't decipherable.*

*All of a sudden, Sadie came bolting out of the woods and across the yard to their house. Her eyes were wild and streaked with tears. There were small twigs in her hair. She ran right past me and into their house. I followed her inside. She was sobbing on her bed by the time I caught up to her. I asked her what had happened and she just cried harder. I laid beside her and ran my hand over her back repeatedly, like my mother did for me when I was upset. I wasn't going to push. I knew I would eventually find out what had happened. Before I could get any more information from her, Jimmy came into her room and sat at the end of her bed.*

*"Listen, Sade. I'm sorry. I never should have invited him here tonight. I knew that you liked him and I know how he is. I'm really sorry. Please don't hate me for it. You're my sister. I will always be the one protecting you." I was still confused and didn't quite comprehend what had happened out there in the woods or why exactly Jimmy was apologizing. She sat up, sniffling and wiping her tears from her eyes.*

*"James, leave me alone. I didn't ask for your help. I don't need protection." I knew it was bad when she called him James. I had only heard her call him that twice, outside of their mother's presence, before that night. They had both been midfight.*

*"I won't leave you alone. Did he hurt you?"*

*"No! He didn't hurt me! It was MY idea!" At this, she broke down again and he hugged her.*

*"I know you like him, Sadie, but he is bad news. Okay? He does things with girls that you are definitely not ready for yet. Also, he is in a rough crowd at school. You need to stay away from him. Promise that this will never happen again?" At this, she laughed a bit and hugged him tight. She kissed his cheek and from then on, it was the three of us. He stopped hanging out with most of those guys and spent a majority of his free time with us.*

After about fifteen minutes of consoling each other, we pull away and look at the black television screen. Neither of us really feels like turning anything on. We just need to share the same space for a bit. It makes everything seem somewhat normal. I'm staring at a dent in the hardwood floor when I feel a cool touch on my hand. I jump.

"Sorry, I didn't mean to scare you."

*It's not the fact that he is touching me that made me jump. It's the way that his cool hands remind me of death.*

"What time do you have to leave?" Glancing at the clock, it's only nine-thirty.

*It feels so much later. Is this how time is going to move now? So slow that I can feel each second crawl by? I hope not.*

"I can stay as long as you want. I don't want to be home right now anyway. It's too hard right now." I lightly squeeze his fingertips at this.

*It has been super hard on me this week to be without her, but I haven't had to walk past her empty bedroom or see her Converse by the door, never to be worn again.*

"Let's put on a movie and lay here for a while. You can stay the night if you want. Mom won't mind. She loves you."

Jimmy slides off his denim jacket and settles into the couch a little more. Closer to me this time though. He rests his head on my shoulder. I can smell his signature scent: sandalwood and peppermint. It's comforting to me. I turn on the television and put on some mindless action film. A weight settles on my left thigh, just above my knee. It's Jimmy's right hand, just laid there lazily as if he didn't realize what he was doing or like an old habit.

*I love the way his hand feels on me, almost territorial. It's nice and makes me feel safe. Not to mention, I have dreamt about him putting hands there and everywhere else constantly.*

"Do you want a drink or anything?" I need to drink something. My mouth is dry from crying and my throat is raspy and hoarse.

"Just a Coke if you have any, please." He didn't seem to notice that his hand was resting on my leg until I moved to get off the couch. He pulled away like I had burned him.

*I've loved him for years, but I've never acted on it. Actually, pretty much the entire time I've known him. For a long time, I hid it from Sadie. I finally had to say something to her because she noticed how weird I got every time that he entered the room. She had squealed with glee when I finally told her. "Gen, marry him! For real! Then we could be actual sisters." From then on, I had avoided showing any of my feelings for him. I was scared that if we did actually date and we broke up that it would tear Sadie and I apart. I've suppressed it around him for years now. Sometimes, I would get a vibe that he felt the same way, but I always shrugged it off as something else altogether.*

## Jimmy

♫

*I just poured my heart out to Gen about Sadie. Any chance that I had with her is probably gone now that she has seen me cry like a full blown baby. On top of that, like a total idiot, I put my hand on her thigh completely uninvited. I just laid it there without even thinking. When she stood up, it hit me how stupid it was. What am I doing?*

*On the other hand though, she invited me to stay overnight. She also allowed me to rest my head on her shoulder and sit much closer to her than I would normally dare. There have been a few times over the years that I have been this close to her, but Sadie was always around to stop anything from happening. It feels different and more dangerous now that we don't have that distraction. I am going to test the waters tonight, I think. I plan on telling her soon, but I want to feel out the situation a little first. I wouldn't be able to handle it if she doesn't feel the same way about me and this ruins our friendship. If I can't have her as my girlfriend, then I at least want to keep her as a friend.*

## Genevieve

I wander into the kitchen and grab two Cokes. I walk back into the living room and Jimmy is now laying down stretching down the length of the couch. I hand him his soda and sit on the hardwood floor beside the couch. The hero in the movie that we put on is suspended from a bridge with a bomb counting down beside him.

"Gen, sit up here. The floor is cold. Sorry, I just needed to stretch out a bit." I tip my head back and look at him upside down.

*He resembles Sadie so much, but yet his face is all its own. He is really handsome, even when he is grieving and exhausted.*

"No, I think I'll stay down here."

"Oh, come on, Gen.  I won't bite." I wait, knowing what he is going to follow up with, *'unless you want me to, that is'.*

*He has always said this to me. Since he was sixteen, he would make comments like that to me just to see me squirm. I think that he knew I liked him then, but he would never admit it.*

I stand up and stretch like an awakening cat. I go to sit near his feet and he tilts up on his side a bit more and pats the couch cushion beside his torso. I stare at the cushion like it might bite me.

*I want to lay beside him so badly, but probably for different reasons than why he is offering.*

I inhale deeply and then lay beside him.

We are laying side by side, but I am being careful to not let our bodies touch too much. He must notice this because he lays his arm over me and tugs me in tighter to his body. We are totally spooning now. His body is so warm against mine. It helps my tense body begin to relax. I inhale his scent deeply and close my eyes.

*I could stay like this forever.*

Suddenly, I realize that I'm not crying.

*I did it! I finally ran out of tears!*

"Is this okay with you? I don't want to make you uncomfortable. I just like knowing that you're here and safe." Jimmy whispers into my right ear as he squeezes me a little tighter.

*And alive. This is the part that he doesn't say, but we both hear.*

"I could never be uncomfortable with you. This is exactly what I need right now."

"Me too, Gen. Me too." He nestles his face into the back of my hair. After a few minutes, his breathing shallows and his arm grows heavy and limp.

*I will gladly lay here all night with him. I imagine what Sadie would say seeing us here together. She would squeak and jump about. I was never afraid of us being together, just the big What If. What if something went wrong and we broke up? Would I lose him and Sadie simultaneously? All I've wanted for years is to be his.*

Slowly, I drift into a, thankfully, dreamless sleep.

The smell of coffee brewing and the sounds of a kitchen alive with the creation of breakfast awaken me. I open my eyes. I'm still snuggled against Jimmy on the couch, in my underwear. I know that, without a doubt, my mother saw us on the couch together before heading to the kitchen.

*Hopefully, she didn't get the wrong idea.*

I slowly remove myself from beneath his arm to attempt some damage control before he wakes up. With bare feet, I pad soundlessly to the kitchen.

"Good morning, Gen." Mom sounds remarkably chipper.

"I wouldn't call it that. It's the day of my best friend's funeral."

"Are you sure you wouldn't say that *something* about it is good?" Mom asks, raising her eyebrows and tipping her head toward the living room. I hold up my index finger to my mouth to quiet her. I'm blushing.

*My body is betraying me. I'm not allowed to feel any sort of joy right now, not today.*

"Maybe it's not *all* bad." I quietly whisper, glancing back toward Jimmy asleep on the couch. I pour some coffee in my mug that Sadie bought for me and sit at the table.

*There are three hours left before we have to start getting ready for the funeral and calling hours. I will be mentally preparing myself as much as possible before then. It will be a long day, but thank God that her parents didn't stretch the events over a few days like some people.*

I sit sipping my coffee in silence. Mom is just staring at the table, waiting for me to signal her that it is okay to speak. "He was the one that found her." I practically whisper it.

"Poor thing! That's not something you forget." She is running her hand through her hair. "Does he like coffee?"

"Black as his soul," I joke.

*This was something that Sadie would always say, trying to seem like a badass, when in reality she wrinkled her nose up at anything without flavored creamer and a sugar packet.*

Mom lets out a hearty laugh and gets up from the table. She grabs a mug from the cabinet and pours some coffee.

"Take this to him. We will all need it today, for sure."

I take the mug and head to the couch. I sit on the edge of the middle cushion and lightly touch his bicep. Even while he is sleeping, it feels freshly toned as if he just worked out.

"Jimmy, I brought you some coffee." I speak gently. His eyes flutter slowly and softly. He blinks a few times to adjust to the natural light coming in through the windows.

"Good morning, Gen." He sips at his coffee a few times before adding with a satisfied hum, "Thank you."

"You're welcome, but Mom actually made it and poured it. All I did was carry it in here."

"I meant for the coffee and for last night. I really needed that." He gently squeezes my hand. I look away, suddenly very self-conscious.

"Me too. You'll probably want to leave soon though, to get ready for the, uh, for today."

"Ugh, don't remind me. I want to ignore today for as long as I can. I'll leave around eight."

"Me too," I say, twirling my friendship bracelet from Sadie around my wrist.

*She had given it to me in tenth grade. It's a silver chain with a bar engraved with 11 to life, which sounded more like a prison sentence than a friendship.*

My phone starts vibrating on the end table. It's a phone call, not a text. The vibration is more insistent. I snatch it off the table and glance at who is calling. It's Maryann, Sadie and Jimmy's mom. I take a deep breath before answering. "H-h-hello." My voice is trembling, all of a sudden.

"Genevieve, dear, I wanted to ask you a question about today." She sounds serious and like the weight of the world is on her shoulders.

*Hell, I imagine it is. She has to say goodbye to her baby today.*

"Of course. Anything."

"Would you stand in the receiving line with us today? You are as much a part of Sadie's family as the three of us are. We would really like you to be there."

*She wants me to stand beside Jimmy, Henry and herself while all of their crying relatives and our sobbing classmates come through to offer their condolences before stopping at the coffin to pay their respects to Sadie personally?*

"If you're sure that is what you want, absolutely."

*How can I say no to her? Her daughter just died.*

"Henry and I really think it is what Sadie would want. We haven't asked James yet, but he will agree wholeheartedly, I'm sure."

"Um, okay, so what time do I have to be there?"

"Ten forty-five."

"Okay, I'll be there."

"Have you heard from James? He hasn't been home since last night. He didn't say where he was going. He just walked out and never came back. Our imaginations are running wild with worry, as you can imagine."

"Um, actually, Jim...I mean, *James* is here. He came by to check on me last night and we talked for a while. He didn't want to go back to your place last night. It was too painful."

*Maryann is always very formal. She never uses nicknames. I am always Genevieve and Jimmy is always James.*

"Oh, thank God! Henry! James is safe! He stayed with Genevieve last night! Thank you! I will see you at the funeral home at ten forty-five." Maryann hangs up, luckily without any questions about why Jimmy had chosen my place over anywhere else to stay.

As I hang up and set down my phone, Jimmy looks at me from above his coffee mug. His face looks puzzled. He just blows on his coffee and then takes a rather large gulp. He then sets his mug down and looks at me again like he doesn't quite know who I am.

"Was that my mom? What did she want?"

"She wants me to stand with you guys today. And then, she was looking for you. You didn't tell her you were coming here last night?" I playfully smack Jimmy in the chest.

"Well, I had been waiting to hear from you all day, all *week* actually; so when you called, I flew over here. I didn't want to miss out on my one chance to see you before today."

"Oh, I'm really sorry. I didn't think you would want to see me."

"Gen, why the hell would I not want to see you?" He looks completely confused and slightly insulted. His brows are furrowing in frustration.

*In this moment, I see Sadie's features. This is how she would look at her math homework.*

"Well, I don't know. Maybe because I'm a painful reminder of Sadie? Maybe because I'm just *'Sadie's friend'*." I make air-quotes as I say Sadie's friend.

*It's the way that he introduced me once to his friends, not with my name, just my position as the friend of his little sister. It has stuck with me. That was when we were twelve. It also happened to be around the time when I first noticed the butterfly feeling I get in the pit of my stomach when he is around.*

"Stop it. You're not just *'Sadie's friend'* and you know it. You're Gen! *Her* Gen! *My* Gen!"

*The way that he said* 'my *Gen' made my heart start twirling around like a drunken ballerina.*

"All I have been thinking about since our call on Tuesday is seeing you and hugging you and making sure that you're alright." Again, my heart is soaring out of my chest.

"So I won't lose you too, will I?" I am feeling comfortable enough right now with the morning light filtering in through the blinds to ask this. Another time or another place and I probably would have banished this thought to the recesses of my brain. He pulls me in towards him and hugs me tightly. I swear I felt him inhale the scent of my hair. He pulls away slightly and cups my face in his hands. He just stares at me for a few moments. He has the same look of bewilderment on his face as he did when I first hung up the phone. "What? Is there something on my face?" I ask quietly.

"You look different today, that's all."

"Different how?"

"I can't explain it. You look like you, but there is something that has changed." My face is still cupped in his hands. He opens his mouth to say something else, but then thinks better of it.

"Oh, well if you figure it out, let me know. I would be interested to know what has changed with my appearance, especially since I've been avoiding mirrors."

"I'll let you know if I place it." He tucks my hair behind my right ear and smiles. It's not a big toothy smile, but a small lopsided grin.

"You never answered me, by the way." I cross my arms, faking annoyance.

"No, Gen. You're not going to lose me too. I'm not going anywhere." His smiling face turns sad and he looks toward the floor. "What are you wearing today?"

"Not black. Sadie only liked rockers in black." As I think of Sadie rolling her eyes at everyone dressed in black on her behalf, a horrible thought creeps into my brain. "Um, Jimmy, is it going to be, um, you know, open?"

"The casket? Um, you know, I'm not actually sure. I hope not." We both sit in silence for a few moments. "I should probably go home and shower. I'll see you in a few hours. Do you want to ride over with me?"

"Um, sure, I guess."

*The thought of riding in Jimmy's car alone makes my insides turn all floppy. It shouldn't. I've ridden with him plenty of times over the years, but rarely without Sadie. Her absence will be undeniable. The laughter as we sang along to every song and talked about everything in our lives. The smell of her poppy perfume wafting through the car as the air conditioner blew. Her Converse tapping along to the beat. Our usual trio, now cut down to two.*

## Jimmy

♪♪♪

*I almost kissed her. I had her face cupped in my hands and only inches from my face. It would have been so easy to just kiss her. Why didn't I? She looked so damn beautiful. She had just woken up and her hair was a mess. She was still gorgeous. I also almost told her how beautiful she is. We need to get through today. Then, when the timing is a little better, I will finally tell her.*

*I have to go get ready for my baby sister's funeral. Once I'm ready, I am going back to pick up Gen. I am so happy that she will be by my side all day. I don't think I could get through this day without her.*

# Chapter Two

## Genevieve

After I watch Jimmy pull out of the driveway, I notice my mother sitting at the table grinning from ear-to-ear like a child holding back a secret.

"What's up with you?" I stare at her suspiciously. Her eyes are lit up like fireflies with reckless abandon.

"You can't hide anything from me, you know." That smile is still plastered on her face.

"I'm not hiding anything. I have literally no clue what you're talking about."

"You've had eyes for James Thompson for years. Girl, I know that you're sad right now and so is he, but the chemistry I just witnessed on that couch is undeniable. You may not believe me right now, but I'm telling you, he is my future son-in-law." She looks happy with herself beyond words. It's as if she just looked into a crystal ball and saw next week's winning lottery numbers.

"Believe me, Jimmy doesn't see me that way. We've never even kissed and you're already throwing me in a bridal suite."

"Call it Mother's Intuition then, but I am telling you, you really will be Sadie's family before all is said and done." She sips at more of her coffee, smiling at herself.

"Yeah, okay, Mom. I need to go take a shower." I walk away, rolling my eyes.

When the showerhead first douses me with warm water, a burst of sandalwood and peppermint fills the air.

*I hadn't realized that I had inherited some of his smell last night. It was calming, just like having his body against mine last night on the couch.*

I can't help but to let out a little smile.

*Maybe Sadie's dream of us really being family isn't so far-fetched as it seemed. I am not going to rush anything though. If something is meant to happen between us, it will of its own accord. I will not force anything.*

After my shower, I step into my emerald green jumpsuit that Sadie had picked out for me on our weekend in Boston during the summer.

*It really does make me look eclectic and very Sadie-esque.*

I pull the hair back from my face and braid it like a halo around my head. I apply my makeup very carefully and deliberately with waterproof eyeliner and mascara.

*I know that I'll be crying a ton today without a doubt. I try to mentally prepare myself for the day that lays ahead of me.*

I slide my vintage Chuck Taylors on that are adorned with carefully written lyrics, an adorable heart and Sadie's signature.

*These will always be my favorite shoes. I remember the day that Sadie propped my foot on her lap in the sun-soaked grass. We were enjoying the warmth and our summer playlist while Jimmy gave us a wonderful air-guitar solo. He also played a set of air-drums. We laughed and applauded him. Happiness was abundant that day. Will I ever feel that happiness again?*

## Jimmy

♪♪♪

*I spent all of last night holding onto the girl that I love. It was the first time since Tuesday morning that I have felt any sort of peace. I could have sworn that I had felt some serious chemistry last night. We have been friends for years, but last night it definitely felt like something more. I may have been imagining it, though. There have been several instances over the last few years that I have felt like we might be on the verge of something.*

*The first time was at the drive-in. Sadie was there though and I didn't want to start an argument with her that would ruin the night. If she hadn't been there, I would have kissed Gen. That connected feeling faded after that night and didn't show back up for months.*

*There was another time at Jake's party. I felt like a string was connecting us and pulling me toward her. There were tons of people drinking and listening to music, but I was keenly aware the entire night of where she was. I was keeping an eye on her, afraid that something might happen. A friend of mine had come over to me and started chatting about school when I noticed this asshole, Damien, was putting his hands on her. I watched for a moment to see if it was unsolicited. When I noticed that she looked uncomfortable, I walked straight toward her. I was going to remove her from the situation, even if it meant fighting someone much larger than myself. Luckily, I got us both out of there without physically fighting Damien.*

*That was the night I first held her hand. I may have told her how I felt that night if Sadie hadn't followed us outside. I've always worried what Sadie would think, but life is too short to keep holding back from what you want. Soon, I'll tell her. Soon, but right now, I need to get ready to say goodbye to my original partner-in-crime.*

As I take off my shirt from last night, I can smell a mix of Gen and Sadie's perfumes. I put on my black jeans and my David Bowie shirt that Sadie bought for me last Christmas.

*We spent so many weekends watching Labyrinth together throughout our childhood. He was one of her favorites. Mom will probably be pissed that I'm not wearing a suit, but Sadie hated me in suits. Why would I do something she hated in her honor? This is what she would want me wearing.*

I look in the mirror. Frankly, I look like shit. I have barely stopped crying this week. My chin-length red hair is wavy and messy. I run my fingers through it to look a little less like I just rolled out of bed. My blue eyes remind me so much of Sadie's. They are the same in shape and color.

"James, it's almost time to go to Rothschild. Are you ready?" Mom calls from down the hall. I already know that she is going to fight with me when she sees what I'm wearing.

"I am, but I'll meet you guys there. I'm picking up Gen." I walk into the living room where Mom and Dad are both dressed in black from head to toe. They glance me up and down.

"James, you know that I hate that. Her name is Genevieve. If her mother wanted to name her Gen, she would have. Is that really what you're wearing?" Mom wrinkles her nose in disgust as she assesses my outfit.

"Darcy even calls her Gen! And yes, Mom, it is. No, I will not change. This is what Sadie would have wanted me to wear. She says I look ridiculous in dress clothes."

I grab my jacket and my car keys. I walk out the door and get in my Focus. I peel out of the driveway, probably a little too fast. My tires squeal and my traction control kicks in. I start to silently cry on my way to Gen's house.

*Everywhere I look reminds me of Sadie. There will never be a day that I don't think of her infectious smile.*

## Genevieve

"Gen, Jimmy just pulled in." Mom yells up the stairs where I've been sitting in my room thinking about memories of Sadie for the past hour or so. I jog down the stairs. Suddenly, I'm bursting with heat. I walk out of the door fanning myself to attempt cooling off. It's a crisp thirty-five degrees outside, but I feel like I have been in a sauna. I walk over to Jimmy's car and instinctively reach for the back door.

"Gen, you can sit up front, you know." Jimmy reminds me, cautiously.

*Sadie always rode shotgun. I would watch her profile from the center of the backseat as she danced and laughed.*

"Sorry, force of habit." I blush a bit, embarrassed that I was still leaving her seat open.

"It's okay. There are a lot of adjustments to get used to now. You look, well, like Sadie dressed you herself." Now it's his turn to blush a bit.

*Was Jimmy trying to compliment me?*

"Really? Thanks. That's what I was going for. I want to keep her memory alive as much as I can."

"You look great...well, not *great*...I mean..." Jimmy trails off as we drive toward the funeral home. As we get closer to our destination, my palms are getting sweaty and my stomach is twisting in knots.

We pull into a parking lot that borders a building that looks like a museum.

*This is Rothschild Funeral Home. I haven't been back here since my father died. I'm already tearing up.*

I carefully wipe my eyes with the sides of my thumbs. Jimmy grabs my hand and gives it a squeeze.

"Are you ready?" His eyes are welling up, too.

"As ready as I'll ever be, I guess." I take a deep breath and get out of the car as fast as possible, before my mind has time to tell my body to quit moving.

As we approach the door, Jimmy quickens his pace so that he can open the door for me. Once I cross the threshold, he steps in beside me and places his right hand on my lower back, guiding me toward the room I am dreading. It is as if he knows that if he lets go, I might flee and will never be seen again.

The Thompsons are waiting for us in the visitation room. Lining the hallway that leads to it are hundreds of photos of Sadie. Most of them include myself and Jimmy. Once we reach the grieving parents, I turn the corner and there she is.

*My best friend. The keeper of my secrets. The one that I knew better than myself most days.*

She is now laying in a cherry casket, lined with champagne silk. Her face is looking at the ceiling, eyes closed, hands clasped. I think about how Jimmy said that she had hit her head. She looks no different than she did when I last saw her on Monday night.

*If she hit her head so badly that it killed her, where is the mark from the fatal blow? I always forget about mortician magic.*

Tears just start falling and I can't hold myself together anymore. She is laying in front of me, like so many times before, but this time there is no sun kissing her skin.

*This is the last time that I will ever see her face in person.*

I fall to my knees and cradle my head in my hands. Jimmy is holding me tightly now. He is crying too. As we sit in a sobbing heap on the floor, the funeral director walks in. He quickly explains how today is going to work. Then, he asks if we want to keep the casket open or not. Maryann looks to Henry, Henry to Jimmy, Jimmy to myself. I look at Sadie. All eyes are on me now, I am the one the decision is being left up to.

"Can we close it please?" As I say this, the whole room lets out a collective sigh. They have all been holding their breath waiting for my response.

"Very well. We will close it up." The funeral director steps past us and gently closes the lid. Now, he is the nervous one. "There is still a little while before we start letting people in for the calling hours. There is actually something that I need to discuss with you, Mr. and Mrs. Thompson."

Their eyebrows simultaneously shoot up. They look completely caught off guard. Maryann is the first one to finally speak.

"Anything that you need to discuss with Henry and I can be said in front of James and Genevieve, as well." She is standing her ground. Firmly but politely, as always.

Again, the middle-aged funeral director in his tailored suit looks nervous. He starts messing with his cufflink and then his burgundy tie.

*What could possibly make a man who deals with death for a living nervous?*

"Well, um, this isn't an easy thing to say. Um, so I guess that I will just say it." We all stare at him in anticipation. "Were any of you aware that Sadie was expecting?"

All of us let out a simultaneous gasp, followed by a chorus of, "Wait. *What*?" He looks at each of us. His forehead is beading up with sweat.

"I didn't think that you did since no one had mentioned it. The autopsy found that she died of a fractured skull due to blunt force trauma. When we did the autopsy though, we also found that she was pregnant. We believe that she would have been about ten weeks."

The four of us just sit here in disbelief.

*Sadie didn't even have a boyfriend, nor anyone that she was flirting with on a regular basis. She wasn't really into one-night stands, either.*

Maryann, after a long moment, looks at Jimmy.

"James, why didn't you tell us? That seems like something very important, that you should have told us about." She sounds angry.

"Mom, I swear to God, I did not know anything about this at all. I'm as shocked and upset as you are." Jimmy is holding his forehead like it might fall off of his face if he doesn't keep his fingers firmly in place.

"Genevieve, darling, did she say anything to you about this? You two told each other everything. Surely she said *something*."

Slowly shaking my head, I respond. "I'm really sorry. She didn't say anything to me at all. She didn't even tell me that she had sex recently. I didn't think she had slept with anyone since Jack..."

*Shit! I forgot that Jimmy doesn't know about her little fling with Jack last Christmas.*

"Wait! *Jack*? Jack Kingsley?" All I can manage to do in response is to nod. "When the hell was that?"

"Christmas." Staring at the toes of my shoes seems like the only acceptable option at the moment. She had made me swear not to tell a soul. She knew Jimmy would flip.

"Well, obviously it isn't from then. That was nearly a year ago." Henry, the voice of reason. "We don't have time to figure this out today. Quite frankly, it doesn't make a difference anyway. We lost them both. Now it's time to deal with the task at hand." Henry points toward the door. He then assumes his position at the foot of her casket. Maryann stands between him and Jimmy. Then, I'm beside Jimmy. Suddenly, I'm feeling like an imposter.

*How could I have not known that my best friend was pregnant?*

The crowd starts to spill into the room with a wave of tears, sniffles, hugging and whispering. I receive the first hugs of each person. Most know me and my position of importance in Sadie's life. Occasionally, one of Maryann's coworkers will bypass the line and go straight to her and hug on to the grieving mother tightly. With every hug, I am becoming more and more unglued. Everyone spills in for four hours and then, we finally get a small break before we have to do the actual funeral.

## Jimmy

*Sadie, my baby sister, was pregnant? This is all that keeps spilling through my mind as I hug all of these people who miss Sadie. I would have been an uncle, now I will never get that chance.*

*Gen is beside me crying her eyes out. I want so badly to just take her into my arms and comfort her like I did last night. The people never seem to stop coming. Every male that comes in is under my scrutiny. I had no idea about Sadie sleeping with Jack last year. What if it's him? Or another one of my friends? Was it a total stranger?*

Even our old teachers are here. Our history teacher, Mr. McCuaig, wraps Gen up in a hug that lasts too long for my liking.

*He isn't even trying to console Gen. He is just squeezing her tightly.*

I am going to step in if he doesn't let go in three seconds.

*Three, two, one.*

He is *still* holding her.

*Time to step in.*

"Uh, Mr. McCuaig, thank you so much for coming." I pat him on the shoulder as I say this. He pulls away from Gen.

*Finally!*

"Jimmy, I am so sorry about your sister. She was one of my favorite students. She was so young and talented and so beautiful."

*Could he be the one that impregnated Sadie? She did always have a thing for him in school. He is young and single.*

I stare at him, hard in the eye as I shake his hand. He is in a navy tweed peacoat. He is only in his early thirties.

*Sadie used to gush about how hot he was all the time. Maybe she decided to act upon it since she was no longer his student.*

He moves down the line to my parents. I lean over to Gen and whisper, "Do you think it might have been him?"

"Mr. McCuaig? No way! If she would have been with him, you *know* she would have told us about it." Gen has a small smile on her face.

*God, I love seeing her smile. It makes everything so much better.*

"I can't stop thinking about it. Who could it have been?"

"No idea, but we will figure it out together." She gives my hand a gentle squeeze to reassure me.

The calling hours are finally ending.

*I don't think I could take hugging one more person, well except for Gen that is. The funeral will be starting in just a few minutes.*

I sit down and try to run this all through my mind.

*Sadie is dead and a mother. I need to know who she was with. If he knew she was pregnant, whoever he is, why wouldn't he contact us or pay his respects to the mother of his child? What kind of guy does that? It's a total dick move.*

# Genevieve

As the funeral starts, Jimmy is the first one to speak. He stands at the podium with bloodshot eyes.

*He is composing himself pretty well. I just want to hold him tight and let him know that I am going to be right here.*

"On Tuesday, my beautiful baby sister kissed my cheek and gave me a sweet smile before going out for a run. That was the last time that I would see her alive. I was the last one to see her alive, actually. I was also the first one to see her dead. There isn't a single memory that I have over the years that aren't scattered with Sadie: her crazy smile, infectious laugh and her pure badassery," he chokes on a small chuckle.

"She was my best friend. The only other person who even comes close is Gen, but in so many ways, she is an extension of Sadie. She is in just as many memories as my sister. They should have been in each other's weddings and had babies to raise together. They were robbed of these chances. Just as I was robbed of the possibility of being an uncle or seeing my baby sister get married or rule the world one day. We all know she wanted to," another small chuckle, "It isn't fair that life can just be ripped from beneath us like a rug. Sadie should be rocking out to David Bowie and dancing around her room right now complaining about the cold, not sitting here behind me in a box. This isn't fair at all. It sucks. I may not have known everything about her life, but I knew enough to know that she deserves more. I love her so much and I will never stop for as long as I live." With that, Jimmy steps down from the podium and takes his seat beside me. I squeeze his hand lightly. He gives me a teary smile.

"Thank you, James. Next up is Henry Thompson, Sadie's father." The funeral director beckons Henry up to the podium. Henry stands and walks like a man taking his final journey down Death Row.

"What can I say about Sadie June? All of you already know how amazing she was. I already miss everything about her. She was secretive and a bit of a rebel, but she was a girl made out of my own heart. She was carefree and happy. She loved without limits. If someone was lucky enough to be loved by her, they were truly blessed. I will never get to walk my baby girl down the aisle or be a grandfather to a mini-Sadie. We will be reminded of her in all that we do, always." Henry begins crying harder and takes his seat beside Maryann again with shuttering shoulders.

"Maryann, did you want to say anything?" The funeral director offers the podium. She simply bows her head and audibly sobs. "Genevieve, dear, would you like to say a few words?" I am frozen in place.

*I didn't prepare anything, but I can't sit here without saying* something.

I move from the safety of my seat beside Jimmy and walk to the podium. I face the crowd and observe the sea of black. My first instinct is to laugh.

"So, you're all probably wondering why I'm laughing when my best friend just died. Well, when I look at you all with your sad faces and sea of black dress clothes, I can't help but think of how Sadie would be rolling her eyes and telling you all to live your lives and to change because only true rockers can get away with wearing black. As you'll notice, I am in a green jumpsuit and Chuck Taylors. The jumpsuit was personally picked out for me by our dear Sadie. The Chuck Taylors have her handwriting all over them in hot pink Sharpie. I cannot think of a better way to honor her.

When I think of Sadie, I think of poppies and bonfires, records and band tees, sunshine and tie-dye. She was full of life, happiness, and spontaneity. Even now, she is still leaving me guessing about things and I knew everything about her. My bracelet that I'm wearing, well that I always wear, says *'eleven to life'*. It's from her. I know, I know. It sounds like a prison sentence, but what it means is that we became best friends at the age of eleven and that will never change until we die. I say when *we* die because even though she is dead, *I* am not and no one will ever take her place. She is in everything I do and think. She always will be. She was supposed to be the maid of honor in my wedding and the godmother of my children, Auntie Sadie.

Please, don't cry for Sadie. I promise I have cried enough for all of us this week. If you want to do something to honor her memory, I urge you to go home and put on your brightest outfit, blast your favorite music and don't take life for granted. It is way too short to worry about everything that could go wrong. I have missed out on some opportunities myself because I kept worrying about what ifs. Sadie always pushed me to do those things anyway, but I didn't. I am going to start though and you all should too."

As I stop talking and peer at the teary-eyed crowd, I see a somewhat familiar face that I can't quite place. He is standing awkwardly in the very back, as for a moment and then I descend from the podium and take my seat beside Jimmy.

The funeral director finishes up the prayers and readings. He then informs everyone that there will be a spring burial due to the ground already freezing. He dismisses everyone and descends the podium. I quickly stand up and turn towards the back of the room. Jimmy looks up at me confused. I start walking toward where I saw that face.

*I have to talk to him. I have to figure out where I know him from and why he was here.*

Jimmy is following closely behind me. I find the face I'm looking for. He sees me making my way toward him and turns walking briskly out the door and around the corner of the building. I jog outside, but he is gone. Jimmy is right on my heels.

"What the hell, Gen? Where are you going?"

"I saw a guy that I kind of recognize. I can't place him, but he acted like he shouldn't have been here. He hung toward the back and made eye contact with me while I was on the podium and then he left when he saw me coming. What if it's him?"

"Him who?"

"*Him!*" I say clenching my teeth tightly together. Then it clicks with Jimmy. He understands why I can't say more as people start flooding out of the building past us.

"We will find him eventually. Come on, let's go back inside and say our final goodbyes." Jimmy places his hand on the small of my back again and leads me back inside.

"Where did you two run off to?" Henry asks with a glint of humor in his eyes.

"Bermuda, Dad. We decided to quickly elope." Jimmy replies sarcastically.

*I wouldn't mind that at all. Just the two of us on a sunny beach professing our love for one another.*

Jimmy quickly glances in my direction to gauge my reaction. I involuntarily let out a sly smile at the thought of marrying Jimmy. He must notice because he winks at me with a lopsided grin.

"Very funny. For real though, where did you go? You practically ran out of here."

"Gen thought she might know who the guy was that Sadie had been with. She was trying to talk to him, but he left too quickly."

"Oh, really? What is his name, Gen?" As Henry uses my nickname, Maryann clears her throat to scold him. "Sorry. *Genevieve.*"

"I don't know, Henry. I recognize him from somewhere, but I can't place it."

We each get one last chance to say our final goodbyes to Sadie. We are each granted a few private moments with her in the casket. I use mine to vow to her that I will start living the way that she has been wanting me to all along. She taught me that life was too short to worry. I'll stop worrying once I find out who fathered her child and why she hid it from us.

# Jimmy

♪♪♪

I use my last private moments with my sister to tell her the truth about Gen. *Finally*. I tell her that I will be letting Gen know about my true feelings as soon as I possibly can. I also tell her how sorry I am that she never got to be a mom or a wife or an aunt. My last words to her are that I love her.

I join Gen and my parents back out in the hallway. Dad has his arms wrapped around Mom consoling her. They are getting their turn with her now. Once they go back to Sadie's casket, Gen and I silently start taking down the picture boards. Each photo is like a snippet of Sadie's life. They span all ages and both towns that we lived in. Once we have removed them all from their easels, we load them into the backseat of my Focus. As we get in the car, I start getting lost in thought.

*Why did I make that joke about eloping? Gen had smiled at it though. I wonder if it was because of it being funny or because it's something she wouldn't mind doing.*

"Hey, do you want to go sit at the park for a bit before we head back to the houses?"

*I hope she accepts my invitation. I'm not ready to be away from her yet. She is the only thing holding me together right now.*

"Huh? Oh, yeah, sure." She seems lost in her own thoughts, too.

*God, she is so beautiful.*

"What was up with that hug from Mr. McCuaig? It seemed a bit awkward."

*I wasn't going to ask this but it slips from my mouth as I drive to the park. It has been bugging me since it happened. Repressing these feelings is not good for me anyway. Might as well let it fall out of my mouth now.*

"It *was* weird, right? It seemed to last forever. Thanks for saving me, like always. I'm such a damsel in distress." Gen giggles a little as she rolls her eyes.

"It was even making *me* uncomfortable." I laugh.

*If she asks why, maybe I'll spill my guts.*

She doesn't. We ride the rest of the way in silence.

## Genevieve

As we leave the funeral home with the backseat full of picture boards, we decide to go to the park for a while before Jimmy drops me off at home. At the park, we sit in silence, staring out the window, for a handful of uncomfortable minutes until Jimmy gives me a look of complete uneasiness.

"Gen, do you think Sadie knew she was pregnant? I feel like if she had known, she would have told one of us."

"I feel like she would have had to have known. If she was ten weeks or longer like that Rothschild guy said, she would have already missed at least two periods." Now, I am trying to count back ten weeks and think about what we did.

*How long were we apart that week?*

"Then why wouldn't she have said something? At least to you?" He looks so worried right now.

*This must really be weighing on his mind.*

I shrug. "She was probably scared. Maybe she was ashamed of who the father was or how you would react. You're her protective big brother, after all."

"Maybe...", he looks like he has moved on to some other thoughts that are weighing him down also, "what were you talking about in your speech? What things was she telling you to do that you weren't doing?" My heart is racing in my chest.

"Following my heart."

*This is the easiest way that I can answer him truthfully without dragging out the whole truth of the I-am-totally-crazy-for-you-and-have-been-for-years thing right now.*

"Me too. She was always so good at following her heart. She got that from Dad."

We stay sitting in his car with hundreds of Sadies staring at the back of our heads for over an hour before heading back to my house. We decide that dismantling the picture boards should be a team effort. Once we get back to my house, that's what we will do with the rest of the afternoon before parting ways. I keep thinking about that face.

*Why did I recognize him and why the hell did he book it out of there? It has to be him.*

## Jimmy

♪♪♪

My brain is so far away right now.

*How did I not know that Sadie was pregnant? She always talked to me about everything. Of course, she didn't mention Jack to me either, so maybe not everything was shared. I should be trying to enjoy the fact that I'm alone with Gen.*

We are parked at the overlook in the park. This is a beautiful view of the city. The trees have a light coating of snow. I turn to look at Gen and I am stunned once again.

*She never ceases to be beautiful. She has been crying all day. Her nose is bright red from wiping it so much. Her eyes are bloodshot and raw-looking, but yet she is still my favorite thing to look at. I almost told her earlier how beautiful she is. Something stopped me though. I want her to know how I feel, but it might be too soon after losing Sadie to get invested in a relationship.*

*If Sadie was in a relationship without me knowing, maybe Gen is too. My biggest fear is losing her friendship. The thought of Gen being with another guy drives me crazy though. I need to tell her. The sooner, the better. Maybe when we go back to her house, I'll be brave enough to have a conversation with Gen about us.*

Gen catches me staring at her. She quickly looks away.

"Is there makeup smeared on my face or something?"

"No, why?"

"You're staring at me."

"I wasn't meaning to stare. I was just kind of zoning out. Sorry. Are you ready to head to your place?"

"Sounds good to me." She shrugs her petite shoulders.

As we drive towards Gen's house, I keep trying to think of how she might react.

*If she says no, it is going to completely crush me. I think about how she looked so different last night. She was still her normal gorgeous self, but there was something vulnerable about her. It's almost as if part of her confidence was tied to Sadie. They had been an inseparable pair for so long that I guess in some ways, they really were one entity. I've never known a Gen without Sadie.*

We stay quiet throughout the ride back to her house. Luckily, the silence isn't awkward. It's a comfortable silence, like an old married couple who read the paper and do crosswords in the same room together without ever saying a word. Being in each other's presence is enough.

## Genevieve

Mom is home when we pull in my paved driveway. We unload the picture boards from the cramped backseat and head for my room. Mom is in the kitchen drinking tea when we walk inside.

"You both delivered beautiful eulogies today." She is quiet and gentle when she speaks to us, as if we might crumble into a million pieces at too harsh of a word. Which if I'm being honest with myself, we just might.

"Thanks", we both mumble in unison as we climb the stairs.

We spread the picture boards all over my room. They are composed of memories from all different ages. There is no rhyme or reason to their placement. In some of them, we are in pajamas eating popcorn on a bed made of blankets. Others, we are in swimsuits or snow gear. There are formal dances, graduations, yearbook photos, and candid snapshots.

A few are from the times that we spent with Jimmy's friends before he became a permanent part of the trio. One in particular jumps out at me. It's from the bonfire where Sadie disappeared into the woods with David. In it, we are all standing beside a huge bonfire, ten of us total. I look at all of the faces staring back at me with huge smiles. One looms from the picture and dares to bite me if I look too long.

"Jimmy." It's nothing more than a whisper. He doesn't respond. I look up and see him staring nostalgically at a photo. I glance down at it. Somehow it was only Jimmy and I, no Sadie in sight. We had great big smiles and were sharing a chair beside a campfire. I remember this picture being taken, but I don't know where Sadie was. I touch his arm lightly to get his attention. He jumps. "Sorry, I didn't mean to scare you. I know who it is." His eyes widen as he stares at me. I hand him the photo from the bonfire. He scans the faces. He doesn't understand. I have to point him out. Jimmy is still stuck in a nostalgic bubble. "It's him." I point to a boy wearing a band tee and skinny jeans. It was the same face that I saw today, just a little younger. Then, it clicks with Jimmy finally. He looks like he might explode.

"It's *David?* You're sure? You have got to be fucking kidding me, Gen."

"That's who ran from me today. Why run if you're just there as a friend to the grieving brother?"

"Did he learn *nothing* from when I pulled him off of her all of those years ago?" I know that he doesn't actually want an answer, so I stifle my response of *'apparently not'*.

"I don't even know how she would have made contact with him. I thought he had dropped off of the face of the earth, honestly. We never saw him again after the fire."

"I'm not sure either but I am damn sure going to find out. I don't care if Sadie is dead or not, if someone knew that he fathered her child and didn't have the balls to say his condolences to her family's face, he deserves to be punched."

Jimmy sits very still, stewing in his own rage. Finally, he looks up at me. His face is still very angry, but not towards me. He grabs my hand gently and pulls it to his mouth. He lightly presses a kiss on my fingers.

"Thank you, Gen, for *everything*. I have to go home, but I'll text you. I promise I will see you soon." With that, he walks out of my room. Now I am surrounded by hundreds of Sadies staring at me, but the photo that had been added even though Sadie was not in it is gone. Jimmy must have taken it with him, but I didn't notice. I pick up all of the photos and stack them neatly onto my dresser. I take off my jumpsuit and slide back into Sadie's Rush tee. It smells of poppies mixed with sandalwood and peppermint. It is the two loves of my life folding and entwining into one. I crawl into bed and pull the covers over my head. It's eight o'clock now, but my body feels like it is past midnight. I drift off to sleep.

*Sadie is dangling off the end of my bed like some strange acrobat. She is giggling as her blood rushes to her face turning it bright red. I'm begging her to just sit up, scared that she is going to be sick if she keeps it up much longer. She finally sits up and collapses face-first into my pillow. "The room is spinning, Gen!" She is laughing at first and then it turns to a panicked whine. "Gen! Make it stop! I think I'm going to barf." I saunter over to her and say, "I told you so," in a singsong voice. We were eleven, I think.*

Suddenly, I am jolted awake by my phone vibrating. It's a text from Jimmy.

I found him! I know where he is
and I'm going to have a little chat with him.

My heart is pounding furiously.

*If Sadie didn't tell me about David, he must have been bad news because she* loved *telling me all about her love life since mine was non-existent.*

James Anthony Thompson!
Don't do anything stupid!
Stay out of trouble!

*Normally he is our protector, but currently I am feeling the strong need to be his for once. He has been through enough this week. He doesn't need to add an arrest to that laundry list.*

Genevieve, I will be fine. Promise.
I'm meeting him in an hour.
He has no clue it's me.

*An hour?* I glance at the clock in the corner of my phone. It's one-thirty in the morning. *Why the hell is he meeting him at two-thirty?*

Pick me up.
I'm going with you.

I didn't even remember David's last name, so I couldn't even look him up on social media.

*How did he find him so fast? And why is David meeting with Jimmy if he doesn't know who he is meeting?*

A knot tightens in the pit of my stomach.

Like hell you are. See you afterwards.
I'll let you know how it goes.

*I know there is no winning this argument. I'll just pray that Jimmy makes it out of this meeting alive and in one piece, preferably with his clean criminal record still intact.*

I force myself to drift back to sleep. This time, I have no memories of Sadie creeping back. Instead, it is just darkness.

# Chapter Three

## Jimmy

Gen figured it out like Nancy Drew. She had stumbled upon an old picture of David in the picture board photos. She is positive that it was David who ran away today. I ran out of her room so quickly. Now, I am driving home, with a photo of Gen and I still unknowingly clutched in my hand.

*Once I get home, I am calling Jack.*

I pull in the driveway and rush inside. Mom and Dad are in the living room when I walk in.

"There you are, James. Did you get Genevieve back home, safe and sound?"

"Yeah, Mom, I did. Listen, I can't really talk right now. I have to go make a couple phone calls."

"Oh, okay. Well, there is some food in the fridge if you're hungry afterwards."

"Thanks."

I rush to my room and dial Jack Kingsley's number.

*Jack was my first friend when we moved here. He took me under his wing and introduced me to the kids that had been his friends since they were in kindergarten. He has definitely changed throughout the course of our friendship, but we have always stayed close. Everything that Gen inadvertently revealed this afternoon really pissed me off. I don't think that I have ever been this angry with him. I have some stuff I need to talk to him about.*

It rings four times before he picks up.

"Yo! Jimmy! It's been awhile. Sorry to hear about your sister, man." He sounds like he has been smoking weed all night, which knowing him, he probably has been. His voice is lazy and low. It's as if speaking to me is taking an unnecessary level of energy. I can picture him reclining back on his gamer chair with heavy eyelids, a layer of smoke hanging in the air around him.

"Actually, Sadie is exactly what I wanted to talk to you about!"

"Really? What about?"

"Did you really hook up with my baby sister behind my back?"

*Don't you dare lie to me, asshole!*

"Hell yes! I enjoyed every single minute of fucking that fine piece of ass!"

*Now my blood is boiling. No one gets to talk about Sadie like that, not even Jack. I have heard him speak about half of the female student body at Hamstead High like this. Somehow, I managed to get through our entire school career without him mentioning Sadie in that manner. He did mention Gen once. He quickly realized that it was a huge mistake though.*

*We were hanging out in his basement, playing video games and snacking until we wanted to puke. Jack and some of the other guys from our group were doing play-by-plays of their 'pussy adventures' like they always seemed to do. It was a Friday night at the end of our sophomore year. That week had been horribly hot and humid. Every girl in school had broken the dress code to avoid overheating. Short skirts, denim cut-offs and spaghetti strap tank tops were in vast supply that week. On Friday, Gen wore her ripped shorts that she normally saved for lazing about with Sadie on summer days. When she walked into school wearing them, I almost passed out. I couldn't believe that Darcy had let her leave the house in those to go anywhere but our house. I had never seen her wear something that revealing in public. Now, I had to endure hearing all of my best guy friends discussing how hot they found her today.*

*"Oooh, man! Did you guys see Porter today? Did you notice what she was wearing?" Jack had actually paused the game to discuss her. He NEVER paused games for anything. Our other friends let out multiple variations of confirmation that they had in fact noticed Gen. How could they not have? Those shorts were so tight and so short. When she bent to grab a book from the bottom of her locker, way too much of her ass was showing. When I caught myself staring, I quickly made an excuse to go stand behind her. I wanted to block her from unwanted ass slaps from the many grotesque boys in our school. I wanted to slap her ass, so I knew everyone else would want to.*

*"Dude, don't. Just stop. Don't talk about Gen. That's crossing the line, man, even for you." I tried to stay level-headed at first. Jack let out a boisterous laugh. He actually thought I was joking!*

*"Jimmy, dude, come on. You know as well as I do that she is hot as hell. I know she is friends with your sister, man, but damn. A freshman that looks like* that*? Can you imagine what she will look like next year? I would totally tap that." That was when I couldn't take it*

*anymore. I snapped. I stood up from my seat on his sectional. I walked over to him and grabbed the front of his shirt in my fist.*

*"Don't fucking talk about Gen. She is off limits. Pick a different girl to fantasize about." I was gritting my teeth. All of the guys were just staring at me in shock. I was the quiet and docile one of our group. This was really out of character for me.*

*"Thompson! What the fuck is wrong with you? It's not like I squeezed her ass or anything. I'm just saying that I noticed how hot she is for once. It's her fault for putting it all out on display! She had her boobs practically out in the open and you could see the bottom of her ass cheeks when she walked down the hall. If she didn't want to show it off, why would she have worn* that? *She doesn't have other clothes?"*

*"You are such a pig, Jack!"*

*"Come on! You cannot possibly tell me that fucking her didn't cross your mind today when you saw that figure walk in! If your sister hadn't been constantly hanging around her, I would totally have pressed her against the lockers and made out with her. Dude, can you give her my number?" With his shirt still balled in my fist, I yanked him out of his chair and punched him directly in the mouth. Everyone else sat there in stunned silence as I released his shirt and sat back in my spot on the couch to take a sip of my soda.*

*"What the fuck! That hurt man! What is wrong with you tonight?"*

*"Genevieve Porter is off fucking limits, man. Do not ever talk about her like that again. I will not put up with that shit. You don't know her, man. You can't just say shit like that about her."*

*"What's so different about her? We always talk about babes. Why can't she be a part of the list now that we are all aware that she is hot?"*

*"Just drop it. I don't ever want to hear* any *of you say her name during one of these conversations again. She is not just another 'pussy adventure' for you to brag about."*

*"Whatever, man. Next time that you punch me, I will be returning the favor, dick."*

*Just like that, we went back into the rhythm of playing video games and drooling over the Hamstead Hotties. Gen's name was very carefully avoided at all costs after that.*

"Do NOT speak about her like that!"

"Sorry! I'm just being honest, man!"

"If you're so interested in honesty, when was the last time that you were with her?"

He scoffs before he answers me. "A few days after Christmas. Why?"

"Because, *jackass*, my beautiful baby sister is dead and it took her death for me to find out that she hooked up with one of my oldest friends. It took her dying for me to realize that I couldn't protect her even though I tried my hardest. It took her death for me to find out that she was fucking pregnant."

"Pregnant? Really? I promise you that I haven't been with her recently. Dude, where the hell is this all coming from? Why are you so angry that I hooked up with her almost a year ago? I don't get it. She is legal, man. She was then, too. And she was hot as fuck. You should be congratulating me like a *good* friend."

"*Congratulating* you? For *fucking* my sister who also happened to be my best friend? Are you serious?" He just grunts and ignores me.

"Do you have any idea who knocked her up?"

"David fucking Jerome! Of all people!"

"Oh man, that might kind of be my fault." *Finally, there is a smidge of guilt in his voice.*

"How?"

"Well, um, I kind of had Sadie meet up with him for a couple deals while we were together."

"Wait. Deals? What kind of *deals*?"

"Drugs."

"So, you're telling me that on top of fucking her behind my back, you also made her do something illegal for you?"

"Come on, dude. It was just pot. Not the hard stuff."

"Give me David's number. *Now*."

"I don't know, man. I don't think he will meet up with you."

"Just fucking give it to me, Jack." He hesitantly texts me David's number. I hang up as soon as I receive the text. I decide to text David anonymously.

*I will just say that I want to do a deal with him.*

I am sweating bullets now.

*I can't believe I'm doing this.*

Yo, you got the goods?

*What am I doing? I have never done a drug deal before and especially not like this. David has always been into drugs and violence. He was an asshole even when we were kids.*

Sure. Soft or hard?

Soft.

Meet me at the old Warren's
Factory at 2:30. Come quietly.

*Done! I will actually be seeing the possible father of my niece or nephew and hopefully getting answers to questions that I can never ask Sadie.*

I look at the clock. It's ten-thirty. I'll be able to get a little rest before I have to go meet up with him. I close my eyes and fall asleep. The darkness is welcoming right now. My mind is completely exhausted from today.

I snap awake. I pat my bed for my phone. It's one-fifteen.

*I should let Gen know that I'm meeting David, just in case something happens.*

I text her and start getting ready to go.

*I'll have to leave quietly so that Mom doesn't notice. Gen is worried about me and wants to go, too. I could never forgive myself if something happened to her. If this goes wrong, I don't want her involved.*

Outside of our house, I start getting second thoughts. Then, I think of Sadie laying in that casket earlier.

*There is no going back. I need to talk to him.*

I drive to the other side of town and down a dark gravel road that leads to a crumbling brick building. Back in the day, this was a bustling watch factory. It has been abandoned for decades. I see a beat up sedan parked by the factory. I pull up beside it and park. He isn't in his car.

*Come on Jimmy, you can do this.*

I get out of my car and quietly shut the door. The factory door is propped open. I step inside as my shoes crunch on some broken glass and gravel.

"I'm back here." David's raspy voice calls out from somewhere near the back of the building. I keep walking toward his voice. When I get to the room where he is waiting for me, he has his back to me. He is in a ragged looking denim jacket and skinny jeans. "Do you care what strain? I have six different kinds tonight. Personally, I would recommend the Purple Haze. It is excellent."

"No, David, I really don't care." He recognizes my voice immediately and turns to face me.

"Jimmy, dude. I didn't know that you were into this stuff now." He is definitely shocked to see me. His jaw drops.

"I'm not. You know that I've never been a fan of the stuff. I am even less of a fan of you. It is getting worse every minute."

"If you're not looking to score, why are you here man?"

"You know damn well why I am here." He starts backing up and then turns like he is going to bolt. He runs face first into the brick wall.

*If I wasn't so pissed right now, I would have laughed.*

"Why the hell were you at Sadie's funeral?"

"I was just trying to give you my condolences. We were something like friends once and I always liked your sister. She was nice."

"Oh, I know that you *liked* her." David tries to run past me. I step in front of him. "She was pregnant, you know?" David looks like I just caught him red-handed. His face is bright red and he is staring at the floor. "So, how long were you hooking up with her?"

"I don't know what you're talking about, man." He is avoiding making eye contact.

*I wonder if it's because my eyes are just like Sadie's. Do they make him feel guilty?*

"Bullshit, David! Bull-*fucking*-shit!" I'm raising my voice.

"Okay, okay, I was with her a few times over the last few months."

"How fucking dare you? Do you never learn?" I push him backwards.

"She came onto *me*! I swear! I mean I loved every single minute of her, but it was her idea, not mine."

"Liar!"

"For real, man! Jack sent her to meet up with me and I recognized her immediately. We hooked up after the second time that he sent her to meet me. Dumbass should have come on his own. I've never forgotten how great of a kisser she was, even when we were younger." As he talks, I am just getting angrier and angrier.

"Why didn't you do the right thing and tell us that she was pregnant when you found out that she died?"

"I don't know. I didn't think it would be a good idea to bring it up when you just had to deal with seeing her limp body in the woods."

"How the fuck do you know that?" David realizes that he just fucked up. He pulls his fist back and punches me directly in the eye.

My anger unleashes and I hit him back as hard as I can. He starts bleeding a little. My head is pounding as he punches me again, harder this time. I push him as hard as I can and he falls on the ground. He is giving me a look of pure anger. "I don't know how you know that, but you better stay the fuck away from my family. That includes Genevieve. If I find out that you so much as *look* in her direction, I will hunt you down and beat the shit out of you."

I turn on my heel and storm out of the factory. I get in my car and reverse out of the spot I'm in and spin around as fast as I can. Dust kicks up all around my car. My heart is pounding in my chest. I can feel my pulse in my ears. I can't see very well out of my eye that David hit.

*It's stinging pretty badly. I don't have time to look at it right now. I'll wait until I'm far from David. All I want now is to tell Gen about what happened and wrap her up in my arms.*

## Genevieve

Again, I'm awakened by my phone vibrating. I grab my phone and see a picture of Jimmy with his goofy lopsided grin. He is calling me.

*It's three-forty in the morning. Why is he calling? Hell, it doesn't matter. It's Jimmy. I will answer his call anytime, anywhere.*

"Hello," I answer groggily.

"Oh, sorry, Gen. I didn't mean to wake you, but can I come see you? I have some information and I really want to see you."

"Um, yeah, of course. I'll go down and unlock the door. Just come on in when you get here."

I drag my body downstairs, half asleep. I unlock the door and curl up on the couch. I drift back to sleep for a few moments. The door quietly shuts and I open my eyes to Jimmy standing in front of me. He has a black eye forming and blood dripping from his nose. His appearance startles me fully awake.

*The normally perfect face has been altered temporarily. Yet, he is still so handsome.*

"Jimmy, what happened?"

"*David* happened."

"How did you even find him?"

"Jack Kingsley."

"Jack still talks to David?"

"Kind of. He's Jack's dealer."

"Dealer? Like a drug dealer?"

"Yeah. Jack swears it's just pot that he is using, but who really knows. Anyway, after I left here, I called Jack. I kind of went off on him about Sadie. He had the audacity to say that he enjoyed every second of, and I quote out of pure disgust, '*fucking that fine piece of ass*'. So then I was super pissed off and I told him about Sadie being pregnant and about David. He told me how to reach him. So I messaged him anonymously."

"And?"

"I met him out at the old watch factory on Hacienda. He was definitely not expecting to see me. He tried to run, but the idiot cornered himself. I told him that she was pregnant. I wish you could have seen his face. He was a textbook-definition of guilty. I asked how long they had been hooking up. He said that she came on to him. Jack, the asshole that he is, sent her on some drug deals to meet up with David. That's how they got back in touch."

"Okay, that explains some of it, but not why you're bleeding?"

"He never asked how she died, Gen, but he *knew*. He knew she died in the woods right where I yanked him off of her all those years ago. How the fuck did he know that? Only you and my parents know that. So I asked him how he knew that and he hit me. I couldn't stop myself. I hit him back. He hit me again and I pushed him to the ground. I told him to stay away from my family and especially you."

"Do you think he was there? Maybe he heard it from someone that your parents told."

"Maybe. I don't know. I'm not sure of *anything* right now."

Now, Jimmy is sobbing uncontrollably. I hug him tightly against me and wait for him to calm down a bit. His chest is unevenly heaving up and down.

"It kind of makes sense now why Sadie didn't say anything. She knew how you felt about David and he was a drug dealer. Her having his baby would definitely have been worse than him making out with her when we were kids."

Jimmy wipes his eyes. I sit here, just staring at him. I can't help it. He is so raw and passionate right now.

*God, I wonder how wonderful it would feel to kiss his lips right now.*

He looks me all over from head to toe.

He sniffles as he says, "You're wearing the same shirt as last night."

"It smells like both of you. It comforts me and makes me happier."

*Maybe he caught that he was included in that.*

He glances down at my bare legs.

"And you're still not wearing any pants." Suddenly, I am keenly aware of how I am practically in his lap.

"Nope. I should probably go put some on. I'll be right back." I start to stand and he grabs my wrist lightly. I sit back down, staring at him quizzically.

"I don't mind that you're not. I was just stating a simple fact that I *noticed.* I mean, how *couldn't* I?" He is definitely blushing a bit. On the other hand, I am blushing so much that my entire face feels like it's caught on fire.

*Without the buffer of Sadie, I can't think of a logical reason to not act on what I have felt for years. He keeps making it harder and harder on me. This week has been so terribly long and all I want is to feel comforted and loved. I don't want grief to be the reason that I act on my feelings though. I want to kiss him when it happens organically.*

"You shouldn't say stuff like that unless you mean it,

Jimmy."

"I meant every single word." He makes eye contact with me with his good eye.

We sit wordlessly staring at each other for a long time. Both of us, trying to will the other with our minds to make a move. His face is still crusted with blood from his nose. It looks like it hurts.

"I'm going to get you a washcloth and an ice pack." I walk to the kitchen to get the supplies to clean up his face. I enter the living room and Jimmy is leaning his head back on the couch. He looks like he is in a lot of pain. "Here, let's go upstairs and get you cleaned up. You can sleep in my room. I don't want Mom asking questions about your black eye. I haven't told her about everything with Sadie yet."

"Are you sure that having me sleep in your bed is the best idea?" He looks reluctantly hesitant.

"Absolutely."

*If he only knew the truth! I have dreamt of having him in my bed numerous times, but none of them were to sleep. He also never had blood crusted on his face in any of these hypothetical scenarios.*

"Where will you sleep?"

"In my bed, next to you."

"What about your mom? Won't she be upset?"

"Believe me, my mom won't mind. She adores you. Plus, I am nineteen and my best friend just died. She isn't going to get mad at me about much right now."

He looks at me with concern in his eyes, like he doesn't quite believe me. I just walk up the steps to my room instead of arguing about it more. He follows reluctantly. Once we are in my room, I check the time. It's four-fifteen.

*The sun will be rising soon. I just want to sink back into that cozy sleep that his call pulled me from. I yearn for those empty, dreamless sleeps right now. The ones filled with memories of Sadie are too difficult.*

I lightly wipe the blood off of his face with the damp washcloth. He places the bag of ice lightly against his eye. Once I am satisfied with the cleanliness of his face, I pull myself into bed and beneath the comforter.

"Do you have an extra blanket?" Jimmy is staring at my solitary comforter stretching across my bed like it might grow claws and attack.

"You won't need an extra blanket. I promise. This one is super warm. Just get comfortable and lay down. It's going to be morning soon. Try to get some sleep." Grudgingly, Jimmy sits on the edge of my bed and removes his shoes. He stands up and reaches for the blanket to climb in beside me. "Jimmy, dude, what are you doing?"

"Um, going to sleep? You said I could sleep in your bed, right?"

"That's not what I'm talking about. You're still in your jeans and belt. You cannot possibly be comfortable sleeping in that."

*I don't know how well I'll be able to control myself with him in his boxers beside me, but I want him to be comfortable.*

"Well, I, uh, I don't want to make you uncomfortable." He winces as he accidentally grazes his black eye as he goes to brush his hair out of his face, his tell-tale nervous twitch.

*Why is he acting so strange?*

"James, look at me." I wait for his eyes to meet mine before continuing. "Seeing you in your boxers isn't going to make me uncomfortable. I've seen you in swim trunks and shirtless plenty of times over the years. Get comfortable and lay down. Get some sleep. Seriously. It's going to be daylight soon."

*If only he knew how* extremely *comfortable I would be with him in his boxers beside me.*

The fact that I used his proper name catches his attention because I don't use it often. He undoes his belt and pants. They slip to the floor in a pile as he removes his shirt. I try my hardest not to stare, or bite my lip. He crawls into bed beside me, very careful not to touch me at all. "Good night, Jimmy."

We lay in silence for a while. As I start to drift asleep, I hear his hushed voice.

"I'm sorry for last night," he whispers. I lay still for a moment, waiting for more. He stays silent.

"Why are you sorry? You didn't do anything wrong."

*I am retracing all of our interactions from last night. I can't think of a single thing he needs to apologize for.*

"Well, maybe nothing *wrong*, but *unwelcome* maybe? It's been such a long week. I just really missed Sadie and *you*. I missed you and just wanted to know that you weren't going anywhere."

I prop myself on my elbow, facing him. The moonlight is casting shadows over him. I take in the view of his bruised eye and his arm draping over his bare torso.

"Jimmy, first of all, I completely understand that you miss Sadie. I do too, so *incredibly* much. We are *always* going to miss her. *Secondly*, I have missed you like crazy this week too. I needed last night as much as you did. I needed to know that you were here with me and *alive*. If I hadn't wanted to lay with you, I wouldn't have. I would have said good night and come up here to my bed. *Nothing* about your existence is unwelcome to me."

*I am so close to telling him how I feel. I'm crying now. I'm not sure when the tears started to fall. It's not an ugly cry, just tears that needed to escape and found an opportune moment.*

I lay my head back on my pillow and shift my body over to his. He takes his arm and wraps it around my shoulders, pulling me closer to him. I am starting to cry harder now, thinking of Sadie and her tiny baby.

*Was this really just an accident of fate?*

My chest is tightening up. I bury my head into his chest and start to sob. He pets my hair and shushes me gently like a toddler who had a nightmare.

"Thank you for not leaving me all alone. Sadie would really appreciate this, you know. And thank you for hunting down David. At least now we have some sort of answers and maybe some more questions."

I close my eyes and try to shallow my ragged breathing. I start drifting asleep. Just as I am about to fully surrender to the abyss of sleep, I once again hear Jimmy let out a barely audible whisper.

"I'm not doing this for Sadie. I'm doing this for *us*."

*Sunshine is breaking through the autumn trees. Sadie is twirling around playing air guitar to something on her iPod. I can't hear the music. All I can see is her crimped hair bouncing with each bang of her head and pure joy radiating from her in that very moment. I had been having a bad day. My dad had been creeping back into my thoughts a lot lately. I didn't want to give in to those memories, fearful of the inevitable slide into depression. Sadie knew that I needed to be with people but still wanted solitude, so we came to the woods behind her house. I was situated on a log, picking mindlessly at the moss covering its bark. She looks at me with a huge grin and starts belting out a cheesy love ballad to me. We were thirteen then.*

Suddenly, I'm woken up by my mother's voice. She is in the hallway, muffled by my door. I know that she is speaking to me, but I can't decipher what she is saying in my half-asleep state. Her voice starts booming louder as she opens my door.

"Good morning, Genevieve. Here is some of your clean laun..." her voice drops off as she looks over to my bed, noticing a second body. In the early morning light, she can't see his blackened eye, but the mess of auburn hair immediately gives away his identity. Her emotions are flicking all over her face. Shock quickly turns to joy and then to embarrassment of what she is witnessing.

"Sorry, I didn't realize you had anyone in here. Um, I'll just go make some, um, breakfast." She is stammering as she is trying to leave the room as quickly as possible. She is rushing too much and stubs her little toe on the corner of my dresser.

"*FUCK!*" Mom grabs her foot and hobbles to sit on my bed. She accidentally sits on Jimmy's foot. He wakes up and sits up quickly, disoriented by his surroundings and his black eye impairing his vision.

"What's going on?" Jimmy asks, groggily.

*His voice has a different husk to it early in the morning. It's sexy and enticing. Honestly, it takes a great amount of concentration to not audibly groan out of desire when I hear it.*

"I just stubbed my stupid toe." Mom answers through clenched teeth. Mom turns her attention from her throbbing foot to Jimmy. She jumps from the spot at the foot of my bed and reaches out to touch his face. He flinches as she grazes the facial bruising with her fingers. "Oh my God, Jimmy! What happened to you? Who did this?"

Jimmy looks to me for some sort of direction on how to proceed. He knows that Mom is still clueless about the baby. I bite my lip and give him a slight nod, signaling for him to tell the truth. She needs to find out eventually. Telling her with Jimmy by my side will make it much easier on me.

"A guy named David Jerome. We got into a fight. He was sort of Sadie's boyfriend, I guess. I met up with him after the funeral. I needed to discuss some stuff and unfortunately it went a little bit...*off-course.*" Jimmy lets out a deep sigh.

"Wait, since when does Sadie have a boyfriend? This is the first I'm hearing of this." Mom sits back down on my bed and looks to both of us, waiting for more information.

"Mom, we didn't know either. Not until yesterday at the funeral home. Apparently, she was, um, uh, *expecting*," Mom's jaw drops and her hand instinctively covers her mouth.

"Pregnant? Really? *Sadie*?" Mom looks distant and bewildered. She looks like a child whose lollipop fell in the dirt.

*Sadie was like a second daughter to her. I know she isn't clueless about Sadie's sex life, but thinking of Sadie being a mother is such a foreign concept to us all.*

"None of us had any idea. We didn't even know about David until our personal Nancy Drew figured it out." Jimmy elbows my arm lightly with a lopsided grin. "She tried to talk to him at the funeral and he ran. Then she recognized him from an old photo. I tracked him down last night, in a pretty stupid way." Jimmy glances over at me, admitting that he was dumb last night for my benefit.

*He has always hated admitting when we were right and he was wrong.*

"Wow. Just, *wow*." Mom is speechless. "I'll go get some breakfast cooking. You two come down whenever you're ready."

*If she wasn't so shocked, she would have winked at us before slipping out the door and down the stairs.*

Once I hear her feet reach the bottom of the stairs, I let out a huge laugh. I can't help it. I laugh and laugh and laugh. Jimmy is just staring at me as if he thinks I'm having a mental breakdown.

"Gen, what is so funny?" He is starting to chuckle now too.

*It feels good to laugh. How long has it been since I had really laughed? Monday was my last real laugh. It feels like it's been years.*

"I think Mom had the wrong idea about what was happening in here last night when she first saw you." My sides hurt from laughing so hard. It's starting to calm down a bit, thankfully. "She came in and didn't notice you at first. But I watched her put the pieces together like a puzzle. A male in bed beside me, shirtless, and for all she knew, naked beneath this blanket. The pile of your clothes on the floor." My eyes are watering and I cough every time that I try to cease my laughter. "She was so flustered. I wish you could have seen her face. She tried to scurry out to avoid an awkward situation, but then she stubbed her toe and woke you up."

"You think that she assumed we had sex last night? *See?* This is *exactly* what I was trying to avoid." Jimmy is tense, his tone growing increasingly annoyed. "I could have slept downstairs. I don't want your mom to get the wrong idea about me. I'm not *that* guy."

"Not *what* guy? One that would consider having sex with me?"

*That was really offensive and uncalled for. I honestly want to hear his answer. Fingers crossed that my tone came out as gentle and not bitchy or sarcastic.*

"I'm not saying that I haven't, *wouldn't*, consider having sex with you. I just meant that I'm not the guy who takes advantage of a girl who is suffering a great loss. I'm also not the kind of guy that has meaningless sex or wastes kisses just for the sake of kissing. If I am going to do those things with someone, I am going to be committed to them first. Sleeping around just isn't my style."

"I think that it's great that you want something meaningful. I doubt Mom has the wrong idea about you. She *knows* you. You're a great guy. Honestly, she would probably be *happy* if we had sex." His eyes fly open with shock.

"Wait. *What?* Why would she be happy about that? If Mom and Dad had known Sadie was sleeping around, they would have flipped. They are *still* pissed and she isn't even *alive* anymore."

"It wouldn't be meaningless sex or sleeping around if it was with you." I look down quickly.

*I can't believe that I just let that escape from my lips.*

I can't make eye contact with him right now. Jimmy is staring at me and searching my face for some sort of clarification. He takes a deep breath and then licks his lips like he is parched.

*God, I want to be the one licking those lips.*

"Gen, what, um, what exactly are you saying?" He starts fidgeting with his bottom lip. He is looking me dead in the eye. He is waiting for some sort of answer.

*Fight or flight! Fight or flight! What the hell do I say?*

"Um, I think we should push pause on this conversation and go eat some breakfast. I smell bacon and coffee."

*Flight, nice choice! I am such a coward! Why is this so hard? It's Jimmy!*

"Okay, but only because I am starving right now. Don't think you're getting out of this conversation though! As soon as breakfast is over, you're answering me." Jimmy is giving me a huge goofy grin as he rolls out of bed. I can't help but to stare at his lean body as he pulls his jeans on. I've never been able to help myself when it comes to seeing him shirtless.

*The first summer that Sadie and I were friends, we went to Cooper Beach with her family. That was the first time that I really got to spend time with Jimmy. We arrived at the beach just in time for lunch. After we ate our sandwiches that Maryann had packed in a small cooler, we decided to play some frisbee before swimming. Jimmy took his shirt off before we started. Even at the young age of twelve, Jimmy had a nice body. Most guys at that point were either scrawny and childish looking or they were pudgy with the puberty weight. Jimmy was nicely in the middle. I looked up just as he was lifting his shirt over his head. I was actually gawking at the sight of him. Sadie caught me and slapped my arm. "Ew! Please stop! That's my brother!" I turned to her and smiled, "I know, but he's so hot." Sadie pretended to dry heave in the sand. "I don't like him or anything. I just like* looking *at him." At this, Sadie rolled her eyes and kicked the sand.*

Jimmy walks out of my room and heads toward the kitchen. I quickly throw on some sweatpants before joining him downstairs. I attempt to brace myself for whatever awkward conversation my mother is inevitably going to start over breakfast and for the conversation I'll be having with Jimmy afterwards.

*He is notoriously stubborn. Once, he bugged Sadie endlessly for three days straight until she admitted that she had taken his last piece of candy. There is no hope that he is going to let this slide. Nothing goes better with bacon and eggs than a side of embarrassment, I guess.*

## Jimmy

*Last night, I was set on telling Gen about my feelings for her. When she pointed David out in that old picture, I immediately became Sadie's relentless protector once again. I got tunnel vision and all that mattered was getting answers about my baby sister. I left Gen's in such a hurry to hunt down David that I didn't realize I was still holding the picture of Gen and I. I remember the night that picture was taken.*

*We were camping at Green Lakes Campground and begged my parents for s'mores all day long until they finally caved. They let us build a fire and tell ghost stories. Sadie sat in a camping chair that we had for years. It was faded from the years of summer sunshine. As soon as she sat down, it broke and her ass fell into the dirt. Gen offered her seat instead. While Sadie went to change her dirt-covered shorts, Gen and I squeezed into my chair together. I was in a blue hoodie and basketball shorts. Gen was wearing a white hoodie and denim shorts. We were both tan with fresh sunburn spread across our faces. Our hair looked like it had been wet all day from swimming. Mom was snapping photos every few minutes. She looked at us and said, "Smile, kids!" We both have huge smiles on our faces and my arm is pulling Gen in close. That was the first summer that I realized my feelings for Gen. Somehow, this photo was added to the picture boards even though Sadie isn't anywhere in it. This feels like a sign that I need to tell Gen the truth.*

*Now, Gen is making me wonder if she feels the same way. She made some comments between when I came back late last night and then again a few minutes ago. She insisted that I sleep in her bed beside her and that I take my jeans off. It took so much willpower to not try something last night. She has now slept beside me two nights in a row in nothing but a t-shirt and her underwear. Not just any underwear, but black lacy ones that don't cover her butt completely. It's so sexy, but in an understated way.*

*The first night wasn't as difficult because I got the chance to hold her close but we were on the couch in the open where Darcy could walk in at any moment. Last night though, that was different and much, much harder. We were in her room behind closed doors. I wanted to pull her close again, but I don't know if I would be able to control myself with her body pressed against mine, practically skin to skin. The only time that I had her within an arm's length was for a short time while she cried. When she was done, she rolled over and fell asleep. I would have absolutely loved to spend the night spooning her again.*

Darcy is plating our breakfast.

*I am going to scarf down my food as quickly as possible. The faster I eat, the faster I get to find out what Gen meant about it not being sleeping around if it were with me. Does she mean that it would be much more meaningful than that? Did I misread the conversation entirely? I tried my hardest to be as respectful as possible last night so that Darcy wouldn't get the wrong idea, but apparently Gen thinks that I failed miserably. I want Darcy to grant us her blessing if we end up getting together. Her opinion really matters to me. As Gen's only living parent, she would be the one that I would need to ask for Gen's hand prior to proposing.*

I get lost in the delectable scent of cooking bacon and freshly brewed coffee.

*Sadie June, Who Were You?*

*Food first, then the conversation that I'm starving to have.*

## Genevieve

Once I hit the bottom of the stairs, I can see Mom and Jimmy at the kitchen table.

*He is eating his bacon and eggs so fast that it seems like he hasn't eaten in weeks. If I ate that fast, I would totally vomit.*

Mom looks up and gives me a smile. I walk into the kitchen and pour myself some coffee before taking my seat at the table. We sit in silence for a moment. I drink a few sips of my coffee. Mom grants me the courtesy of letting me wake up a bit before diving into being nosy.

"Thank you so much for the food, Darcy. It's fantastic."

*Jimmy is laying it on thick this morning, I see. He must be trying to get back into her good graces, though I am sure that he was never out of them.*

"Absolutely! You need to regain energy after last night." Mom winks at me.

*Oh my God! I am so mortified.*

"Mom! Stop it!"

"Sorry! Sorry!" Mom is laughing so hard that I think she might snort. *Laugh it up, lady!* "What else am I supposed to think when I walk into your room and find you two in bed together?"

"Darcy, I promise you that nothing happened. I wouldn't disrespect your house or Gen that way. I just needed to sleep and Gen thought her bed would be a better idea than the couch."

"*Gen* thought, huh?" Mom smiles and raises her eyebrows at me suggestively.

"Mom, it was nothing like that. I swear."

"Whatever you say. All I know is that when I was your age, if I had a person of the opposite sex in my bed, it wasn't to sleep."

My shocked "*Mom!*" is paired with Jimmy's "*Damn, Darcy!*" as Jimmy starts choking on his coffee.

"Well, I am just saying that I know what it's like to be nineteen and twenty. I also want you to know that I'm okay with you staying here whenever you need to. I love you like family, Jimmy." Mom reaches across the table and rests her hand on Jimmy's, oozing motherly affection.

"Thank you, Darcy. I love you, too." Jimmy smiles at my mom and then glances in my direction. "I've finished my breakfast." He beams at me and winks.

"Let me finish my coffee first." I slowly sip from my mug.

*I am going to savor every last drop of this quarter-cup to make sure I prolong this conversation. I am* so *not ready for this.*

"Well, I'll meet you upstairs. I am going to freshen up a bit." Jimmy walks out of the kitchen and takes the steps two at a time. Mom looks at me.

*I know what's coming now.*

"Okay, Gen. You *have* to tell me! Don't hold out on me! What's going on with you two?"

"Nothing...*yet*."

"*Yet*?" Mom squeals like a schoolgirl.

"He pretty much asked me this morning how I feel about him and I have to go discuss it with him when I finish my coffee."

"Yay, yay, yay!" Mom is rapidly clapping. "I'm so happy for you two."

"Mom, I don't even know how he feels about me. For all I know, he could think of me as his sister. Also, it's too soon after Sadie to even *think* about this happening."

"Well, I have *never* seen a guy look at his sister the way that Jimmy just looked at you. It was full of flirtation! And as for Sadie, I think this could only bring you two closer."

"I think I am going to refill my cup..."

"No, you're not. You are going to go upstairs and tell him how you feel. *Finally!*" Mom stands up and takes my mug from my hands. "Go!" She waves me up the steps, shooing me away like a fly.

I walk up the steps as slowly as I can. As I reach the landing, I notice my body is trembling.

*I don't think I can do this. I have been building this moment up for years in my head, often in my dreams. It always ends differently.*

*One dream, we were stuck in traffic when I told him. He laughed in my face and he made me get out of the car and walk eight miles back home. That was one of the bad ones. Another, we were in the middle of grocery shopping and he pinned me against the frozen food aisle and started making out with me. That was one of the nice ones. One of the* very *nice ones. There was also one where we got together but then we broke up and Sadie refused to be friends with me anymore. That was the one that made me decide I was not going to act on my feelings no matter how badly I wanted to.*

I deeply inhale as I turn the door handle. Jimmy is lounging on my bed like he has always belonged there.

*I should make him stay just like this forever.*

The sunlight falling on his face makes his blackened eye look shiny.

"So, Gen, what *was* it that you meant earlier? You tried to avoid answering me pretty hardcore, but no more procrastination." Now, he is sitting cross-legged on my bed and pats the mattress beside him. I walk over and sit next to him.

"Well...it wouldn't be sleeping around because it would only be you and sleeping around normally implies two or more partners."

*Nice attempt at skirting around the truth!*

"Gen, that is *not* what you meant. If it was, you wouldn't have been so weird. What's *really* going on?"

"Okay...promise me you won't laugh?"

"I won't laugh. Pinky promise." Jimmy holds up his right pinky. We lock pinkies. I look at his face, his lovely freaking face. He looks sincere.

*I know that I can trust him. I have to do this. He is serving me the perfect opportunity on a silver platter. It's now or never.*

"Well, I, um, I, I, um, I really like you. I have for a really, *really* long time. That's sort of why I've never had a boyfriend or anything. And the reason my mom wouldn't mind is because she knows how long I've liked you and she has this crazy notion that you feel the same way about me. She actually called you her future son-in-law yesterday. Her and Sadie have been trying to convince me to tell you for years."

*Once I start talking, it all spills out extremely quickly. I'm rambling frantically and I'm out of breath.*

My heart is racing and I'm just staring at Jimmy. He is just looking at me, but not saying anything. He is totally stone-faced.

*Oh shit. This is it. This is the moment I've been dreading. He is about to tell me how much he* doesn't *see me in that way.*

"God, Jimmy. Say something. *Anything*. Just rip off the damn band-aid." I'm whining while my heart is in my throat.

"Years? How many years?"

"After everything that I said, *that* is your first question?"

"Yeah. I seriously want to know. How many years?"

"Um, this is kind of embarrassing..." I fidget with my cuticles while avoiding eye contact. "Eight."

At last, his face is no longer straight and emotionless, instead his jaw is wide open and his cheeks are starting to turn up into a smile.

"Eight years? You've been hiding this for *eight years*?" He starts laughing and is rocking in place. He claps his hands on his knees.

"*Hey!* You promised you wouldn't laugh at me!" I make a pouting face.

"I'm sorry, Gen. I'm *sorry*. I'm not laughing at *you*. I'm laughing at *myself*."

"What? Why?"

"Well, um, to be honest, I've liked you since I was fourteen. So, we've both been hiding this for almost seven years. We could have been dating for six years already." Jimmy is laughing hysterically.

*I love when he loses himself in laughter. It's one of my favorite things. He is so goofy and adorable.*

"Wait. You *like* me? Like, actually *like* me?" My heart feels like it's trying to jump from my chest. It's fluttering.

*This is crazy.*

"Are you *kidding*, Gen? How could I *not*? Why do you think I was so worried about what Darcy thought went on last night?"

"Why didn't you ever say anything?"

"*Sadie.* I was afraid she would kill me for even considering it." Now, it's *my* turn to laugh.

"I told her, but I hid it for a while at first. I thought she would hate me too."

"You told her? How did she react?"

"She squealed and told me to marry you. She wanted me to be her real sister." Tears are streaming, but I'm smiling. He is tearing up, too. "I really miss her. I bet she is spying on us right now from wherever she is."

"Totally." Jimmy chuckles as he wipes his tears away lightly.

We just sit here for a few minutes looking at each other. It's like we are both trying to figure out if this is real life or a dream. I wipe the tears from my eyes and bite my bottom lip. "So, um, what happens now?"

"*Now?* Now, I go home and get ready."

*The hurt from that statement is so real and raw. It feels like he just slapped me.*

I turn away a bit and look at the floor.

"Oh. Uh, okay. I guess I will, uh, see you later then."

*Don't cry. Don't cry. Not until he leaves.*

"Yeah, you *will* be seeing me later. You will see me at three when I pick you up for our first date."

"Wait. What did you say? First date?"

"It's extremely overdue, don't you think?"

I start laughing. "Uh, yeah, I guess so."

"Later, Gen." Jimmy flashes me a huge smile and grabs his stuff. He grabs my hand and lightly squeezes it before he walks out the door. The sensation of his hand touching mine lingers long after he lets go.

I wait until I hear the front door open and close to let out a squeal of joy. Mom hears me and rushes in. She must have been waiting in her room to find out what happened. She looks like a little kid on Christmas morning.

"Was that a squeal I heard? I'm assuming it went well."

"It did! Better than I could have imagined." I am beaming.

"So, how did it feel to finally kiss James Thompson?"

"I wouldn't know. We didn't kiss."

Her smile falters with slight confusion. "You said it went well?"

"He went home to get ready. We are going out on our first date this afternoon." I get up from my bed and hug Mom tightly.

"That is so exciting! I can't wait to hear all about it tomorrow. I have to work tonight. I am so happy for you, honey."

Mom gives me a tight squeeze and leaves my room. I walk over to the stack of Sadie's old photos. I pick them up and start looking through them. About halfway down the stack, I find one of my favorites of our trio.

*It was taken in the middle of winter on a snow day. We are all decked out in our winter gear. We spent the day playing in the snow like small children. We had a snowball fight that resulted in all of us being strewn with fresh powder. We made snowpeople. Jimmy gave his snowman a mohawk or attempted to anyway. It was our junior year and Jimmy's senior year. Sadie is in between us. Our cheeks and noses are bright red from the cold. We are all beaming and covered in snow.*

I decide to stick this photo in the frame of my mirror, so that I can always see it. Sadie is beautiful and full of life in it.

"Well, Sade, I did it. I finally told him how I feel. Fingers crossed!" I touch her face in the photo and start to tear up. "I love you. I wish you would have told me about David and the baby."

I start putting away my laundry that Mom brought in my room this morning. Mixed in with my laundry, I find a pair of Sadie's jeans.

*She was always leaving clothes here and borrowing mine. Our closets have become so intertwined that I normally can't remember if something is mine or hers. These jeans though were her favorites. They have a permanent streak of black from where she spilled her liquid eyeliner.*

I put them away in my drawer. My phone vibrates.

Gen, thank you for telling me.
I can't wait to see you later.
BTW, my parents asked what
happened to my eye.
All I said was that I was in a fight.

I can't wait either, Jimmy.<br>I'm going to get ready.<br>I'll see you soon.

# Jimmy

My mind is reeling.

*Gen actually likes me! She has liked me longer than I have liked her. Why the hell didn't I say something sooner? I am such an idiot. I could have spent all of my teenage years with her. We would have been high school sweethearts. Hell, I would have already proposed by now! I know exactly where I want to take her for our first date today. She deserves romance and happiness. I am going to give her as much as I can.*

I walk into the house beaming for the first time since Sadie died.

"James, where have you been?" Mom is in the kitchen with her back turned to me.

"With Genevieve." At this, she turns around to look at me. She notices my eye immediately.

"What happened to your eye?"

"I got into a fight." I shrug and say this while still beaming.

*She must think that I have lost my damned mind.*

I walk to my room to start getting ready. I need to shower before we go out later. As I get to my room and start picking out my clothes for our date, there is a single knock on my door and then Dad walks in.

"Who did you get in a fight with? You seem pretty damn happy for someone with a black eye."

"Just some asshole. And I *am* happy! I finally did it, Dad! I told her how I feel."

"Wow! About damn time, son! You stayed at her place again last night, huh? How did that go?" He raises his eyebrow at me.

"I would say it went well." I still cannot get this huge smile off my face.

"Were you careful, at least?"

"Dad! No! I mean, yes. I mean, *no*, because we didn't do anything. I just told her about my feelings this morning. Do you really think I would just sleep with her without telling her first?"

Dad holds his hands up in mock surrender. "I didn't know the timeline and I guarantee that if you *had* slept with her first, you wouldn't have needed to tell her how you feel. It would be written all over your face! I'm happy for you."

"Thanks, Dad. I'm going to get in the shower and start getting ready."

I get in the shower and start daydreaming about showering with Gen.

*Damn! That's a mental image I never want to lose. But now I am fully active. This isn't going away for a while, not on its own at least.*

I turn the water to ice cold.

*I am not going to use up any of that energy without her with me. I've spent enough time with myself over the years thinking of her. Not now, though. I am going to wait for the real thing now that it's finally in reach.*

After my shower, I throw on my clothes and head for my car. Dad winks at me as I pass by him while I try to avoid Mom. She is staring at me with daggers in her eyes.

"Where do you think you are going? You just got back."

"I'm going to see Genevieve. I don't think she should be alone right now."

"Weren't you just there? I'm sure that she will be fine for a few days. Plus, she has Darcy."

"Mom, I'm almost twenty-one. If I want to go see her, I will. Bye, Mom."

*She has been awful since she found out about Sadie's pregnancy. She is acting like a strict prude. I am not letting her get her way. She is being ridiculous.*

I walk out the door and get into my car. As I back out of the driveway, Mom steps outside and stares at me disapprovingly with her hands on her hips.

## Genevieve

Mom leaves for work around one-thirty. She works twelve hour shifts as a home health aide at the local assisted living facility. As soon as she leaves, I turn on Sadie's favorite Spotify channel and start getting ready.

*What am I supposed to wear on a date with someone who has known me for years and has seen all of my wardrobe options?* I stare at my closet. *I don't even know what we are doing today or where we are going. I have no clue what to expect.*

I decide to put on an oversized yellow sweater and what Sadie always called my "*great ass*" jeans. After I get my clothes on,

I brush my hair and braid it to the side. I put on some mascara and black eyeliner. My green eyes are wide open and not bloodshot for the first time since Tuesday. I steal a glance at the time on my phone. It's almost time for our date. The butterflies are fluttering in my stomach again. I put on my shimmery lip balm and smack my lips together a couple of times.

I take a good look at my reflection.

*Sadie would be proud of how I am pulling myself together right now.*

I strike a few poses in the mirror and make kissy lips. I let out a small giggle.

*I look ridiculous, but I've done this a million times before with Sadie by my side.*

The doorbell rings. I jump a little, startled.

*He's here. Deep breaths, Gen!*

I walk downstairs to open the door.

My hand is trembling as I turn the door handle. Jimmy is wearing black skinny jeans, gray Chelsea boots and a black sweater. His hair is pushed back from his face.

*He looks so damn perfect and he smells amazing. He always looks like he doesn't even have to try.*

He has a huge smile when he sees me open the door. He is looking at me from head to toe, taking in every detail. His eyes are lighting up as they dance over my body.

"Hi." I say sheepishly. I can feel the blush rising to my cheeks.

"Hey." He flashes me another award-winning smile. His hands are shoved far within his pockets. He is slightly rocking back and forth on his heels.

*Is he nervous or just cold?*

"Are you, um, ready to go out?"

"Oh, yeah. Of course. Let's go." My heart is thumping in my ears. I close the door behind me as Jimmy turns toward the driveway. His hands are still inside his pockets. I follow him, awkwardly fidgeting with my hands. He opens the passenger side door for me, smiling. "Um, thanks."

*This is really weird.*

I sink into the passenger seat and buckle up. He closes the door lightly once he knows that I am fully inside the vehicle. He jogs around the front bumper to the driver side and gets in. He quickly buckles and turns the keys in the ignition. He definitely seems nervous. As Jimmy starts to drive toward the business district, I ask him where we are going.

"We, my dear Genevieve, are going to the river. Well, *eventually*. I have to make a quick stop first." He glances at me with smiling eyes.

"That sounds like fun!"

"I'm hoping you'll like it."

"I'm sure I will. You know that I'm pretty easy to please." I smile before realizing that I'm still fidgeting with my hands.

"Are you nervous?"

"Not gonna lie. I have never been this nervous before in my *entire life*." I laugh at my own expense.

"Honestly, I'm nervous too. I just want it to be perfect."

"It's silly. We have known each other for so long. Why are we nervous? It's just *us*!"

"I know, but I think that's *why* I'm so nervous, because it *is* us! What if this makes things weird between us?" Jimmy chuckles nervously and pulls over in front of my favorite bakery,

Cameron Cookies. "I'll be right back out." He gets out of the car and heads inside.

I nervously pull out my phone and aimlessly click apps. I check the weather and then my email before scrolling through my text messages.

*I keep hoping that if I act like this is just an ordinary day with Jimmy that my brain will calm itself.*

Jimmy opens the driver side door and hands me a to-go coffee cup before sitting in his seat again. "Here, this one's for you."

He sets his own drink in the cup holder between us and hands me the bag of goodies that was just hanging from his wrist. I glance at him suspiciously and take a sip of my drink as he starts to drive away from the bakery. It's a soy chai tea latte, my favorite.

"Thank you! It's delicious. How did you know that was my favorite?"

"Do you think I haven't been paying attention to what you like all of these years? I am pretty much an expert in knowing what you like."

"Well, then how do you explain not knowing that I liked *you* for the last eight years, huh?" I raise my eyebrow at him coyly as I tease him and sip at my latte.

"You know, I'm not really sure. I keep running that back through my mind. I thought you did for a while, but then I figured I was just imagining things because I *wanted* you to like me."

"You were definitely not imagining it."

"Well, obviously I know that *now*." Jimmy laughs and takes his right hand off the steering wheel for a few moments to let his fingertips graze my hand. My mind instantly flashes to the first time that he ever held my hand.

*I was sixteen and we had gone to a party that one of Jimmy's classmates was throwing. Everyone was drinking and having a good time. It was like a party scene from any teen drama on television. An older guy, who's name I still have never learned to this day, was hitting on me nonstop. I kept ignoring it for a while, but then he started touching my arm, followed by my back. Just as his hand was making its way toward my ass, Jimmy swooped in and saved the day. He had noticed what was happening from across the room and pretended to be my boyfriend. He came straight toward us, shooting daggers at the guy the entire time with his eyes.*

*"Hey, baby. I've been looking for you everywhere. Come on, let's get out of here." Jimmy grabbed my hand, interlocking our fingers and leading me out of the party and toward his car. We walked the entire way to his vehicle, hand in hand, until we reached the safety of his front seat. Sadie had spotted us from the kitchen while grabbing a beer. She quickly bee-lined it out of the door, following us. Almost as soon as we had gotten in the car, she was climbing into the backseat and slamming the door shut.*

*"What the hell is going on guys? Am I missing something? Is there something you're choosing not to tell me?" She kept frantically looking from Jimmy to myself and back again.*

*"No, Sade. Chill. I was just getting Gen out of a bad situation before it got any worse." Those words cut into my very soul. I know that he didn't mean for them to be hurtful, but it felt like he was saying that he was only doing me a favor and could never see me in that light. I tried to conceal my feelings more after that night for a while. Those few*

*precious moments of having his hand in mine only cemented my feelings more. It felt so natural to slide my hand into his.*

"What are you going to do about it now that you know it's the real deal?" I can't peel my eyes off of him as I sip my latte. I study every detail of his face while he is driving.

*He is such a beautiful creature.*

"You'll just have to wait and see!" He grins from his own amusement. He knows how much I hate surprises.

We turn down the road that leads to the river. It's more of a rural area. There are very few houses out this way. The ones that are out here are old farmhouses that are spread pretty far from their neighbors. Jimmy drives about a quarter mile and then pulls over. He puts the car in park before unbuckling. I am so confused.

*What the hell is he doing? We are in the middle of nowhere.*

He reaches into the bag from the bakery and hands me a box. The white cardboard is housing two peanut butter blossoms and a brownie. He has an identical box of baked goods.

"Are we just going to sit on the side of the road and eat these?" I start laughing as I take a bite of a cookie.

"Well, kind of. We are going to eat these yummy snacks and enjoy our drinks. Then, I am going to show you something that I think you'll like."

"Okay, whatever you say." I am speaking with a fresh bite of cookie in my mouth. I am sure to finish that mouthful before speaking again, reminding myself that I'm on a date and should be acting as such. "Let's play a game."

"What kind of game?"

"Ask Me Anything. So, go ahead. Ask away."

"I don't know what to ask."

"Is there anything that you've always wanted to ask me but haven't or anything that you're curious about? If so, now is your chance."

He studies one of his cookies while he contemplates his answer. "Um, well yeah. There are a few, I guess."

"Okay, shoot. One at a time though please."

"Why haven't you ever had a boyfriend?"

"Well, a few reasons, I guess. Number one is *you*. Plus, I had Sadie. I didn't need a boyfriend. I had her to take up all of my free time."

"Me?" He seems genuinely shocked.

"Yeah, *you*. I didn't like anyone else. I liked *you*."

"Oh." Jimmy is blushing a bit, but also beaming with pride.

"Okay, my turn. Are you, um, you know, a virgin?" I'm so nervous that my palms are sweating and clammy.

*I'm terrified of his answer. I have always wanted to ask him about this, but it is the one topic that our trio always seemed to avoid at all costs.*

"Are you?" He stares at me seriously from over his coffee cup.

"I asked you first!"

"Don't laugh!" He is smiling at me and pointing his finger in my face. I am holding my breath in this moment, anticipating his answer. "Yes. I am. I know that sounds ridiculous since I'm almost twenty-one, but it's the truth." He almost looks ashamed.

*It's the answer that I was hoping for!*

"It doesn't sound ridiculous. I just wasn't sure because you only dated Hilary and that was a really long time ago. Plus, I didn't know if you had maybe hooked up with anyone on the down-low at parties or anything."

*I am so damn relieved.*

"Hilary and I made out all the time, but neither of us was ready for that. We moved to second base a bit, but that was it. We were only fourteen."

"Hey, I know people who had sex at fourteen!" I'm holding my hands up in surrender trying to prove that this isn't some crazy notion.

"Oh yeah? Like who?"

"Like Sadie."

*I probably shouldn't have said that, but I can't lie to him.*

"What?! With who?"

"Lucas Holmes."

"Really? At *fourteen*? What the hell was she thinking?" Jimmy looks pissed even though this was five years ago.

"I don't really know. It was only the one time though and then she didn't do it again for a long time."

"I don't want to think about that. Ugh, *yuck*." He shakes his head like he just ate something disgusting, like orange juice right after brushing your teeth. "But you still never answered me. Have *you* slept with anyone?"

I chuckle lightly. "I've never had a boyfriend, remember? I thought we just went over this."

"Having sex and having a boyfriend are two totally different things, Gen." As he says this, he pops the last bite of his brownie into his mouth and takes a swig of coffee.

"I know, but remember how you were talking about not doing things without a commitment first? That's how I feel about it too. I'm not going to just hook up with some random guy."

"That's a good thing, Gen." He smiles at me sweetly. "Okay, my last question for right now. When was your first kiss?" He bites one of his cookies while looking at me expectantly. I glance at the floorboard of the car.

*I can't look him in the eye right now. This always embarrasses me.*

"Um, actually, I haven't had it yet."

Jimmy almost chokes on his coffee. He is staring at me with a look of pure shock.

*This is always how people react when they find this out. Most people have their first kiss before turning fifteen. I have always dreaded being asked this question. I would always find a reason to leave the room if this topic came up at sleepovers or parties.*

"What? Seriously? You haven't been kissed *at all*? How the hell is that even possible?"

"No one ever tried, so it just hasn't happened." I shrug.

*It really isn't as big of a deal as people make it out to be.*

"No one has ever tried to kiss you? *Ever? Really?* I'm sorry. I don't believe that for a second. I mean, *look at you*."

"It's the truth. Sadie was always the one getting kissed. With her around, no one really even gave me a second glance. You know how she was. People always gravitated toward her."

"No first kiss, huh? Well, I plan on changing that sometime soon, if you don't mind." I look at him and can't help smiling. His eyes are twinkling at me.

"I wouldn't mind that at all."

"You have no idea how happy it makes me to hear you say that." Jimmy holds my hand and rubs his thumb over the back of my hand as our fingers are intertwined. "Come on. I want to show you that thing now." He opens his door and gets out. I check to make sure no cars are coming down the road and then I get out too.

"Where are we going?"

"Through here." Jimmy points to the woods beside the car. He holds his right hand out behind him so that we can hold hands. I gladly intertwine my fingers in his. "Watch your step." He starts ducking under branches that I can easily walk under. The ground is covered in leaves and patches of snow.

*It's breathtaking in these woods, but I still don't know where he is taking me. My brain keeps wandering to all of the true crime documentaries where girls are murdered and left for animal food in the woods. If this was any other guy, I would be worried about a scenario like that.*

We keep walking hand in hand for about a half mile. "It's just ahead, only a little bit farther."

We walk for about another five minutes and then he gently tugs on my arm, signaling for me to go ahead of him. The woods open up into a clearing that is nestled on the bank of the river. The water is rushing by, sparkling blue in the sunlight. Right beside the river is a table and two chairs all made from old tree stumps.

"Jimmy, this is so beautiful."

"I knew you would like it. Plus, it gives more privacy than down at the main river area. I thought it would be a perfect spot to spend a bit of today together. Once we get too cold, we can obviously go somewhere else though." He squeezes my hand gently and smiles. "Do you want to sit or we can walk beside the water?"

"Let's go close to the water and walk a little. I don't want to sit and get my butt wet."

"I didn't even think of that! I'm such an idiot. Walk, it is." We start walking along the river. The mist that is spraying up into the air is just hanging around us.

"You're not an idiot! I love it here! I would sit, but I'm afraid it would make me a lot colder."

"I've been coming here a lot on my own the last few months. It's a great spot to think and just clear away some stress. There is a bunny and a few deer that will come right up to you."

"Oooh, really? That is so awesome!"

"They are great listeners, too. I can just come out here and talk to them without any fear of judgment."

"What kind of things do you talk to them about? You know that you could always have talked to Sadie and I about stuff. We would never judge you."

"Well, actually, I would talk to them about *you*. They were the only ones I could really open up to about you and say everything that I was thinking. That's another reason that I wanted to bring you here. It just feels right to me."

"Honestly, *everything* about this feels right to me." I kick a small stone into the water with the side of my foot as we walk.

"I think so too." Jimmy stops walking, prompting me to spin towards him to see why he stopped. He is just looking at me. He grabs my other hand so that both of my hands are in his. "Gen, thank you so much for giving me this opportunity."

"Of course! Thank *you* for bringing me on a date. You know that you didn't really have to do this since I already know pretty much everything about you, right?"

"I wanted to do this the right way. If I am even going to have the *slightest* chance to be with you, I am going to make sure that I earn every second of it. I don't get some territorial claim to you just because you've been in my life for so long. You deserve me pulling out all of the stops."

He lets go of my hands. His left hand moves to my hip and his right moves up to cup the side of my face. With one slight step forward, he closes the space between us. He stares into my eyes and then leans his forehead against mine. We just stay like this for a few minutes, feeling our chests move against each other as we breathe. The feeling of intimacy in this moment is overwhelming. Tears start to spring into my eyes. I just keep breathing in his scent. The sandalwood and peppermint mixture is intoxicating.

*Crunch. Crunch. Crunch.*

We pull away from each other to look in the direction of the crunching snow. From about ten feet away, we see two beautiful deer walking toward us and the river. I stand utterly still, petrified that they may have one rogue deer just waiting to attack. Jimmy just smiles at the graceful animals in our presence.

"Hey, Casper and Jasper! How are you two doing today? This is Gen. The girl I have been telling you about."

"They are so amazing, Jimmy. Look at them! They are beautiful." I am starting to shiver now.

*I don't want to leave here though. It's so private and pretty.*

"Gen, come on. Let's head back to the car. You're shivering!" I was too busy staring at the deer to notice that Jimmy had been looking at me. He grabs my hand and starts leading me back into the woods.

"I'm not ready for today to be over yet though."

"Over? Oh, nope. We are just getting started."

"Good!" I beam as a violent cold chill momentarily overtakes me.

"For the rest of the night, we have some options. We can either go to a restaurant and movie or we can get take out and watch movies at one of our houses if you'd like to continue with the privacy theme."

"I'm not ready to be around too many people just yet. Let's go back to my house."

"Oh I get it! You just don't want to be seen with me." Jimmy winks at me with a smile.

On the drive back to my house, Jimmy holds my hand the entire time. The radio is set to a local rock channel and we are both mindlessly singing along.

*I am still nervous. Actually, I am more than nervous now. I'm beginning to panic.*

*We are going to my house alone. I shouldn't be nervous. We have been together at my house plenty of times. This is only the third time without Sadie's accompaniment though. Also, it's the first time sans Mom. It's just Jimmy! Why am I so nervous? Remember, Gen, he won't make a move without commitment first. This is a key thing to keep in mind. Ugh, Genevieve Porter, snap yourself out of this.*

The butterflies in the pit of my stomach are surreal as we pull into my driveway. "You can park in front of the garage. Mom is at work."

*Crap, now he knows that the house is empty. What if he expects something to happen?*

"What do you want to order for dinner? We can do pizza or Thai if you want." When Jimmy and I reach the front door, I pull the house key out of my pocket and attempt to unlock the door. The temperature is starting to drop. I can see my breath now. My hands are trembling so badly that I can't get the key to go in the hole. It takes a few tries. Jimmy touches my lower back. "Do you need help, Gen?"

"Uh, yeah. Sorry. I don't know why my hands are shaking so badly."

*Yes, I do. I am so freaking nervous.*

"It's just really cold out." Jimmy takes the key and opens the door effortlessly. He is calm and collected.

*Why is he not freaking out as much as I am? Maybe he doesn't actually like me as much as he thought he did. Maybe this is too weird for him now.*

"It really is. Let's grab some blankets and pick a movie to watch. Then we can decide on dinner." I slide my shoes off inside the front door and head to the hall closet to grab some blankets. I grab a few blanket options off the shelf and return to the living room. Jimmy is sitting on the edge of my couch, taking his shoes off. I set the pile of blankets beside Jimmy. "I'm thirsty. I think I am going to grab some water. Do you want anything?"

"Some water would be great. Thanks." Jimmy sets his shoes by the door and flashes me a carefree smile. I walk into the kitchen.

*I am going to take my time filling the two water glasses. I need a moment to compose myself. This could be my first and last date with Jimmy if everything doesn't go smoothly. I really don't want to blow this.*

"Do you want me to get Netflix started so that we can choose a movie and then chill until we get dinner?" Jimmy speaks loud enough for me to hear him in the kitchen. I let out a small chuckle and fill the two glasses. I return to the living room.

"*Netflix and chill*, huh?" I raise my eyebrows at him teasingly.

"Oh my gosh. I'm sorry! I totally didn't mean it like that. That was a bad choice of words." Jimmy is blushing fiercely.

"It's okay even if you did mean it like that. I mean, we *are* on a date after all." I hand him his water and grab a red fleece blanket from the pile. I sit on the couch beside him, cross-legged, and cover up to get warm.

"That's very true, but it is our *first* date." Jimmy drapes his left arm over my shoulders as he scrolls through the options on Netflix. "Should we do horror, drama or romance?"

"I don't think I can handle a drama this week. I say horror."

"Gory horror or storyline horror?"

"Hmm, storyline!" I settle myself closer to Jimmy beneath his arm.

*His body is so warm against mine. Having him this close relaxes me.*

Jimmy scrolls through until he finds a movie that seems to fit the bill. It's about a group of paranormal researchers that go to Scotland for an investigation. He presses play and the opening scene shows a moss-covered mansion with chipping paint.

# Jimmy

♪♪♪

*Relaxing on the sofa, snuggled up with Gen, feels so natural. She seems so nervous today. I just want her to be comfortable around me like she normally is. I don't want the fact that we revealed our feelings to make things weird between us. So far, I think that everything has been going pretty well, except maybe for that Netflix-and-chill faux pas. I didn't mean it in that way at all, not that I haven't dreamt about that countless times before. This is only our first date, after all. I want to let things happen naturally. I don't want them to feel rushed or forced.*

*I haven't even kissed her yet. Why the hell haven't I kissed her yet? I came so close by the river. My deer friends interrupted us just as I was becoming courageous enough to do it. The timing hasn't seemed quite right just yet. Plus, isn't there some sort of code in Girl World about not kissing on the first date?*

So far, this movie has had quite a few jump scares. Each time one of those scenes comes on, Gen jumps a little and scoots a tiny bit closer to me.

*I don't know if she is doing this on purpose or if it is completely unintentional. But either way, I am not complaining.*

Two of the paranormal investigators have this strange sexual tension happening, but neither of them is willing to acknowledge nor act on it.

*It reminds me a lot of us, honestly. I wonder if Gen sees the similarities, too.*

I pull her in closer, soaking up every single second that I can of her body touching mine. Her hair smells so nice, like apples or something fruity.

## Genevieve

♡

"So what do you think of our date so far?" Jimmy now has his hands clasped in front of us, so I am in a strange sort of hug. My head is resting against his chest, but I am looking at the tv even though my ears are focusing more on listening to his heart beating within his chest.

"It's great, Jimmy. Thank you."

"Thank you for giving me a chance to do this the right way. Are you a little less nervous now?"

"A little bit, but I am still pretty nervous though. I'm sorry. I can't help it."

"Gen, don't be sorry. I'm nervous, too. I want this all to go perfectly. I feel like there is so much riding on this."

"You don't *seem* nervous. I can't stop shaking and the butterflies keep coming."

"Well, I am. I mean, it's *you*! How can I *not* be nervous? You are so important to me. I don't want to mess up what we already have."

"Neither do I." I drape my left arm across his torso and give him a small hug. His hands aren't clasped anymore. Now his left hand is resting on my hip as if it has always belonged there.

"I'm really hoping that if I do everything right, it will just make what we have even better." I smile and start to tear up, thankful that he isn't looking me in the face right now. We just sit in a comfortable silence for a little while watching the movie. I snuggle into him even more.

*There is nowhere I would rather be right now.*

*Buzzzzz. Buzzzzz. Buzzzzz.*

My phone is ringing in the kitchen. I don't want to get up, but no one ever calls me so I hate letting it go unanswered. I apologize to Jimmy and remove myself from the couch. I grab my phone off the kitchen counter. It's Mom calling me.

*Why is she calling me? She is supposed to be at work.*

"Hey, Mom. Is everything okay?"

"Hey, sweetie. Everything is fine. I just got a quick break and wanted to call and see how the date is going."

"It's, um, pretty good."

"Pretty good, huh? Not great?"

"Well, it is. Definitely. He is right near me though, so can we talk about this later?" *Way to make things awkward, Mom!*

"Has he kissed you yet?"

"Not yet. We are watching a movie at our place. I've got to go. I love you, Mom."

"Love you! Go kiss him, for God's sake!"

"Bye, Mom!" I hang up and walk back to the living room rolling my eyes at her meddling ways. "Since I already have my phone out, what do you want to order for dinner?"

"Whatever you want to get is fine with me."

"Okay, I'll just order pizza. Is Father Tony's okay?"

"Sounds great." Jimmy smiles at me. I go back into the kitchen to place the order. I order us a medium pizza and wings over the phone and set delivery up for forty-five minutes. When I walk back into the living room, Jimmy pats the couch cushion beside him. "Who called?"

"It was just my mom."

"Oh, no. Is everything alright?"

"Yeah, everything is fine. She just wanted to give me the third degree about our date."

He laughs lightly. "Really? What was she asking?"

"She wanted to know how it was going and if you had kissed me yet or not." I roll my eyes and run my fingers through my hair.

"Same old Darcy." Jimmy laughs lightly. "What did you tell her?"

"The truth. I told her not yet."

"Well, yeah, not quite yet." *Those words make me feel like I've been slapped. It stings that he hasn't kissed me yet.* I quickly look down at my thumb and start picking at the cuticle. I feel tears starting to sting my eyes. I quickly blink to keep the tears away. "Gen, what's wrong?" Jimmy touches my hand lightly.

"Nothing. Well, not really *nothing*, but I'm okay."

"Gen, tell me what's wrong. You can tell me anything. You know that, right?"

"Yeah, I know. I'm okay, really. It's stupid. My emotions are just all over the place this week." I blink again to keep the tears away, but this time one falls onto Jimmy's hand. His hand moves up to my face. He lightly turns my face toward him so that he is able to look me in the eye.

"Oh, Gen. Don't cry. Please. I hate seeing you cry." Jimmy brushes his thumb beneath my eye to wipe away the stray tears. "Whatever it is that is making you cry, you can talk to me about it or if you don't want to talk about it, I can just hold you so that you can get those feelings out. You know that bottling it up doesn't help. It just prolongs the suffering."

"What if *you're* the reason I'm crying? Can I still talk to you about it?"

"*Especially* if it's because of me! Wait. *Am* I the reason you're crying?" Jimmy is looking at me with horrified wide eyes. He looks terrified and hurt. I just lightly nod my head. "Gen, I am so sorry. I never meant to make you cry. What did I do? Do you want me to leave? I can just go home and forget about all of this. Just forget that I told you how I feel. Everything can go back to how it has always been. It's too soon after Sadie. I shouldn't have pushed you. I'm so sorry." Jimmy is hugging me tightly against him and speaking frantically. I can feel his heart pounding rapidly against his ribs. He sounds like he might cry, too.

"No, I don't want you to go home. I want you to stay here with me. You didn't *do* anything. I'm just really nervous that you won't actually like me or want to be with me now that I'm attainable. Why won't you kiss me yet? Has being on a date with me changed your mind about your feelings for me? Do you not actually like me like that now? Is it too weird because we are friends?" Now, I am the one speaking frantically. I am also crying really hard. I am getting Jimmy's sweater all wet from my tears.

He pulls back from the hug and looks at me with a small smile on his face.

"Genevieve Kathleen, is that what this is all about? Because I haven't kissed you yet?"

"Well, yeah, kind of. I mean, if you really like me as much as you say, why haven't you kissed me? I told you how I feel about you this morning. You've had all day to kiss me."

"I was trying to be respectful of you, Gen. Most girls don't like to kiss on the first date, not until the end at least. I don't want to do anything that you're uncomfortable with. I don't want you to feel pressured. I have waited this long to get a chance with you. I am not about to mess that up." Jimmy has both of his hands wrapped around both of mine in my lap.

"Oh. Well, thank you, but I am completely okay with you kissing me at any time, Jimmy. I've been okay with you kissing me for eight years. At any moment in the past eight years, if you had just walked up to me and kissed me, you would have made my entire world. You have no idea how many times I daydreamed about something like that happening."

"Gen, I promise you that I *will* be kissing you before the night is over. Honestly, the only reason I am holding back right now is because if I start kissing you, I don't know if I will be able to stop myself. I've kept all of my feelings for you bottled up for so long that if I take the lid off, it is all going to just explode out of me and there will be no stopping it." Jimmy tucks some of my hair behind my ear. "Is that okay?"

I nod, lightly biting my lip. Now thoughts of him not being able to contain himself are flooding my mind.

*That sounds absolutely perfect to me but also completely terrifying. What if I'm not any good at kissing or the other stuff? I have absolutely no clue what I'm doing.*

We turn our attention back to the movie and I lean back against his shoulder. The investigators on the movie are walking around the mansion using night vision on the camera. They hear a floorboard creak. Just as they all turn to face the noise, the doorbell rings.

*Ding dong. Ding dong.*

I jump and let out a small shriek. I turn my head toward the door.

*I totally forgot that I had ordered pizza.*

I get up to answer the door and Jimmy follows behind me. I open it and see Andrew Collins. He graduated with Jimmy. As he hands over the food, he offers us both his condolences about Sadie. We thank him and send him on his way.

Jimmy takes the food into the kitchen. I follow closely behind and grab two plates from the cabinet. When I turn around to set the plates on the table, Jimmy is right in front of me. He takes the plates from my hands and sets them on the table.

"Why don't you go sit down and I'll bring you your plate?" Jimmy opens the pizza box and raises his brow at me. I take the hint and return to the living room to sit. When Jimmy comes into the living room a minute later, my plate has two pieces of pizza arranged in the shape of a heart. "Food for my lady."

"Thank you, sir."

*We have always done cheesy stuff like using formal titles or fake British accents. It feels natural to just be together like this.*

I take a bite of my pizza as I watch him return to the kitchen for his own plate. He grabs his food and joins me on the couch. "*Yummmm.*" I moan from the pizza's deliciousness.

*I didn't realize how hungry I was. The pizza is fitting exactly what I need right now.*

"Gen, you *really* shouldn't be making noises like that around me." Jimmy winks at me and smiles before taking a bite of his food.

"Oh, yeah? Why not?" I tease.

*I know exactly where he is going with this, but why not play dumb?*

"It makes my mind wander to all of the other ways I could hear those noises from you. By the way, I *do* plan on being the reason you moan like that eventually." Jimmy is staring me dead in the eye with only a tiny bit of blush spreading across his cheeks. I bite my lip. My imagination is going wild with me now.

"You do, huh?"

"Absolutely. It might not be anytime soon. It might be weeks or months or even *years* from now. However long it takes for you to be ready, but it *is* something that I am *really* looking forward to." Jimmy rests his hand on my thigh, just above my knee and gently runs his thumb back and forth on my leg.

"I would *really* like that and I promise you that it won't be years." I bite my bottom lip and smile, making eye contact with him the entire time. I finish my pizza and take my plate to the kitchen.

While Jimmy finishes his food, I am going to take the opportunity to go pee and freshen up. I head upstairs to the bathroom. After I pee, I wash my hands and brush my teeth to banish the pizza smell. I reapply my lip balm and head downstairs. Jimmy isn't in the living room and the movie is over. I glance at my phone. It's already seven o'clock. "Jimmy? Where did you go?"

"I'm in here." Jimmy's voice comes from the kitchen. He is at the sink washing the dishes that we used.

"You don't have to do those. I can do them later."

"I've got it. Don't worry about it. I don't mind." He dries the plates and sets them on the counter. He turns and looks at me. He is only about a foot away from me. I'm acutely aware of every inch between us. He steps toward me, closing the distance between us once again. His hand is on the side of my face and wraps beneath my hair at the base of my neck. He tilts his head slightly, parts his lips a bit and kisses me. He just kisses me very lightly on my lips and then pulls away to look me in the eyes. His entire face is smiling. "I've been waiting to do that for so long."

Before I realize it, he is kissing me again, but more insistently this time. His mouth is warm against mine and his tongue slips between my lips. I kiss him back and instinctively press my body against him. Jimmy moves his hands down my sides and cups my butt lightly. I let out a small moan.

*I have wanted this for so long.*

I don't want to ever stop kissing him. I pull away and smile at him.

"Let's go upstairs to my room." I grab his hand and head toward the stairs. Jimmy stops walking. The abrupt stop halts me in my tracks, yanking me back toward him.

"You know, maybe we should stay down here." Jimmy starts to walk toward the living room.

"Come on. Let's just go to my room. It will be more comfortable up there."

"That's what I'm afraid of." Jimmy kisses me again and pulls me close.

"I'm not afraid of what might happen, James. Come on. Let's go to my room." I grab his hand and head up the stairs. This time he is following me. We go into my room and I shut the door behind us.

Jimmy sits on the end of my bed nervously.

*Now, he's the nervous one? Seriously?*

I walk over and sit beside him. He looks at me and kisses me lightly. I grab both sides of his face and kiss him intensely. I lay down on the bed and pull him down beside me.

*I can't stop making out with him. It feels so perfect to finally kiss him.*

I press my body against him as much as I can. I'm instinctively grinding my hips against him and his hands are pulling me in closely. Jimmy's body is so warm against me. His hands slowly start to move beneath my sweater and toward my bra. I let out another small whimper of anticipation. All of a sudden, Jimmy pulls away and sits up. "What's wrong?"

"I should probably go. I've had such a good time today, but if I don't leave now, I don't think I will be able to stop myself. I really don't want to go, but we don't need to rush things. We have time." His hair is tousled and his face is flushed.

"I don't want you to leave. Stay with me tonight."

"Darcy will be home soon. I really should go."

"Please? For me?" I stick out my bottom lip like a pouting child.

"Gen, you have no idea how badly I want to stay."

"Then stay! We are both adults. There is no reason why you can't stay here. You've already been here the last two nights anyway. The only difference between then and now is that we kissed." I kiss him one more time lightly on his lips. "I *love* kissing you, by the way."

"Is it everything you imagined it would be?"

"It's better, so incredibly better." I smile and kiss him again. "I have been wanting to do this for so long."

"Me too, Gen. Me too." Jimmy kisses me and lays us back down. I roll on top of him and grind my body against his. I can feel him getting hard through his jeans. I slip my tongue in his mouth. He twitches in his jeans. "Gen, babe, we need to take a break for a second."

"Mmm, I like hearing you call me that." I kiss him again deeply before rolling off of him onto the bed. I lay on my side facing him. "Why do we need to stop?"

"I want to talk to you about us for a minute."

*Oh, God. Here it comes.*

"Um, okay." *The whole we-need-to-talk vibe is making me nervous. That rarely ends well.* "What do you want to talk about?"

"Okay. So warning: this might seem a little straightforward. Remember how I said that I don't take intimacy lightly? Well I was really serious about that. I know that this is only technically our first date, but I already know that I don't want to be with anyone else. I would really like for you to be my girlfriend. I want to know that I'm the only one kissing you."

"Jimmy, I'm yours. I've been yours for years, whether you knew it or not. You're the only one that I have ever wanted to kiss or even considered having sex with. You will never have to worry about me kissing someone else."

"That makes me so happy." Jimmy kisses me and pulls me into him. "Wait, did you just say that you've considered having sex with me?"

"Well, of course I have. I might be a virgin, but I still have *needs*." I nuzzle my nose into his neck.

"Mmmm, Gen. Don't tease me like that."

"I'm not teasing you. I'm serious. Everytime that I have ever pictured my first time, it's been you. It has *always* been you."

"Really?" Jimmy looks shocked but pleased. I nod and bury my head in the bend of Jimmy's neck again. "I need to run outside really quick. I'll be right back." Jimmy gets out of the bed and jogs down the stairs.

I get out of bed and take my sweater off. I start rummaging through my drawers for a t-shirt to wear for bed. I find one of my senior year shirts and take it out. As I am taking my bra off, Jimmy walks back into the room.

"Mmm, hey there." Jimmy wraps his arms around my waist from behind and kisses my neck lightly. Then, he pulls away nervously. "Sorry, I couldn't help myself." I quickly put my shirt over my head and walk to my bed. "By the way, those jeans look really hot on you."

"Thanks. Sadie used to call them my '*great ass*' jeans." I flash a smile and start to blush. "I need to take them off to get ready for bed. Do you want to leave the room?"

"I'll just turn the other way if you're uncomfortable, but you have been in just underwear the last two nights."

"Do you think we could control ourselves tonight if I don't put pants on?"

"I've done pretty well the last two nights, haven't I?" Jimmy looks proud of this accomplishment.

"Absolutely. You've been nothing but a gentleman." I slide my jeans off and set them on my dresser.

*If we can't control ourselves, oh well. This is Jimmy. I love him. I've been in love with him for years.*

Jimmy bites his lip as he looks me up and down. I notice what he brought inside for the first time now. It's his duffle bag. "What's in the bag?"

"Clothes for tonight and tomorrow. I packed a bag just in case."

I walk to his side and have him set the bag down. I lay down and pull him down next to me. He kisses me once and then sits up to remove his sweater. Now, Jimmy is shirtless beside me. I run my hand along his torso and keep kissing him. He starts running his hand along my back beneath my shirt and removes it in one slick move over my head. He runs his hand down to my hip and then back up my torso until his fingertips graze my breast.

"Genevieve, you're so beautiful." Our kissing grows more and more intense. Before I know it, I am unbuttoning Jimmy's jeans and trying to slide them off. "You are really testing my willpower." Jimmy lightly nibbles on my lip.

"Jimmy, anything that happens, happens. Don't think about it too much. Just relax and do what feels right in the moment." I grind my body against him with our underwear as the only barriers between us.

"Gen, I want you so, so, so badly. You have no idea how badly I want this, but let's not do this tonight. Just kissing you and holding you is enough for me. We have plenty of time for sex. We don't need to do it all at once. I know we both have years of bottled up attraction to let loose, but we will in time. Today you went on your first date ever and had your first kiss ever. Let's take baby steps." Jimmy keeps kissing me between sentences. We lay there in nothing but our underwear making out for hours until we finally fall asleep with our bodies completely entwined, our lips swollen and red.

## Jimmy

♪♪♪

*I kissed her. I finally kissed her.*

She is laying in her bed beside me now after spending quite a while letting our tongues mingle and explore each other's mouths.

*Her body is so soft and warm against me. Keeping myself from having sex with her right here, right now is so difficult. She is definitely providing me with a warm welcome, but I cannot bring myself to make too big of a move right now. I want to make sure she is completely ready. I mean, it's Gen. I never want to hurt her. I will wait until she is in the right mindset. I will not push her.*

She has already fallen asleep. I'm just laying here with our bodies completely melding together.

*I'm soaking up every single ounce of happiness that I can from this moment. This still doesn't feel like real life. It has been almost seven years since I first fell for her. For all of that time, I saw her as strictly off-limits. I already know that she is The One. It's been years that I've known that she is the woman I am going to marry. Anything that happens from here on out will only further cement that fact. She seems ready and willing for sure.*

*I still can't believe that she never had her first kiss until today. Holy shit! I was Genevieve Porter's first kiss! It just hit me how monumental this is. Now, all I can do is hope that I'm her last first kiss. I would marry her right this very second if I could. Over the years, I have envisioned our future: marriage, a house and two or three children. The only difference now is that Sadie won't be a part of that future. She had always been in those visions too. She would have been the maid-of-honor and godmother, as well as aunt. In my earlier days of loving Gen, I even envisioned taking her to prom. They would be in corresponding dresses and both beaming beautifully. Unfortunately, I was too scared to let that happen. I really wish I would have. I finally drift to sleep envisioning our future together.*

# Chapter Four

## Genevieve

My bedroom door creaks and I hear a high-pitched squeal. I prop myself up on my elbow and squint toward the light flooding in through my open door. Mom is standing there clapping like a little kid at a magic show. She whispers for me to come downstairs and then closes my door. I carefully remove myself from beneath Jimmy's arm and put on a shirt and shorts. When I get downstairs, Mom is at the table, still in her scrubs. I glance at the clock. It's three in the morning.

"Hey. How was work?" I rub my eyes and yawn.

"It was work. Same old, same old. I'm more interested in how *your* night was." Mom raises her eyebrows at me.

"It was perfect!"

*I can't stop smiling.*

"Details, details!"

"We kissed. A lot. It was really nice."

"What I just walked into looked like a lot more than just kissing."

"It was just a lot of making out. You know Jimmy. He is a gentleman. He wanted to make sure that I was totally cool with everything that was happening. He wanted to just kiss me and hold me tonight."

"He is definitely one of the good ones. You should try to hold onto that one."

"That's my plan. You know that I've been in love with him for years."

"Have you told him that yet?"

"That I love him? On our *first date*? Are you *insane*?"

Mom looks at me like I'm a complete dunce. "Come on, Gen! You already know that you love him! You've been in love with him for years. It's not like you just met. You know practically everything about each other."

"Well, he *did* tell me that he wants me to be his girlfriend. He also said that he wants to be the only one kissing me." I have a dopey grin plastered on my face.

*James Thompson asked me to be his girlfriend! I've dreamed about this for so long.*

"Ooh, Gen! That is so awesome! Sadie would be so stinking happy!" Mom gives me a huge squeeze. "Go back upstairs to your *boyfriend*! I am so happy for the two of you. You two deserve happiness. I love you. Good night."

"Good night, Mom. I love you too. See you tomorrow."

I head back to my room and crawl back into my bed beside Jimmy. I lean over and place a gentle kiss on his temple before settling back into bed. He gently tugs me against him in his sleep. As we start spooning, I can feel him hard against me. I let out a small moan and grind my ass against him.

*I don't mean to do it. It's purely instinctual.*

He has his face buried in the bend of my neck and he mumbles, "I love you, Gen". My heart rate instantly speeds up.

*Did he really just say that? He's asleep though. He probably has no idea that he even said it. He is probably just dreaming. He won't remember this in the morning. Just close your eyes and go back to sleep.*

*It's Sadie's birthday. We are dancing in her driveway with music blaring from Jimmy's car. We are preparing for our other friends to come over for our birthday festivities. Sadie's hair is blowing crazily in the wind. I start spinning in circles making myself dizzy. I lose my balance and start to fall towards the pavement. A pair of hands catch me by the hips before my body can make contact with the hard ground. Jimmy pulls me into an upright position. The world is still spinning all around me. I can't take a single step. Jimmy pulls me tightly against his body and holds me upright until the world stands still again. Sadie stops dancing and winks at me. I quickly pull away from Jimmy.*

*"Uh, thanks for catching me." I nervously stare at the ground while I talk.*

*"I couldn't let you smash that pretty face, now could I?" Jimmy winks and flashes me a devilish smile.*

*This was three years ago. This moment has replayed itself time and time again inside my mind. Sometimes in daydreams. Sometimes at night. No matter the time of day though, it always ends in a kiss.*

"Good morning, my beautiful girlfriend." Jimmy kisses me lightly on the cheek and smiles. He looks bright and chipper. He is still in nothing but his boxers.

*I want his body against mine as much and as often as possible. Even with bedhead, he is still gorgeous. Some of my favorite mental images of him are from early morning breakfasts at Sadie's house. We would be in our pajamas at the table enjoying copious amounts of cereal together. His hair would be all tousled and his face would still have that sleepy look.*

"Good morning, boyfriend."

*God, I love the way that sounds.*

"Where did you disappear to last night?"

"You felt me get up? I'm sorry! I went downstairs to talk to Mom."

"Oh, shit! Darcy saw us? We were practically naked."

I chuckle softly. "She did. Don't worry. She wasn't upset or anything. She actually couldn't have been happier."

"That's good. I'm so glad that she is so cool about all of this. I felt you get back into bed, but I wasn't sure how long you had been gone."

*So maybe he wasn't as asleep as I thought last night.*

"Me too. She really is awesome. I'm actually really worried about Maryann and Henry finding out though."

"Why? They love you."

"Well, you said that they reacted badly when they found out about Sadie and David. I don't want them to start hating me. Do you think they are going to have a similar reaction?"

"No, I truly don't. We aren't Sadie and David. They would hopefully realize that this isn't a purely physical relationship and you're not pregnant...*yet*." My jaw drops. "*Kidding*! I am totally kidding!" Jimmy starts laughing. "But, seriously, I think the reason that they were so freaked about Sadie and David was because she hid it from all of us. Plus, I think that finding out your sweet teenage daughter was hiding a pregnancy from you would make any parent freak out a bit."

I mindlessly chew the inside of my bottom lip from nervousness. "Have you told them anything about us yet?"

"Not exactly. All I told them yesterday was that I was going to spend some time with you. I didn't want to jinx anything, but Dad knows how I feel about you. He always has."

"I don't want them to feel blindsided by it."

"I'm sure that they will be totally fine with it. I was actually thinking that maybe we could go talk to them about it over lunch."

"I would love to, but I actually have to work today. I go in at eleven. I'd be happy to come for dinner though."

"Okay, dinner it is! I'll let them know that you are going to join us for dinner. I can take you to work if you want."

"What time is it anyway?" I pat around the bed searching for my phone. I can't find it.

"It's almost nine." Jimmy checks the time on his phone.

"Good. I don't want to get up quite yet. I'm happy right here." I cuddle my body into Jimmy and give him a small squeeze around the waist. "I have to start getting ready for work soon, but I want to stay like this for a few more minutes. Today is my first day back. I don't know if I'm ready for that yet."

*Sadie and I both got jobs at Paper & Joe during our senior year. It's a small indie bookstore with a coffeehouse attached. Originally, they would put Sadie and I together. They quickly learned that we were never going to be very productive that way. We were still scheduled for the same shifts most of the time, but one of us would be placed on book duty while the other made drinks. When I called Rhea, the owner of Paper & Joe, to tell her that Sadie had passed away, she told me that she would cover as many of my shifts as I needed. I knew that if I didn't set myself with a return date right away that I might never go back. My week of not leaving my bed is all that I am allowing myself. This all feels way too familiar. I cannot and will not go through the shit that I did when Dad died again.*

"I can't believe that it's been a week." Jimmy is just staring off in the direction of my wall.

His eyes are starting to well up. His breathing is becoming more ragged. He is about to break. I can feel it. All I can do is hold him close to me and tell him that I'm here, over and over. He lets go of all of his bottled-up emotions that he has been trying to hold back and starts sobbing harder. I hold him tighter and begin petting his hair. I'm not sure when I started, but I am crying now too. We spend the next thirty minutes or so laying in my bed, holding one another and crying. Finally, our breathing begins to calm down and we wipe our eyes.

"I'm so sorry, Gen. I didn't mean to break down like that. You shouldn't have to deal with me crying all of the time."

"Jimmy, it's totally fine. We will get through this together. You know that I am here anytime that you need me." I kiss him lightly and lean my forehead against his. "I have to go take a shower and start getting ready for work. Mom is probably down drinking coffee if you'd like to join her." I plant one last kiss on his lips before leaving my bed.

Once I'm in the bathroom, I start the shower water and stare at myself in the mirror. My face is smeared with yesterday's eye makeup. My hair is a tousled mess of bed head. My eyes are bloodshot from our crying session. I see all of these imperfections jumping out at me, but somehow through all of them, Jimmy still called me beautiful. I am smiling, truly smiling.

*James Thompson called me beautiful when I looked like* this.

I undress and get in the shower. Once again, I am surrounded by the smell of the shampoo that Sadie bought for me. She would absolutely hate me crying all of the time over her. I know that she would want me to keep living my life and be as happy as possible.

"You know, Sade, I still can't believe that you hid a *baby* from me. We would have gotten through it together, just like everything else." I whisper as if she can hear me.

*Who knows? Maybe she can.*

I give my hair and body one final rinse and turn off the water. I step out and grab a towel. I dry off and then wrap it around me. As I walk down the hall to my room, I can hear Jimmy's voice floating up from the kitchen. He must have taken me up on the offer to join Mom for coffee. I get myself in my uniform for Paper & Joe, a black polo with a stack of books topped with a coffee cup embroidered into the right breast and a pair of black jeans. Then, I wrap the towel around my wet hair and descend the stairs to the kitchen.

"Hey sweetie. Jimmy was just telling me about the place that he took you to yesterday. It sounds absolutely beautiful." Mom smiles at me from over the rim of her coffee cup. She keeps glancing from Jimmy to me and back again. It seems like she is trying to decide if we look any different or not since last night.

"It really was. It was so secluded and peaceful." I rest my hand on Jimmy's shoulder where he is seated at the table. I glance at the clock. It's already quarter after ten. "I'm going to be late if I don't finish getting ready. We will need to leave really soon."

After brushing my hair and teeth, I slip on my flats. I press my fingertips to my lips and then place them on the photo of Sadie that I hung on my mirror before whispering, "Help me out Sadie. Let me handle this with a smile." I turn to walk out of my room and run directly into Jimmy. He quickly apologizes and hugs me tightly.

"Are you ready, Gen? It's time to leave."

"Yeah, let's go." I grab his hand and walk to the coat closet. I put on my gray bomber jacket, yell goodbye to Mom and walk out the door. On the way to his car, Jimmy makes sure that he is a few steps ahead of me so that he can open my door. "You don't have to do that everytime we get into your car now, you know? I am capable of opening a door by myself."

"I know, but I don't mind opening it for you."

Giving Jimmy a thankful smile, I sink into the passenger seat and close the door. He gets in the driver seat and backs smoothly out of my driveway. As he shifts the car into drive, he holds my hand.

*This feels like life has always been meant to be like this. The only thing missing that would make this perfect is Sadie.*

I hold Jimmy's hand and stare out of the window for the drive to Paper & Joe while listening to oldies on the radio. When we pull up to work, I turn to look at Jimmy. He is staring at me with admiration in his eyes.

"What? Is there something on my face?"

"No. I was just thinking about how pretty you are and how crazy it is that you're *finally* my girlfriend. This week has simultaneously been the worst and best week of my life so far." Jimmy gently pulls my hand to his face and kisses my fingertips.

"Mine too." I lean over the center console and kiss Jimmy. He kisses me back and almost instantly we are full-on making out in his front seat. I give him two more deep kisses and then pull away breathlessly. "I have to go. It's time for me to clock in."

"I'll see you tonight. What time are you done? I'll pick you up."

"I get out at four." I steal one more kiss before getting out of the car and walking to the front door.

The normal breakfast customers have already cleared out, so the store is pretty quiet when I enter. Once I clock-in, I will be preparing for the lunch rush. I walk to the back and trade my coat for an apron. Rhea is washing some dishes in the sink behind the register. Her black hair is hanging down her back in a long braid.

"Hey, was it busy this morning?"

"Just a typical Tuesday. How are you holding up?" Rhea leaves the sink and leans on the counter beside me.

"I'm pushing through. I know she wouldn't want me to be depressed. I miss her like crazy though." I stare at the bracelet residing on my right wrist.

*I forget that I'm wearing it on a daily basis. It's just three simple strings braided together. I've never taken it off since the day that Sadie tied it onto my wrist years ago. I remember her tying it on my wrist, but I can't remember exactly how old we were.*

"Is there anything else that you want to talk to me about?" Rhea smiles, lightly elbowing me while raising her eyebrows.

"Um, no. I don't think so." I shoot her a confused look.

"Oh come *on*! There's *nothing* else that you want to discuss?" Rhea scoffs and gives me an offended look.

"No. Nothing that I can think of, Rhea."

*What is she going on about?*

"That's crap and you know it! I saw you out front!"

*Oh shit! She is talking about my little makeout session with Jimmy in his car. I'm so embarrassed.*

"Oh! You saw that? I'm sorry!" I can feel my cheeks heating with embarrassment.

"Don't apologize! Correct me if I'm wrong, but wasn't that Jimmy Thompson? Your best friend's brother that you have been pining after the entire time that I've known you?" A smile creeps across my face.

"You're right. Yes, it was." Thinking about what just transpired in his front seat is causing me to smile this huge dopey grin.

"I want details! When? How? Don't hold out on me, girl!" Rhea rubs her hands together, preparing to hear the best gossip.

"Yesterday." I continue divulging all of the information from our last couple of days together until a customer walks through the door. A middle-aged man wearing a cardigan and horn-rimmed glasses walks in. He orders a latte and browses the books while we prepare his drink.

*It's nice to have some sense of normalcy.*

After his coffee is ready, he grabs his to-go cup and walks out the door. I start cleaning up the latte mess.

"So, I have a question. You and Jimmy both mentioned secrets the other day in your eulogies. What was up with all of the secret talk?" I take a deep breath.

"You have to swear that you won't tell a soul." I whisper. Rhea nods and leans closer. "Right before the service, Mr. Rothschild told us that Sadie was pregnant."

"*What!*" Rhea exclaims this so loudly that if we had anyone in here right now, their attention would most definitely be turned toward us. "How is that even possible? I didn't think she was seeing anyone."

"Neither did we!" I shrug and spin my *11 to life* bracelet. "I think she was ashamed. She always followed her heart, no matter what others might think."

"Oh, believe me, I know! I warned her to steer clear of Jack and look at how well that turned out." Rhea rolls her eyes.

The bell by the door rings as a few people meander through the door. That squashes the conversation that we were having. As the lunch rush begins, we work in silence for the remainder of the day.

During the week, we close at half-past three. We spend the last half-hour cleaning, restocking and preparing for tomorrow morning. At three-fifty, Jimmy's car pulls up out front. I smile as I glance out the window and see Jimmy singing along to the radio and drumming along on his steering wheel.

"Ooh! He is dropping you off *and* picking you up? *Nice!*"

"We are eating dinner with his parents tonight. We want to talk to them about us." I finish wiping off the counter and clock out. I grab my jacket from the back.

"Good luck. Is this your first time going over there since, you know, *last week*?" Something catches in my throat. I had somehow managed to not consider that.

"Yeah. It is. I mean, I have to go there eventually. I might as well just rip off the bandaid." I'm starting to cry.

"Well, I'll be thinking about you, hon. I'll see you tomorrow. You're opening." I give a small wave and wipe my eyes as I walk out the door to Jimmy's car. He is still singing along with the radio.

*He looks so carefree in this moment. I've missed this version of Jimmy.*

As I get almost to the car, he turns to look at me approaching. He gives me a huge smile.

*It's like a warm welcome made just for me.*

I open the passenger door and slide into the seat.

"How was work?" Jimmy puts the car in drive and heads toward the Thompson household. He holds my hand and leans over to kiss me at a stop sign.

"Busy. I made like fifteen in tips today. I have the breakfast rush tomorrow."

*The smell of coffee beans is overwhelming. I need to change as soon as we get to his house.*

"Are you ready for dinner? Mom made rigatoni. Dad should be home from work in an hour or so."

"I'm starving. I need to change out of my uniform when we get there. I should still have some clothes in Sadie's room."

"You have more than enough clothes in there. You have free reign of the closet."

"No. Those belong to Sadie."

"Gen, she has no use for them anymore. You two have always shared everything anyway."

"But still..."

I stare out the window and blink away tears.

We pull into the Thompsons' driveway. Jimmy parks in his normal spot beside Sadie's car. My chest is tightening up.

*I don't know if I'm ready to do this yet. Being here without her is too weird. Reminders of her are literally everywhere.*

I look toward the front door and see Maryann waving. I plaster on a fake smile and give a small wave. I unbuckle and get out of the car. As we walk toward Maryann, I notice that Jimmy doesn't take my hand in his. He trails behind me walking into the house instead. I try not to overanalyze it.

"Oh, Genevieve! Thank you for coming for dinner tonight. I think we could all use a distraction. Plus, we definitely need to stick together." Maryann hugs me. "Mmm, coffee. You smell just like Sadie always did after work."

"I know. I'm going to change into some of my clothes from her room."

"I can't bring myself to go in there yet. I don't know if I'll ever be able to. Everything is exactly how she left it." Maryann sniffles a little before returning to the kitchen to man the oven.

Jimmy and I walk down the hall to Sadie's room. Her white door is shut. I turn the handle and step in. A wall of her poppy perfume hits me in the face. Her hairbrush and lip gloss are still out on her vanity from when she last got ready. Her pajamas from last Monday are still in a crumpled pile on the floor beside her bed. I start crying.

*It's as if she has never left. Everything looks utterly normal, just as it has thousands of times before.*

Jimmy wraps me into a hug from behind. I can tell from his ragged breathing that he is crying too. I wipe my eyes and walk toward her closet to grab some of my clothes. I stop as I pass her nightstand. Her phone is still on the charger. I stare at it as if it's a vicious snake that might attack at any moment. Jimmy notices what I'm staring at. I look up at him with wide-eyes. I know we are both thinking the same thing: *what other secrets was Sadie hiding?*

I reach for the phone and unplug it. The screen lights up and asks for the passcode. I enter it as I always have. As it unlocks, I immediately notice that she has three unread texts. I open the messaging app and see two bolded names looming up at me. The top one is my own.

Morning, Sade! What are
we going to do with a glorious
day off?

*I sent that fifteen minutes before Jimmy called me. She was already dead at that point, but I had no idea.*

The other unread messages are from David.

The oldest–

I'll meet you in our usual
spot at our usual time. We really
need to talk.

That was sent twenty minutes before Sadie kissed Jimmy on the cheek and ran out the door. The second one from him was sent at two in the morning on Thursday.

Sadie, I'm sorry. I didn't mean it.

As I read the last one, my jaw drops and I begin shaking.

"Jimmy. Didn't you tell me that David never asked you what happened to her?" I say this slowly, in a sort of trance. My eyes never leave the phone, fearful that if I blink the message will disappear.

"Yeah. Why?"

"Look at this." I hand him the phone. He reads the screen and crinkles his forehead before looking up at me, wide-eyed.

"What. The. Fuck. I have to tell Mom and Dad, or the police, or someone." He looks like he might vomit.

"Let's not tell your parents tonight. It's still too raw. Wait until the morning. We could even take it to the police first. We have barely any evidence. It's just speculation. Let's not hurt your parents more than necessary right now." I gently hold his arm.

"You're right. The police are probably a better option anyway."

I kiss him softly and grab a change of clothes. I go into the bathroom connected to Sadie's room and change out of my uniform. I put on my favorite blue thermal and gray jeans. When I walk back into Sadie's room, Jimmy is scrolling through all of her messages looking for clues. He is perched on Sadie's bed and has his brows furrowed with concern.

*I hope that he doesn't let this ruin tonight. There is so much to process. No matter what happened a week ago, nothing is going to bring her back to us. His mom wants a night of good food and nice conversation to distract her. I am going to honor her with that. She has been through enough.*

"Let's go to your room until it's time for dinner. I can't handle being in here anymore right now." I grab his hand and lead him down the hall to his room. His room has red walls and black bedding. His extensive vinyl collection is lining his walls.

*Even though I've been in here plenty of times before, tonight feels different. It feels more momentous. For the first time, it feels like I'm in a* guy's *room, not* Sadie's brother's *room.*

I'm suddenly very aware of how clean it is and how much it smells like him.

He grabs a vinyl and puts it on the turntable. I'm getting nervous again. My palms are getting clammy with sweat. I stick them in my back jeans pockets. I'm awkwardly perched beside his window, staring down at the woods where Sadie died. He plops himself down onto his bed and just stares over at me.

"Come here, Gen. Come lay with me for a bit. You've been at work all day. Get a little rest before dinner."

I crawl into bed beside him. Resting my head on his shoulder, he wraps his arms around me and kisses the top of my hair. I close my eyes and try to concentrate on his breathing. He sounds calm and relaxed. After a few minutes, his grip around me loosens and I realize that he has fallen asleep. I just lay there with him until I hear the front door open signaling that Henry must be home from work. I get up from Jimmy's bed and check my reflection. My hair is a little messed up from where I've been laying on it. I tousle it a bit and put it into a messy bun. I nudge Jimmy awake.

"Hey, I think your dad is home. We should probably go out there."

Jimmy groggily sits up and yawns. He stretches like a newly awoken cat and rubs his eyes. He stands up, smiling, and walks over to me. He gives me a single deep kiss that makes me let out a small moan into his mouth.

"You and those noises!" He smiles and kisses me once more. "Let's go eat." Jimmy opens his door and heads down the hall. I trail a few feet behind him. Again, he doesn't hold my hand.

Maryann already has the dining room set with four plates heaped with rigatoni and salad. She also has glasses of wine at all of our seats. This puzzles me. Maryann is a textbook law-abiding citizen. She would never normally offer alcohol to two people who are underage. Henry sits at the head of the table. He is still in his dress clothes from work. He loosens his tie as we sit. Maryann walks in and joins us at the table.

"I hope you guys like it. I poured some wine, too. I think we could all use something to lighten the mood tonight, so enjoy." Maryann gestures for us to start eating.

"Thank you, Maryann! It smells amazing like always." I pick up my fork and take a bite of the delicious and cheesy pasta. This has always been a favorite of mine.

"Well, thank you dear. Feel free to drink the wine. I'm sure your mom won't mind if you have a glass or two. You've had a long week. We all have." We fall into a comfortable silence as we eat.

"Genevieve, we are very grateful to you for how great of a friend you've been to Sadie all of these years and how much you have been helping James through this." Henry addresses me as he sips at his wine.

"I am lucky that I got to have so much time with Sadie. I am completely grateful for every moment that I got to spend with her and your entire family. I love you guys."

"We love you too Genevieve. We don't want to stop having you around just because Sadie isn't here anymore." Maryann reaches for my hand. She smiles at me with motherly love in her eyes.

"Well, Mom, I am really happy to hear you say that." Jimmy smiles at me and lightly grazes my foot beneath the table. Maryann gives him a confused look.

*Is he really doing this right now?*

"I have a feeling that Genevieve will be over just as much as before, if not more." Jimmy winks at me and sips his wine.

*He thinks he is so slick.*

"James, as much as we would all love that, I highly doubt that Genevieve will be here nearly as often now without Sadie being here." Henry finishes off his first glass of wine and pours a second while he speaks.

"Well, she would if she were my girlfriend, right?"

Maryann spits wine across the table and starts coughing. "Wait. Your *what*? Did I just hear you correctly, James Anthony?" Maryann is frantically glancing between the two of us, hoping one of us will say we are joking.

"You did, Mom. Genevieve is my girlfriend now." Jimmy is smiling broadly.

"Attaboy, Jimmy!" Henry gets up and claps him on the back, laughing. "About damn time!"

"Thanks, Dad." Jimmy is blushing but his smile isn't fading at all. Maryann is still sitting in her seat, staring at Jimmy in shock. "Mom, are you okay? Please say something."

I swallow hard and stare at her. "Maryann, I totally get if you're not okay with this. I know this probably seems really out of the blue. If it makes you feel any better though, I have not liked or even thought about anyone other than Jimmy, I mean *James*, sorry, for the last eight years." I speak rapidly out of raging nervousness.

"Oh sweetie, it's not that I'm against you two dating. I love you like a daughter. I think it's just going to take me some time to process this. It feels like everything I have ever known to be true is being challenged this week. My kids are definitely keeping me on my toes."

"Maryann, James has been telling me for *at least* the last five years that he has been in love with Genevieve. He didn't want Sadie to know. That's the only reason I didn't tell you." Henry pours more wine into his wife's glass.

"Really, Henry? You didn't think that this was something you should have told me? The girl that he liked for years spent numerous nights under the same roof as him. Many of those in the same room if not the same bed. What if he had acted on it?" Maryann is starting to sound frantic. Her voice is starting to raise. Jimmy looks like he wants to hit something.

"Woah, woah, woah. Mom. *Stop*. First of all, I would hope that you know me better than that. Secondly, do you really think that Sadie would have ever let anything happen?" Maryann completely ignores him and looks at Henry again full of anger.

"He has also spent the past three nights at her house. You still didn't mention it. There is no more Sadie for me to tell. So *now*, what's your excuse?"

*Maryann is not taking this well at all. This is pretty out of character for her.*

"Well, frankly Maryann, I didn't think it was any of your damn business. He is an adult. If he wants to spend the night with a woman, he has every right to."

*Henry is getting defensive now. Over the years, I have witnessed a handful of fights between them. Whenever Henry starts getting defensive, Maryann always gets even angrier.*

"It's all fine and dandy until he gets someone pregnant!" Maryann is in full hysterics.

"Oh my God! Mom! *Stop*!" Jimmy pushes his chair out and walks away from the table. His hands are gripping his hair and his face is turning bright red.

"I *thought* Sadie was smarter than that, but look at what happened to her! She was pregnant and *hiding* it from us." Maryann is about to cry.

*I'm not sure if it is from anger or just grief.*

"Maryann, I'm a *virgin*. Plus, James has always been a complete gentleman. He has never once tried to make a move on me."

*I don't know why I feel the need to make a comment, but I can't just sit here silently while she berates Jimmy.*

Maryann completely ignores me and looks straight at Jimmy. "What the hell would Darcy say if you knocked up her daughter?"

"Honestly, she would probably be ecstatic, Mom! She is extremely happy that we are together. She is in our corner." I am just staring at Jimmy.

*Although he is probably one-hundred percent correct, I cannot believe he just said that to his mother. She is obviously not in a good state of mind right now. She just lost her daughter, for God's sake!*

"James, why don't you take Genevieve to your room while your mother and I have a little chat?"

"I don't want them in his room together!" Maryann is practically screaming now. Her voice is strained and growing hoarse.

"James, go. You're an adult. You are allowed to have your girlfriend in your room if you want." I glance at Jimmy. He pulls my chair out for me and takes my hand. We quickly exit toward his room.

As soon as we shut his bedroom door, I can hear Maryann raising her voice at Henry again. Jimmy turns the volume on his turntable up louder.

"What the hell was that? She has *never* behaved this way ever before." Jimmy sits on his bed and hangs his face into his hands. "Gen, I am so unbelievably sorry. I never imagined she would react like that in a million years." He pulls me onto his lap and hugs me.

"It's totally fine! I'm fine. Her emotions are all over the place. She just lost her only daughter and first grandchild at the same time. Now, she finds out that her son and husband were keeping a secret from her for years. It makes sense that she is upset." I lean into Jimmy and he wraps his arms around me tighter. There is a small knock at the door and Henry walks in. He sees me sitting on Jimmy's lap and he genuinely smiles.

"Please forgive Maryann or at least *try* to anyway. She is very emotional this week. She *really* is happy for you two, somewhere deep down. There is dessert, too. Please come back out and eat with us. I promise she will behave better this time."

We follow Henry to the dining room where there is warm apple crisp and ice cream in bowls on the table. I sit in my seat and shyly glance in Maryann's direction. She is taking tiny spoonfuls of her dessert and eating in silence.

"Mom, I promise you that this isn't just some petty fling. I am in this for the long haul. I will continue treating Genevieve with all of the respect that she deserves." Jimmy holds my hand across the table and smiles at me. "Plus, if she did end up getting pregnant, I would be the happiest guy around. I would be by her side throughout the entire pregnancy."

At this, I choke on my dessert. Maryann does too. Henry just laughs.

*I can't tell if Jimmy is being completely serious right now or just saying this to get under Maryann's skin.*

"A little ahead of ourselves, aren't we?" Maryann asks snidely.

"Not really, Mom. Honestly, if I hadn't been afraid of Sadie's reaction, I would already be over six years into this relationship." Jimmy flashes me a smile from across the table. "In some ways, I kind of am actually. Why do you think I haven't had a girlfriend at all?"

"You had Hilary." Maryann is still being snarky.

"I also broke up with Hilary as soon as I realized that I had feelings for Gen." I stop mid-bite and just stare at Jimmy.

*He has never told me that I'm the reason he broke up with her before.*

"I should have told her right away. Then, I could have taken her to prom three times." He never breaks eye contact with me while he continues talking. "For six years, almost *seven* actually, I enjoyed just being in her presence without ever telling her how I felt about her. That was a huge mistake. The biggest one of my life. If I would have just put myself out there and told her, we would probably be living together or hell, even *married* by now." Maryann looks thoroughly disgusted by everything that he is saying right now. My heart is doing somersaults.

"Well then." Maryann is speechless. She is sitting as still as a statue with her jaw clenched tightly. She is staring directly at Jimmy.

"Personally, I think that is absolutely wonderful James. I'm so happy for you." Henry is beaming and has a tear in his eye. Maryann pushes her chair out and leaves the table without a sound. "I'm sorry. I think she just needs to sleep on it. Give her some time. I know she will come around. She loves you both." Henry, giving us an apologetic look, leaves the table to follow his wife.

"Did you mean all of that?" I am staring at Jimmy in awe.

"Absolutely. Every single word. Hell, if you would let me, I would marry you tomorrow." Jimmy lifts my hand to his face and kisses it gently. My heart is fluttering.

"Really? You would marry someone that you just started dating?" I tease him and raise my eyebrows.

"Well, no, I wouldn't, *but* I absolutely would marry you without ever giving it a second thought. I already know pretty much everything about you. I've been in love with you since I was fourteen. Dating is supposed to be when you take the time to learn about the other person and slowly fall in love with them. I feel like I've already been doing that for all of our teenage years." Jimmy gets up from his seat and comes over to me. He grabs both of my hands and helps me up. "Come on. Let's go to my room."

We walk down the hallway to Jimmy's room. He shuts the door behind us and locks it. Now my nerves are getting the best of me again. I sit on the end of his bed and kick my feet like a small child. Everything Jimmy just said to his parents keeps running through my head.

*Has he really been holding himself back from all of the girls that have undoubtedly hit on him over the years because of me?*

Jimmy sits beside me on his bed. He lightly kisses me a few times until our kisses grow more insistent. I let out another one of those small moans that Jimmy teases me about. This time though, he doesn't tease me; instead, he lays me back on his bed and climbs on top of me, never breaking from our kiss. His hands wander along my torso until he reaches my bra and he just keeps kissing me more passionately. I run my hands along his back and into his hair.

*It feels like I cannot get enough of his lips. Something has unleashed inside of me. I don't want to stop making out with him. Ever.*

I let another small moan escape.

*Knock. Knock. Knock.*

Jimmy pulls his lips from mine and sighs. He looks completely disheveled from our makeout session. He gets up from the bed and doesn't even *try* to compose himself before opening his door. Maryann is standing just outside of the door. Her eyes first take in her son's messy hair and wrinkled clothes before looking at me on his bed, red-lipped and frizzy-haired. Her eyes are wide saucers. I can tell that she is holding back her irritation right now.

"I'm sorry to, um, *interrupt*. I just wanted to apologize for my behavior. I really am happy for you guys if this is what you truly want. I will support you in whatever decisions you make.

Just please be smart about everything." She is wringing her hands from nerves.

"Mom. I turn twenty-one in a couple of weeks. You are not seriously going to attempt a sex talk, are you?" Jimmy scoffs at her.

"Well, no. I guess not. I just love both of you and would hate to see you ruin your lives because of one bad decision." I see Jimmy's shoulders tense up.

"Okay, Mom, noted. Is that all you came in here to say? Can I get back to enjoying my girlfriend's company now?" He isn't trying to hide any of his disdain for his mother at this moment.

"Oh, uh, yeah. I'm sorry. You'll probably want to get her home soon though." Maryann is visibly hurt.

"Thanks for the advice and apology. Good night, Mom." Jimmy closes the door in Maryann's face and locks it again. "Now, where were we?"

"Your mom is right. I should probably be going soon." I stand up and kiss his cheek.

"Well, if you really want to go home, I'll take you back in just a minute." Jimmy looks as pathetic as a wounded puppy.

"It's not that I *want* to leave. I have to open tomorrow. I need to be there by six and I'll be alone so I will need all of the rest that I can get." I look down at my feet. *I don't want to go.*

I leave his room and head outside as Jimmy follows slowly behind.

# Chapter Five

## Jimmy

*Dinner didn't go quite as well as I hoped that it would. At least I got to tell Gen some things that I've been keeping bottled up. If Mom hadn't interrupted us when she knocked, I would probably be kissing a half-naked Gen in my bed right now.*

I try to hide my disappointment and resentment towards Mom while I drive Gen home.

*I don't want to let her see me upset again this week. She has seen enough of my emotional turmoil.* My mind keeps wandering back to those messages on Sadie's phone. *I absolutely have to take it to the police. What if he hurt her? I will seriously contemplate murdering him if I find out that he was involved in her death. My beautiful and spunky little sister didn't deserve this.*

While Gen was working earlier, I went home and laid in my bed staring at the ceiling. I tried to process everything that has happened in my life over the past week. The first thing running through my mind was the amazing makeout session that I just had with Gen in my car. Then, thoughts of Sadie's death and all of the terrible things accompanying it started streaming in. When I had told Mom that Gen would be coming for dinner, she seemed to be in a much better mood than she had been in all week. She seemed excited to have another female in the house. I've always been more deeply connected with Dad than with Mom. We have that natural father-son bond. We are best friends. Honestly, he actually reminds me a lot of Darcy.

I glance in Gen's direction in the car, but it's too dark to truly see her. I can see shadows cast upon her face.

*All I know for certain is that I don't ever want to lose her. She has been the bright spot in my life every day, even when she was deeply suffering from depression. I plan to put a ring on her finger as soon as I possibly can. I cannot wait to make her Mrs. Genevieve Thompson.*

I begin imagining her in a beautiful wedding gown walking down the aisle towards me.

*I need to get out of my parents' house as soon as possible. I cannot live here without Sadie's presence filling every room.*

We had been talking about getting an apartment together soon before she passed. I have been saving a majority of my money since my first job when I was sixteen. I have a nice little nest egg set aside.

*The fact that Gen is working early in the morning tomorrow is really bumming me out. Sleeping with her by my side and waking up beside her the last few days has been absolutely amazing. If she didn't have to work, I would probably stay tonight too. Neither of us wants to be alone and together is truly the best place to be. Spending the nights alone is really painful right now. Being by myself gives me too many chances to think of Sadie and how much I miss her. Our house seems so quiet and dark without her presence.*

# Genevieve

♡

Once we get back to my house, Jimmy walks me to the door. He stands there awkwardly on the front step. Giving me a small peck and turning away, he mumbles, "Good night, Gen."

"Where are you going?"

"Home. You said you needed to rest tonight, remember?"

"It's not that late. You can come inside for a while."

"No. I really should go home and let you have some time alone. My mom is right. I'm likely to move too quickly with you if I stay another night. My willpower is waning." I grip his shirt in my hands and give him another kiss.

*I really don't want him to go.*

"Like you said, it's as if we have been together for years already. I don't think anything would be considered too quick. Regular timelines don't seem to apply for us."

"Maybe they don't, but tonight isn't the right time. I'll see you tomorrow."

"Okay. Good night, Jimmy. I'll see you tomorrow." I try and fail at keeping the disappointment out of my voice as I turn to go inside.

He gives me one more deep kiss before turning towards his car. I wait until I see him get in the car and start the engine. I give him a small wave and head inside.

Mom is sitting on the couch with her favorite blanket. She turns and smiles at me.

"How did dinner go, honey? Where's Jimmy?"

"He went home for the night. Dinner was...*interesting*."

"Oh no. That doesn't sound good. Is everything okay? What happened?"

"Maryann was a little freaked out about us, to say the least. Then, she kept acting like he was going to knock me up and ditch me." I run my hand through my hair with frustration as I sit beside Mom on the couch. I'm still trying to process all of this evening's awkwardness.

"Does she know her son at all? Jimmy is one of the most respectful men I have ever known. He is very genuine. I don't think he even has the ability to consider turning away from his responsibilities."

"I know, right! Jimmy kind of let her have it actually. He said that he would be happy if I ended up getting pregnant. He also said that he wishes he would have told me how he felt when he first realized it so that we could be six years into this relationship already." I am smiling while replaying tonight's events in my head. "He even said that he would marry me tomorrow if I would let him."

"Marry him! You've loved him for years already!"

"You sound like Sadie." I laugh. "I think I will eventually. I mean we *just* started officially dating."

"That might be so, but the chemistry you two have is what makes for great marriages."

"You really think so?" A giddy warmth fills my chest.

"I do. Go get some beauty sleep, kid. You open tomorrow, right?"

"Yeah, I do. Can I use your car?"

"Of course. Good night."

I walk upstairs and strip down to my bra and underwear. I'm so exhausted from constantly carrying around the weight of the past week that I just sink into my bed. I start drifting off to sleep. My mind keeps replaying Maryann's reaction to the news of our relationship. As I fall deeper into sleep, I walk down the aisle to Maryann's rhythmic sobs. As I am about to say my vows to Jimmy, my phone vibrates and wakes me up. I squint at the time in the brightness of my phone screen. It's three in the morning. It's a text from Jimmy.

Genevieve, I just want you
to know how hard it was for me to
leave your side and not stay at your
house tonight. I've been kicking myself
in the ass for not following you inside
since I hit the end of your road. I
promise that if you'll let me, I will make
it up to you tomorrow.

This message makes my heart flutter inside of my chest.

I'm done work at 1.
Make it to up me then?

My phone starts ringing as Jimmy calls me.

"Hey." I can tell that my voice is tense and strained from waking up.

"Hey, babe. Did I wake you up?"

*He called me babe! Ugh, I seriously love that!*

"Yeah, but it's okay. What's up?"

"I love you, Genevieve."

My heart starts to beat frantically in my chest.

"James, I love you, too. So incredibly much."

"That's all I needed to say. I just really needed you to know that I *do*, in fact, love you. I don't care if we have only technically been dating since Monday."

"You know that I've been yours for so much longer than that."

"God, it feels amazing to hear you say that. I have known that I've loved you for years. Good night, Gen. Go back to sleep. I love you. I love you. I love you."

"Good night, Jimmy. I love you too."

Falling back asleep isn't as difficult as I thought it would be. My sleep is dreamless and ends quickly. My alarm goes off at five. I roll from my bed and throw my uniform on. I look in the mirror at the reflection of an exhausted girl. I definitely need to drink some coffee before I go to work if I want to look less like an extra from *The Walking Dead.*

After brewing myself some coffee and pouring it into my mug, I get a good morning text from Jimmy. This is all it takes to plaster a huge smile on my face while I drive to work and prepare for my day.

The breakfast rush is enough to occupy my brain. Falling into the ebb and flow of the early morning customers is almost a sort of meditation. There is nothing else in my brain except for fulfilling the orders.

When Rhea comes in to join me, it is just before lunch. She doesn't even attempt to beat around the bush with small talk before she asks me about last night's dinner.

"Trainwreck would be putting it politely."

"Oh no! What happened?"

Her eyes are twinkling with a very unwelcome sympathy. I'm sick of people looking at me that way lately.

"Maryann freaked the fuck out. Just flew straight off the deep end! She started preaching about unwanted pregnancies and saying that she didn't want us being alone together."

"You're both consenting adults. Why is she being like that?"

I shrug. "She is dealing with a lot right now. She isn't normally like this." I'm trying to be as understanding as I can and not take her new attitude personally. "Jimmy didn't improve matters though. He told her that he would be happy if I had his child and that he has been committed to me solely for the past six years already."

Her eyes are large saucers now. "Oh shit! He actually said that to his mom? Was he drunk or something?"

"Not drunk. He had a little wine, but I think it was just enough to loosen him up. I choked when he said that though. I couldn't believe it. I still can't actually."

The lunch rush begins and by the time it's over, so is my shift. I say my goodbyes to Rhea and drive home. The wind is blowing snow drifts over the road the entire drive home. As I pull into my driveway, I notice that Jimmy's car is parked outside. I park and walk inside, smiling. Jimmy isn't in the living room or kitchen. I walk upstairs to my room to find Jimmy is sitting on the edge of my bed staring at the floor. He looks nervous, but gifts me with a huge smile as soon as he sees me.

"I hope you don't mind that I'm here already. Darcy let me in. I knew you'd be home soon."

"Of course I don't mind! I'm so glad that you're here. Just let me get changed and then we can do whatever you want."

"Can I talk to you for a second, first?" Jimmy is all nervous and twitchy. He almost looks like he is tweaking. This is making me tense up.

"Yeah, of course. What is it?" He gently pulls my hand and guides me so that I am standing directly in front of him.

"I want to give you something." He settles me into his lap and kisses me.

"A present?"

"Let me see your hand." Jimmy takes my hand and slides something into my palm. He encloses my fingers around it and kisses me. I open my hand and take a look.

In the center of my palm is a gold ring with a black stone in the center. The sides of the ring have the torch for National Honor Society and music notes. Around the stone says *Hamstead.*

*It's Jimmy's class ring. I remember when he first got it. Sadie and I were so jealous that he had his class ring already.*

"What's this for?"

"It's a promise."

Arching a brow at him, I ask, "What kind of promise?"

"One that ensures another ring *will* be coming. I meant every single word of what I said at dinner last night, Gen. I know that you're the one for me. You're who I want to call my wife and you're the one that I want being the mother of my kids. I have actually known this for a very long time, probably longer than I should have honestly. I knew that *eventually*, I would be making a move whether Sadie hated me or not." I quietly whisper his name as I let out a small squeal and slide the ring onto my middle finger. I give him a small kiss. "I want to talk to you about something else, too. This might be a little forward, but I want to discuss it with you and at least get your opinion."

"Go ahead. What's up? I'm all ears!"

"I have some money saved up. I am thinking about looking at getting my own place. Living with my parents is too difficult without Sadie."

"That's awesome! I think that's a wonderful idea. You should totally do it."

"I was also wondering if you would possibly consider moving in with me. We could even do a two bedroom apartment if you wanted."

"I would absolutely love to live with you. We should definitely look into it. I'll talk it over with my mom, too." I kiss him and hug him tightly.

"Only if you really want to though. I will totally understand if you're not ready for that."

"If I'm not ready after eight years, I don't think I ever will be." I chuckle, removing myself from his lap and grabbing some clothes to change into. I take off my uniform shirt with my back turned towards Jimmy. I quickly replace it with a long-sleeve V-neck. I then slip off my pants and slide into a pair of yoga pants.

"Gen, you're going to start a frenzy doing things like that." Jimmy is biting his lip, staring at me. His voice is huskier than usual.

"Would that be such an awful thing?" I run my fingers through his hair and smile down at him.

*Knowing that the attraction is reciprocated makes me bold. I think I kind of like it.*

"No, not awful. Not even close, but Darcy is right down the hall."

I give him a flirty smile. "Well, she won't be there tonight. She works again."

"I need to run Sadie's phone over to the police station. Do you want to come with me?"

"If you don't mind, I think I'll stay here and eat some lunch. I'm starving. I haven't eaten anything yet today. I'll see you when you get back."

*Before Jimmy left for the police station, he told me that he had a terrible night's sleep last night. He kept having nightmares about David murdering Sadie. They all started the same way: Sadie would kiss him on the cheek and head out the door. Then, in some of them, Sadie and David would be fighting about the baby and he would ask her to get an abortion which causes a physical fight to ensue. Others, they would meet up for a rendezvous where David would mention Sadie gaining weight causing her to run away crying and smack her head. He had his mind set before we spoke on the phone in the middle of the night that he needed to tell the police what he knew. They need to at least question David. After quite a bit of contemplation, Jimmy chose that he is going to tell them all that we know so far and give them her phone as evidence. He decided that Sadie deserves to have the truth known. I completely agree with him and fully support his decision.*

After Jimmy leaves, I go to the kitchen and help myself to some salad and iced tea. While I'm eating my first meal of the day, Mom comes in and sits at the table. As I lift a forkful of lettuce to my mouth, Mom grabs my wrist. I try to assess what she is doing and furrow my brow at her. She rotates my hand toward the ceiling so that she can look at the ring that is now inhabiting my right middle finger.

"What is this?"

Keeping my expression deadpan, I say, "A ring."

"Well, duh, *smartass*. It's Jimmy's class ring. I would recognize it anywhere. What I mean is how did it make its way into your possession?"

"He gave it to me. He wants me to wear it."

"Under what context?"

"As a promise."

"A promise ring? Gen, that is so exciting!"

"He said that it's a promise that another ring will be replacing it. He also asked me something that I want to discuss with you."

"What? Did he propose or something?"

"Not exactly." I nonchalantly sip at my iced tea.

"Not *exactly*? What does that even *mean*?"

"He said that he has known for years that I'm *The One*. He said he wants to marry me and have kids with me."

"Wow. That is amazing. Most people never even know if they have found *The One*." Mom is staring blankly at the table with a cheesy smile on her face.

"He has money saved up to get an apartment. He plans to move out of Maryann and Henry's soon. It's just too painful living there without Sadie."

"That's great! I can't even begin to imagine how difficult it is to be living there without Sadie."

"He, um, asked me if I would, um, maybe want to get an apartment with him."

"Wait, what? Are you serious?" Her jaw drops a bit.

"Yeah, I am. That's what I wanted to talk to you about. What are your thoughts?"

"I mean, if that's what you want to do, I'll absolutely support you. Just don't do it if you aren't ready."

"I think I do want to, but I don't want to leave you all alone. He said we could even get a two bedroom and be roommates if I wasn't ready to share a room yet."

"I will be fine, Gen. I work all the time anyway. I had mentally prepared myself for this already. I figured you and Sadie would be getting an apartment together soon anyway. It's just a different Thompson than I had thought. Jimmy can stay here anytime that he needs to until he finds a place of his own."

"Mom, I love you. Thank you for being so cool about this." I give her a huge hug.

*She really is an incredible mom. I am so blessed.*

"I really do love him like a son, Gen." Glancing around the room, she seems to realize that he isn't here anymore. "Where did he go anyway?"

"The police station." I mumble under my breath.

"Excuse me, did you just say the *police station*?" Mom's face is wrinkled with worry and confusion. "What the hell is he doing there?"

"He has to talk to them about Sadie. We aren't totally convinced that it was an accident."

Mom looks completely shocked. She is fidgeting nervously with her necklace that she always wears. It's a diamond pendant that Dad bought for her before he got sick. I tell her all about finding Sadie's phone and the incriminating text messages.

"Oh, honey, are you okay?" Mom hugs me tightly. Then, she pulls back just far enough to look straight into my eyes.

"I have to be. I can't let myself fall back into my old depression habits. I'm going to go lay down for a bit. My alarm seemed to go off really early this morning. Have a good night at work, Mom." I kiss her on the cheek and head to my room.

Once I'm in my room, I start flipping through the old pictures of Sadie. There are beaches and fall leaves, amusement parks and camping trips, birthdays and school dances. All of these moments are from after Sadie and I became friends. Toward the bottom of the pile, I find three photos that are of Sadie and Jimmy.

The first one is of toddler Jimmy holding newborn Sadie for the first time ever. He is looking at her with a scowl on his face. He definitely does not look like the proud older brother that I know he grew to be. They are sitting on a couch that screams nineties.

The second one is from Sadie's first day of Kindergarten. She is in a floral dress with a bright pink backpack on. Her smile is taking up her entire face. She is so tiny and her face is sprinkled with freckles. Jimmy is now the picture-perfect proud big brother smiling over her shoulder. He is in a red polo shirt and jeans. His smile and freckles match hers perfectly, minus the missing tooth from Jimmy's mouth.

The last one is from a trip to the drive-in. I remember taking this photo. It's crooked from my poor attempt at artistic perspective. We were thirteen and had begged Maryann and Henry to let us go. They didn't want to see the horror film that was playing, so they refused to take us. My mom ended up caving in. She faced the car away from the screen and allowed us to camp out on the trunk of her car. Sadie has licorice vines sticking out of her mouth like walrus tusks and she is cross-eyed. Jimmy is laughing as he is getting covered in a rain of popcorn. It was a memory perfectly captured in time. I lay down while still holding the photo. I stare at it and keep replaying that night in my mind as I drift off to sleep.

I wake up to a hand brushing hair out of my face. I open my eyes and see Jimmy staring down at me, smiling.

"Hey, sleepy head. If you're tired, I can go home. We can take a rain check for tonight."

"No. Stay. I didn't mean to fall asleep. I was just looking at old pictures and accidentally fell asleep." Jimmy looks down at the photos still in my hand.

"You know, that picture is from the first night that I realized that I wanted to kiss you."

"Wait, really? What made you realize it that night?"

"Well, in the movie, there was this kissing scene and while it was playing, I was suddenly very aware of your presence. I looked around at all of the couples around us making out instead of watching the movie. I started to notice every movement of your lips and I wanted so badly to know how they tasted, how they would have felt against mine."

"You're lying." I search his face for any sign of a tell, but I can't find any and I know all of his tells.

"Can you imagine how different things would have been if I had acted on it?"

I start laughing at the thought of Maryann's reaction if she had caught Jimmy at fourteen kissing his baby sister's best friend. "Maryann would have killed you."

"She definitely would have, but I would have done things so differently." Jimmy has his hand on the side of my face and is staring me right in my eyes. "I wasted so many opportunities with you. I'm never going to squander opportunities with you again." Jimmy presses his lips against my forehead and closes his eyes. "Oh, I almost forgot. I brought you some dinner. I stopped at that Thai place that you like on Harrison Street."

*Dinner? How long was I asleep?* I glance at the clock. *Three and a half hours. Yikes!*

We go to the kitchen so that I can eat my dinner that Jimmy so thoughtfully picked up for me. He tells me about what the police plan to do with Sadie's phone. They are apparently going to bring David in for questioning. They even mentioned possibly going to Rothschild Funeral Home to take a look at Sadie's corpse. The thought of an investigation into Sadie's death makes me sick to my stomach.

"Let's change the subject. Please. Talk about something else, *anything* else." I plead with Jimmy to take my mind off of Sadie.

*I am so sick of crying. I don't want to cry tonight.*

He thinks for a moment like he is at a loss for words that don't revolve around his dead sister. I watch his eyes light up as he catches a thought that will take us out of the sad topic. "I found a couple of apartment options. I am going to look at them in person after work tomorrow. I would really like for you to come with me, even if you don't want to move in with me, I would still really like to get your opinion. I want you to be comfortable wherever I end up living." Jimmy is leaning against the counter drinking a glass of water. He is effortlessly attractive. His eyes are extra vibrant thanks to the aqua band tee that he is wearing. His summer freckles have fully faded now.

"I would love to go with you tomorrow. What time are you done with work?"

"Four. The first meeting is set for quarter-after. I want *my* home to be *your* home. I think you'll really like the first one. It's right downtown between Paper & Joe and the library. We would both be able to walk to work."

"Oh really? That would be perfect!" I am daydreaming of us living together and decorating our place with things that would meld both of our styles.

"That's what I was thinking, too. It's only a one bedroom though, so maybe not..." Jimmy looks down at his feet, fidgeting nervously.

"Still perfect. Even if we had two bedrooms, we would probably only ever use one." I smile at Jimmy and kiss his cheek right beside his ear. He gives a small shiver. I move down to his neck and kiss him tenderly.

"Mmm. Gen, you make it so hard for me to hold myself back." He pulls my body against his. I am highly aware of every single point of contact. I press myself against him even more, leaving very little to the imagination.

I kiss him deeply and then teasingly pull back with my tongue lingering between his lips, lightly flicking it against the inside edges. His breathing quickens. He pulls away slightly to look me in the eye. He has a crazed excitement in his eyes that I've never seen before, at least not in real life. He kisses me again deeply. His grip on my lower back tightens, pulling me into him even more. I can feel how hard he is through his jeans. A small moan escapes from my mouth as I instinctively grind my hips against his.

"I don't want to hold back anymore." Jimmy manages to say between hurried kisses.

"Then don't." I smile, never breaking away from his kisses. Now, it's his turn to let out a small moan. He kisses me more, just as passionately. His hands are wandering all over my body, mapping out every curve and dip of my shape. "Come on, let's go upstairs." I pull away and meander quickly up the stairs and into my room. Jimmy is right on my heels.

"Genevieve, are you sure?"

He looks hesitant, but only for a moment as he absorbs the intensity of this moment and what is actually about to happen. My only answer to him is wordlessly pulling my shirt off over my head and staring him dead in the eye. He glides across the room and is on top of me kissing me intensely in one swift movement.

His hand moves to my chest and cups my breast through my bra. My hands reach for the top of his jeans. I slowly undo his belt and unbutton his jeans. He pulls away long enough to pull his shirt off over his head and slide his jeans off. He then reaches for my bra and unlatches the clasp in back. I let my bra slip off of me. He bites his lip and inhales sharply as he sees my bare torso.

"I've wanted this for so long, Gen."

Jimmy starts kissing my neck and then makes his way down my chest. He kneads my breast as he runs his tongue over my nipple. A small sound escapes from somewhere deep inside of me. This excites him even more and he makes his way further down my torso. He hooks his fingers inside the band of my yoga pants and slides them off with my underwear in one clean motion. He bites his lip as he glances between my thighs and all the way back up my body. "You're so beautiful."

He puts his lips against mine and kisses me lightly. His hand slides lightly across my skin, first down the length of my torso and then slowly circling along my hip bones. He slides his hand further down my pelvis achingly slowly. My breathing is growing ragged. My heart is racing. He lightly rubs between my legs. Another small moan passes from my lips. I can feel Jimmy smiling through the kisses. He slowly slips a finger inside of me and pulls it back out even slower.

*If he keeps going slow like this, my body may seriously implode.*

When he slides it back in quickly, I flinch, causing Jimmy to pull away.

"I'm sorry. Did I hurt you?"

"No. Not at all."

"You're sure? You flinched. I just want to make sure you're okay."

"I'm positive."

I kiss him and reach my hand into his boxers to prove to him that I'm completely fine. He quickly slides them off. I run my hand tenderly over the length of him. He is so hard in my hand and the skin is so warm and soft.

*I'm starting to get really nervous now.*

As our fully naked bodies ease against each other for the first time, I lose myself in his kisses. His fingers find their way inside of me once again, but this time he moves them in a pulsating motion instead of removing them completely. I moan into his mouth. Just as he is lowering himself into position to ease himself into me for the first time, the doorbell rings.

*Ding dong. Ding dong.*

"You have *got* to be kidding me." Jimmy rolls off of me onto my bed. He is trying to catch his breath. I look at his nude body beside me, so obviously ready to deflower me. It takes all of my mental capacity to pull my stare away from him.

"I'll go see who it is." I push off of my bed and throw on my underwear, some shorts and Jimmy's shirt. I kiss him quickly and head downstairs.

I open the door slightly to see who caused this horribly timed interruption. I use the door to shield my bare legs from the cold breeze. A decent-looking middle-aged man with slicked back hair in a suit and tie is standing on my doorstep. I have never seen him before. "Uh, hi. How can I help you?"

"I'm looking for Genevieve Porter."

"Uh, I'm Geneveive." I tell him with concern in my eyes.

"I'm Detective Ramsey from Hamstead PD. I need to talk to you about your friend, Sadie Thompson."

"Oh, um, of course. Come in." I open the door wider for him, inviting him to step into the entryway. I lead the detective to our kitchen table and motion for him to sit down. I perch myself awkwardly in the chair across from him.

"Can you tell me about Sadie's history with David Jerome?" He asks as he pulls a small notepad and pen from the inside pocket of his suit jacket. He clicks the pen open, readying himself to take down whatever details I may know. Something churns inside my stomach.

"Gen, is everything alright? I thought I heard a guy's voice." Jimmy calls out as he descends the stairs, shirtless with nothing but his jeans on. He stops dead in his tracks when he walks into the kitchen and sees the detective across from me. "*Oh*, Detective Ramsey, hello again."

"Mr. Thompson." Ramsey nods his head in Jimmy's direction as he clears his throat, obviously suppressing a smile. Jimmy swallows hard like a small child caught with his hand in the cookie jar before dinner. "Sorry, it seems as though I have interrupted something. I just need a few moments of Miss Porter's time."

"Oh, um, yeah. Gen, I'll be upstairs." Embarrassed, Jimmy bee-lines it for my bedroom.

"Ms. Porter, I just need to get some information and then, I'll let you get back to your, um, *evening*." He clears his throat, choking on something that must have been a nervous laugh.

"Well, there isn't really much for me to tell. Up until her funeral, I thought the last time that Sadie had spoken to David was when we were thirteen."

"What happened back then to make them stop talking?"

"He had taken her into the woods behind her house and started making out with her. Jimmy found them like that and yanked David off of her. She really liked David, but Jimmy said he was bad news and that she needed to stay away from him."

"Okay, and you had no knowledge of them resuming their relationship over the last few months?"

"No, not at all." I shake my head while wringing my hands and glancing at the floor. "We were pretty much always together. I don't really know how she would have had time to see him without me knowing about it."

"Thank you for your time, Miss Porter. I think this is about it for tonight. I may be calling on you or Mr. Thompson again at some point. Have a good evening. Sorry again about the *interruption*." I escort the detective to my front door and watch as he leaves my house. Then, I go back upstairs.

"What was up with you down there? You looked like you were caught cheating on a test or something." I laugh as I address Jimmy who still looks pretty guilty.

"Having the freedom to be with you without repercussions is still so new and fresh. I instinctively felt like I was going to get yelled at or punished for being with you. There would have been no use in making excuses to try and cover what we had been doing either. It was so *obvious*." Jimmy is fidgeting nervously with his hands.

"Was it really that obvious?"

"Are you kidding?" Jimmy laughs loudly. It is a real true laugh, like a million I had heard prior to Sadie's death. "I came downstairs shirtless and you were wearing the shirt that I had been wearing when I saw Detective Ramsey earlier today. What else could we have been doing? It was pretty obvious that we were just naked with each other."

"That's true." I chuckle. I kiss Jimmy lightly. "I'm sorry that we got interrupted. We were so close, *finally*."

"We don't have to rush it, Gen. If you want to hit the pause button and just chill on the couch for the rest of the night watching tv, I'm totally fine with that. Maybe this wasn't supposed to happen tonight since we got interrupted. If you want to pick up where we left off though, I am *absolutely* okay with that too."

"Why don't you just kiss me and we will see what happens?" I lean back on my bed, inviting Jimmy to join me. He leans down and kisses me.

"I really do love you, Gen." Jimmy is staring down at me and brushing my hair out of my face. "I still can't believe that I'm actually getting the chance to be with you. I have wanted this for so long; not just the sex, but us together. It seems surreal."

"I know exactly what you mean. I love you too, Jimmy."

We kiss slowly and intentionally, allowing our lips and tongues to savor and linger. We melt into one another and before I can mentally grasp what is happening, we are naked again. We are kissing so intensely and with so much passion that it's making my head spin. Jimmy positions himself so that he can slowly enter me for the first time. For a moment, there is a sharp tinge of pain that quickly passes. I let out a small whimper as he gently thrusts.

*Oh my God, this is actually happening. This is real life. I am losing my virginity to Jimmy.*

He is taking his time and being deliberately gentle. I can tell that he is holding back. After a few minutes, it's like an extra barrier lets loose inside of me and he suddenly slides deeper into me. We both let out a small approving moan at the unexpected change. Movements are seeming much easier now with little resistance. He starts to speed up his thrusts and his kisses are growing more insistent by the second.

*I've never felt anything like this. My whole body feels like it's pulsating now.*

Another small moan escapes me. Jimmy thrusts a few more times in response, deeper and faster. I let out a louder moan and then I feel his entire body start trembling as he is about to finish. He thrusts two more deep and rapid thrusts before collapsing into me breathing heavily.

"Thank you." Jimmy whispers, trying to catch his breath.

He rolls over to lay beside me. He is panting and has his eyes closed. His face is all flushed. I just lay there listening to his breathing and trying to process all of the different things that my body is feeling right now.

*My entire body feels like jelly right now. Emotionally, I am exhilarated and elated that this finally happened. I also feel something different hanging in the air between us, like the string that has connected us for all of this time has gone from one string to an entire rope.*

"I can't believe that we actually just did that. I have thought about having sex with you so many times before that it seems impossible that this really happened."

"How was it? I mean, obviously you don't have anything to directly compare to it in real life, but was it okay? Did it hurt?"

"It only hurt for a second."

"Good, I was so afraid that I was going to really hurt you."

"Jimmy, it was wonderful. I promise."

We lay beside each other in my bed, just enjoying being skin to skin. We lay here for a long time, wrapped in each other's arms before I end up falling asleep.

I wake up in the middle of the night needing to pee. I climb out of bed realizing that I'm still naked. I throw on a pair of underwear and Jimmy's shirt before heading to the bathroom. I walk a few steps before I feel the soreness from losing my virginity a few hours ago. In the bathroom, it burns to pee and the pain intensifies as I empty my bladder.

*No one ever discusses the pain associated with having sex for the first time.*

After I finish in the bathroom, I head to the kitchen to grab a glass of water. When I walk into the kitchen, Mom is sitting at the table. I glance at the clock. It's almost three in the morning, which means she must have just gotten home from work.

"Are you okay, Gen? You're walking like you're hurt or something."

"I'm fine. I'm just a little sore." Mom looks at me and glances me over from head to toe. Then, she raises an eyebrow and gives me a lopsided grin.

"*Sore*, huh? From what?" There is a knowing grin on her face. She knows that I suck at lying to her.

"Uh, nothing. I don't really know." I can feel my face turning bright red.

"Well, I have a wild guess." *Oh God, here it comes.* "Jimmy is here. You're wearing his shirt and your underwear, your hair is a disaster and you're walking like you just rode a horse." She punctuates each of her points by counting off on her fingers.

"Shut up. You're crazy." I am fully blushing and have a guilty smile. It's not even worth trying to hide it.

"Oh my God! I'm right, aren't I? Gen, this is *huge*!" Mom squeals.

"I know it is! I still can't believe that it actually happened."

"Go back upstairs and be with your man! *Eek!* I am so happy for you two!" Mom is doing her rapid clapping that she does when she is really excited.

After I finish my glass of water, I return to my room. Jimmy is still asleep, completely naked. I throw back the comforter to crawl into bed beside him and I pause to look at him for a moment while he is in all of his godly perfection. I crawl beside him and just as I start to fall asleep, Jimmy jolts awake. He sits straight up and is breathing rapidly like he's been running a marathon.

"Jimmy, what's wrong? Are you okay?" I grab his arm.

"I am so sorry."

"For what? I was already awake."

"For tonight."

"What? Why?"

"Well, um, I just remembered something really important."

"What is it?"

"Gen, I, um, I don't know how to say this." He pauses to catch his breath. "I didn't, um, use a condom."

"Yeah, I know. I was there too. So what? It's not like either of us have STDs or anything. You haven't been with anyone else, right?"

"Right, but Gen..." Jimmy is looking at me with sad and serious eyes. "Condoms prevent things other than STDs." My brain fully awakens and his point sinks in.

"Oh..." I lean my head against Jimmy's back. "If anything happens, it was obviously meant to be that way. I'm not going to freak myself out and worry about this. I am not sorry for tonight at all, not even for a second." I turn his face toward mine and kiss him to reassure him that I mean every single word.

"Let's try to not tell Mom about this anytime soon, okay? Wait until we get our own place, maybe?"

"Agreed! She would freak out, but my mom already knows."

"Darcy knows? How?"

"She guessed! Apparently, I am walking a little strange."

"*Oh no!* See? I *did* hurt you."

"I'm okay! I'm just a little sore. It's to be expected. I'm sure I'll be fine by tomorrow night."

"Okay, I hope so. I love you, Gen." Jimmy lays back down beside me and closes his eyes. I settle myself beside him. As I fall asleep, I drift into a dream.

*It's a rainy spring day of our junior year and Sadie is complaining about some rain leaking through her window. I'm laying on her bed reading an issue of Seventeen magazine. There is an article about the do's and don'ts of kissing. I'm reading it aloud and Sadie is agreeing with some of it based on her own personal experiences. All of my input is about how I wonder what it would be like kissing Jimmy.*

*"He's right down the hall, Gen. Just go kiss him! If you want, I can just call him in here right now." Sadie flashes a huge smile at me and opens her bedroom door. "Jimmy! Come here! Gen needs you for something." Sadie yells down the hall toward Jimmy's room.*

*"Shut up, Sadie! Shut up! Please!" I smack her with the magazine just as Jimmy walks into her room. He leans against the door frame and flashes me a flirty smile.*

*"What did you need, Gen?" I panic as I try to think of something to say.*

*"I was just wondering if you could play us a song later on your guitar." God, that sounds so stupid. Literally anything else would have sounded better.*

*"Oh. Uh, yeah, sure." He looks at me like I'm crazy. He turns and leaves the room.*

*"You should have just done it! I served you the perfect opportunity."*

In the morning, I wake up to Jimmy getting out of bed. I see him putting his clothes back on and I can't help but to feel sad because he isn't in the bed beside me anymore.

"Are you trying to sneak out and run away on me?" I tease, groggily.

"No, not at all. I really do have to go home though. I need to shower and get ready for work." He leans down and kisses me.

"Ugh. Okay, fine, if you have to. I am meeting you at the library at four, right?"

"Absolutely. Thank you again for last night." Jimmy smiles and kisses me again, leaning on my bed.

"You don't regret it though, right? You seemed pretty freaked out in the middle of the night."

"Genevieve, I could *never* regret making love to you. Ever! I promise."

"Even though it was unprotected?"

"I honestly never even thought about it until I woke up panicked. I was too caught up in what was actually happening during. My only concern was you."

"I'll go grab you some today while you're at work so that we will have some for next time."

"Next time, huh?"

"Well, duh. It's not going to just never happen again!"

"Very, very true!" Jimmy smiles and kisses me playfully. "I really have to go now. I really, really don't want to though. I wish I didn't work in two hours. I love you. I'll see you tonight." Jimmy walks out and I cover my head with my blanket. I'm not quite ready to get out of my warm, comfortable bed.

# Chapter Six

## Jimmy

♪♪♪

*I did it. I finally slept with Gen. It felt even better than I ever imagined, both emotionally and physically. I can't believe that we both got so caught up in the moment that we forgot about protection.*

*Come to think of it, I'm not even sure if Gen is on birth control. I never thought to ask. I will need to find a time to bring that up. I've never seen her take any, but that doesn't mean that she doesn't have it.*

*After all of that fuss that Mom made about us being together, we still managed to forget and Mom made such a point of freaking out about the consequences of unprotected sex, too. How did we forget?*

*Gen is right though. If she gets pregnant, it's meant to be. I'm sure we will be fine. It can't be that common to get pregnant on the first try, right? I don't have time to worry about this right now.*

I have to go to work soon, but I definitely need to shower first. When I walk into my house, Mom is on the couch working on her daily crossword puzzle in the newspaper.

"Did you spend the night with *Gen* again?" I can't tell what mood she is in. She is so difficult to read anymore.

"Yeah, I did. Where else would I have been?" I am preparing myself for an argument. She is so quick to jump down my throat lately.

"I have no clue, James. With a male friend, perhaps? A man from the police came by. His name was Ramsey. He was asking questions about Sadie." Mom is tapping her pen repeatedly against the edge of her crossword puzzle. She is definitely agitated.

"Oh, really?" I plaster faux-shock on my face.

"Oh, come on, James. As if you didn't already know that! He said that he has information from Sadie's phone that might insinuate that her death wasn't an accident. The only way that he would have gotten ahold of Sadie's phone was if you or Genevieve took it to him."

*Oh here we go!* She is treating me like a child and she is starting to be bitchy once again.

"Okay, yes, Mom. I did take it to him. We found some messages on her phone when Gen went into Sadie's room to change the other night. If I hadn't taken it to him, there is the possibility that someone would have gotten away with murdering Sadie. I couldn't let that happen."

"Another secret? Really, James? Anything else that you're hiding from me? I'm not okay with things being withheld from me. Your sister hid a *baby*! I really need to know if you're hiding anything else. It's really important to me that you are being honest with me." Her voice is growing all high-pitched and stretched tight like she is struggling to hold back tears.

Having her scold me like I am ten years old again sends me over the edge. "You know what, Mom? I'll tell you *everything.*

So, buckle up because it's a lot. Sadie was messing around with David Jerome. He was bad news then and he still is now. He made a move on her years ago, but I physically removed him from her presence. She recently got back in touch with him apparently. We think he was the baby's father. He is the one that texted her, too. He is also the reason that I have this black eye." I'm unintentionally raising my voice. Mom just sits in shock as I let loose.

*I might as well just tell her every little thing while I have the floor.*

"Also, after work today, I am going to look at an apartment with Genevieve. I gave her my class ring, too, as a promise that I will be proposing to her eventually, but if all goes well, it will be sooner rather than later."

*Okay, maybe not* every *little thing. The sex secret should probably wait a bit longer.*

"Wait, an apartment? Are you moving out?" Now she looks offended. Tears are welling up in her eyes.

"I can't stand being here anymore without Sadie. It's too painful. I keep expecting her to be hanging out in her room or watching one of her shows on the couch. Plus, you don't seem too happy about my relationship with Gen. I don't want her to feel unwanted when she spends time with me." My voice cracks like I'm still going through puberty.

"I already told you that I am happy for you both. I don't think you need to move out right now when everything is still so new. Were you even going to tell us?" She has the audacity to stick her bottom lip out in a pout. "Also, your class ring belongs on *your* finger, not hers. I want you to take it back when you see her later today."

*This conversation is really starting to piss me off. She is being so childish and petty right now. She has loved Gen as a second daughter for so many years. I don't understand why she is acting this way toward her now.*

"The only way that I am ever taking it back is when I replace it with her engagement ring. I meant what I said the other night, every single word of it. Genevieve *will* be my wife and the mother of my children."

Mom puts down her crossword puzzle and stands up. I brace myself for an impact, afraid that she might slap me. Instead, she walks over to me and embraces me in a hug.

"James, you *truly* love her?"

She is crying now and actually smiling.

"Yes, Mom. I do. I have been completely in love with her since I was fourteen."

*I can't believe that she is asking me if I really love her. Of course I do! Has she seriously not noticed me pining after her for the last seven years?*

"Wait right here. I'll be right back." Mom disappears down the hall.

*Where is she going?*

I bewilderedly stand in the living room and await her return. When she comes back in, she hands me a burgundy velvet ring box. I give her a confused look.

"What is this?" I carefully open the lid on the ring box. There is a stunning diamond ring with a couple of emeralds encrusted in the gold band. I look at the ring and then back up at Mom. She is tearing up and has a small smile on her face.

"It was your great-grandmother's engagement ring. It's a family heirloom that I promised my mother I would give to you for your own engagement. If you're really this serious about Genevieve, it's yours."

*Mom is so damn confusing lately. Conversations with her since Sadie are an emotional rollercoaster ride, especially when it comes to Genevieve and I. Her moods can change in the blink of an eye. I'm just thankful that I have my normal, loving mother at the moment.*

"Wow. Thank you, Mom. This is very thoughtful. I, uh, have to go get ready for work now, but for real, thank you so much."

*This seems like some sort of test: if I decline it, she will think that I'm not serious about Gen, but if I accept it, she will be hearing wedding bells. I am going to take a shower before Mom changes her mind and demands the ring back.*

I walk into my room and set the box on my dresser before getting ready to take a shower. I start daydreaming about how it is going to look on Gen's finger.

When I first step into the running water, a huge cloud of Gen's scent wafts up all around me. It instantly gets my heart racing.

*I really hope that we get this apartment today. I would absolutely love being able to wake in her presence every day and stay by her side for as long as I can.*

Through the roar of the shower water, I can hear Dad's voice.

*That's weird. I thought he was working. He must have forgotten something. It isn't anywhere close to lunchtime yet.*

I get out of the shower, towel off, and head to my room to get dressed for work. I walk into my room with the towel wrapped loosely around my hips. My bedroom door is cracked open and I can see Dad's shoes at the end of my bed. I walk into my room, giving him a sideways glance, and head straight for my boxers.

"Uh, hi Dad. What's up?"

*It's not like him to sit on my bed. He is making me nervous.*

"How did things go with Genevieve?"

"You know what? They went great actually!" I cannot help but to beam brightly at him.

"That's perfect! I wanted to talk to you quickly about Sadie."

"Uh, okay. What's wrong?"

"You took her phone to the police without even warning us first. Can you imagine how it felt to have a detective show up asking questions about our recently deceased daughter who we believed was taken away from us by accident? Ramsey wants information about some David guy. Who is he?"

"I'm sorry. I need justice for Sadie if someone hurt her. I wouldn't be able to live with myself otherwise. I didn't tell you because I was afraid you would try to stop me. Do you remember the whole bonfire incident?"

"You mean when you flipped out because Sadie was kissing some friend of yours?"

"*Friend* is being said very loosely. He *was* that guy! He is also the guy that Gen saw at the funeral that ran from her and that's who I got in a fight with."

"Uh, okay. So, she was hiding him because she knew you wouldn't approve? Why did you fight him? It's not like you to fight someone, not without good cause anyway."

"When I went to talk to him, he never asked how or where Sadie died. He *knew* she died in the woods. How would he know that unless he was there?"

I watch as Dad processes what I just told him.

"Then, you were right to go to the police." Dad stands up and is about to walk out of my room when he catches a glimpse of the ring box on my dresser. His jaw immediately drops open. "Woah. What is *that*?"

"Oh, uh, that is great-grandma's ring apparently." I tousle my wet hair nervously.

"Shit! You're proposing?" Dad's eyes are the size of half dollars.

"Well, *eventually*, yeah."

"Your mom has said for years that if she didn't like the girl that she thought you were going to marry, she wasn't going to give you the ring. Lucky for you, she loves Gen. She has also always said that she wouldn't give it to you until right before you were planning on doing it. So, when are you proposing?"

"I think she only gave it to me because I gave Gen my class ring as a promise that another one will be on its way at some point. Sooner, rather than later if I can control it."

"Ah! So *that's* why she gave it to you. She must think it's inevitably right around the corner."

"Have you talked to Mom at all since I got home?"

"No. She had to run out to the grocery store. Why?"

"Well, I told her some other news that I haven't told you yet. Gen and I are looking into getting an apartment together."

"One bedroom or two?" Dad has an inquisitive smirk on his face.

"One." I answer shyly.

*If I was a turtle, I would have retreated into the safety of my shell.*

"*Damn*, Jimmy! Go get her!" He claps me on the shoulder.

"Can I tell you something else that I *didn't* tell Mom?"

I'm nervously wringing my hands in front of me. Dad looks like he is growing nervous now, too.

"Of course. What's up?"

"Well, since I don't really have any super close guy friends to talk to, I need to tell you something. I need to tell someone because I am about to burst at the seams. I need to get this out there. I need someone else to know."

"Okay. Shoot already!" Dad's face is filled with anxious anticipation.

"I slept with Gen!"

I spill it out really fast. Dad gapes at me, as a smile slowly creeps across his face.

"Wait, like *for real*? Not just sleeping in the same bed as her? As in you two actually *had sex*?"

"Yes. For real! We did last night."

He scoffs out an obnoxious laugh worthy of a frat boy.

"About damn time!"

"Are you sure it's not too soon? I mean technically, we have only been dating three days."

"You even said yourself that you have six years invested in this relationship already. I don't think any of this is too soon honestly. Generally, I would steer people clear of jumping into bed or an apartment with someone that they just started dating, but you two are different. I don't think standard relationship rules apply to you."

"I seriously cannot imagine life without her in it. Waking up beside her is the best feeling. Dad, kissing her is *incredible*. It is better than I ever could have imagined. It feels like I will never be able to get enough of her. I don't know how I got so lucky."

"Son, do me a favor. Propose to her the very first chance you get. Everything that you just said is exactly how I *still* feel about your mother to this day. You've held yourself back from her countless times over the years. You both have. Stop doing that! Follow your heart and everything else will fall into place."

At that, Dad walks out of my room, leaving me to get ready for work. I already know that my day at the library is going to be filled with thoughts of Gen and the apartment that we will hopefully be living in together. I have spent many of my days categorizing the library's inventory thinking about her. I send her a text before I get dressed.

I can't wait to see
you again after work.
Have a great day, my
beautiful girlfriend!

I put on some of my library-appropriate attire and think about that box on my dresser. I am very tempted to carry it with me constantly, just in case the perfect moment arises unexpectedly. Right now, I only have two fears swarming my brain: the possibility of Gen rejecting me and the possibility that she finds the ring before I give it to her.

*It's time to head to the library. I cannot wait to get this day moving so that we can get to the apartment faster.*

On my way out the door, Mom stops me. She just got back from the store. She has two grocery bags still around her wrists from carrying them inside.

"James, can you eat with us tonight? Genevieve, too. I really want to have a redo of the other night. I feel foolish for how I acted. I love you both so much."

"Uh, yeah, probably. I'll ask Gen just to be safe, but I am pretty sure we will be here."

"Thank you. See you tonight."

I hug Mom and leave the house. As I climb into my car, I can faintly smell Gen's perfume. The smell makes me think of how it feels kissing Gen and of last night.

*I am still finding it difficult to grasp that she is actually dating me. I have wanted her for so long that this seems like a dream that I might wake up from at any moment, but if this was a dream, Sadie would still be alive. If she was here, she would be helping me plan the perfect proposal and we would be looking for a two bedroom apartment so that we could all be together. I hate that she is gone. This isn't fair. I miss her so much. Shit! Now, I'm crying again.*

I park at the library and wipe my tears before checking my reflection. My blue eyes are encircled in red.

*There is no way to hide that I was just crying. It is glaringly obvious. This will have to do.*

I get out of my car and lock the door before entering the library.

Janet, the head librarian, is sitting behind the counter, knitting. She finishes her row before looking up at me with a sorrowful look in her eyes.

"How are you holding up, Jimmy?" Her red reading glasses are perched on the bridge of her nose. She is glancing at me over them.

"It's terrible being without her. I can't stop crying."

"It is going to be that way for a while unfortunately. You simultaneously lost your sister and your best friend."

"I know. That's very true, but I do have Gen, too."

"Is she okay? They were inseparable. I've never seen one without the other."

"She is getting there. We are trying to work through this together."

"Good. So, she is still talking to you?"

"Yeah. Well, a little more than talking."

I can't help myself. There is a huge smile on my face and I am blushing so much that my face feels tingly and hot. Janet perks up at this. She has been listening to me spill my guts about Gen for the full three years that I have been working here.

My senior year the guidance counselor thought an internship at the library suited me because of my love for music and books. He got me all set up for the internship. After graduation, my internship became a paid job. All I do is catalog and sort out the returns, new arrivals and inventory, but it's a great job and I love it.

"Jimmy Thompson! Spill the beans! Come on! God knows I'm not getting any younger." Janet always acts like she is an elderly woman in her eighties, but in reality she is only in her mid-fifties. She stopped dying her hair about a year ago and now it is all of her natural gray.

"Well, where would you like me to start?"

"The beginning! Duh! Would I pick up *Sense and Sensibility* and start reading at page fifty?"

"On Monday, the three of us went to a movie together. I decided that I was going to tell her how I felt on Tuesday, but that was before Sadie died. I didn't see her again until Saturday. On Saturday, I went over to her place to talk to her and ended up staying the night there."

"*Oooh!* Go on! Go on!" Janet is eagerly smiling.

"It was nothing like that. We just talked and comforted each other for a while and then we fell asleep, spooning on the couch."

"Spooning, huh? So she definitely likes you back. Friends don't spoon friends."

"I swear it was just innocent spooning." I hold my hands up in surrender. "Then, I spent Sunday night, too."

"You *rascal*!"

"Again, nothing happened. We slept in her bed, but all we did was sleep. In the morning, her mom caught me in her bed though."

"*Shit!*" Based on the way Janet is sucking up this information, I am assuming we have no bibliophiles around at the moment.

"Oh, it gets better! Her mom was actually *happy* about it, but anyway, I'm getting sidetracked. We were talking after her mom caught us in bed together and Gen made a comment about sex."

"That she wants to have it with you?"

"Well, *kind of*, but she said that if it was with me, it wouldn't be meaningless. That drove me crazy! I had to know what she meant! So, I had to pry it out of her after breakfast."

"*And?* Come on, I'm *dying* here!" Janet is eating this story up like a delectable dessert.

"She ended up telling me that she has liked me for eight years. *Eight!*"

"That's perfect, Jimmy!"

"It really is."

"*Soooo*, how did it feel to finally kiss her?"

"Incredible! So much better than even my wildest fantasy. Everything about her drives me crazy."

Janet squeals with excitement like a small child.

"I'm so happy for you! It's been a long time coming. She has pretty much already been your girlfriend the entire time that I have known you."

"More like six, almost seven, years actually."

"Jimmy, by that point in a relationship, most couples are engaged or married."

"I know, Janet...can you give me an honest opinion? Take all of your bias away. I want your *actual* thoughts on this."

"Um, yeah. Of course."

"Do you think we should be taking it slowly?"

"What do you call both of you suppressing your feelings for six years?"

"So you don't think it's too early for us to be having sex?"

"*Oh my God, Jimmy!* Are you?" If she smiled any larger, she would put the Cheshire cat to shame.

"Well, we did once last night, but I'm worried that maybe it was too soon and we should have waited. I mean we have only actually been dating since Monday."

"You've known each other for half of her life. I don't think it's too soon at all. If you are having second thoughts though, make sure you tell her sooner rather than later."

"I'm not having second thoughts at all. I just don't want people to judge her for how soon it was. I love her, Janet. I plan on marrying her."

"If someone judges her for that, I will personally tell them to fuck off. You have both been waiting long enough and you are two consenting adults."

"See? *This* is why you're my favorite."

I smile at Janet and she laughs. "Alright, go get some work done. There are a couple of full carts to put back."

I locate my cart and start putting books away while daydreaming about what might happen with the apartment today. I can already picture Gen's clothes sharing dresser space with mine, her shoes slung carelessly by the front door, and her favorite mug in the kitchen. I see Gen sprawled on the floor watching a movie and snacking on popcorn. I also imagine her dancing around the kitchen to some of Sadie's favorite songs with something shiny glittering on her hand in the light. It's the ring that Mom gave me. It's the ring that is now residing in my glovebox. I made sure to pocket it on my way out of the house.

*As much as I really want to, I don't think I'll be giving it to her anytime this week or even this month. The holidays are coming. Maybe a Christmas Eve proposal? New Year's Eve might even be nice. Our first holidays without Sadie are already going to be miserable. Maybe the celebration of an engagement would make this all less dismal.*

*Thanksgiving is coming up so quickly. I wonder if Mom and Dad would let me invite Gen and Darcy. Maybe if we have an apartment by then we will be able to host. I'll mention it to Gen later and see what she thinks of that idea.*

I'm finishing up my first cart of books when I hear footsteps heading my way. I look up expecting to see Janet, but it's just a patron. I give a customer service smile and go back to my duties. I push the empty cart back to the desk near the entrance. Janet is still knitting away when I return beside her. I realize that I haven't told her about my bruised eye and she hasn't inquired.

*One great trait of Janet's is that she knows when to stay silent. I also haven't mentioned Sadie's baby, but I don't think that I am quite ready for that discussion yet.*

She glances up from her project, smiling at me.

"Jimmy, I've been thinking while you were working."

"That's a dangerous pastime, Janet."

"I know it is, but I couldn't help it." She gives me a devious grin. "I was thinking about this whole situation with you and Gen. I think your sister is still playing a hand in this. How else would you explain the timing? It's *fate!* Also, I would like my wedding invitation hand-delivered, not mailed."

"It's probably not going to be anytime soon. I mean, I haven't even given her the real ring yet."

"*Real* ring? *Woah.* I need more information! What you're implying is that you've already given her a ring?" I affirmatively shake my head.

"My class ring." Janet inquisitively raises her eyebrows at me. "It's a promise of a proposal to come."

"Jimmy, that is a huge step! I do find it very fitting though that the girl who you loved all throughout high school is wearing your class ring."

"Right? I feel exactly the same way. Mom wasn't very happy about it at first, but then she turned around and gave me her grandmother's engagement ring to give Gen. She is so bipolar lately. One moment she is jumping down our throats about using protection and then the next, she is giving me a family heirloom to propose with. I never know which version of her to prepare myself for."

"She did *not* seriously attempt a sex talk with you, did she? You're almost twenty-one." Janet is laughing ridiculously.

"She did, *during dinner*, with Gen right there." I rub my forehead with my fingers.

*I still can't believe that Mom acted that way.*

"Oh my God! Poor Gen! That is hilarious." She is laughing even harder now. She takes a deep breath to try and compose herself. "Okay, okay, I think I am better now. So, anyway, you have the real engagement ring? When are you going to pop the question?"

"I do have it, but I honestly have no clue. I am planning on keeping it with me constantly in case the perfect moment arises. It's in my car right now."

"*Ooooh!* Can I see it?"

"Uh, yeah, I guess. Let me go grab it."

I walk outside and unlock my car. I open the passenger side door to get into my glovebox. Gen's lingering perfume is a lot stronger on this side of the vehicle. I inhale deeply.

*I love that smell. It makes me think of everything good in this world.*

I grab the ring box out of the glovebox and open it. I stare at the ring for a long moment, admiring how the sunlight dances off the diamond.

*This ring looks like it was custom-made for Gen. It's elegant and beautiful, yet simple, just like her.*

There is a huge unyielding smile on my face as I head back inside after locking the car again.

I take it to Janet, expecting her to be enthralled in whatever knitting project she is currently working on, but she is just sitting there expectantly. She reaches out her hand for me to place the ring box in. She takes it and lightly runs her fingers over the velvet.

"Beautiful box!" She slowly opens it and her eyes turn into gigantic discs when she lays her eyes on the ring. "It is so pretty! Can I marry you instead? I would love to have this beauty on my finger."

"Nope. Sorry, I am already pretty set on who will be my bride." One side of my mouth turns upward into an amused smirk.

"Keep me in mind just in case she says no!" Janet jokes as she hands me back the ring box. I push it into my front pocket. It's a tight fit, but it is going to have to work for now. I am not about to go back outside at the moment.

"Do you think that she might? I am seriously petrified of her saying no." My heart is pounding in my chest and my palms are starting to get clammy.

"It was a *joke*! No, I don't think that there is even a remote possibility of her turning you down. If she has truly been in love with you for as long as you say, she would probably marry you right this minute if you asked her to."

"If she wanted to go to the courthouse right now and elope, I would drop everything and go in a heartbeat without ever giving it a second thought."

"I really don't blame you! You've been crazy about her for practically ever. You have an hour and a half left to do two more carts of books. Think you can quit daydreaming long enough to get them finished?"

"I think I'll manage." I wink at Janet as I grab the next cart.

I spend the next hour putting books away in the kid and mystery sections. Once I empty that cart, I return it to the front and grab the last one. It's only partially filled, but it has an assortment of books from all over the library. This one may actually take a while.

After I put away a few biographies about various public figures, I come across a book about pregnancy. I head toward the reproductive health section to get this on the shelf as fast as I can. It's making me think of Sadie and the tiny person that was growing inside of her.

*Maybe one of these days I will be strong enough to open one of these books and read about what the baby would have been like when they were both taken from us.*

I place the book where it belongs and quickly move from that section. Next up are a bunch of harlequin novels. As I'm placing some Fabio-clad book in its proper place, I hear a familiar voice from behind me.

"Are you studying seduction techniques?" I turn around to see Gen leaning against the end of a nearby bookshelf.

"*Hey, you!* What are you doing here?" I am smiling at her and suppressing the need to kiss her. I know that if I give in and start kissing her right now, I won't be able to stop.

"It's almost four. Mom brought me by a little early and your car was locked, so I came in to stay warm."

"Did you come looking for me or for a book? This section is just a lot of smut-filled books that middle-aged women use to get off. I don't know if you'll find anything of interest." I tease her.

*She has always read romances from the young adult section. Those actually tend to have quite a bit of smut, too. I have always been able to tell if she gets to one of those scenes in her books. She pulls one knee up toward her face and bites her bottom lip just a tiny bit. Her eyes flick from side to side violently as she devours every word on the page. If you say her name when she is in the middle of those sections, she looks up at you quickly over the book and her face turns bright red. I purposely do this any chance I get.*

"I was looking for the Kama Sutra actually." She laughs joyfully. "Kidding. Totally kidding. Janet told me where to find you. She seems to be in an especially good mood today."

"She is. What time is it?"

"Three fifty-five, so it's almost time to go."

"Oh good! I only have to wait five more minutes to kiss you then."

"Says who?" Gen raises her eyebrow teasingly at me.

"Well, Miss Porter, I don't think I will be giving you a choice." I wink playfully at her and start pushing the cart back to the front. Gen lingers behind me.

*I am so aware of her presence. I can feel exactly where she is behind me as if we were connected by a tether.*

I park the cart beside Janet. It's almost empty. "I'll finish these up next time. I need to get to a meeting."

"Oh I bet you do." Janet winks at me and glances over to Gen. "I hope I will be seeing you around more, Gen."

"I'll try to stop in more often. Have a great night!" Gen walks over to me and grabs my hand. We walk out to my car hand in hand. As soon as we are beside my car, I pull Gen into me and kiss her deeply. "God, I've been thinking about doing that all day! What's in your pocket?"

*Shit! The box is still in my pocket.*

"Oh, uh, nothing. Come on. Let's get over to the apartment." I quickly try to change the subject.

*I need to find a way to get the ring from my pocket to the glovebox without Gen noticing it. That will be impossible though since it is directly in front of her. Hopefully she will just forget that something mysterious was ever in my pocket.*

"I'm excited to see it. Where is it?" Gen is bouncing in her seat like a small child on the way to the apartment.

"Right down the street. We will be there in just a second." I answer her while at a red light. I drive another block before turning into a paved driveway. The apartment is on the front half of a brick duplex. "Here we are!"

"I already love it!" Gen is beaming. We get out of the car and walk up the sidewalk to the front doorstep. I knock and put my hand around Gen's waist while we wait for the door to open. There is a light breeze blowing her hair around her face.

A tall and broad man, who introduces himself as Gregory, opens the door. He is the landlord of this property. He welcomes us into the quaint apartment. This place is adorable and definitely a great first place. Gen's eyes are filled with wonder like a toddler in a candy shop.

There are technically only three rooms because of the open floor plan. There is a countertop forming a bar as the only thing definitively separating the kitchen from the living room. A small hallway leads to the bathroom and only bedroom. I can easily picture us taking up residency in this apartment and transforming it into our home. Once our tour is finished, Gregory invites us to sit at the bartop in the kitchen with him.

"So James, what are your thoughts? Would you like to look at some more properties?" I glance at Gen beside me. She looks so happy and beautiful sitting in this yellow kitchen.

"Actually, if you have a lease with you, I will sign right now. I think it's perfect."

"Really? That's fantastic! Let me go grab the papers." Gregory gets up and leaves the kitchen to get the paperwork from his vehicle. Once his work boots stop sounding on the floor, I turn to Gen.

"You seem to really love it here. I've been watching your eyes light up the whole time that he has been showing us around. Are you still planning on living with me? No pressure though!"

"Of course I do! It's perfect." Gen squeezes my hand tightly and smiles.

"Well after Gregory comes back in here, it's *ours!*" I kiss Gen on the forehead just as he walks back in with the manila folder.

"Okay, so down to business. The apartment will be move-in ready by Saturday. Rent is six hundred dollars a month. That includes water, utilities and trash removal. In order to move in, it will be the first month's rent and an additional four hundred dollar security deposit. I'll have you look it over and then you can sign it. On the lease, you will also need to list the names of every person that will be living here. If something changes with your living situation, I will need you to inform me so that I can make the proper updates. If someone moves in or out, I need to know."

Gregory hands me the lease and a pen. I read it over. It's fairly general rules that pretty much break down to being respectful of the property and neighbors.

I sign my name in both spots that it is required and then write both of our names:

James Thompson and Genevieve Porter.

*It feels amazing to be writing our names together. It will feel even better moving our belongings in together and morphing our lives into one.*

"Perfect! Now, I'll need the money before I can hand over the keys. So, just call me when you're prepared and I will meet up with you to do the trade off."

"I have it in cash. I can meet up with you again this evening."

*The money is at my house, hidden in the back of my drawer. I have almost twenty-two thousand saved up. I keep about three thousand in cash. The rest is in the bank in my savings account. I cannot wait to get the keys to our first apartment.*

"I have some other engagements this evening. I can meet up with you at some point tomorrow if that's alright with you."

"That's perfect! Have a great night." After I shake Gregory's hand, Gen and I walk out to my car. Once we are in the car, Gen lets out an excited squeal. She has a huge smile on her face. I lean over the center console and give her a passionate kiss. "I cannot wait to live with you! Oh, my parents want us over there for dinner tonight by the way."

"So that your mom can be all weird again?" Her huge smile has instantly changed to a frown.

"No. She wants to make it up to us, especially to you, for how she acted the other night. Plus, this will be the perfect time to tell them about the apartment." That brought her smile back. She looks truly happy right now.

*I will do absolutely anything in my power to make sure she looks like this every day for the rest of our lives.*

## Genevieve

♡

*The apartment is perfect. It has an open floor plan. The kitchen has a bar and it looks into the living room. Then, there is a small hallway that leads to the carpeted bedroom and sea blue bathroom. Mom will absolutely adore it. I hope that the Thompsons feel the same way. I'm really nervous for dinner there tonight. It's dumb because I have spent so many dinners there over the years. Last time though, Maryann went a little nuts on us and that was only telling them that we were dating. Now that we are about to tell them that we are going to be moving in together, I can only imagine how she is going to react. I am mentally preparing myself for the worst case scenario.*

We pull up to the Thompsons' house. As we get out and walk inside, I notice the lump in the front pocket of his jeans again. I felt it against me earlier when we kissed outside of the library.

*It's hard, whatever it is. He wouldn't tell me what it was earlier, so I am going to try my hardest not to pry even though it is going to drive me crazy. If he won't tell me, then it's obviously none of my business. He isn't a very secretive person normally.*

Maryann is sitting on the tweed couch when we enter the warm house. The smells of a home-cooked meal being prepared are wafting out of the kitchen. Henry's voice is humming somewhere in the kitchen.

"Gen, I'll be right back." Jimmy disappears down the hall, near his room. I sit down on the loveseat, caddy-corner from Maryann. I am wringing my hands in my lap.

*I am so fucking nervous!*

"Genevieve, I want to apologize for my behavior the other night. I just can't believe that Sadie was hiding so many things from me. I thought that we were closer than that. I want you and James to feel comfortable talking to Henry and I about anything."

Maryann seems to be sincerely apologetic. Before I can respond, Jimmy is back in the room. He comes to the loveseat and sits beside me. He sits close enough that the full length of our legs are touching and he places his arm around my shoulder.

I'm hesitant to react, for fear of Maryann's reaction. I look over at her timidly. She is smiling at us, truly smiling.

"It's nice to see you both smiling. I've missed it. That's a nice ring, Genevieve." Maryann gestures toward my hand. I look down and rub my thumb over the stone of Jimmy's class ring.

"Oh, um, thank you. It's Jimmy's. I mean, *James*. Sorry."

"I'm aware that it's his. I *am* the one that bought it, after all. It looks nice on you though."

"Thank you." I'm scared that she is going to flip out again.

"Everything looks better on Genevieve, Mom." Jimmy smiles as he squeezes me closer to him while I blush.

"I'm sure it does." Maryann seems like she is getting a bit snooty again. This is getting pretty uncomfortable.

"How are you doing, Maryann?" I feel like turning the conversation away from me is probably the best idea.

"As well as can be expected, I guess. I'm still crying a lot. I can't go into her room or move anything that belongs to her. I'm so emotional lately." Maryann looks raw and vulnerable.

*I just want to hug her and make her feel better.*

Acting on that impulse, I get up from the loveseat beside Jimmy and go to her side. I give her a tight hug.

"Thank you, Genevieve. I really needed that." Maryann is crying now and starts wiping her tears away. "I really am happy for the two of you. I can't believe that I missed your potential relationship right under my nose all of these years. I mean, looking back on it now, there were signs here and there; small glances between you two, longing looks, lingering touches. I never imagined that you two would actually get together. I wonder what Sadie would think about all of this."

"Actually, Sadie knew about my feelings for James." I smile and look over at Jimmy. "She told me to marry him so that we could actually be sisters."

"Well, maybe someday you will." Maryann seems a little more genuine with this comment.

"Is everyone getting along in here?" Henry says, entering the room while drying his hands with a kitchen towel. He smiles at all of us. "Dinner is ready. Let's all go eat."

We all get up from the couches and file into the dining room to sit at the table. Dinner is roasted vegetables and chicken. It looks delicious. My stomach starts growling since I barely ate today. As we start to eat, Maryann and Henry make small talk about work. We fall into the comfort of a family dinner and I am so thankful that there isn't any discussion about us. I eat a forkful of vegetables. I didn't realize exactly how hungry I was until the food started hitting my mouth.

"Genevieve, that's an interesting ring you have there." Henry winks at Jimmy. "Where did you get it?"

*Oh great, here we go.*

"Um, it's from James actually."

"Oh really? What is that for?" Henry has his trouble-causing smile on his face.

*He loves to get under Maryann's skin. I swear that it's some weird form of foreplay.*

"He said it's a promise."

"Promise of what exactly? That he won't be a jerk?" Henry chuckles.

*He is feeling feisty tonight, I see.*

Jimmy shoots his father a dirty look from across the table.

"Uh, that another ring will be coming, um, you know, eventually." I'm extremely nervous and fidgeting.

*Why is he asking me this stuff?*

"So, James, you have another ring?" Henry sips at his drink and glances at Jimmy, then to Maryann. Now Jimmy is the one who looks nervous and embarrassed.

"Dad." Jimmy says, sternly. He rarely uses that tone of voice with anyone, but *never* with Henry.

"What? I just asked a simple question."

"Can we talk about something else please?" Jimmy is clearly frustrated.

*Why is he being so weird? A simple no would have sufficed.*

"How did your day go?" Maryann tries to ease the tension between the males.

"It was quiet today. There were only a couple of patrons. Janet sends her condolences."

"Be sure to tell her thank you." Maryann leaves the table with her empty plate. "I'll grab the brownies."

*This has been a very weird dinner so far.*

Maryann returns a few moments later with a plate stacked high with brownies. She hands them to Jimmy and we pass them around the table. As we start eating our chocolatey dessert, Jimmy speaks up.

"We have some news."

*He is really going to do this* now?

"News?" Henry looks confused.

He already knows that there hasn't been a proposal. He also glances at my stomach as if he is trying to decide if we could possibly be hiding a baby.

"We signed a lease this afternoon."

"Really? That's huge! Where is it? When do you move in?" Henry seems pretty excited for us and a bit relieved that we weren't announcing a pregnancy.

"We get the keys tomorrow. It's downtown near the business district." Jimmy is beaming at his parents. Maryann seems like she is still trying to process what he just said. "I don't know when we will actually move in. We haven't gotten a chance to discuss it yet. I do know that it will be soon though."

"How big is it?" Maryann asks before taking a bite of her brownie.

"Uh, it's one bedroom and one bath. It has an open floor plan. It's really nice, Mom. I think that you'll really like it." Jimmy is eager to please his mom.

"*One* bedroom?" Maryann coughs as she chokes a little on her dessert.

"Um, yeah." Jimmy gives me a sly smile.

*We both know how this is about to go over with his mother. Even before everything happened with Sadie, this would not have gone over well. Maryann is very prim and proper at all times.*

"With *two* beds, I presume?" Maryann challenges. I have to fight back my sarcastic response: *Oh yes, Maryann, just like Lucy and Desi.*

"Nope! Just one, Mom!"

"Genevieve, are you sure you don't want your own space?"

"I, um, actually enjoy sharing a bed and all of my space with Jimmy." Jimmy is giving me an approving smile. He is trying to stifle laughter. Not only am I about to make Maryann's head spin for confirming that we have been sharing a bed, but I also just broke her formal name rule.

"James, do you really think that it's a good idea to only have one bed?"

"Mom, I don't think it's a good idea. I *know* that it's a *great* idea." Now, he can't hold back the laughter. Henry is laughing, too. I keep waiting to see Maryann snap, but she is surprisingly smiling too.

We finish up our dessert and go to Jimmy's room.

*It's still bugging me that Jimmy got so irritated at Henry for just asking a simple question.*

I sit down on his bed and watch as he shuts and locks his door.

*It's crazy to think that a few weeks ago, we wouldn't have had any need to lock it and soon we won't even need to shut the door because we will be in a place of our own.*

"Can I ask you something, Jimmy?"

*I don't know if it's necessarily my place to ask and he might get angry with me, but I need to know before it drives me nuts.*

"Of course. Anything."

"Why did you get so mad at your dad? He just asked a simple question and I'm sure he was just joking around."

"I just didn't want to discuss it."

"There's no pressure, you know. You don't have to propose any time soon or spend a ton of money on a ring. I'm just so happy to finally have *you*. Hell, you never even have to propose if you don't want to. I'm not going anywhere, ring or not."

"Gen! Of course I want to propose to you! It's nothing like that! It's just that he already knows the answer to that question. He was only asking to see me squirm. I hate when he does that. It's one thing to try and get a rise out of Mom because that's like their *thing*, but come on."

"Oh, well I don't get why you couldn't have just said a simple no. There was no point in getting so mad about it." I am watching him pace around his room.

*He looks nervous or angry. There is all of this tense, negative energy coming off of him. Why is he being so strange tonight?*

"For one, I seriously suck at lying."

"Wait, *what*? You already have a ring? For real?"

"Well, I might."

"You're being so weird and secretive today. This whole ring thing with your dad and avoiding telling me what was in your pocket earlier."

*It just clicked!*

"*Oh my God*! It was the ring, wasn't it? That's why you wouldn't tell me! Why did you have it on you though?"

"Okay, yes. I can't lie to you. I couldn't even if I wanted to. I had your real ring in my pocket. I didn't want you knowing that I had it yet." I try to hide my excitement. *Somewhere in this house, probably in this very room, is my future engagement ring!* "Side note: if you turn me down when I do ask, Janet has requested to take your place at the altar. She absolutely loves the ring." He laughs.

"She is much more *experienced* than me. I'm sure that would be quite the learning experience." I start laughing so hard that I snort. The mental image of Janet trying to seduce Jimmy is too hilarious.

"Um, *ew*!" Jimmy laughs and pretends to throw up. "The only learning experience I need is with *you*. Practice makes perfect, you know?" He comes over to me and kisses me flirtatiously.

"I wouldn't mind some practice." I kiss him back. We move ourselves to laying down on his bed while never breaking from our kisses. I'm on top of him and pull away for a moment to look at him.

*I need to remind myself that this is real life.*

"Jimmy, I love you."

*Everything about his face is perfect to me, even this close up.*

I lean my forehead against his and close my eyes to better soak in the feeling of this moment.

"I love you too. You are so beautiful. The ring is going to be absolutely gorgeous on you."

"I can't believe that you already have a ring."

"Well, I did tell you that I plan on marrying you. I can't wait to make you my wife. I've known for so long that you're who I want. It's killing me having you this close to the ring and not giving it to you."

"Don't give it to me until you are completely ready. You have all of the time in the world to propose. I won't ever be going anywhere."

"I don't think I'll be able to wait very long. I want to marry you as soon as I can. I wasted enough time not making you mine."

"*Yours*, huh?" I grin at him.

"Well, I mean, not *mine*. It's not like you're my property or anything. I'm not like that. I mean, you know me. I would never stand for a male treating a female like property. I just meant..." Jimmy is frantically stammering while trying to explain himself.

"I knew exactly what you meant. I like being *yours*." I kiss him again. "We need to tell Mom about getting the apartment."

"Let's go to your place. We can tell her and then I'll stay if you want me to."

"Sounds perfect. I'll go tell your parents goodnight while you pack a bag." I kiss him once more before getting off of his bed and going to the living room.

Maryann and Henry are cuddled up on the couch watching an old sitcom.

*They look so happy and peaceful to just be in each other's arms. I remember when my parents used to have moments like this one. I have always dreamed that I might have that someday.*

# Chapter Seven

## Jimmy

♪♪♪

*Dad really pissed me off so much when he put me on the spot so badly at dinner. If I said no, both of my parents would be upset with me for lying. If I said yes, Gen would have wanted to know more. It was a double-edged sword. I want to give it to her soon, just on my own terms. Plus, I really need to show it to Darcy and talk to her about it first.*

I grab some jeans and a long sleeve shirt for tomorrow and throw them into my old gym bag. Then, I reach all the way to the back of my middle drawer and grab the cash for tomorrow's deposit. I also make sure to retrieve the small box from the back of my sock drawer and place it in the bottom of my bag beneath my clothes.

*I am going to find an opportunity to chat with Darcy tonight one-on-one, even if I have to wait for Gen to fall asleep.*

When I get to the living room, I see my parents sitting on the couch holding onto one another like they used to when we were little kids.

*It's been a long time since I've seen them like this. For a while, I don't think I even saw them ever touch one another. It was a change that I didn't really pay attention to until recently. I'm so glad that they have each other. If they can get through this, they can get through anything together.*

Gen is just standing by the door watching them. She looks completely mesmerized.

*During moments like this, I am very aware of the fact that Gen lost a parent. She hasn't gotten to see a happily married couple first hand in years. My goal is to make sure that we are that couple. I want to make sure that our children see exactly what love looks like. Gen deserves that kind of happiness and more. She has been through so much.*

"Good night, guys. I'll see you at some point tomorrow. We are going to head over to Gen's house. We want to talk to Darcy about the apartment and then I think I will just spend the night over there. Love you guys."

"Love you." They both say in unison while slightly glancing in my direction.

*They have a sense of calm and ease right now. I feel like they are learning to find some kind of peace while playing this shitty hand they were dealt recently. I am so grateful.*

While driving down the familiar roads to Gen's house, we sing along to the radio with our fingers entwined. The sky is so dark and overcast tonight that the only lights on the drive are our headlights and porch lights on the houses we are passing by.

When we pull into Gen's driveway, I am thankful for the dark. It is hiding the fact that I am really nervous. My hands are getting clammy and I'm trembling. I grab my bag and get out of the car to head inside to tell Darcy about our news.

*I really hope that I will get a chance to speak to Darcy about the ring too.*

Darcy is relaxing on the couch in her pajamas watching a movie when we walk in.

"Hey kids! How was the apartment today?"

"We signed the lease!" Gen is beaming from ear to ear. "Jimmy gives the deposit tomorrow and then we will get the keys!"

"I can help you two move in this weekend if you want."

*Darcy is always so cool about this kind of stuff. If anything positive came out of Gen's dad passing away, it would be the way that the bond between Gen and Darcy strengthened. They are more best friends than mother and daughter.*

"That would be great, Darcy! Thank you so much!" I give Darcy a small hug.

"Thanks, Mom! Jimmy, I'm going to go take a shower." Gen gives me a quick peck on the lips before jogging up the stairs. I wait until I hear the water running.

"Darcy, can I, uh, talk to you about something?"

I am fidgeting quite a bit. I sit on the couch, opposite of Darcy. My leg starts bouncing like a jackhammer as soon as I sit down. It takes a lot of concentration to get it to stop.

"Sure, Jimmy. What's up? Is everything okay?"

"Uh, I'm really nervous. Sorry." I wipe my sweaty palms on my jeans.

*Deep breaths, Jimmy!*

"I, um, I want to ask Gen to marry me."

"Oh my God, Jimmy! For real? That is absolutely amazing."

"Would you really be okay with that? Do you think I should wait longer? I don't want to do anything that you won't approve of."

"Of course I'm okay with it! I'm more than okay with it actually. Gen has been in love with you for practically half of her life. Marrying you would make her so happy."

"I am so happy to hear you say that. Do you want to see the ring?"

"Wait. *What?* You have a ring? Are you planning on proposing like *tonight*?"

"No, not tonight. Here, let me show you the ring."

I take the box out of my gym bag and hand it to her. She opens it and immediately starts tearing up.

"It's so beautiful, James. She is going to absolutely love it. I can't believe that my baby is going to be getting engaged soon! This is so exciting."

"I want everything to be perfect. I would have asked Sadie to help me plan it all out, but obviously that isn't an option. Any advice on when or how?"

"Just wait until it feels natural. Planning out some huge romantic thing normally ends in disaster. Ask her when you're alone. I think that will make it more special."

I hear the shower turn off. I quickly put the ring back in my bag. I whisper my thanks to Darcy and head to Gen's room. She walks in and shuts the door as I'm setting my bag on her dresser. I turn her around to see her with dripping wet hair, wearing nothing but a towel.

*Damn! She is tempting me so much. How am I supposed to hold back when she comes in wearing just a towel?*

She smiles as if she can read my mind and kisses me lightly. Her lips are so warm and soft. I cup her face in my hand and kiss her passionately. She lets out one of those small moans that drives me absolutely crazy. She drops her towel to the ground while she is kissing me. My hands start exploring her body. Her skin is still damp from the shower. I slide my hand down her back and cup her ass lightly as I pull her into me. She keeps grinding her hips against me. Her bare body is pressed against mine and I can't resist it anymore.

I move us over to her bed and lay her down on her back while never breaking from our kisses. I stop kissing her long enough to pull my shirt off over my head. I have this primal need to feel her bare skin against mine. I lay on top of her and kiss her making sure that our torsos are touching as much as possible. She starts reaching to undo my pants. I eagerly help her to remove them. I'm throbbing against her. I *need* to be inside her. Just as I am ready to enter her, a thought occurs to me. I pull away from her lips, but I don't move my face more than a few inches from hers.

"Gen." My body is still pressed snuggly against her. "Did you ever get a chance to go to the store today?"

"The store? No. The only place I went today was to the library." She kisses me again. Her kisses are growing more fervent.

"We should probably slow this down then."

*This is absolutely killing me to stop this right now. I want her so badly.*

She has moved from my lips to my ear and neck. These kisses are giving me goosebumps all over my body.

"What? Why?"

*She totally forgot.*

"We don't have any condoms. You said that you were going to grab some today." She isn't stopping her torrent of kisses that have now traveled to my collarbone and on to my chest.

*This definitely doesn't feel like she is planning on slowing down.*

I pull myself off of her, forcing her to stop. "Gen, for real, we should really stop." Gen looks really hurt.

*I don't want her to take this the wrong way. I really want Gen, but I am also trying to be smart about this and do the responsible thing.*

I can't help but to look at her naked body beside, ready and waiting.

*I must be insane to be stopping this. Certifiably. Fucking. Insane.*

"What if I don't want to stop though?" Gen looks at me flirtatiously as she grazes her fingertips lightly along my torso, sending what feels like an electric shock through my entire body. As she reaches right along my hip bone, I shiver in anticipation.

"I really don't want to stop either. I want you so badly."

I lightly drag my fingers down the side of her body and then let my hand rest on her butt. Her skin is so soft. I never want to stop touching her. She lands passionate kisses on me with her warm mouth.

*I could get lost in her kisses so easily.*

She climbs on top of me while intensely kissing me. This position takes away any sense of control over this situation that I thought I had. My willpower is fading quickly with her body on top of mine.

She starts kissing her way down my body. My entire body is trembling. I close my eyes for just a moment and as I do, Gen takes me into her mouth.

*Oh my god!*

My eyes roll far back in my head. Before I can stop it, a deep moan escapes from my lips. I'm not sure how loud that was.

*Did Darcy hear that? Oh well, right at this very moment, I don't care.*

Every single intricate movement of Gen's tongue feels electrifying. She pulls away, gives me a tight tug and a smile before moving back up my body to kiss my mouth.

As she starts kissing me frantically, she lowers herself onto me. She moans into my mouth. She feels perfect riding the length of me. With me deep inside of her, it feels like our bodies were truly made for each other. We fit together like two perfect puzzle pieces. We are both fully lost in this moment. Moans are escaping between kisses from both of us. Our bodies are moving in unison like a well-oiled machine. Our movements grow faster and faster.

Gen starts kissing my neck again causing me to completely lose control. I roll us over so that I am on top of Gen. After a few more quick and deep thrusts, I climax. The room is quiet except for our chorus of panting.

*Shit! So much for slowing it down! That was an epic fail.*

I roll myself onto the bed beside her. I keep alternating from staring at the ceiling to closing my eyes to calm my brain and body down.

"That was," Gen is panting, "*amazing*. Thank you so much for that. I love you."

"Gen, thank *you*." I kiss her once on those soft plump lips. "It really was amazing."

We just lay here in silence beside each other as we try to calm our breathing. I am lying here with my eyes closed and a smile plastered on my face. I start drifting asleep when Gen's voice startles me and brings me back to this side of consciousness.

"Jimmy, I'm sorry." Her voice is barely audible. She sounds like she might start crying.

"Why in the world are you sorry?"

"Well, you wanted to stop, but I kind of lost control and forced you into that."

"Gen, I didn't *want* to stop. I was just trying to be responsible. I promise you that absolutely none of that was forced."

"We *were* pretty stupid, huh? I should have listened to you and quit. I just got so caught up in the moment. I'm sorry."

"Please don't start regretting it, Gen. I don't regret it at all, not even for a second."

"I don't want to ruin your life by accidentally getting pregnant." Gen is crying now.

*I hate seeing her cry.*

Her whole body is trembling with trepidation.

"That would not ruin my life at all, Gen. You and our future together *is* my life." I pull her in closer. She is still crying.

"Are you sure?"

I kiss her lightly on the lips and stare into her tear-filled eyes. "Genevieve Porter, I am absolutely positive. All I want out of life is to marry you and start a family with you. I *love* you."

"I love you too." She hugs tightly onto me. She is still crying, but the tears seem to be slowing down.

*I should just propose to her right here and now.*

"We should probably get dressed since Mom is downstairs."

"Do you think she heard us?" I chuckle nervously.

"I guess we will find out when we go downstairs." Gen is laughing now too as she gets up to put on her pajamas. We both get dressed and head downstairs.

## Genevieve

*I have nearly a decade of bottled up desire for Jimmy and it seems like it has been unleashed since I have actually been able to act on it. I can't help but to get as much time with him as I can. After my shower, I walked into my room with him and dropped my towel. I practically jumped him. I couldn't help myself. I have been dreaming of doing that for years. I saw the opportunity arise to make it a reality and took it. I never even thought about the fact that Mom was right downstairs.*

Now that we are both dressed again, we are going to go downstairs, get some popcorn, and watch a movie. As we walk past Mom on the couch, she turns and smiles at us.

*She definitely heard us. Oh well.*

I pop two bags of popcorn while Jimmy fills some water glasses. Once we take our snacks to the living room, Mom scoots over on the couch making room for us to sit side-by-side.

"What kind of movie do you guys want to watch?" Mom is still smirking.

"We don't care. You can choose whatever." I say, munching on my popcorn.

Mom searches for something to watch. She puts on a classic comedy starring the Brat Pack. Jimmy looks over at me and places a kiss gently on my mouth. His lips are salty from the popcorn.

"Hey, you two. Didn't you get enough of that upstairs?" Mom teases.

"Nope, I don't think I'll ever get enough." I say before kissing Jimmy again.

"What about you, James?" Mom is smirking at him. She loves trying to embarrass him.

"I plead the Fifth, Darcy." Jimmy is matching her smirk.

"Don't think that I don't know what was happening up there, Mr. Thompson!" Mom is chuckling.

"Mrs. Porter, I have no idea what you're talking about." Jimmy is trying so hard to keep a straight face.

*He is a terrible liar. He always has been.*

"It's fine. I really don't mind. If Clark was still alive, we would be doing it like rabbits twenty four-seven."

"Mom!" *I can't believe that she really just said that. I have never really thought about the fact that Mom gave up that entire part of her life when she lost Dad. She hasn't dated anyone since he passed. At least none that I know about. I remember them being very loving to one another before he got sick. They were never shy to make out in front of me, or anyone for that matter. They were very proud of their marriage. I think Jimmy and I will have that kind of marriage, too.*

"What? Sorry Gen, but I still to this day am completely attracted to your father. It isn't fair that fate stole him away from me, away from us. We still had so much left ahead of us." Now, Mom's eyes are misting.

*She doesn't bring Dad up very often. It is still a very raw topic with her. The love of her life was ripped out of her grip and there was nothing she could do to stop it.*

"Darcy, I will try to not let that happen under your roof again. I'm really sorry. We definitely shouldn't be doing that when other people are around. It's really inconsiderate. We will be moving into the apartment soon."

"It's really not a big deal. I'm truly happy for you two. Remind me to always knock when I go to your place, just in case." Mom winks at us. She is back to smiling again.

"Still. I will try to keep your daughter off of me." He is laughing and nudges me with his elbow. I am blushing scarlet.

*I cannot believe that he just said that to my mom.*

"Don't let her be a bad influence on you." Mom laughs. They are both finding this banter hilarious while I, on the other hand, am completely embarrassed.

We are all becoming enthralled in this movie again. Mom lays her head on the arm of the couch. I'm sure she will be asleep in a few minutes. This is normally her tell.

Just as we are getting comfortable and our eyes are getting heavy, I hear my phone ringing. I remove myself from the couch to answer my phone in the kitchen. The number is blocked.

"Hello."

"I heard that you went to the cops." The voice is raspy and hushed. It doesn't sound like anyone that I know.

"Who is this?" My heart is beating loudly in my ears. I feel like I'm in a horror movie.

"That doesn't concern you. You should have never gone to the cops. This will not end well for you." The line goes dead. A bit concerned, I walk back to the couch scuffing my feet. All I want right now is to feel safe in Jimmy's arms.

"Who was that, babe?"

*He called me babe!* My heart is fluttering happily now. *I love that he is calling me that.*

"I don't really know. I think it was David."

*Maybe it was.*

"David? Why would he call you?"

"He said that he knew that we went to the cops and that this isn't going to end well for me."

"What?" Jimmy's eyes have a fire burning within them. "Gen, I will kill him!"

*I have rarely seen him this angry over the last eight years. All of them except for one have been when he is being protective over myself or Sadie. The other one was during the only really bad fight that Sadie and him ever had.*

*It was during our sophomore year. Sadie had been in an especially bad mood for almost three weeks. Jimmy and I kept trying to figure out what was wrong with her, but it was just making her more irritated. She told Jimmy to mind his own damn business. He tried to explain that since he was her older brother, it was his business. She didn't like that in the slightest. She pushed him, but she knew he would never push her back. When he didn't push her back, she kept pushing him again and again until his back slammed against the wall in their living room. I just stood in place, frozen in shock.*

*"Sadie, stop, seriously." He was gritting his teeth. His eyes were angry and burning with that same cold, intense fire.*

*"No. Hit me. Come on, wimp. Push me back. Are you just going to let me sit here and do this to you?"*

*"I'm not going to do that and you know it."*

*"You are such a pussy. You're going to let a girl beat you up? No wonder you don't have a girlfriend and never get fucking laid."*

*"Chill the fuck out, Sadie. What the hell has gotten into you?" He tried to get around her and leave the living room, but she blocked him. I could see that he was getting angrier and angrier with her. "Sadie, move the fuck out of my way. Don't do this." He was speaking slowly and trying to keep himself level.*

*"I'm not moving until you make me. Come on. Don't be such a coward." She kept pushing him with all of her weight. She looked certifiably insane.*

*"I'm not being a coward. I am not going to hit you. One, you're my little sister. I am not going to be that kind of asshole that hurts his own sister. Two, there is obviously something going on with you that you don't want to talk about. Beating the shit out of me is not going to make you feel any better. If you don't want to talk to me about it, fine, but at least talk to Gen or Mom. You've been an emotional wreck and now you're just turning into a royal fucking bitch. Can I leave the living room now?"*

*She got this look of utter shock on her face and then broke down sobbing. He wrapped her up in a huge hug. She just kept sobbing. She never told him why she freaked out on him like that, but she ended up telling me later that day when we were alone. This was after her second sexual partner, Jackson Balleros, decided that with her he was going to be one and done. She really liked him, but he just used her for sex and then criticized her performance. She had been hiding it from me for almost a month and it was making her a total bitch.*

"No, Jimmy. I don't even know for sure that it was him."

"You need to at least call Detective Ramsey. It's not okay for someone to be threatening you."

"Okay, I'll call him in the morning. It's getting late."

"Do you really think you should wait?"

"I think it will be okay to wait until morning."

"Alright. I think we should make sure that everything is locked up and head to your room to get some sleep." Jimmy locks the front door while I lock the back. He also checks all of the windows before climbing the stairs to my room.

We crawl into my bed and I curl up beside him. He wraps his arms tightly around me and squeezes lightly. "Genevieve, I will never let anyone hurt you. I promise. I am going to protect you until the day I die." He kisses the top of my head.

"You always have. You've been my protector for as long as I can remember."

"I'm serious when I say that if David tries to lay a finger on you, I will murder him."

"No, you won't. I can't have you going to prison for murder charges when I just finally got my hands on you." I squeeze him tightly around the waist. The thought of being torn apart kills me inside.

"Okay, I won't kill him. Can I at least hurt him a bit?"

"To protect me? Sure."

I smile and kiss him on the end of his nose.

We drift off to sleep. I toss and turn all night with nightmares of David attacking Jimmy and I. Then, I have a few of him fighting with Sadie.

*That's it. In the morning, I am going to call Detective Ramsey. I can't keep looking over my shoulder in fear because someone threatened me.*

I wake up to my body folded into Jimmy's. We are spooning and he is holding me tightly with his one hand resting on my breast. He is still asleep, so he doesn't realize that he is totally copping a feel. Against my ass, I can feel Jimmy hard and ready to go.

*Feeling him against me like this is sending my body into a hormone-fueled frenzy. I keep trying to calm myself. He is completely unaware of how he is affecting me right now. I can't just wake him up and then jump on him. Actually, maybe I can. We are going to be living together soon anyway. Mornings like this are bound to happen.*

As I push my body against him more, I can feel his hardness rub against that precious bundle of nerves between my thighs. My whole body tightens at that teasing touch. I grind against him again but much slower and with more pressure this time. At this, Jimmy lets out a pleased moan and pulls me tighter against his body. The hand that had been cupping my breast is now descending to my underwear. He kisses my neck just below my ear as he slides a finger in me. I let out a small moan.

*I already need this so badly that I'm aching.*

## Jimmy

♪♪♪

*This is one hell of a way to be woken up. I thought I was dreaming at first. I felt Gen rubbing her body against me like I have dreamed of so many times before. Then, I realized that I was in bed with her. My head is spinning right now. I don't think I will ever get used to having sex with Gen. This will forever be my favorite way to wake up. Her naked body is against mine, relaxed and warm.*

"Good morning." Gen is smiling against my chest. I can feel the small muscles in her cheeks turning upward.

"Good morning. I can't believe that this is real life." Even I can hear the pure happiness in my voice.

"Honestly, neither can I but I am so glad that it is." She kisses me lightly and smiles at me. I just stare into her gorgeous green eyes.

*She is beautiful.*

"I cannot wait for you to be my wife, Genevieve Porter." Our eyes are locked. Her eyes have flecks of hazel in their seas of jade.

*I could get lost in her eyes for hours.*

"Your *wife*, huh? I'm sure your mom would have an absolute conniption if we got engaged."

"I wouldn't be so sure." Her hair is falling onto my face. I tuck some of it behind her ear. "Genevieve, I love you so much."

"I love you too, James Anthony." Smiling eyes are looking back at me.

*I should just give her the ring now. It's such a perfect morning.*

"Hey, let me get up for a second." I slowly start to pull myself from beneath Gen.

"Where are you going?" Gen looks sad that I am getting out of bed.

"Nowhere. I am just grabbing something." I walk over to her dresser where my bag is sitting. I reach in to grab the ring box out. As soon as I feel it in my palm, I turn towards Gen. I keep the box clenched tightly in my hand behind my back. "Gen, I am so thankful that I am finally yours after all of these years."

"I have always been yours. You just didn't know it." Her expression is so serene.

"I want to talk to you about something." I am trying not to let my nerves show. I slide into bed beside Gen once again.

"Of course, anything." Gen looks anxious and concerned.

"I, uh, well, I have something I want to give you." I'm shaking from my nerves.

*Ding dong. Ding dong.*

"Hold that thought! Let me go check the door." Gen gets off the bed, throwing on some sweatpants and a hoodie before leaving the room. I can hear her feet rhythmically descending the stairs.

*Maybe this is a sign that it wasn't the right time. I was seconds away from officially proposing. That damn doorbell interrupted me. I'm hoping that my courage doesn't wither.*

I wonder who is at the front door while silently cursing them.

# Genevieve

*Jimmy is acting a little strange today. He said the dreaded "we need to talk" line. It must be something serious. He looks pretty nervous. Just as he was starting to stammer it out, the doorbell rang. I am certainly not expecting anyone. I feel awful postponing our discussion, but I have to figure out who is at the door.*

I practically run down the steps. I open the door to Detective Ramsey.

"Good morning, Miss Porter." Ramsey smiles and tips his head at me. "May I come in for a moment?"

"Oh, um, sure." I step out of the way to let him inside.

"I just wanted to let you know that we have been unable to locate Mr. Jerome. Do you have any idea of people that might know where he is or how to find him?"

"I don't actually. Maybe Jack Kingsley? He is the one that gave Jimmy the number to find him before."

"Any idea on how to get a hold of Mr. Kingsley?"

"Jimmy has his number. Give me just a minute. I'll go get him."

"Oh, is Mr. Thompson here?"

"He is upstairs. I'll be right back." I run up the stairs to my room. "Jimmy, Detective Ramsey is downstairs. He needs Jack's number." Jimmy jumps. He still looks really anxious.

"Let me throw some clothes on and I will be right down."

I give him a look of concern and then return downstairs to the awaiting officer.

"Jimmy will be right down." I say as I walk into the kitchen and sit at the table. I gesture for the detective to take a seat. Mom isn't on the couch anymore. I'm not sure where she disappeared to. Jimmy comes down the stairs to break the awkward silence.

"Good morning, Detective. Has there been any progress with Sadie's case?"

"As I was just telling Miss Porter, we have been having some difficulty locating Mr. Jerome. She said that you might know someone who can track him down?"

"Jack buys from him. He told me that he always knows how to get him. I can write his information down for you."

"That would be great. Thank you."

"Did Gen tell you about the call from last night?"

"Call? No. What call?" Ramsey is glancing from me to Jimmy and back again.

"She thinks it may have been David."

"What happened on that call?"

"It was an unfamiliar voice. The person was pretty much whispering. They said that they knew that I had talked to you. They said that I shouldn't have gone to the cops and that this wouldn't end well for me."

"What? Why didn't you call me?"

"It was pretty late. We were going to call you first thing this morning. You beat us to it."

"Let me make a few phone calls really quick." Ramsey walks over to the window and dials someone on his phone.

I look at Jimmy. He looks so upset. "I'm sorry that we got interrupted. Once he leaves, we can pick up where we left off." I say quietly as I smile up at Jimmy.

"It's okay. It can wait until later." He shrugs off the apology.

*I can tell that whatever he had wanted to talk about upstairs is still weighing on him, but now the wounds from losing Sadie are being torn back open before they ever get a chance to scab up. Our perfect morning that we were having is quickly taking a turn for the worst.*

"Gen, have you seen my green –AHHH!" Mom lets out a scream from the stairs. She didn't realize that the detective was here. I peer around the corner and see Mom in her bra on the stairs.

"Mom, sorry. This is Detective Ramsey. I didn't realize that you were awake. I would have warned you." I say while outwardly cringing.

"I've been awake for about an hour." Mom seems frozen in place from embarrassment. She is covering her chest now with her forearms. Jimmy is carefully avoiding even so much as glancing in my mom's direction. "I'm sorry, Detective. I didn't realize anyone was down here."

"My apologies, Mrs. Porter."

"It's, um, Darcy. I am going to go put a shirt on. Excuse me." Mom turns and runs up the stairs.

*If I didn't know any better, I would think that Mom finds Detective Ramsey attractive.*

"I have spoken to some of the patrol cars that come into this area. They are going to keep an eye on the house to make sure that whoever called you doesn't try anything. I also think it would be a good idea to not be alone for a while."

"I won't be leaving her side." Jimmy has his hand resting on my shoulder lovingly.

"I also want you two to call me immediately if anything else happens. I can't help you if you don't inform me."

"We will. Definitely."

*Jimmy's reassuring presence is the only thing keeping me from freaking out right now.*

He lets go of my shoulder to write down Jack's number. As he is writing, Mom walks into the kitchen to join us.

"Is everything okay, Detective?"

"Well, we are having some trouble finding our suspect. Your daughter and Mr. Thompson are helping us get some leads."

"I'm really sorry for earlier." Mom is blushing and twirling her hair around her finger like a schoolgirl.

*I haven't seen her flirt with anyone since Dad.*

"It's completely fine. I showed up to your home unannounced. I should be the one apologizing." Ramsey is also blushing a bit. I glance down at his hand and notice the absence of a wedding ring on his finger. This confident, no-nonsense detective actually looks nervous to be in my mother's presence.

"Here is the information for Kingsley."

*Jimmy obviously senses the awkward exchange that is taking place right now.*

"Will you be calling us once you have some more information?"

"Of course. We will be in touch." Ramsey smiles and heads for the door. Mom is staring after him longingly.

As he reaches the door, he turns around and says, "Mrs. Porter, I would feel better about this whole situation if you had my business card. Here is my number. Please call me if anything out of the norm happens." Mom eagerly takes his card from him. Ramsey leaves and Mom is standing motionless, staring at his business card.

"He's pretty handsome." I say, looking at my mother. She is still in a trance. "Hello. Earth to Darcy." Mom snaps out of whatever trance she was in and looks up at me.

"Did you say something?"

"I was just saying that Ramsey is pretty handsome."

"Handsome? Um, yes, most definitely." Mom is blushing again. She is the shade of a ripe tomato right now. "I wouldn't mind doing what you two were doing earlier with him."

*Shit! She heard us.*

"I have no idea what you're talking about." I attempt to play dumb. Mom sees right through it and raises an eyebrow at me.

"Oh you don't? Well, maybe James does." She looks at him with a knowing smile and her eyebrow cocked.

"Can I plead the Fifth?" Now, it's Jimmy's turn to blush. Mom just laughs.

"You can, but it's pointless. I already know the truth. I have ears, you know. Even if I hadn't heard you, I would have been able to tell just by looking at the two of you."

"Sorry, Darcy. In my defense though, she started it." Jimmy points at me and starts laughing.

"*Jimmy!*" Now, I am blushing hardcore.

*Did he have to say that to* her *of all people?*

"Hey, I don't blame you! He *is* pretty cute. If I had an attractive boyfriend in my bed, I would too." Mom nonchalantly shrugs her shoulders and winks at me.

"Sorry that you had to hear that. We will try to make sure that it doesn't happen again until after we are in the apartment." Jimmy looks at me apologetically as he says this. We both know that this will be a difficult promise to keep.

"I'm not going to make you hold off on my account. *Some*one should be getting laid in this house, but if you *do* feel the need to do that while I'm here, at least try to be quieter." Mom chuckles as she elbows Jimmy. "I mean, sure it has been quite a while since I've heard a guy make noises like that, but you don't forget what causes them."

Now, I'm laughing hysterically. Partly from my own embarrassment and partly from the look of complete mortification on Jimmy's face right now. Mom is laughing too.

"On *that* note Mom, I really think you should ask Ramsey out." Her face goes suddenly serious.

"I couldn't. It would be a conflict of interest or something because of Sadie's case. Plus, a guy like him would never be interested in someone like me."

*Where is this self-conscious version of Mom coming from?*

"It's not like you're *Sadie's* mom. He seemed to be *very* interested in the preview that he got on the stairs." I raise my eyebrows now at Mom like she had at us. This is my attempt to take some of the embarrassment off of us and put it onto her.

"I wouldn't even know how to do it. I haven't gone on a date in twenty-two years."

"It hasn't changed much, Mom."

"Plus, I would have no clue how to make small talk or anything."

"Darcy, call him! That's all it will take." Jimmy is providing the encouraging male perspective that we need to convince Mom right now. "I'm telling you that as a guy, if the girl has the courage to speak up first, that is a great sign and a total turn-on." He smiles in my direction.

"I'll think about it. I have to run out to the store. Do you guys need anything?"

*Condoms.*

"Nope, I don't think so."

I grab Jimmy's hand and lead him back to my room. Once we get back into my room, I sit on the floor by the foot of my bed and smile up at Jimmy. I pat the floor beside me. He sits down and gives me a small kiss.

"So, what were you talking about before I went downstairs? You looked upset or something."

"Oh, that? It's not important right now. It can wait."

## Jimmy

♪♪♪

*I want to propose to her so badly, but I don't want to rush it either. I was hoping that Gen would forget about the conversation that we were having when she left her room. I don't know why I even entertained that idea. She could tell something was off with me this morning. What do I tell her?*

She is sitting beside me with sunlight bathing her face in golden light.

*Her eyes are much more vibrant in the sunlight. She is truly gorgeous. Some girls have to cake makeup on to look even slightly pretty, but not Gen. She is naturally beautiful. Even when she had acne from puberty, she was still a ten out of ten. I can't lie to her. I couldn't even if I wanted to. She knows me too well for that.*

I just keep staring at her, trying to find the words to say.

"Jimmy, *seriously*. What's up? We have all the time in the world now." She is holding my hand in both of hers. She looks genuinely concerned. "Is it Sadie?"

"No, it wasn't about Sadie. I miss her like crazy and I really hope that Ramsey finds David, but that wasn't it." I'm staring at her hands on mine.

*Her skin is so soft.*

She has chipped blue nail polish on.

*Her and Sadie used to do each other's nails all the time. I wonder if that's why she hasn't fixed it yet.*

"Is it about the apartment? If you're having second thoughts, I can stay here. I don't have to move in if you don't want me to."

"I promise you that it wasn't about that. I'm absolutely *not* having second thoughts about living with you."

*I can't believe that she thought I might be changing my mind.*

I kiss her deeply to reassure her. I don't want her doubting my feelings for her, not even for a second.

"Well, then what is it? Did I do something? Was this morning not good for you? Or were you not okay with something that I did? You can tell me. I won't be upset. It's a learning curve to find out what we both like and what works for us." She is furrowing her brow at me with a truly perplexed look on her face.

"Gen. *Oh my god.* Are you *crazy*? This morning was *perfect.* Also, I have loved *every* moment of us being together." My heart is pounding.

*Why on Earth would she be questioning my satisfaction with this morning? It was even obvious to* Darcy.

"Jimmy, please tell me what's wrong. Tell me what made you upset. I want to make whatever it is better."

"I wasn't *upset.*" I take a deep breath and let it out slowly. "I was *nervous.*"

"Nervous? Why were you nervous?"

"Well, because I needed to discuss something with you." *I don't want it to happen like this.* "Something really important."

"Then why do you keep putting it off now?" She looks genuinely confused.

*Good question, Gen.*

"Do you really want to know?"

She is squeezing my hand and staring me right in the eye. I kiss her lightly. Her lips are as soft as butter against mine.

"Of course I do! Don't you know by now that I want to know everything when it comes to you?" Gen flashes me an adorable grin.

"Well, I wanted to tell you how happy I am to be with you. I spent so much of my life being completely head-over-heels in love with you but knowing that I could never have you. Now that I do, I never want to let you go. Being away from you for any length of time is physically painful." I am smiling, but starting to tear up as I ooze my heart out to her. "Losing Sadie has shown me how short life truly is. I refuse to waste anymore of it. Gen, you are my best friend. I can't imagine ever living without you. I could never endure the thought of losing you."

"You're not going to lose me, Jimmy. I promise you that I'm not going anywhere." She is tearing up now too. I wipe a tear from her cheek and kiss her on the forehead.

"Genevieve Porter, I want you to be mine forever."

"I already am." She smiles brightly at me with sparkling eyes.

"I absolutely love hearing you say that." I kiss her lightly, but I don't pull my face away from hers. I leave our foreheads and noses touching. We are close enough to feel each other breathing. "Gen, I love you so much."

"I love you too." Her lips graze mine as she speaks. It's such a sensual feeling. She kisses me again. I cup her face in my hand and lightly entwine my fingers in her hair at that nape of her neck. "Do you want to get ready and go look at apartment stuff?" She changes the subject.

*Thank God! I was so close to proposing, but I want the moment to be perfect. It definitely feels like we are right on the cusp. That ring is going to be with me at all times.*

"Yeah, yeah, absolutely. I'll go call Gregory and see when we can meet up."

"I'll go take a shower while you do that. I can't wait to move into the apartment." Gen gets up and bounces out of her room toward the bathroom. I grab my phone and call Gregory.

"Good morning. This is Jimmy Thompson. I have your money all set. When can we meet up?"

"Meet me at the apartment at two."

"Sounds great. See you then."

## Genevieve

*Something is definitely on Jimmy's mind today. I can see it in his eyes. I want to do my best to help him shake whatever is getting to him as much as I can. The fact that the police can't track down David is definitely going to put a bit of a damper on both of our moods today. Whenever Jimmy would be having a bad day, Sadie would go out of her way to make him smile. I loved those days because we would do absolutely anything to see him smile, no matter how immature or obnoxious. Now, it's all up to me. I hate seeing him upset. I hope I can fix this.*

As I wash my hair, I hear the bathroom door open. I peek out of the curtain to see who entered. Jimmy is leaning against the sink basin, smiling at me. His eyes are home to a devilish twinkle. I bite my lip lightly and smile back at him.

"Did you just come in here to watch me shower?" I chuckle lightly.

"No, I came in to tell you that we can get the keys at two. Watching you shower is just a perk." He walks over to the shower and kisses me intensely. This kiss is making me weak in the knees.

*Even though we just had sex this morning, I still would like to have my way with him right here and now. If he doesn't leave the bathroom quickly, I just might end up inviting him into the shower with me. What's wrong with me today? I have absolutely zero willpower when it comes to Jimmy.*

"I'm almost done. I'll be right out." I pull the shower curtain shut and finish rinsing my hair. I wait for the sound of the door opening and closing again before I start washing my body.

*This could very well be my last shower here. This is so weird.*

After one final rinse, I step out of the shower and towel off. When I enter my room, Jimmy is perched on the end of my bed counting a wad of cash. My jaw hinges open.

"What the heck is that? Pimping money?"

He chuckles at me lightly. "*This* is seventeen hundred dollars. It's the allotment that I brought for the apartment today." Jimmy sticks the money in an envelope from his bag.

I grab my clothes and step into my closet to start getting dressed.

*If I stand right in the middle of my room like I normally would, I don't think either of us would be able to keep on task.*

"You brought that much with you in cash?"

*I've* never *held that much money on my person at once before.*

"Yeah, it's only part of my savings. I figured that it's enough for us to give Gregory his money and still have cash to get stuff for the apartment. Do you think it's enough?"

"Are you seriously asking me if I think seven hundred dollars is enough to buy stuff for the apartment? Did you forget who you are talking to? I am a bargain hunter. I've never spent more than two hundred dollars at one time on anything before."

"I know. I don't want us to settle for something that we don't want just because it's cheaper. I want you to be happy with everything we put into the apartment."

"I'm not picky, Jimmy. We can get stuff at the thrift store for all I care."

"No, we are going to get brand new stuff that is just *ours.*"

Grinning from ear to ear, I say, "I love the sound of that. *Ours.*"

"So do I." Jimmy kisses me. "I have enough money saved up that we can get anything for the apartment that we want to."

"How much do you have saved anyway?"

*He rarely splurges on anything, but I have never seen him stressed about money.*

"Quite a bit actually."

"How much is *'quite a bit'*?"

"Over twenty thousand." Jimmy murmurs under his breath.

"Wait. *What?* Really? How is that *possible*?"

*Did I hear him correctly?*

"I've been working at least twenty hours every week since I was almost seventeen. I don't spend much. I just pay what bills I need to and then save the rest. The only big purchase that I have made was my car."

"Holy crap! I was thinking like seven thousand or something. That is insane."

"I know! It's a lot. I even shock myself sometimes when I look at my balance. My parents have no idea that I've been saving up."

I am legitimately impressed. "You must be really good with money."

"I try to be. I don't ever want to be in a panic. If my car needs a new part or there is an emergency, I would like to have a cushion to fall back on. Plus, this way we have money to live our life however we would like and pay for whatever kind of wedding you want."

"I'm sure that you didn't have a wedding in mind when you were saving." I playfully elbow Jimmy.

"Actually, I *did*...well, an engagement ring at least. I wanted to make you mine for so long. I wanted money for *our* future." Jimmy pulls me into him and kisses me.

"That's so sweet. Come on. Let's go shopping." I can't help but to smile.

# Chapter Eight

## Jimmy

♪♪♪

We are walking the aisles at Decor N' More filling our cart with rugs, pillows, and blankets. We are almost to the bedding sets when it dawns on me that we haven't discussed the bed situation other than to say that we would be sharing one.

*Do we take mine or hers? Do we buy a brand new one?*

"Do you want to pick out a new bed set?" I glance at her.

"Sure, what size is your bed?"

*Okay, she answered without me even needing to ask.*

"It's a queen. So we are going to take my bed with us?"

"Well, I just *assumed* that we were. If you want to take mine instead, we totally can. I didn't even think about whose we would use. All I thought about was the fact that we would be using the same one." She smiles and kisses me. "Do you want to get something like this?" Gen holds up a navy bed set with tribal embroidery. It's not terribly feminine. I really like it.

"Anything you want. As long as you're beside me, I don't care what it looks like." I wrap my arms around her waist and pull her into me. I catch a whiff of her shampoo.

*It's taking a copious amount of willpower to not start ravaging her right here in the store. I need to calm whatever thing inside me has been awakened since we got together.*

I place a small kiss on the curve of her neck.

"Yo! Thompson, is that you?" I hear a familiar voice from over my shoulder.

I pull away from Gen and turn to see Grayson Copeland, one of my old classmates.

*He has the total douchebag jock vibe. He walks around with swagger like he knows that he is the best person in the world. Gray played a sport every season. His favorite pastime though is picking up girls. He has hooked up with pretty much every female within the surrounding counties.*

"Gray! Man, long time no see. How are you?"

"I'm pretty good. Just getting back from a trip to Houston. I'm sorry about your sister. I just found out today when I got back into town."

"Thanks." We just stand here in awkward silence.

Grayson glances around the store like he is trying to think of something to say in order to squash the awkwardness. "So are you just in the habit of groping pretty girls while shopping now?"

"What? Oh, sorry. This is Gen. You might remember her from school. She is one of the only girls that you *didn't* sleep with." I chuckle with a sly grin.

"Well, hello *Gen From School.* Are you in the habit of letting guys grope you in stores or just this charmer here?" He has his classic flirting face that I have seen him use on tons of girls before.

"Don't you get any ideas, Gray. I would have to fight you and I really would rather not do that."

"Ah, so *territorial*! She must be, like *what*, your girlfriend or something now? Wasn't she like Sadie's lesbian lover?"

"Only on days that ended in Y." Gen speaks up for the first time since he walked up and I can't believe the words coming out of her mouth.

*She still manages to impress and surprise me after all of these years.*

"But seriously *Gray*," her top lip curls in disgust as she addresses him with a snarl, "I am completely off limits so take whatever schoolboy fantasy you were picturing out of your mind. I am Jimmy's fiancee."

*What did she just say?! My what?!*

My jaw is wide open and my eyes are gigantic saucers.

"Woah! Congrats, man! I had no idea! Hey, stay in touch, okay? I've got to go."

Gray does one of those typical guy-on-guy hugs with the awkward handshake between the two bodies. Once he is out of earshot, I turn to Gen.

"What the hell was *that*? I mean, kudos to you for putting him in his place like that, but damn! Warn me next time before you floor me like that!"

*Her badassery is definitely not helping me hold myself back. That was honestly such a turn-on.*

"Sorry. I totally spoke out of turn and lied. I just couldn't help it. He was making that comment about Sadie and I just couldn't let that slide. He has always been such a misogynistic *asshole*." Gen looks ashamed and is blushing a violent shade of red.

"Well, it wasn't exactly a *lie*. I mean we *are* going to get married eventually. The question just hasn't been asked yet." I lift her chin so that she is looking me in the eye. "Hearing you refer to yourself like that though sent a surge of electricity through me. I absolutely loved the sound of it. My *fiancee*." I can still see a tinge of sadness or embarrassment in her eyes. "I love you, future Genevieve Thompson."

"I love you. I'm really sorry that I just said that to Gray. He is probably going to tell a ton of people now. Most people don't even know that we are a couple yet." Her eyes are studying the ground again.

"I really don't mind at all. You just surprised me."

"I'm still really sorry. I shouldn't have done that."

"Gen, if you want to tell the entire world that you're my fiancee, feel free! I already have your ring, so you know that it is inevitable."

"I'm not trying to pressure you into proposing or anything. I won't be telling anyone else that. I promise. At least not until it's the truth."

"Why don't we go pay and then head to the park for a bit before we meet up with Greg?"

We head to the register and stand in line mindlessly checking out the goodies that they keep near the register to sucker you into adding onto your order. Once we check out with our three hundred dollars worth of goodies, we take our treasure trove to my car and load it all into the backseat and trunk.

*I can't get that comment from Gen out of my head. She shocked the hell out of me when she told Gray that. Gen has never had an issue sticking up for herself before, but the fact that she roasted Gray in the middle of the store is hilarious. She made telling him off look so easy.*

While we are driving away from the store, I watch her. She is staring out the window.

"You're so beautiful."

"What?" She snaps back to reality. She was obviously daydreaming or lost in thought.

"I said that you're so beautiful." I grab her hand and smile.

"Oh...thanks." She sounds sad and distant.

"What's wrong, Gen?"

*I'm concerned about that tone. It reminds me of all of the times before when she was at all of her low points where Sadie and I would have to drag her out of the ditch that depression pushed her into.*

"Nothing. I'm just thinking a lot. Sorry."

"What are you thinking about?"

"A lot of stuff: Sadie, us, the apartment, your mom, that whole incident with Grayson." She sounds increasingly emotional. I glance at her and notice that she is starting to cry.

"Gen, talk to me. I want to help you through whatever is going on in your head."

"It's okay. I'm fine, really."

She tries to sneakily wipe tears out of her eyes with her sleeve. I pull over onto the side of the road.

"Gen, babe, look at me. I know you better than that. I know something is up. Please just talk to me. You don't have to do this alone. I'm right here." I am holding both of her hands in mine.

"No. It's stupid. I'm totally fine. Just drive."

"If it's making you cry, it isn't stupid. I'm not driving again until we talk about it. I know that you're not fine. You can tell me you are all you want, but I know you better than that."

"I'm just sad about Sadie. I miss her so much. There are so many times every day that I want to call her or text her and then it hits me all over again that she is gone. I want to tell her about us. I want to act like a total moron with her. I just want my best friend back." She is sobbing.

"I miss her like crazy too." I kiss the back of Gen's hand. I just sit here for a few silent moments running my thumb over the back of her hand. Once she seems to be calming down a bit from the Sadie revelation, I try to ease more information out of her. "That covers the Sadie portion. What about the rest? Talk to me."

"The whole apartment thing is just really overwhelming. There is so much to do and it's such a huge step and..."

"And we will be totally fine! We will work on it together. Don't stress! We can take our time. There is nothing saying that we have to move in right away."

"I know. I know. It just seems like a lot."

"We've got this! I promise! You mentioned Mom. What were you thinking about *her*?"

"The other night just keeps running through my head. Her reaction was bad to say the least. That was only announcing that we were dating. How is she going to react if we get married? At first, I gave her the benefit of the doubt and thought that it was because of everything with Sadie but the more I think about it, the more I start to doubt that. What if she loves me as *me*, but doesn't love me for *you*? What if she doesn't think that I am good enough for you?"

"Gen, she told you that she is happy for us and that she loves you. I swear that you have nothing to worry about."

"I'm just really scared that she is going to end up hating me. What if something happens and I end up pregnant or we get married, will she still like me or will she completely hate me for ruining her son's life?"

"You will *never* ruin my life and I promise you that she won't hate you. I think the thought of us being together is so new that the idea of us having sex scares the shit out of her. It's just the fear of the unknown. When we do actually get married, she will be so happy for us. She will be ecstatic when we start a family, no matter when it is."

"Whatever. If you say so." She still looks really upset. She keeps looking at her feet or occasionally she will lift her head to look at a car zooming by us.

"Well, I *do* say so. What about *us*?"

She takes a deep breath and releases it in a sputtering exhale before answering me.

"What if down the road you realize that I'm not actually the person you want? What if your idea of me isn't something that I can live up to? What if the novelty of liking me wears off? I will be completely crushed."

"Oh my god, Gen! That will never happen, *ever*! I promise. I have wanted you for so many years. I've always wanted you more and more each day. I don't have some unrealistic image of you in my mind. You aren't up on some imaginary pedestal. I see every single piece of who you are, good and bad. I love it all. I promise you that there are only two ways that you'll ever lose me: if you decide that you don't want to be with me anymore or if I die. If you ever do decide that you don't want to be with me anymore, I won't stop you from leaving but I will be utterly inconsolable."

"You even loved when I lied about our relationship?" Tears are streaming from her eyes.

"Gen, are you still worried about that whole thing with Grayson? Honestly, *yes* I did. First of all, I loved hearing you call yourself that. It sounded so right and natural. Second, it was hot as hell."

"Yeah, but now he is probably going to blab to people. You know that stuff like this spreads like wildfire around here."

"Let him tell people. The more he tells, the less announcing we'll have to do."

"There's nothing to announce."

"Do you want there to be?"

"I don't know. Maybe. I mean, *eventually*, yes."

"You say the word and I will have the ring on your finger that instant."

"I don't want to rush it. Whenever you're ready, go ahead and propose."

"Want to know something funny? I almost proposed to you this morning. *Twice*, actually."

"You did? When?" She looks less sad finally. "Oh my gosh. Is that why you were acting so weird in my room earlier?" All I can do is nod my head in confirmation. My confidence is waning quickly. "Why didn't you then?"

"Well, Ramsey interrupted the first time. I am *really* starting to hate that guy's timing, by the way. The second time, you changed the subject. It must have just not been meant to happen this morning."

"I'm sorry that it got ruined." She looks depressed again.

"It's fine, Gen. Hey, are you sure that you're okay? You seem really upset today, just in general. Do you want me to take you back home?"

"I'm alright, mostly. My depression is just sneaking up on me really badly today. Being home by myself is the last place I should be right now."

"Please promise me that you won't shut me out if it gets bad again. I can't lose you." I am starting to tear up.

*Gen's history with mental health issues totally terrifies me. I've already had to live through the pain of her attempting suicide once already. I can't do that again.*

"I'll try not to. I just feel really overwhelmed and stressed out. I also feel like a total fuck-up this week."

"You are *not* a fuck-up."

"Yes, I am."

"*How*? I don't think you're one at all."

"So many ways. First of all, I had no clue that you liked me all of these years. Then, I was totally clueless about Sadie and David and the baby. Then, your mom totally freaked out about us. I forgot to buy condoms. I ruined what would have been your proposal. I snapped on Gray in public. Should I continue?" She counts on her fingers as she lists each thing she thinks she messed up.

"Gen, you're a human. You're allowed to make mistakes. None of those things were your fault. I hid my feelings as much as I could. *None* of us knew about Sadie. Mom was just an emotional wreck this week. Gray is a total tool and deserved it. Please stop blaming yourself for everything. Can you do that, for *me?*"

"I can try. I never do anything right though."

"Genevieve, I love you. I have *always* loved you and I always *will* love you. You will never be a fuck-up in my eyes." I give her a reassuring kiss. "By the way, I'm completely okay with us never using condoms. We both know that neither of us have any STDs and it's amazing not having any barriers between our bodies."

"Your mom would totally disapprove if she found out."

"Well, frankly, it's none of her business. She can't tell me how I can and cannot have sex with my wife."

"I'm not your wife yet."

"You will be and no matter what the label of our relationship is, she has zero say over it. We can do whatever you're comfortable with. If you want to start using condoms, we will go get some. If you'd rather keep going all natural, that is completely fine too."

"Maybe we should take a break."

She is staring at her fingers and picking at a torn cuticle.

"What? A *break*? What do you mean?"

*She cannot seriously be breaking my heart already, can she?*

"Not like a *Ross and Rachel* break, but like a *sex* break. Just until we are in the apartment officially."

"That is going to be extremely hard, but if that's what you want, you've got it. I have pretty much mastered the art of ignoring my sexual impulses when it comes to you."

*I can't believe that she already wants to take a break from sex. We just started having it!*

"I know it's going to be difficult, but maybe that will keep your mom from being on our backs so badly. I can't handle the fear of her not liking me. It's really important to me that we stay on good terms with her." Gen is crying steadily again.

"Gen, we can absolutely do that if it's what you really want. I promise you though that Mom completely adores you. She really is happy for us. Can you promise me something?"

"What is it?"

"Please promise me that you're not going to let this whole Mom situation come between us. I love you so much and I've waited way too long to finally have you. I'm not letting you go."

Her eyes are so sad right now.

*Seeing her like this kills me.*

"I'm not going to let her come between us. I just want her to approve of our relationship. She has been a second mom to me for years. Disappointing her kills me."

"I promise you that her behavior the other night was not a representation of her actual feelings on us. Her and I have discussed it since then. She is truly happy that we are together and she just wants us to be happy. She only snapped like that because she was upset about Sadie. You are such an extension of Sadie in her eyes that I think her brain just needed to take it out on you. She knows that our relationship is nothing like Sadie and David's. She is not disappointed in either of us. She is actually being really supportive of me proposing to you."

"I highly doubt that she is overly thrilled with the idea of us getting engaged anytime soon."

"Okay, I wasn't going to say anything, but you're leaving me no choice." I sigh, exasperated. "Can I tell you something so that you'll believe me that she is totally fine with us being together?"

"You can try. I don't know if it will change my mind though."

*I didn't want to tell her about this yet, but here goes nothing!*

"I was really irritated with her for how she treated you the other night. I told her that I was going to be proposing to you whether she liked it or not. I thought she would get angry again and start another fight with me, but she didn't. It went in the totally opposite direction actually. She went to her room and brought out a family heirloom for me to propose with."

Gen sits there staring at me, mouth ajar, with a look of surprise on her face.

"Really? I didn't think she would ever do something like that." She looks like she is trying to solve a difficult crossword. Her face is all contorted with concentration. "So that's how you got a ring so fast, huh?"

"Well, I would have gotten one by now anyway. I had been planning to go buy one that same day. If you would prefer not to have an old hand-me-down, I will absolutely get you a brand new one of your very own."

I have my hand stretched across the center console and I am running my fingertips along the length of her fingers. They look so empty right now, other than her middle finger that is home to my class ring, which looks pretty mammoth on her petite hand.

"If it is a part of your family history, I would be absolutely honored to wear it. It will make me feel like a real member of your family."

"You already are! You have been for years. Now, you'll just have the last name to go with it. I'm glad that you'll be wearing the ring soon." I give her a deep kiss. "Come on, let's go to the park for a bit." I pull back onto the road and start driving again.

Once we get to the stone wall that lines the park entrance, I pull onto the side of the road and park. I unbuckle and look at Gen. She is silently staring out the window at something off in the distance.

"Let's go enjoy some sunshine."

She turns toward me and gives me a tiny smile as she gets out of the car. I meet her at the front of my car and hold her hand as we walk along the road.

We walk silently, hand in hand, just enjoying each other's presence. The breeze is crisp and cool. It's blowing Gen's hair back from her face. The ground is covered in fallen leaves and a small amount of snow. Some of the leaves are still vibrant reds and yellows while others are a muted brown.

I can tell that Gen needs to have some time to get lost in her thoughts, so I just stay quiet. The warmth of her hand in mine does something wonderful for my soul.

*My body may be cold but I can't feel it with her here. Even though she is having a crappy day, I still couldn't be happier to be spending it with her.*

We walk to the wall made of natural stone that overlooks the entire city. I spin her toward me and kiss her. She gives me another one of her small smiles and kisses me back. We lean against the wall looking at the array of roofs below us. The girls and I used to come up here all of the time.

"Sadie always wanted to take photos of us up here. I never understood why." She stares at the city below and continues speaking to the air more than to me. "I mean, it's pretty and all but I could never figure out why she wanted to take our pictures here. She didn't necessarily have an eye for photography or anything. It just seems really random to me."

"Well, we did spend a lot of time up here. Maybe that's why? Plus, why not have photos of two beautiful friends in front of a gorgeous view?"

"No, not her and I. Me and you." She gestures to the air between the two of us.

"*Us? Really?* You're right. That does seem pretty random."

"She always told me that this spot was *'magical'* and it *'spoke to'* her. She said that it made her feel the way that all of her favorite eighties songs did. It made her feel like love was possible."

"Two of her favorite people in a place that made her happy makes more sense."

"Sometimes I wonder if she thought the so-called *'magic'* of this place would make us fall in love if she took our picture here." She has this dreamy look in her eye.

"Knowing Sadie, I bet that's *exactly* what she thought. If only she had known that she wouldn't have needed anything magical to make us fall in love."

I smile down at her and wrap her up into an embrace with my hands on her waist. Looking at her pretty face, her nose and cheeks are getting red from the cold. It is pretty chilly out here.

"Well, she knew that I loved you. I can't keep a secret as well as *you* apparently."

"The more that I think about it, I think that she knew deep down that I loved you too. I just wonder why she didn't push us together harder."

"*Harder?*" She starts laughing really hard. "One time, she called you into the room to make me kiss you. Oh and there was the time that she bought me that awful red bikini that barely covered anything because she knew that you would be seeing me in it." She lets out a snort.

*I love her laughter. She loses herself to pure joy when she laughs. It transforms her entire presence from beautiful to downright magnificent.*

"*Oooh*, yeah, I *definitely* remember that bikini." I give her a devilish smile and plant a small kiss to the bend of her neck.

"Then, her plan partly worked." She is arching her neck to give me more room to kiss. I kiss her neck once more.

*If I don't stop myself, we will have to get back to the car quickly.*

"Partly? If the plan was for me to notice you, it completely worked. You were *so* hot! That entire summer, I had to stay underwater anytime you came outside wearing that or my attraction to you would have been *extremely* noticeable."

"Well, part B of her grand scheme was to get us at least making out by the end of summer."

"I wish someone would have revealed her evil plan. I would have happily obliged."

"We are making up for it now at least."

She smiles up at me with shining eyes. The sunlight is enhancing the color of her eyes.

"Do you still have that bikini by chance?" I tease her.

"I just might!" She gives me a flirty smile.

*She is acting more like my normal Gen now. Thank God!*

"Maybe I'll break it back out next summer." I'm glad that I got her to smile again.

"Are you ready to head towards the apartment?"

"Let's go! I cannot wait to get our keys."

Once we get back to the warmth of my car, we rub our numb hands together and blow warm air on them to try and bring back some of the feeling. I turn on my car and drive us to our apartment.

*This is a huge step. I wish Sadie were here to see this. Two of her favorite people are not only in love, but they are also moving in together. She would have been so happy.*

## Genevieve

*Today is one of those really terrible depression days. It is bad enough that I'm even annoying myself. I feel like I am going to burst out crying any second about literally anything. I really think that I might need to go to the doctor to get back on an antidepressant. I feel totally worthless. I just keep messing everything up. If I don't get myself back in check soon, I am afraid that I might end up suicidal again. Jimmy is being amazing about my moods, like always. Him and Sadie have always been the ones to pick me up and brush me off when I have a really down day or week. Now that Sadie is gone, all of that responsibility is going to fall on him. I hate making him feel like he really needs to keep a constant eye on me, but unfortunately I cannot help it when it comes to my anxiety and depression.*

*Today is a perfect example of what's wrong with me. I should be extremely happy. We are going to pick up the keys for our very first apartment together. Instead of being filled with joy, I am an emotional wreck. I still can't believe that I made such a scene in the store with Grayson. I made such an idiot move of lying to him about our relationship status. Grayson just made me so fucking angry. It was one thing when people would make comments like that about Sadie and I when she was alive, but now it feels wrong that she isn't able to defend herself. Plus, Gray always puts so many moves on anyone with female anatomy that it is sickening. I'm not some plaything that he can borrow for an afternoon if he wants to. I don't regret telling him off, only the lying part.*

We pull up to the apartment and Gregory is perched on the front step, smoking a cigarette. He is spinning a key around his index finger. My heart is thumping rapidly in my ears. This is starting to feel really overwhelming and scary. Jimmy puts his car in park and squeezes my hand.

"Are you ready to go get our keys and make this official?" His mouth is smiling at me, but I can see concern still in his eyes. It is still holding residency from when we pulled over and had our heart-to-heart before the park.

"Do you think he will let us put the new stuff that we just bought inside until we move in?"

"Probably. Once he puts the keys in our hands, it's ours!" Jimmy cannot stop smiling. He turns off the car and gets out. I follow suit.

"Well hey there, lovebirds! Are you ready to get your own place?" Gregory smiles at us. He seems very chipper today.

"We most definitely are. Here is your money." Jimmy pulls an envelope out of his coat and hands it to our new landlord. He counts the money and then hands over the keys.

"When do you plan on moving in?" He smiles in my direction.

"Probably over the next couple of days. We don't have anyone to help us with the big stuff until tomorrow. We do have some stuff in the car though. Is it okay for us to put it inside?" I ask, feeling hopeful that we can actually get a start in our new place tomorrow or Sunday.

"Absolutely! She is yours now, after all! Remember that rent is due on the fifth of every month and feel free to call me with any issues that might arise." He claps Jimmy on the back and shakes my hand before leaving us on the front step of our apartment.

Jimmy puts the key in the door and unlocks it with a satisfying click. As he opens the door, he turns to me beaming from ear to ear.

"Come here." Jimmy steps a little closer to me and bends a bit. He put one arm behind my back and one behind my knees scooping me up into his arms.

"What on Earth are you doing?" I laugh and give him a quizzical look.

"Carrying my future bride over our threshold." He carries me a few steps into the house before placing a gentle kiss on my lips.

"You are so cheesy. You know that, right?" I can't help but to laugh. My crippling anxiety is finally fading into excited giddiness.

"That may be true, but you know you love it." His smile is bright enough to light up the entire apartment. "Can you believe that this is real? This is actually *ours*!"

"It seems so crazy to me. Not only am I moving out of the only house I have ever known, but I am moving in with *you*."

"So, when do we get to christen the apartment?" Jimmy smiles flirtatiously and kisses me deeply. I can feel the smile forming on his lips as they are against mine.

"Well, preferably after we have some sort of furniture in here." I look around at the empty hardwood floor. *That would definitely be uncomfortable.* "We aren't doing that stuff right now though anyway, remember?"

"Okay, okay, it was worth a shot." He holds up his hands in surrender while wearing a small smirk. "Do you want to grab the stuff from the car now and bring it inside?"

"Come on!" I walk happily out the door and back into the cold breeze of this mid-November day.

I open the backseat and begin grabbing as much as I can. I take a few bags of decor and other household goods inside and set them on the floor of the living room. Jimmy follows right on my heels with the remaining loot from our shopping trip.

"Hey, Gen, I want to run an idea by you to get your opinion." Jimmy empties his arms carefully onto the floor in front of us.

"Okay, shoot."

"So, today is the fifteenth."

"Yeah, and?"

*What the hell does today's date have to do with anything?*

"That means that Thanksgiving is in less than two weeks."

"Ugh, don't remind me."

*I don't even want to think about Thanksgiving. This will be our first holiday without Sadie.*

"Since we will be living here by then, what would you think about us inviting our parents here for Thanksgiving?"

"Wow. That is actually a really good idea."

"I do get those occasionally."

"That's not what I meant! Mom always gets really down in the dumps about Dad on the holidays at our house. I'm sure it will be the same way for all of us at your house this year because of Sadie. Let's do it! We will host Thanksgiving!" I can already picture the five of us gathering around the table covered in food. A happy family with a huge gaping hole in the shape of Sadie.

"Perfect! Let's make sure to give them a heads up this weekend in case they need to start planning." Jimmy smiles at me and pulls me in close. "I cannot wait to move in with you, Gen."

"I can't wait either! Let's start moving what we can today and leave the big stuff for tomorrow when Mom can help out. We need to start packing." I am filled to the brim with anticipation and nervous energy.

*I am so excited about the move, but I am also terrified. This is a huge step. What if something happens and this ruins what we have?*

I grab his hand and walk quickly to the car.

## Jimmy

♪♪♪

Just as we are about to start packing up Gen's belongings, I realize that we don't have any boxes yet. I scan her room trying to figure out what she plans on putting all of her stuff in. Gen starts loading up her stuff into her duffle bags. I watch as she grabs handfuls of clothes from her dresser. Her hands are trembling.

*She seems a bit off kilter today. I'm starting to worry about her.*

"There's a suitcase in the hallway closet. If you grab that, we can get a lot more moved at once. We don't need to waste money on boxes. These will work just fine."

*Gen is trying so hard to seem totally normal, but I can see that something negative is lingering just beneath the surface.*

As I grab the suitcase from the hall closet, I swear that I hear Gen sniffle like she's crying.

"Hey, are you sure that you're alright Gen? You seem like something is bothering you still. Is it the same stuff that we talked about earlier or is there something else going on?"

"I'm fine. I just want to try and get as much done as possible today." She doesn't look like she is about to cry, but there is a small change in her voice that is telling me she is definitely not fine.

"I need to pee. Do you want me to grab your toiletries and stuff while I'm in there? Do you need any medicine from there?"

I seize the opportunity to indirectly ask if she is on birth control.

*I feel weird asking her straight out. I'm not sure why though. It seems too personal to ask, even though I know everything else about her. We have been as up close and personal as two people can be together but this still seems like it's not my place, especially not today.*

"Uh, sure. That would be great. Thank you and no, I don't need any medicines. I'm not on anything right now. If you want to check the cabinet just in case, grab anything with my name on it."

*So, that seems like she is definitely not on birth control, but maybe she doesn't consider that a medicine.*

After washing my hands, I open the mirrored door above the sink. The first thing I spot when I open it is a blue pack of birth control pills. It looks just like the ones Sadie used. I flip it over to look at the label hoping that I would see *Genevieve Porter* in bold print, but instead I see *Sadie Thompson.*

*So, that would be a no.*

I check the rest of the bottles in the cabinet.

*I've never seen a medicine cabinet so empty. My parents always keep theirs fully stocked.*

The only thing in the cabinet with Gen's name is an allergy medication. I grab it and take it to Gen.

"You did have one thing in there. I thought the birth control might be yours, but it was Sadie's."

"Oh, that was still in there? I totally forgot about it, but yeah, I'm not on any birth control. What did I have in there? I haven't taken any medicines since Markowitz took me off of my antidepressants."

*Well, there we go. I got my answer.*

"Just an allergy medication."

"Oh, yeah. I only take the allergy meds every once in a while. I try my hardest to not take anything."

"Didn't she take you off of those a while ago?"

"Two years ago, almost."

"You seriously haven't taken anything since then? I take ibuprofen at least twice a week."

"Well, honestly, I think I might need to get back on something soon. Dealing with everything has just been extra hard lately. I don't think I can keep doing this on my own. It was getting bad again anyway and then everything with Sadie..." She trails off with sad eyes. She is crumbling into pieces before my eyes.

"Oh, Gen! It's okay to not be okay. I am here to help you whenever you need me. All you need to do is say the word. If you think you need to get back on medication, call and schedule an appointment. I'll go with you if you want me to."

*I just want to comfort her and make her feel better.*

I walk over to her and rest my hand on her lower back.

"I'm so scared. What if it gets bad again and I can't be pulled out of it?"

She has her head in her hands. I wrap her up in my arms. Her breathing is uneven and shallow. She is about to cry for sure.

"Gen, babe, I promise you that I will do everything in my power to make sure that doesn't happen. I know I can't cure you, but I want to try to at least make it a little better. I will *not* lose you! If you need time alone, I'll give it to you. If you need to go back to therapy, I'll drive you. Anything you need from me, it's yours." I squeeze her tighter. Her breathing is getting more and more uneven.

"I don't deserve you. You're so great to me all of the time. You always have been, even when I was just your sister's annoying friend." Gen is crying now.

"First of all, I *never* found you annoying. If you don't deserve me, it's only because you deserve better. I love you so much."

I lift her chin so that she is looking at me. I wipe away her tears and press my lips tenderly to her forehead. I squeeze her firmly against my body. She is trying to calm herself down, but it's not working. She is starting to hiccup.

"I don't understand why you would ever want to live with me or even *be* with me. Look at me! I'm a complete trainwreck. I can't even make it through a day like today, that is supposed to be happy and exciting, without sobbing. I'm useless, especially now that I'm without Sadie."

"You are *not* useless. Not even close! If I told you the entire list of reasons that I want to be with you, we would be here for at least two full days. If you need to cry, cry as much as you need to! Just promise me that you won't hide it from me. Don't shut yourself away from the world anymore. If you feel the need to do that, at least close me in with you." I give her a small lopsided smile.

"I really think that I need to call the doctor and get back on something for my depression." She closes her eyes tightly and drops a few tears down her cheek. "I just don't want to do anything to mess this up." She moves her hand in the small amount of space between our torsos.

"You could never do anything to mess this up. You're stuck with me, lady! Why don't you go ahead and call to book an appointment? I will pack up some more of your stuff." I let go of her and stare at her for a moment.

*I hate seeing this sadness taking her over.*

She breaks eye contact with me and looks at the floor before turning to leave her room.

Once she is walking down the steps, I grab a pile of her neatly folded laundry and place it in the suitcase on her bed. I walk over to her dresser and open the top drawer. The drawer is filled with Gen's delicates. I try my hardest to not picture her in each and every item as I place them in her suitcase. Some are lacy while others shimmer a bit. They are all different cuts and materials. I recognize some of them from trips to the mall with her and Sadie.

*On the days when they would pull me into the lingerie store, I would try my hardest to not pay attention to anything Sadie grabbed. No one wants to think about what unmentionables their sister insists on buying. I also tried not to be too obvious that I was* very *interested in what Gen picked out.*

When the drawer is empty, I notice a small green journal. All of my better judgment tells me that I should respect her privacy and not open it.

*Just place it in the suitcase and move on, Thompson!*

Something deep inside me is screaming at me to read it. I take a deep breath and slowly open it. The first page is covered in doodles of hearts and 'Mrs. Genevieve Thompson' written over and over in blue ink.

The next page is where the writing starts. The initial entry is about someone bullying her for never being kissed. I keep growing angrier the more that I read of this. I look at the date.

*It was on her birthday, June 15th, of all freaking days!*

I flip through more pages, barely glancing at the words until a sentence in purple pen catches my eye:

Jimmy gave me this look from across the living room tonight and I really thought that he might have wanted to kiss me.

I check the date on that entry. It was four years ago.

*If I'm being honest with myself, she was probably right. I probably* was *going to kiss her. I have almost done it and then chickened out at the last minute so many times over the years.*

I flip a ton of other pages until I come across one with a smear of blood on it. My heart starts racing. I read the entry. This is from this past May.

Tonight, Sadie and I got into a huge fight. She wanted to ditch me for some guy and then wouldn't even tell me who it was! When I had finally had enough, I told her that she was acting like a stupid bitch and she lost it. She started saying some really shitty things to me. Things that a best friend should never say to you. She accused me of being jealous because she has guys practically lining up to be with her. She said that I'm just mad because no one wants me. Apparently, I am weighing her down and she wishes sometimes that I wasn't her friend.

I started crying like an idiot, not just small tears but actual ugly crying. Instead of caring that she had made me cry, she told me to quit acting so needy. Then, JIMMY of all fucking people had to walk into the room! JIMMY!!!! He immediately noticed that I was crying. I mean, how could he not? I was sobbing like a baby. He tried to comfort me and Sadie told him to fuck off. I don't know what the hell has gotten into her lately. Something is really weird with her. I feel like I am losing my best friend and the worst part is that I don't even understand why. I had

Jimmy drive me home because I didn't want to keep cramping Sadie's slutty style. She very obviously didn't want me around anymore.

No one ever wants me around anymore. What's even the point of me living anymore? It's extremely obvious that Jimmy will **NEVER** want me. I have been with him daily (more or less) for years and he has **NEVER** tried to make a move or show any sort of interest in me. It's obvious that we are never going to happen. I love him and I can't help it. I want him so badly, but he doesn't want me. Sadie doesn't want me. She thinks that I suck now. Hell, my mom would probably even be better off without me around.

**FUCCCCKKKKKKK!** I **CANNOT** keep doing this! I can't keep fucking up everyone else's lives with my existence. I need to isolate myself. Human interaction makes everything worse. What the fuck is wrong with me? I just need to stop wasting other people's oxygen already.

*She was suicidal again? May wasn't that long ago! How did I not pick up on the cues? Now she is throwing all of these signs at me that she needs help. Does she really want my help or is she trying to distract me so that I will be thrown off of the scent of her suicide plan? The blood on the page* has *to be from her cutting herself again.*

I flip through some more pages and a straight blade falls from between the pages to the floor with a clank.

*Shit!*

I pick it up and it still has dried blood on it. I slide it back between the pages.

As I am getting ready to slide the journal into the suitcase, I hear her reach the top step.

*I can't believe how much I just violated her privacy! What is wrong with me? If I had ever read Sadie's journal, she would have murdered me.*

I rush to put the journal away and move on to another drawer so that she won't know what I've done. The blade falls to the floor again with another metallic clank against the hardwood. I bend to pick it up and when I stand straight again, Gen is standing just inside the door staring at me. Her green eyes are huge and she looks completely horrified. I'm scared she is going to run downstairs.

"I can explain." She starts stammering. "It's not what it looks like."

"Gen." She seems to be preparing herself to be yelled at. I am not going to be angry with her. I work very hard to keep my tone level. My concern is clouding my anger at the moment. "Why didn't you say something to someone? If you didn't feel like you could've told Sadie, you could have at least told *me*."

"Tell you what? That I was suicidal again? That I had a really shitty day and thought that cutting would help to make me feel better? I didn't have to draw too much blood before I realized that I should stop. I don't *want* to die, but sometimes I have a really hard time trying to remember why."

*Those words cut into me like she just stabbed me directly in the heart.*

"If you *ever* need a reminder of why, just come to me. I will remind you of everything you have to live for." *I just want to keep her safe.* "Does Darcy know about this? Gen, can you please promise me that you're not going to cut anymore?"

"No. She doesn't know and she won't be finding out either. She doesn't need to be involved with this. There is no sense in making her worry over me. I don't cut myself anymore. It's been months."

"Can you please actually *promise* me that you won't do it again? How do you think I would handle it if I lost you? If you committed suicide, do you have any idea what that would do to me or to Darcy?"

"I promise that I'll try to speak up if I feel myself slipping again."

"I will be right here no matter what. Nothing you could say or do could ever scare me away." I pull her into my arms and press my face against hers. My lips are right beside her ear. "I remember that night, by the way. When I drove you home, you cried the entire way. It was just us. You should have told me how you were feeling. I would have stayed with you as long as you needed me to. I would have tried harder to cheer you up. I would never have let you go inside alone if I had known. I would have kept you busy all night long and stayed until you felt better."

"I'm sorry. It's hard to admit that I want to stop living, especially to the person that I am head-over-heels in love with. I mean, now it would be a little easier than when I thought that it was unrequited. I didn't want to scare you away." She leans into me more. "*This* is exactly why I need an appointment. I need to get back on medicine. They can't get me in for a few weeks though."

"A few weeks? Really? That seems like a really long time for something like this."

*Don't offices treat mental health issues as a priority? What if she commits suicide before that appointment because they waited too long to get her in?*

"I guess that's the only opening. My doctor is on vacation for Thanksgiving apparently." The look on her face is really concerning me.

"Well, in the meantime, let me know if you start feeling even *slightly* like you want to hurt yourself. Please." I pull her tighter against me and kiss the top of her head.

*All I can think about is when she had those bandages on her wrists. At school, she wore thermal shirts with thumb holes in the sleeves or hoodies to hide them from people who may ask too many questions. Our house though was one of her only safe places where she could let them show. It was an outward sign of her depression for the world to see, for* me *to see. Knowing everything that I do now, I almost wonder if I was partly to blame for her depression back then. I always thought that it was just because of losing her dad, but now I'm not so sure. Normally, I am so used to seeing those white scars running down her wrists that I rarely notice them. Right now though, those scars are all that I can see. It's like they are screaming at me to help her.*

"Mmm." She slightly nods in agreement without lifting her head to look at me.

"Gen, listen. I am going to get rid of any blades that I find. I just want you to know that before you start finding them in the trash. Am I going to find any more?"

*I feel like an admonishing parent using a stern tone with her, but I need to do what I can to save her. If I have to tear this entire room apart to search for blades, I will if it means protecting her from herself.*

"I don't think so. I think that's the last one."

"Okay, but if I do come across any, they *will* be gone. I'm not going to let you keep anything that might tempt you. I love you, Gen. I've already seen you with bandaged wrists once. I don't want to do that again. It was horrible enough the first time and next time, you might not be as lucky."

*When Gen had done the damage last time, the doctors told Darcy that if Gen had put the blade just a few centimeters closer to the center that she would have died within fifteen minutes.*

"I know. I really do try not to cut. I only cave sometimes when things get really hard. I have to force myself not to cut at all with this whole Sadie situation. I know how much it would have hurt her if she knew that I cut because of her."

"Good. I'm really glad." I kiss the top of her head again. "Hey, can I ask you something?"

"I guess. You can say whatever you want around me, you already know that."

"Did you ever cut because of me? I mean, you don't have to answer that if you don't want to but it's been weighing on my mind."

*Why the hell did I ask that? Do I really want to know the answer?*

"Um...a few times. It wasn't your fault though. I don't want you to feel guilty. You didn't do anything to *make* me do it. It was just the stress of the whole situation between us."

"I really wish that I would have told you sooner. Maybe we could have avoided all of that."

*If I had just told her instead of being a total wimp, I could probably have saved a few of those scars from being on her wrist.*

"Do you want to help me finish packing up your dresser?"

"Yeah, I will. Hey, speaking of dressers, how is that going to work? Are we going to share a dresser or are we going to bring both?"

"I don't mind sharing. Just don't go stealing my boxers." I chuckle. "I think mine is probably heavier than yours though. Let's take my bed and your dresser."

"Less heavy lifting! Good idea."

Gen is grabbing sweaters from her closet and putting them in the suitcase neatly as I empty another drawer filled with pajama bottoms. We keep packing up her belongings into the suitcase until she has barely anything left to wear in her closet. We completely emptied her dresser.

I reach for the photos stuck in the frame of her mirror. One of them is of the three of us.

*I love this picture. Sadie looks so happy in it. We all do, actually. I remember that day. We had so much fun.*

"She was so pretty. I really miss seeing her face. I feel like we should all be packing up to move into this apartment together. I'm still not used to the fact that she is gone." I'm not really speaking to Gen, more to the air really. I can't peel my eyes away from Sadie's smiling face. "I wonder what her baby would have been like. Man, I would have loved that kid like crazy. It wouldn't matter to me that David was the father. All that would matter to me would be that it was a part of Sadie. I can't believe that I'll never have nieces or nephews. Well, that *we* won't. I had always looked forward to being the cool uncle."

"I'm sure that the baby would have been absolutely adorable and would have loved their Uncle Jimmy very much. Can you picture Sadie with a big ol' pregnant belly inside of her band tees? That would have been a sight." Gen is laughing and has a smile on her face but her voice sounds like she might cry.

"That really would have been hilarious, especially in her tutus. What about Sadie in a Mommy and Me group, like those ladies who walk the mall with their strollers? That would have been entertaining."

"A kid would probably have turned her into a total basic soccer mom." We are both laughing now.

*Sadie was anything but basic.*

I take the rest of the photos down and place them on the top of the suitcase. "I think this is enough stuff for the first load from here. Do you want to go home and pack some stuff too before we go back to drop this off?"

"I don't know. Do you feel up to going over there today? Mom is home and you know that there are reminders of Sadie everywhere."

*With her mood today, I don't know if I am willing to expose her to a possible tantrum from Mom.*

"Yeah. Let's go. Plus, I want to grab something from Sadie's room to put in our apartment. There should be something of hers there, too." She smiles at me as she zips up the suitcase and grabs it off of the bed.

I follow her out to my car and help her load all of the luggage into the backseat.

*She doesn't seem to be shaking anymore. Talking about Sadie seemed to help her even out a bit. It helped me a lot too actually. My chest feels warmer now and almost like I am starting to heal my heart just a tiny bit. It's almost therapeutic to talk about her.*

As we drive to my house, I zone out listening to Gen hum along with the radio and occasionally sing some of the lyrics. She is staring out the window with her head back against the headrest. I start thinking about a drive that we took a few months ago.

*We were bored and looking for something to do. Gen had been having a crappy week and Sadie was fighting with our mom. We all decided to load up in my car and get out of town for a little bit. We drove for hours before we found a small town to eat lunch at. When we got to the restaurant, our voices were so hoarse from belting out all of the songs on the radio that we were all practically whispering our orders.*

*Sadie ordered a ton of fried food and forced us to eat it. She also ordered three milkshakes, but they only had enough ice cream left to make two. Gen decided to let me have the one that was left. I saw the sad look in her eye when she saw us both sucking the thick cookies and cream mixture up the striped straws. I grabbed an extra straw and stuck it in the other side of my shake for her. At first she refused, but I insisted because I knew she was just trying to be polite. She took a long sip out of the shake and I wish I would have gotten a photo of the smile after that sip. Something so simple made her smile glow through her entire body. I would give anything to see that smile again right now.*

*After our lunch, we went into all of the small businesses around the restaurant. Sadie and Gen's innocent shenanigans wreaked havoc on those stores. None of the owners were prepared for these two innocent-looking girls to giggle so loudly and dance in circles around their merchandise. By the time we got back in my car to head home, we had been asked to leave four different stores and had received many dirty looks. Sadie looked around one of the stores noticing the looks of disdain on everyone's faces and proudly proclaimed, "What? Did we stumble into the town from* Footloose *or something?" with all of her normal Sadie spunk. I miss her sarcasm and sense of humor so much. It helped me through so many days in my life. Now, I'm starting to tear up. I don't think the tears for Sadie will ever stop.*

We pull into my driveway and can see my mother cleaning the windows from inside of the house. She smiles at us and gives a small wave with the rag still in her hand. We both get out and head for the front door. Mom is already waiting with it open when we get up to it.

"What are you guys up to today?" Mom sounds genuinely interested. This is actually pretty shocking.

"Packing and moving some stuff actually." I slide my shoes off just inside of the front door.

"You're moving already?"

"Well, slowly over the next few days. We will probably spend our first night there on Sunday."

"Oh really? That seems really fast! You can take your time!"

"I know, but we actually want to be in and settled as soon as we can."

"Maryann, is Henry home? We want to talk to you about Thanksgiving."

*Gen must have been able to sense the impending argument forming with my mother.*

"He's in the kitchen reading the paper. Go on in. I'll be right there." Mom sprays window cleaner on the front door and wipes it down. Gen walks into the kitchen ahead of me and sits herself beside my father at the table. He glances at her sideways and smiles.

*He has always enjoyed her company, even before he knew how I felt about her. She has always been able to banter with him and carry an intelligent conversation.*

"I see you're still wearing the class ring."

"Well, of course I am. I'm not taking it off." She is staring at the way the light dances off of the stone in the ring and smiling.

"I figured it would have been replaced with the real one by now." This time, he glances at me over the rim of his reading glasses that are perched on his nose and smiles.

"Oh. Nope, not yet. Maybe sometime soon though." She smiles at him and then looks to me for some more feedback. I just smile and shrug my shoulders. Mom comes into the room behind me.

"Genevieve, you said that you two wanted to discuss Thanksgiving?"

Mom props herself against the counter.

"We were thinking that since we will be moved into the apartment by then that we could host Thanksgiving. We want the two of you and Mom to come over. If you still want to cook something to contribute, go ahead. If not, just let us know and we will make sure that everything is there."

"What a wonderful idea! We can bring the turkey if you just want to focus on desserts and sides." Mom shockingly seems excited to have it at our place. She is genuinely smiling. "Henry, did they tell you that they are starting to move their stuff into the apartment today? What do you think about that?"

"Wow. Today, really? Do you need any help? I would love to help you out. We can even use Sadie's car and mine to get stuff moved over there faster."

"Sadie's car? Dad, I don't think any of us are quite ready for that yet. It's a nice idea, but I think it's still a bit much."

*There is no way that I am ready to get in the car that smells just like Sadie and is filled with her stuff. Also, there is no way in hell that I am going to put Gen or Mom through that.*

"Well, you can still load stuff in my vehicle and I will bring it over for you."

"Thanks Dad. Can I use the suitcase from the basement?"

"Of course. Go down and grab it. It's in the normal spot."

"Thanks! I'll be right back up, Gen."

I jog down the wooden steps to the basement. It's musty and cold down here. The only light is provided from a small window filtering in sunlight and a single bulb suspended from the rafters. It takes a few seconds for my eyes to adjust to the dim lighting. I find the gray suitcase on the top shelf. I yank it off the shelf quickly and start shaking it in hopes of banishing whatever nasty creepy crawlies may be calling it home.

The sound of something hard, but wrapped in plastic, falling to the ground behind me echoes off the wall. I turn in a circle squinting. I keep trying to place whatever made that sound. I see a plastic sandwich bag holding something wrapped in newspaper.

*What the hell?*

I pick it up and open it carefully. I unwrap a glass pipe and a tiny baggie with a few ounces of marijuana.

*Who the hell would hide this down here? Mom said that she doesn't want there to be any more secrets, so I am going to confront them about this without beating around the bush. I'm about to move out anyway. Who cares if they get mad at me?*

Carrying the suitcase in one hand and the bag of mystery paraphernalia in the other, I return to the kitchen.

Gen is listening to Dad read some article in the local paper. She is so effortlessly pretty. Her hair is cascading lightly down her face. Looking at her is making me lose track of my thoughts.

*No, Jimmy, focus! You have something important to discuss. You can drool over Gen later.*

"Did you find it alright?", Mom asks as if she can't see the suitcase very obviously in my right hand.

"It's not the only thing that I found. You two want this to be a secret-free family. I am going to ask you something and I would appreciate honest answers. Remember: I'm an adult and I can handle it." I place the contents of the bag on the table in front of my parents. They both take in the sight of the items that look so foreign on their table before giving me a look of total bewilderment. “Which one of you hid this downstairs? How long have you been smoking? You were always on our backs about abiding by all laws and then you go and do this?”

“James! You cannot seriously think that this belongs to either of us!” Mom looks completely offended.

“Well, it sure as hell is not mine! I wouldn’t be dumb enough to hide mine in the basement if I had any.” I retort.

“I don’t use drugs, James! I don’t even speed, for God’s sake! Your father hasn’t smoked since college. Right, honey?”

“That’s right! I haven’t touched anything like that since the night of my graduation. Don’t get me wrong though. I’m not saying that I haven’t craved any or that seeing this in front of me isn’t tempting, but I would *never* hide it where anyone could find it either.” Dad looks perplexed.

“Well, it doesn’t belong to you guys and it doesn’t belong to me. So, who else could it belong to?” As I say this, it is as if my parents and I are all on the same wavelength. We all turn to stare at Gen.

“Hey, don’t look at *me*!” Gen puts her arms up in surrender. “I don’t smoke at all. Jimmy, you know that I can’t stand any smoke being near me.”

“Well, that covers the only four people who are ever here.” I cross my arms outwardly showing my irritation. It dawns on me, all of a sudden. “Gen, do you think this was Sadie’s?”

Gen shakes her head gently before staring at her cuticles. “I mean, I don’t know. With everything that has happened this week, I keep feeling like maybe I didn’t know her as well as I thought. Not this new version of her anyway. I was totally clueless about David and the baby. Now, smoking too? I would say that she is the only logical owner of this stuff though. We already know it doesn't belong to any of us." Gen's eyes are filled with sorrow.

"Do you think I should turn this into Ramsey?" I look to my father for some advice.

"You have enough to worry about already with the move. I'll take it to him." Dad bags up the paraphernalia and heads for his shoes. He isn't wasting any time. Mom is right on his heels.

*Part of me thinks that they might chicken out of taking it to the police and keep it for themselves instead. Dad was definitely right about me being busy though. I have so much to do.*

"Come on. Let's go pack!" We walk down the carpeted hall to my room. For some reason, my parents refuse to tear out the terrible shag rug in the hallway.

In my room, I set my suitcase on the bed and assess the packing situation in my room.

*Hmm, what am I going to use for transporting my records? A box!*

"I'll be right back! I'm grabbing a box." I return to the kitchen alone to get a box from the recycling.

*I am still trying to process what has been happening in my life lately. I am still so confused by the weed. Whenever we smoked, it was together and at a party. It was always provided. We never bought any for ourselves. Sadie was hiding David, which I kind of understand. She knew how I thought about him. I still can't grasp the drugs though. Why wouldn't she tell me? Was she hiding more? What's next? Heroin and prostitution?*

# Genevieve

♡

The dresser in Jimmy's room is composed of six long drawers that are in columns of three. I slide a drawer open to start emptying into his suitcase and it is filled with t-shirts. I scoop all of the shirts into one heaping armful. I toss them lightly into the suitcase. I move on to his jean drawer. This time it takes me two armfuls to get it emptied. The bottom drawer is filled with his hoodies. After I add them to the suitcase, I notice that there are pictures laying face down in the bottom of his drawer.

*What the hell are pictures doing in here?*

Out of curiosity, I pick them up and flip them over.

The first photo is of me laughing while laying in their lawn. It's sunny and bright. It must have been summer. I am in a bikini. Sadie is just out of frame.

*I don't remember this photo ever being taken. It's a really nice photo of me though. I look happy and pretty.*

The second one looks like it was taken on the same day. I'm wearing the same bikini and I'm in the middle of doing a cartwheel.

*When did he take these? I can't think of any time that he had his camera on him during the summer.*

The next one is only featuring me again. I'm completely drenched from head to toe. My hair is hanging around my face like a wet mop. Makeup streaked down my face. My jeans and hoodie look like they probably weighed a few pounds each from all of the rain. I'm smiling again in this one. This time though, I am smiling directly at the camera, directly at Jimmy.

*The smile though was for him, not the camera. I actually remember him snapping this one.*

*We had decided to walk from the movie theater to their house instead of getting a ride home. Unfortunately, in the middle of the three mile walk, it started to torrential downpour. We were all being stubborn and remained committed to the walk that we had already started. We were fully determined that we would not be asking for a ride. By the time that we got back to their house, we were all chilled to the bone, completely soaked but could not stop smiling. It was such a refreshing feeling to have the unrelenting rain beat down on us.*

*That day, the dramatic rain scene from* The Notebook *kept playing in my head, over and over. You know the one where Allie and Noah fight and then make up with a passionate kiss? Only in my head, it wasn't Ryan Gosling and Rachel McAdam. It was Jimmy and I.*

*Once we were back inside, we changed into dry clothes, made popcorn and hung out in the living room watching old cheesy teen movies.*

*That was one of my favorite days ever. I think that it probably always will be.*

The last photo in the stack is of Jimmy and I together. Neither of us seems to be aware of the photo being taken. We are sitting side by side on the couch, listening to Jimmy's iPod. We are each wearing one earbud. It looks like we were singing along to whatever we were listening to. In this photo, if I didn't know any better, I would think that these two young teenagers were a couple. Our knees are touching and we look absorbed in our own little world.

*I want to frame this and hang it in our apartment. I love it. I wonder why he kept these in a drawer. Kudos to him for finding a place that Sadie would never have found the hints of his fondness for me. Besides the cartwheel shot, these are all actually quality photos of me which is not something that I ever really say or think.*

I set the photos down on the top of the clothes in the suitcase and move on to the other side of the dresser.

Jimmy walks in with a box for his records. He places it on the floor and starts loading it up. He turns and smiles at me before walking over to me and kissing me lightly.

"Thank you for packing those up for me, babe."

"Of course. I love those photos, by the way."

"What pictures?" He looks really confused.

"The ones of me from your bottom drawer." His face looks like he just saw a ghost.

"You found those?" He is going from pale white to bright red.

"Yeah. They were right under your hoodies. I really like them! I want to frame the one of us."

"Sorry that they were in there."

"Why would you be sorry? I just told you that I thought they were nice pictures of me. I never like how I look in pictures, but somehow in those ones I do."

"Well, it's kind of embarrassing."

"It's not embarrassing. It makes sense. You didn't want people knowing you liked me."

"It's still embarrassing for me. First off, I shouldn't have hidden you away in a drawer. Secondly, I *may* not have had the best intentions when I took some of those photos."

"What?" *He is all fidgety and weird. What is happening right now?* "Oh. My. God. Did you use these to, um, *you know*?"

"Sometimes." He is the shade of a lobster and won't break eye contact with the ground. He won't look up at me. I laugh, partly from shock and partly from nerves.

"So you *actually* thought about me like that, huh?"

*I can't believe that he was actually attracted to me enough that he hid photos of me to use. Most guys used lingerie catalogs that they swiped from their mothers or sisters. I have never felt pretty enough to even have the inclination that someone would think of me in that way, but this whole time Jimmy was wanting me way more than I ever knew.*

"Of course I did! Honestly, I have since I even started having thoughts like that. But, I didn't use *all* of them for that. Some of them I just kept because I loved them and I really wanted to hang them in my room. I just didn't want to upset Sadie, so I kept them in there instead. The swimsuit one though....that one I took strictly because I loved the way your body looked. You know how people say '*Take a picture. It will last longer*'? Well, that's exactly what I did. I'm sorry for that. It was oafish of me."

"Don't be sorry. It's totally fine that you wanted to have it. I really don't mind at all that you thought about me. I'm glad that it was me and not some model or pornstar that I could never live up to. We knew that you did that sometimes while we were here." His face is even redder, if that's possible.

"You knew? How?"

"There were just *signs*. You would disappear into your room or the bathroom for a while and lock the doors. When you would come back, your face would be all red." I laugh a little.

*I know that I am adding to his embarrassment, but this is fun. I love teasing him.*

"I didn't know that you two ever even suspected what I was doing. One thing I can assure you though is that it was *always* you." He sheepishly glances up at me.

*Jimmy is so mortified right now by this conversation. I'm enjoying making him squirm a bit though.*

"Well, we weren't *total* idiots. It was totally normal. You were a teenage boy. We didn't care. You know that we would totally have called you out on it if we did."

"Thanks for not harassing me about it. I still feel bad though and like I did something wrong."

"You didn't do anything wrong at all. I'm happy that you didn't just go find someone else to fulfill those needs for you. It makes it a lot more special for us now."

"No one could ever live up to you. You're my dream girl, literally. I dream about you all the time. Sometimes they are just normal dreams or weird snippets. Other times they are really, really good dreams." At this he actually smiles at me. His embarrassment seems to be fading a bit now. I kiss him firmly on the lips and let the tip of my tongue graze just inside his top lip.

"Really, really good, huh?" I shamelessly flirt with my man. I press my body against him and hook my fingers in his belt loops, pulling him closer.

"A few times, you were in the same room as me or right down the hall when I had those ones. It was so difficult to just not wake up and ravage you. One of them was actually the other night when we were on the couch. I kept praying that you wouldn't wake up and feel me pressing against you like that. I tried so hard to think of anything I could to make it go away, but then you would breathe a little bit deeper and your body would rub against me again. It was of no use." He kisses me and presses his forehead against mine.

"Next time that you have one of those, feel free to wake me up. I'll help it go away. I would have helped you all of the other times too without a second of hesitation." I kiss him deeply and let out a small moan.

*We are supposed to be packing, not getting distracted like this.*

"How did I actually get lucky enough to get my hands on you?" He kisses me again.

"Well, for one thing, you're just completely amazing. Secondly, it helps that you're so hot." I place a firm kiss on his lips. He squeezes my ass a bit. "We are never going to get packed if we keep this up. Plus, I thought we were going to take a break until we actually get moved into the apartment."

"Poor room. It has never seen any real action." He laughs, glancing around his room.

*It's weird that soon he won't be calling this room home.*

"But, you're right. You said earlier that you think we should take a break, so I will get myself away from you and back to packing before we cave."

I turn away from him and open the next drawer to start packing. When I get to the back of the drawer, I find an envelope. I open it and look at its contents. It's filled with cash. I can feel my eyes getting huge. Jimmy glances at my hands.

"That's thirteen hundred. The rest is in the bank. That is just my security blanket that I keep in cash just in case I need it."

"What the hell would ever come up that you would need thirteen hundred in cash for? I can't believe that you kept this much cash in here. What else do you have hidden in this dresser?" I set the envelope down and start searching the remaining drawers.

"Car trouble, bail money for you and Sadie, funds for one of our impromptu road trips, lots of stuff. I don't have any other stuff hidden in there right now. Your ring was in there, but it's not now."

"You just keep all of your secrets in your dresser, don't you?"

"Doesn't everybody? I mean you kept your journal and blade in yours."

"Yeah, I guess I did. It seems like a safe place." I am refolding a shirt that came unfolded when I pulled it from the drawer before putting it in the suitcase. An idea dawns on me. "I'll be right back."

I rush out of his room and down the hall to Sadie's. I rip open her bottom drawer first, yanking everything out and throwing it on the ground. Nothing. I do the same to the next one up. Again, nothing. I grab the middle drawer and pull out two handfuls of shirts. As I throw them to the ground, I hear something hard hit the ground. I stoop down and dig through the mess of clothes that I made.

I find a black makeup bag in the middle of the clothes. I quickly unzip it and empty it onto her bed. There is now a pregnancy test, two small unlabeled vials of something amber-colored, a syringe, a small baggie of various pills and photos of her with David spilled onto her mattress.

*Damn it! How many secrets was she hiding? I am almost certain now that those drugs in the basement were hers. I wonder if there is anything else.*

I turn back to the dresser and finish emptying the remaining two drawers of their contents. In the very back of her top drawer, I find two folded up letters. As I start to unfold the first one, I sit on her bed. I start reading the first letter just as Jimmy walks into the room.

"Woah, Gen! What happened here?"

"Secrets are kept in dressers! I emptied it to find hers!"

"What did you find?"

"A pregnancy test, photos, letters, and what I think might be heroin." His jaw drops.

"Excuse me, what? Did you just say heroin?"

"And pills." I point to the pile of things on the bed beside me.

"*Sadie June!* What the hell were you thinking?" Jimmy is looking down at the secrets and shaking his head.

I read the letter.

*Sadie,*

*Listen, I feel weird about selling to you. You're way better than all of this shit. You shouldn't be destroying your body with this junk. We can still meet up, but I don't want you buying anything else from me. I know that you think the sex is better when you're high, but you're not you. I don't want to be the one dragging you down. Jimmy already hates the idea of us enough. Adding drugs into the equation is just going to make it that much worse. If you want this whole thing to work out, I need you to stop using. One of my favorite things about you is your innocence.*

*Keep it.*

*XO*

*D.J.*

"She was definitely using. Read this letter." I hand it to Jimmy. I watch his face as his emotions take over.

"As much as I hate him for selling to her in the first place, I'm glad that he was trying to get her to stop. I wonder how long this was going on." He looks up from the page.

"There is another one too."

I open the second note and start reading.

*Sadie,*

*I'm sorry. I never meant for this to happen. I never intended for you to get pregnant. We can't have a kid. Look at us. We are two trainwrecks. Do you realize how fucked our kid would be? A drug dealer for a father and a bitchy barista for a mother? There is no way that we can do this. Plus, your family would totally hate me. It's not like we could ever get married or be a serious couple. I'm not that kind of guy. I don't do commitment. If I ever did though, it would be with you. I'm just not at that point right now.*

*Sorry.*

*D.J.*

*What an asshole! That confirms that he was the dad though. Sadie would have been a kickass mom in spite of him. She loved with her whole heart so there is no doubt that this was torture for her to read.*

Disgusted, I hand it to Jimmy. He reads it and looks completely crushed.

"How could he do that to her? It's one thing to just hook up with her, but then to duck away from his responsibilities after getting her pregnant? You and I both know that she would have wanted to keep that baby no matter what. This would have totally crushed her." Jimmy looks distant and sad.

Maryann is in the doorway with a look of shock on her face as she stares at the mess that I made.

"What the hell happened here?"

"Maryann. I am so, so sorry." I start stammering.

"Mom, we were just looking for answers. We're sorry."

"You two will be cleaning this up. Did you at least find anything worthwhile when you destroyed your sister's room?"

"Incriminating is more like it." Jimmy says while looking at the pile of things on the bed. Maryann walks over to get a closer look.

"Are those *drugs*?" She looks like she might vomit as her eyes scan over the items beside me.

"I think we know who the other stuff belonged to now." Jimmy looks reluctant to say anything more.

"I'll get this cleaned up, Maryann. I'm really sorry." I stoop down to start picking Sadie's belongings up and tears drop onto the carpet beside my hand. I look up at Maryann. In one hand, she is holding one of the letters. In the other, she has the positive pregnancy test.

"How could he not want a baby with her or even a relationship? Excuse my French, but he is a fucking *asshole*. I would like to punch him, personally." We both stare at Maryann with utter shock. She never swears.

"I really don't know." I stand and hug Maryann as she cries.

"Gen, how about you go get Mom some tea? I'll clean everything up in here." Jimmy starts folding Sadie's clothes back up.

"Come on, Maryann. Let's go to the kitchen." I give Jimmy a small, grateful smile as I lead Maryann from the room.

In the kitchen, I put a kettle full of water on the stove to boil. I sit beside my future mother-in-law and watch as she cries with her head buried in her hands.

"How did none of us know that she was using? Were there any signs? You and James saw her more often recently than me."

"No. There was nothing even weird with her. She was happy and normal Sadie. Part of me wonders if she only bought from him to have a reason to meet up with him. She wasn't into drugs. She would smoke weed at parties every once and awhile or drink socially, but she never did anything else that I know of."

"But what about all of the stuff in her room and the basement?"

"The fact that it was still there makes me think that maybe she didn't use any of it. The syringe looked clean. The vials looked full. I mean, I can't guarantee that she didn't use any of the weed or pills, but the other stuff looked untouched." I am trying to offer any sort of consolation that I can.

"What made you check her dresser?"

"Um, well honestly, Jimmy and I both uncovered some secrets of each other's while packing up our dressers. It just seemed like a good place to look. I kind of got tunnel vision and just started emptying it."

"Oh." Maryann is staring at the salt shaker on the table while she processes the information. "Wait, you two had secrets that you kept from each other? I thought you two knew pretty much everything about each other."

"Yeah, we did. A couple, at least."

"You're not mad at him for keeping things from you?"

"No, I'm not. I love him. Everyone has secrets. It doesn't change how I feel about him. Plus, he told me the truth when I confronted him about it, no matter how embarrassed it made him. I think in comparison, my secret was worse anyway."

"Do you still have any secrets that you're keeping from him?"

"Honestly, no. I've been pretty open with him over the years. The only secrets I had really were about him or about, um..."

*I don't know if I should continue or not. I'm not really sure how Maryann feels about my mental health issues.*

"It's okay. You can say whatever it is. I won't be upset. Were you lying about being a virgin? Is that the problem?"

"No! Nothing like that!" *God, is that how terribly she really thinks of me?* "I, um, had a bit of a relapse earlier this year. I was self-harming again. I hid it from everyone, including Sadie. He knows now though."

"You were suicidal again?" Maryann's eyes are filled with shock and concern.

"Uh, yeah...well, *kind of.*" I start twiddling my thumbs. This is my first time ever discussing this with her, really.

"*Kind of?* Are you still?"

"No, not right now. At least not yet, I feel that my depression is kicking into high gear though." I can't bring myself to make eye contact with her.

"I'm here if you need to talk. I had no idea that you still had problems like that." Maryann stares blankly at the space between us for a few moments. She is silent the whole time.

Taking a deep breath, she says, "Is James okay with all of that? What happens if you try to kill yourself again? How is he going to handle that? Losing Sadie and you, both, would destroy him."

"He will help me get better before I ever get to that point again. If I had just talked to him about it the last time, he would have stayed with me as long as I needed. I don't plan on ever hurting him. I want you to know that."

"Genevieve, while I have you alone, can we talk about your relationship with James?"

"Uh, yeah. I guess we can." She is making me really nervous.

"Do you really think that this is the real thing? Are you ready to actually commit your life to *one* person? You've never even had a boyfriend before."

"I am more than ready to commit myself to Jimmy and *only* Jimmy. He is the *reason* that I've never had a boyfriend. I've been in love with him since I was eleven years old. It's definitely the real thing, Maryann."

"I am truly so sorry for acting so crazy the other night. I want you to know that I am truly happy for the two of you. I will be very lucky to have you as my daughter-in-law someday."

"Thank you. It makes me really happy to hear you say that. Honestly, I am petrified of disappointing you. You're like a mother to me. Your opinion matters to me just as much as Mom's. If I did something that upset you, it would kill me." I glance up from my cuticles and look her in the eye to show her my sincerity.

"Promise me that you two won't keep secrets from me? I hate secrets. I always have, but everything with Sadie has made it even worse."

"We won't be keeping any secrets. We are pretty hurt by all of the things that Sadie was keeping from us too." I can feel the tears trying to come out and burning my eyes. "None of it sits right with me though. I mean, maybe the drugs would explain her mood swings back in the spring. Sadie wasn't an addict though. She wasn't the girl that snuck around behind everyone's backs. She definitely wasn't the girl that would hide a *baby*. She absolutely loved babies. Telling me about her sex life was one of her favorite pastimes."

*Oops! I shouldn't have just said that to Maryann.*

"Her *what* life?"

"Come on, Maryann. You know that she wasn't a virgin. She was pregnant, for God's sake! Don't get me wrong. She wasn't like a slut or anything, but she was definitely experienced. She would spend hours telling me about her latest conquests. Other than talking about how much I liked Jimmy, I had no love life of any sort to tell her about, so she made sure that I knew every single detail of hers. She never mentioned David though. I know that she was probably afraid that Jimmy would've killed him, but I wouldn't have judged her for it. I knew how she always felt about him. I would have tried talking to Jimmy for her." I'm sobbing now.

*I can't believe that my beautiful Sadie is gone. I want to go through more of her stuff and see if I can find anything else. I feel like there has to be more information somewhere.*

The kettle lets out a high-pitched whistle. I get up from the table and finish preparing the tea.

"Maybe she thought that you would side with him since you liked him so much. I guess we will never really know."

"I'm going to keep trying to find out more. There have to be more pieces to this puzzle. Hey, do you mind if I take something from her room to put at the apartment?"

"Absolutely feel free to take whatever you'd like. I still think that you should do two beds, by the way."

*I knew this was going too well.*

"I'm sorry Maryann, but we aren't going to do that. We will be sharing our bed just like we have every night that we've stayed together." I am probably just confirming her worst fears at the moment.

"Won't that amount of temptation make it difficult to wait until you're married?" Maryann sounds serious.

"Wait for *what*?"

"Um, well, being *intimate*." *Did she really just say that?*

Just as I am about to retort, Jimmy walks into the kitchen. He has definitely been crying by the look of his eyes.

"Are the two of you seriously discussing intimacy? What dimension is this?" Jimmy looks thoroughly confused.

"Your mom was. She thinks that us sleeping in the same bed is going to be too tempting for us to wait."

"*Wait*? Like for *sex*?"

"Until we're married." I nod, trying to keep a straight face. Jimmy bursts out laughing. His mother looks at him like he might be having a mental breakdown.

"What's so funny, James?"

"Come on, Mom! I'm *twenty*!"

He is still laughing all the way from his toes like this is the funniest joke that he has ever heard.

"So? You can still wait until you're married."

"No, Mom. We can't." *Shit! What is he doing?!*

"What are you saying?" Maryann is growing irritated. Her arms are crossed over her chest.

"Mom, I have already had sex with her. Plus, we are going to be living together this weekend."

"You *what*?!" Maryann is raising her voice.

*Here we gooooo.*

"Do you really think that we wouldn't have already? Not only are we both adults, but we have already waited long enough for each other. We weren't going to wait any longer." I wish I could just fade into the wall behind me as Maryann turns her head toward me.

"Well, you did say no more secrets. I should probably just be happy that you told me the truth."

She definitely does not sound happy, but you can tell that she is trying to compose herself. This is going to be a huge feat for her.

"Yeah, you should be." He crosses his arms like a pouting toddler.

"I just don't know what to think."

"Mom, I'm marrying her as soon as I can. We've already had this discussion. She is *It*!"

"I still see the class ring on her finger though."

"It will be gone soon. I promise."

"Okay. Whatever you say." Maryann looks down at the table in defeat. She looks like she is fighting to hold something back. She looks up at us, parts her lips like she is going to speak but doesn't. She averts her eyes back to the table and inhales a very deep breath before turning her stare to Jimmy. "Please tell me that you are at least protecting yourselves."

At this, Jimmy doesn't say anything. He just stares at his mother for a long moment, and then looks to me like he is searching for something to say.

*I don't have an answer for him. I brace myself for whatever he decides to say. No matter what comes out of his mouth, this is going to end badly. If he tells the truth, she will freak. If he lies, she will probably catch him and then be more pissed that he lied. He inhales sharply before speaking.*

"Honestly, I don't see how that is any of your business."

"You're my son. That's how it is my business. I think if there is a possibility of me having a grandchild, I should know about it."

"Mom, you're talking about Gen and I. Of course we will tell you if we are expecting. Whether or not we use protection though only concerns the two of us." Maryann looks completely taken aback.

"While you're under my roof, I expect you to use protection."

"Maryann, you wanted honesty and he gave it to you. That is a hell of a lot more than most guys his age would have done. We all know that it's way more than what Sadie did. By the way, just for your peace of mind, we haven't had sex here."

"I am glad that you told me so that there are no more secrets, but I still wish the two of you would have waited until marriage."

"We waited for *each other*, isn't that enough?" Jimmy is beginning to raise his voice. "Why do you have such insane standards that you hold me to? I have been head over heels in love with the same girl since I was FOURTEEN! I didn't sleep around in high school like Sadie. I didn't kiss anyone, other than

Hilary. I always had good grades. I've never been pulled over or arrested. I don't do drugs. I occasionally drink, but never to the point of acting ridiculous. I haven't done anything to warrant you treating me this way. Gen *definitely* does not deserve this." He is bright red from anger. He never yells like this. It is honestly pretty frightening. Henry walks into the room to assess the commotion.

"What is going on in here?" He looks from his wife to his son. They both look at him with frustration painted boldly on their faces.

*I want to turn and bolt to the safety of his bedroom. I have only ever witnessed Jimmy and Sadie act this way toward their parents a few times and they all ended very, very badly.*

*One time, Sadie was having a horrible hormone day and Maryann had the audacity to ask her how a quiz went at school that day, which she had totally bombed. Sadie started screaming at her mother that it was none of her business. She also said that she was never speaking to her again and that she absolutely hated her. That was the first time Sadie threatened to run away. After screaming at her loud enough for the entire street to hear, Maryann grounded her and forced her to go to her room. She gave me the option of going home or spending the night still, but I could only hang out with Jimmy and not Sadie. I chose to stay. That night, Jimmy and I laid on the living room floor watching dumb reality shows and munching on popcorn. Sadie's punishment was lifted the next day. Maryann figured that hearing the two of us enjoying each other's company without her was punishment enough. It was a long time before she screamed at Maryann like that again.*

"Why don't you ask your son?" Maryann's nostrils are flared with anger.

"James?"

"I think your wife should actually take the reins on this one, Dad. She started it."

"You two are being so childish. Genevieve, would *you* like to tell me what's going on?"

"Do I have to?"

*Please don't make me recap this. I am mortified enough.*

"Well, I would prefer one of the ones yelling to tell me, but since they won't you're my only option."

I sigh heavily. "They are fighting about Jimmy and I again. This is a vicious cycle."

Henry rubs his temple out of frustration and takes a deep breath before speaking. He always tried to be the calm and collected one in the Thompson family. "Maryann, we've talked about this. You were going to be better, remember? You were going to try harder to be accepting?"

"That was before James told me that they aren't waiting until marriage."

"Wait? For what? Sex? That is ridiculous, Maryann! We aren't in the 1950's anymore. They are old enough to make that decision without your input."

"You sound just like James!"

"Maryann, he waited until he was *twenty*! You should be proud of that!"

"Proud? Seriously?" She looks flabbergasted. "Henry, you just said wait*ed*, as in past tense. Did you already know?" Her anger is flaring in Henry's direction. If her eyes could shoot out flames right now, they would.

"Um, well, yeah I did."

"Another secret?"

"I already told you that I don't think his sex life is any of your business. Sorry." Henry nonchalantly shrugs.

"Did he also tell you that they aren't using protection?" Maryann is just taking digs at us now to irritate us.

"No, he didn't. I also never asked. Whatever is happening in the bedroom is for them alone to worry about."

"Mom, I never said that we weren't."

"You insinuated it and it's written all over your face." She punctuates the end of her sentence with gritted teeth.

"Would having a grandchild sometime soon really be such a bad thing, Maryann? Put it into perspective a bit. Gen and Jimmy are the only way that we are ever going to have a grandchild. Do you really want to discourage that?" *Henry, always the voice of reason.*

"Well, of course not, but they just got together and what if this doesn't work out?"

"It's not like they just met though. They know everything about each other: the good, the bad and the ugly. Even with knowing all of that, they have still been in love with each other for years. This isn't some puppy dog love that is going to die out in a month or two, Maryann. They are getting married, for God's sake!"

"I'm sorry! It terrifies me! What if they aren't ready?" Now she is speaking to her husband as if we aren't even in the same room.

"That's the beautiful thing about pregnancy, Maryann! It gives you time to get prepared. Plus, we have seen these two grow up together. They would be great parents and they make a wonderful team. You and I weren't exactly *ready* when you got pregnant for James. If you remember, that wasn't planned at all. It happened at literally the *worst* time, but look at how that turned out."

"We were different. We were married already. Kids are expensive. How would they afford that on their pay?"

"Mom, I have savings. We would be totally fine. I still don't understand why you're treating me like such a child. I turn twenty-one in less than three weeks. Plus, like I already said, I have been a pretty good person so far."

"James, you are a great person. I just want what's best for you and I don't want to see you ruin your life."

"Oh my *God*, Mom! For the last *fucking* time, there is not a single thing that could happen between Gen and I that would ruin my life besides us breaking up. Having a family with Gen and spending the rest of my life with her is *exactly* the life I want."

*I cannot believe that he just swore not only in front of Maryann, but* at *her.*

"He is the age I was when we got together, but he is a hell of a lot more mature than I was. I barely had two nickels to rub together on any given day, but he actually has savings. Do you know how rare that is? We raised an amazing son, Maryann. He is an adult. You need to let go. He can make his own decisions and he makes pretty damn good ones, by the way. Plus, it's not like he brought home some random girl off the street that he just met! He brought home *Genevieve*! We know her and love her. She will be an amazing wife and mother. She cares about everything she does with her entire heart."

*Alright, this is getting awkward.* I am turning scarlet. Maryann looks from Henry, to Jimmy and then to me. As soon as our eyes meet, she starts tearing up. She stands and hugs me tightly.

"Genevieve, I am so sorry. You know that this isn't me. I'm just so upset over everything with Sadie. James is right. You don't deserve this. Neither of you do. Henry is right, too. We will be very blessed to call you our daughter-in-law. If you think you can handle the consequences of being unprotected, then I'll leave you two alone about it. I just don't want to see either of you go through any more pain that you've already had to."

"It wouldn't be a *'consequence'* if I got pregnant, Maryann. A baby isn't a punishment. I almost wonder if this attitude right here is why Sadie hid it from all of us. It's obvious she was crazy about David." *I can't believe that I just said that to my future mother-in-law. She is really getting on my nerves lately and I am obviously in a fighting mood today. First, Gray and now, Maryann. Hopefully she doesn't end up hating me for this.* "She kept him hidden away in a drawer. The same girl who didn't give a single eff what *anyone* thought of her felt the need to hide the person that she loved from all of us. She never wanted to disappoint any of you."

Now, Maryann starts crying harder. Henry walks over to hug and console his grieving wife. I take the opportunity to exit the room and incidentally this conversation. I walk to the bathroom and lock myself in. I stand with both hands on the sink, staring down at a smear of toothpaste in the bowl. My chest feels tight. I can hear my heartbeat in my ears. I'm shaking.

*Today is too much. It's too hard.*

I look up to face my reflection. I barely recognize the girl staring back at me. *When did my face change so much? When did I get these dark circles and sharp cheekbones?*

## Jimmy

♪♪♪

*One of the many things that I love about my dad is that he never fails to mediate family conflicts. He has always been the rock that has kept Mom from losing her mind. He is truly the calm to her storm.*

I'm standing awkwardly in the kitchen while he comforts her.

*Whatever conversation that I walked into between Mom and Gen went seriously off course. They left Sadie's room as a united front trying to make sense of Sadie's secret life. That was only half an hour ago. Now, Gen ran down the hall and locked herself in the bathroom. My mom is sobbing now. I wish Sadie was here right now to help with this mess, but if she was here, this wouldn't be happening.*

Dad pulls away from my mom, lightly rubbing her lower back. He looks at me with sympathetic eyes.

"Where did Gen go?" Dad didn't notice that she had bolted at the first chance she got.

"She needed some space from this conversation. She is in the bathroom."

"I didn't even hear her speak."

"That's because she didn't."

Dad looks completely puzzled.

"Then how do you know where she went and why?" Mom is equally confused. Her face is wrinkled from a mix of crying and confusion.

*She looks so much older right now. All of this stuff with Sadie is really taking its toll on her.*

"I just *know*, Mom. I could tell by the look on her face and her body language." *Does she really think that I wouldn't recognize the signs of Gen being in emotional distress? I have pretty much made her happiness my sole mission in life.* "I'm done living here. I will be staying at Darcy's until we get the apartment ready. This needs to stop. I am not going to stand for you causing drama with Gen every time that you get upset about Sadie. She may have been her best friend, but she *isn't* Sadie. Stop taking all of your anger and resentment out on her. It isn't her fault that Sadie is gone. It certainly isn't her fault that there were drugs in Sadie's room."

"Wait, what drugs? What are you talking about?"

*Shit! Dad didn't know that yet!*

"We found some stuff hidden in her dresser. There were, like, pills and something for shooting up. It was all with pictures of her and David."

*This day has been exhausting so far and telling Dad this is making it that much worse.*

"Where is it?"

"I left it on her bed. I picked up the rest of the mess that Gen made though."

Dad rushes from the kitchen and down the hall to Sadie's room. Mom and I follow quickly behind him. This is the first time that he has gone in her room since she died. He walks straight to the bed and picks up the vials. He rolls them around in his hand and then picks up the syringe. He holds it up to the light and squints. He puts those back down and picks up the baggie of pills. He flips them over in his hand and then squints again.

"Well, I have a little bit of good news. This needle has never been used and these are completely full. So, Sadie never used these. Bad news is that by the looks, this is heroin and there is no way to tell if she had more before. The pills look like ecstasy."

"Uh, Dad. I don't think I even want the answer, but how do you know all of that?"

"You know that I have a past of partying. I've dabbled with a little bit of everything unfortunately."

"But this kind of stuff, really? This isn't the stuff that you just *'dabble'* with." Dad just nods silently. "What do we do now?"

"Call Ramsey. Have him take this stuff off our hands." Dad looks at the pictures on her bed. "You know, she actually looks really happy in these."

"I really hate to say it because I can't stand him, but she truly does."

*My baby sister's whole face is lit up with a smile in the photos, except for in one of them kissing. Something about her body language still looks really happy in that one too. Luckily, she is fully clothed in them all, unlike a couple of the photos I had hidden away of Gen.*

Dad picks up the letters to start reading them. Mom looks at him, waiting for his reaction. "Dad, don't read those. I promise you that all they will do is cause more pain. Leave it be for now. Today is rough enough."

I remove the papers from his hands and put them back on the bed. Dad gives me a defeated look as he leaves the room. Mom follows behind him.

I run both hands through my hair and grip my head. I am trying to wrap my mind around all of this. I walk out of the room and when I am about to step into my room, I realize that Gen is still in the bathroom.

I stand outside the door. I listen but don't hear anything. I lightly wrap my knuckles against the door a couple of times. Still not a sound. I try to turn the handle, but it's locked.

"Gen, babe, are you okay?" I call through the door. Still nothing. *What the hell?* "Come on, Gen. Open the door." Again there is no response. I am starting to worry.

I rush to the kitchen and rip open the junk drawer. I dig through the mess of belongings in the drawer to find an Allen wrench to pop the door open. I rush back to the bathroom door. "Gen? Gen, please answer me!" I put the wrench in the small hole on the door handle. I hear the click of it unlocking and I push the door open afraid that I might see her in a pool of her own blood.

Gen is sitting on the floor of the shower, hyperventilating with her knees tucked to her chest, eyes closed and hands covering her ears. She is in the middle of a panic attack.

*It has been so long since I've had to see her like this. It still hurts just as much, if not more. I remember that the last time I saw her like this was after one of her senior finals. She was sure that she had completely bombed it and wouldn't be allowed to graduate. She didn't want to be near anyone. She wanted to just be left alone. I stayed close, but just out of sight. I brought her a bottle of water and waited just in case she needed me. Sadie sat in the corner, reading a book and listening to music. She always just let Gen work through these without doing anything.*

"Hey, are you okay?" I squat down beside Gen and pet her hair gently. She tries to calm her breathing. She breathes in really deep and exhales while sputtering like a horse. Slowly, Gen opens her eyes and moves her hands from her ears. She looks at me with an entire world's worth of sadness in her eyes. Gen shakes her head no and frowns before she looks at the shower drain at our feet. "I am really sorry about the whole thing in the kitchen. I told Mom that she needs to stop because I am not going to put up with her causing issues with you."

"You shouldn't have done that. Now she is going to be pissed at you and it's going to be all my fault." Tears are still streaming down her face.

"Oh fucking well! Let her be mad at me all she wants! She is not going to treat you like that. I don't care if she's my mother. I'm not going to let her act that way toward you! You've done *nothing* wrong, Gen." I wipe Gen's tears from her cheeks and give her a sympathetic smile. I place a soft kiss on her forehead. "Whenever you're ready, we will go back to my room and finish packing. I'm done living here. I am not spending another night in this house. I will be staying with you and Darcy until we get the apartment ready." She inhales deeply before pushing her palms off of the shower floor to stand up.

"Let's go pack and get the hell out of here. Today is way too difficult to be here. I love your mom, but she is being a total bitch. I can't deal with it. I don't have the energy." She walks briskly to the bathroom door. She enters the hallway like a warrior preparing for battle.

*I've always found it amazing how she can dust herself off and still be so strong. When she gets to her breaking point, she escapes to where no one can see her before letting her emotions wash over her.*

I follow her into my room and watch as she quickly loads armfuls of my records into the box that I brought in earlier. It is so obvious that her fight-or-flight response is in full swing. She is staying silent and I can tell she is holding back tears. I keep watching her as I take clothes from my closet. I am afraid that if I look away for even a moment too long that she may start to crumble.

"I miss her so much. I don't know how to function without her. She was the first person that I would talk to every day and the last voice I would hear every night. Somehow I still missed so much about her. She loved him. She actually *loved* him! She hid him away like you hid me. I feel terrible that she didn't feel comfortable enough to tell us about him and her happiness. The drugs, she hid those too. What the hell! She knew *everything* about me, except for the cutting. How could she betray us like this? Now your mom keeps getting so upset with me when I was in the dark just as much as her. I hate when she gets mad at me! Sadie looked so much like her. I feel like it's Sadie getting angry with me. It takes me back to that night in the spring. I just don't understand! What did I do?" Her back is turned to me for the entire rant while she is stacking more records in the box. I don't have to see her face to know that there are tears streaming down it.

I empty my hands and walk over to her. Lifting her from beneath her elbow, I help her to stand. She faces me with red, blotchy cheeks that are drenched in tears. I pull her into a tight embrace against my chest.

*I wish I could bring Sadie back. Will Gen eventually get to the point where she can't stand to look at me because of my resemblance to my baby sister? I really hope not.*

"Come on. Let's get out of here. You don't need to be here today. I can come back later to grab the rest of my stuff." I brush her hair from her face. I release her from the hug and hold her hand as I grab my suitcase to leave my room. Mom and Dad are sitting in the living room silently staring at the floor. "Bye guys. We are taking this over to the apartment. I'll be back later to grab more stuff." They briefly glance up at us, but say nothing.

*I can't tell if they have been fighting amongst themselves or if they are mad at me. Either way, I don't care at the moment. I only care about getting Gen as far from here as possible. If everything today is taking her back to that fight with Sadie, she may want to cut again. I can't let that happen.*

I lead Gen outside to the cool, fresh air. I want to help her feel better. "Let's go grab some coffee before we head back to the apartment."

I drive us to Paper & Joe. Gen is silent the entire ride, but she isn't actively crying.

*That has to be a good sign, right?*

After I park in front of Paper & Joe, I open Gen's door for her. Once she is out of the car, I give her a huge kiss before leading her into the cafe. We open the door and our noses immediately fill with the scent of freshly brewed coffee. We are greeted with a cheery, "Welcome to Paper & Joe", by a distracted Rhea.

"Hey, Rhea!" Surprised by an unfamiliar male voice calling her by name, she spins around. Her long black braid twirls behind her like a whip. I'm glad no one else is behind the counter. They would have been hit by that at full speed.

"Oh my God! Hey, guys! What's up?" She is beaming as she takes in the sight of us together, especially my arm around Gen's waist.

"We came to grab some coffee on our way back to the apartment." I answer since Gen is off in her own little world. Rhea's jaw drops.

"Um, apartment?! You two are full of good news today, aren't you?" I give her a puzzled expression.

"What are you talking about?" Gen finally speaks.

"Oh, shoot. Maybe I wasn't supposed to know yet!"

"Know what?" Gen and I exchange a confused glance.

"About the engagement?" Rhea looks extremely perplexed by our mutual reaction of shock. "Morgan came in and said that she heard about it from Grayson. She had no idea that you were even a couple. She said that she has speculated about it for a while, but never had any real evidence. I didn't even know that you guys were close with Grayson. I was kind of shocked that I was hearing it secondhand and not straight from you, Gen."

*Oh great! Exactly what Gen was afraid of happening is unraveling before our eyes.*

"It's a long story...can I get a macchiato with an extra shot please?" Gen looks like she may break down again as Rhea checks the time.

"Lucky for you, I have time for a long story! It's closing time. Sit down and I'll grab your coffee. What do you want, Jimmy?"

"Just black coffee, if you have any left." Rhea starts getting our drinks and we sit down at the table in the corner.

*I'm worried about how Gen will handle this conversation with Rhea.*

I hold her hand on top of the table. I take in her appearance for a long moment. All of a sudden, I am completely overwhelmed with my love for her. It feels like my heart is about to burst from my chest. I whisper, "Hey, Gen. I want to ask you something." When she looks up at me, she has so much nervous energy radiating off of her.

*She is definitely panicked about explaining this to Rhea.*

"What?"

"Will you marry me?" I whisper across the table. Her eyes are huge. She definitely wasn't expecting that to come out of my mouth, at least not right now.

"Stop it. You aren't being serious right now."

"Yes, I am. I *want* to marry you, Genevieve. I keep waiting for the perfect moment, but I think I just realized that every moment is the perfect moment."

"You don't want to marry the trainwreck of a person that locks herself in the bathroom after having a difficult conversation with your parents."

"*Yes*, I do! So, what's your answer?" I whisper, smiling at her coyly.

"You already know my answer." She is slicing right into my soul with her green eyes.

"Ugh, okay...I guess I should call Janet then and let her know that she needs to join me on the altar." I tease, pretending to dial Janet's number on my phone.

"Oh, quit it! You know that it's a yes!" She is beaming at me now with happy tears filling her eyes. I give her a deep kiss before looking over to see what Rhea is doing. She is still making Gen's drink. Letting go of Gen's hand, I reach into my pocket for the ring box. I struggle for a moment to get it out of my pocket. I open the box beneath the table and remove the ring. Gently, I pull Gen's left hand under the table. I gently slide the antique ring on her finger.

*I can't get her out of this conversation with Rhea, but hopefully I just made it a lot easier for her. I know how much she hates lying.*

She places her hand on top of the table and admires the ring. After staring at it with awe for a few moments, she locks eyes with me and truly smiles. "I love you, Jimmy."

"I love you, Mrs. Thompson." I smile and kiss her quickly as Rhea walks our way.

"Alright, lovebirds! Spill!" Rhea grabs a chair from another table and straddles it facing us.

"Well, we ran into Gray in town and he was being his normal player self. Gen totally let him have it! It was great." I start laughing remembering how well Gen handled herself this morning.

"It *was* pretty awesome, wasn't it?" Gen is laughing now, too. "I pretty much told him to get over himself because he was never getting a chance with me since I'm Jimmy's fiancee."

"Good for you! He totally deserves it most days!" Rhea is smiling, too. "So, can I see this ring?" Gen holds up her left hand for her boss to examine her ring. "Oh my God! It's beautiful! You did good, boy!" When she smiles at someone, it seems like her entire body is smiling. Rhea's charcoal black hair even seems to light up.

"It was actually my great-grandmother's."

*I find it fitting that Rhea is the first to know. She was the first one outside of our parents that knew we were officially together, too. The ring fits Gen perfectly. It was definitely meant to be hers.*

"Oooh, a family ring! Very nice, Mr. Thompson! Now, tell me about this apartment! You two have been very busy this week catching up for lost time!"

"You could say that..." Gen gives me a flirtatious smile.

"Genevieve Porter, you scandalous broad! You slept with him, didn't you?!" Rhea's cheeks may break if she smiles any harder.

"What can I say? She seduced me!" I wink at Rhea.

"Oh, I'm sure it took *a lot* of convincing." Rhea says sarcastically, laughing. Gen would normally be blushing at comments like this, but right now there is a huge smile plastered on her face. As I catch myself staring at her, I can't help but to wonder how I got so lucky.

"Tons of it!" Gen laughs hard enough that she actually snorts. This is the most carefree that I have seen her all day.

"Have things gotten better with your mom?" Rhea turns to me as I sip at my coffee.

"Um, not really. There was kind of an explosion again today. It was bad enough that I have officially moved out. We won't be in the apartment for a few more days, but I'll be at Gen's. Mom is a little cray-cray right now."

"How did she react to the engagement?"

"She doesn't know yet. I mean, she knows that it's coming soon obviously, but she doesn't know that it actually happened yet." Rhea's jaw drops.

"Does Darcy know at least?" We both look at each other and then back to Rhea. "I'm assuming that look means no. Guys, as the older and wiser one here, I am telling you to get the hell out of my cafe and go talk to your parents before they hear it from someone else. It was one thing that *I* heard it from someone else, but your *parents*? Totally different story! *Go*!" She stands up and points to the door. We both grab our cups and move quickly to my front seat.

*Rhea means business!*

As we pull into traffic, I feel the sudden need to apologize.

"Gen...I'm really sorry if that was anticlimactic. It was about as *unfairytale* as it gets. I didn't even kneel for God's sake!"

"It was perfect! Honestly, it was great! It was just us, quiet and intimate. I don't care about some extravagant proposal from a movie. You could have proposed with a ring from a gumball machine and I still would have said yes. The only thing about it that matters to me is *you*."

"I had this huge list of things that I wanted to tell you before I proposed. I didn't say a *single* one of them!"

*I royally screwed up my own proposal.*

"You have forever to tell me the things on your list. I'm not going anywhere!"

"Do you want to tell your mom first or mine?"

"Actually, can we just go to our place and drop the stuff off that we already packed? Our parents can wait. They all know that it's coming anyway." Gen flashes me a small smile.

*I think having some time that is just the two of us is really going to help Gen.*

"Are you feeling any better now? You really scared me earlier."

"I'm sorry...I just couldn't handle it anymore...it was way too much at once. I definitely feel better now though. Also, I think that whole break thing that I mentioned earlier is kind of stupid."

"When you said it earlier, it really sounded like you meant it...I think we should still try to stick to it."

"Well...we are officially engaged and living together now...that changes things a bit, don't you think?" She seems pretty adamant.

"Not if you're uncomfortable or worried about it! I don't want to do anything to jeopardize your happiness."

"I think my break idea was just my fear of your mom's reaction, but she knows now so there is nothing left to fear." She shrugs, giving me a half-smile. I'm still not totally convinced.

*I'm not going to initiate anything until we are officially in the apartment; however, if she initiates something, it's game on!*

Parked in front of our new residence, we start unloading the backseat. Gen grabs my box of records and carries it inside while I load myself up like a packing mule. With my hands completely full, I realize that the key is still in my front pocket of my jeans. I set down the suitcase from Gen's house quickly to dig in my pocket for the key. Once we walk into the apartment, we unload our bundles on the middle of the floor of our future living room.

*It is weird to see our two lives just piled together in the middle of a floor.*

"We really need to get something to sit on in here." I glance around the barren house as I speak. My voice echoes off the walls.

"We have the barstools that came with the house!" Gen sits in one of the barstools and spins in circles, kicking her feet like a small child on a Ferris wheel.

"Those aren't very comfortable though. That also means that we can only have two people over at a time." I try to make a mental note of everything that we are lacking. "Oh, we will definitely need to invest in a table if we are going to host Thanksgiving. It needs to fit at least six people."

*I am starting to understand why Gen was so overwhelmed earlier. I got so caught up in the excitement and happiness of living with the girl of my dreams that I completely blanked out on some things that functioning adults actually need to have in their home. The things that are always in a home, but you never really think about until you have to furnish your own home. Things like a t.v., or table, or couch, or those things that you hang bananas on.*

"Let's go look at that fancy furniture store on Harrison! We can afford stuff there, right?" She just looks at me with inquiring eyes. I watch as her face goes from inquisitive to guilt-ridden in a flash. "Oh shit! I am so sorry! I just said '*we*' as if I had some hand in your finances. I meant, '*you*'. Nevermind, actually! We can just go to Target or something. I just got paid this morning, so I have like three hundred dollars to burn through. I'm sure we could find something simple at Target. At least a table this week and then save up for a couch for a couple of paychecks. We might need to just get a futon or something for now." She is ranting frantically about the faux pas that she thinks she made.

*She is so self-conscious sometimes.*

I let out a small laugh. She is acting nervous again like she did on our first official date.

"Gen, chill! You were right when you said 'we'. It is *our* money now, not just mine! Yes, we can afford the fancy place on Harrison. We can go there and then grab some Thai?"

"I would love that. It would be fun to go look, but we don't have to buy anything. Like I said, we can just go to Target or somewhere simple."

"We are going to get a couch that we love. Not some uncomfortable futon. This isn't a frat house or some smelly bachelor pad with cheap beer. Also, we are going to get a nice table. There is no sense in spending your hard earned cash on something flimsy that we hate and will need to replace in a year."

"Only if you're sure...I don't want to blow through all of your money."

"If we blow through all of *our* money in one trip buying furniture, then we have some serious problems." I start laughing.

*I don't really know how expensive furniture is, but I highly doubt we could burn through all of my money buying two pieces of furniture since I've been told that I have enough to buy a brand new car in cash.*

"Come on. Let's go cause trouble at that fancy, grown-up store!" I smile and wink at Gen. I hold out my hand for her to take on our walk to the car.

*The last time that we went to this furniture store, I was sixteen and the girls must have been fifteen. Sadie and Gen jumped on all of the mattresses in the bedroom area laughing hysterically the whole time. We sat on every couch and chair that we could. There was this huge gray velvet chaise lounge in one set and both girls squealed as soon as they saw it. Sadie started to caress the fabric.*

*"James! Be the best big brother ever and buy this for me!"*

*"Where would you put it?"*

*"I don't know. I'll get rid of my bed if I have to!"*

*Gen and I both laughed at her even entertaining this ridiculous notion. Then, Gen threw herself on it dramatically and reenacted the scene from Titanic.*

*"Jack, draw me like one of your French girls!" She said breathily before letting out an overly dramatic sigh.*

*"The name is James, actually. I'm Jack's friend." I shot her a huge smile and a playful wink.*

*If only she would have known what that did to my hormone-enraged teen brain. That night and many nights after, I had dreams of her lying naked on that just like Kate Winslet did in the movie. Even thinking about it now, my jeans are growing tighter. Hopefully she doesn't notice from beside me in the front seat.*

I immediately feel out of place when we get to the furniture store. A graying woman in a form-fitting dress welcomes us to Feindman's Furniture. I glance around at the huge selection. It's a bit overwhelming.

*Where do we even begin?*

We naturally walk toward the right side of the store through mock living rooms. A man in an expensive, tailored suit approaches us.

*I think I recognize him from the library.*

"What brings the two of you in here today? Shopping or browsing?"

"Shopping definitely. We are in desperate need of a table and couch."

"Let me show you our old floor models that are marked down." He starts trying to lead us toward the back corner on the opposite side of the store.

*He must assume that we are on a crunched budget because of our age. I'm sure that we look quite out of place with my black eye and our obvious discomfort of being here.*

"Um, we actually don't mind paying full price. We just want something nice that we both like." I clear my throat and nervously tousle my hair.

"Oh...okay, then did you have a style or color in mind?"

"I think the table should be black!" Gen scans the store looking for something that may catch her eye as she speaks.

"Black is lovely! Simple, elegant, modern. I love it! We definitely have some nice options. What about the couch?" He reminds me of one of the Fab Five, but I can't place which one.

"A sectional might be nice. Do you think we have room for one, Jimmy?"

"Totally! The living room is pretty big, but can we get cloth and not leather? Leather is cold in the winter and sticky in the summer. It drives me nuts."

"We have some nice options right this way." The salesman directs us toward the couches near the center of the store. "My name is Aaron. I will give you two a bit to take a gander and then I'll come back to see if you need any help." He smiles and turns away. Once he is out of earshot, I turn to Gen and we both burst out laughing.

"Did he really just say that?" Gen is laughing so hard that her eyes are about to water. "*Take a gander*? Seriously? Who says that?"

She definitely seems much better than she did earlier. As she starts to calm down, she runs her fingers through the front of her hair to move it away from her face. I catch the light sparkling off of Gen's ring. I almost forgot that it was on her finger.

*Holy shit! I am actually engaged to Genevieve Porter, like officially. This is insane. I have to be dreaming.*

"What do you think about this blue one?" I point at a couch made of navy blue microfiber.

"Do you think that blue would be hard to match? Maybe we should do a neutral. Ooh! What about a dark gray?"

"Sounds good to me! Let's see what we can find." We walk around a fake wall for one of the living room set-ups and see a green version of the chaise lounge that she sprawled herself on last time we were here.

*I wonder if she remembers that.*

I look at the chaise and then to her. As soon as our eyes meet, it is obvious that she remembers. "Think we should get it?" I flash a smile and wink at her.

"Maybe we can eventually." She smiles at me with a devilish sparkle in her eye. "Let's get the important stuff first!"

"Look at this one over here. It's perfect! What do you think?" I walk over to a couch that is covered in pillows and looks overly comfortable. I take a seat, patting the cushion beside me. Gen plops down, wiggles her butt into the cushion and lays her head on my shoulder. I rest my hand on her knee.

*I could stay like this all day.*

Just as I am about to get up, Aaron approaches us to see if we need any help.

"How is it going so far? Have you found any winners yet?"

"We want this one!" Gen is beaming up at him as she runs both hands over the fabric on either side of her legs. "How much is it?"

"Twenty-three hundred." When she hears the price, her eyes practically bulge out of her head. She is definitely not used to this kind of spending. "Is that a problem? If so, I can show you some cheaper options."

"Not a problem at all! We'll take it! Can you also help us find our table please?" I interject.

"How many people does it need to fit?"

"At least five. We are hosting Thanksgiving this year."

"How nice! How large is your current table?"

"We actually don't have a table currently." Aaron gives me a puzzled look. "We are just moving into our first place."

"How exciting! Have you bought any dishes yet?"

*Shit! I totally forgot about dishes and silverware. It looks like we will be needing to make a Target run after all.*

"Not yet."

"Let's go take a look at our table selection and see if we can find the perfect fit for your place." Aaron leads us to the right part of the store. I glance around at the options. I run my hand along the one beside me. It's smooth and cold. Gen is biting her lip and staring at the choices before us. I'm trying to read what she is thinking by the look on her face.

*I wish Aaron would leave us alone again so that I could talk to her.*

"Do you see anything that you like?"

*Jeesh, he's pushy!*

"Gen, what are you thinking?"

"They are all really nice, but I think these chairs are my favorite though." Gen takes a seat at a black table with high-backed tweed chairs that are the color of sand.

"We will take this one!" I smile at Aaron to show him our excitement.

"Let's go ring you out. Would you like this delivered?"

"Absolutely!"

"The soonest available delivery will be on Tuesday. Do you want the warranties?" I make eye contact with Gen before agreeing to the warranties. Neither of us really knows what we are doing with this kind of thing.

Gen sits in a leather chair nearby and pulls out her phone while I finish up with Aaron. She looks like her thoughts are getting heavy again. I sign what feels like fifty papers before swiping my debit card to pay for the furniture.

When I finish, Gen looks like she is in a trance staring at her phone. I glance at it and notice that she is on Sadie's social media page. The main photo is of them singing into hair brushes together. I took it a few years ago. Gen looks like she is about to cry. I don't want her to break down in the middle of the store.

"Hey, babe. Let's go get dinner!" I try to sound as cheerful as I can. Her eyes are holding back so much pain as she looks up at me.

"Huh?"

"We are all set! Let's go pig out on some Thai food!"

"Oh...um, yeah...okay."

*She seems like her depression is in high gear again.*

She stands and I take her hand in mine. We walk out to the car and before she gets in, I make sure to give her a tender kiss.

*Maybe a kiss will calm her heart a bit.*

# Chapter Nine

## Genevieve

*I should never have logged onto Sadie's page. There are a ton of posts from classmates and acquaintances sharing their condolences including photos and memories on her page now. Reading them now makes it feel like she just died all over again.*

I'm struggling to breathe and my chest feels tight.

There were still unread notifications from things she tagged me in on Monday night. I've been avoiding all forms of social media like they carry the plague. Her last status that she posted was about the three of us going to the movies together. She had attached a picture of the three of us sitting in the dimly lit theater awaiting the previews.

*Her and I are looking right at the camera in normal selfie fashion. Jimmy is beside me and looking at me instead of at the camera. I hadn't noticed that when we checked it over for imperfections before posting it. If I had noticed that on Monday, there would not have been a single doubt in my mind about Jimmy's feelings for me. The look in his eyes holds all of his longing and love in it. He has one of his signature lopsided grins on his face. I love when he smiles like that.*

*Picking out furniture felt like something that we should have been doing with her. It should have been the three of us. The salesman was so chipper and sickly sweet. At first, I thought he was acting condescending toward us because of our age. At the end though? It seemed like he was flirting with Jimmy. Did we get a special deal? I kind of want to fight him for eyeing my future husband.*

After we eat dinner, we drive back over to the Thompson household. Henry is laying across the couch when we walk in. He glances up at us. Right now, the resemblance between Henry and Jimmy is unmistakable. Normally, Henry looks very businesslike. Tonight, he is relaxing in flannel pajama bottoms with slippers dangling from his toes over the arm of the couch.

"What? No knock? I thought you said that you weren't living here anymore." Henry asks, stone-faced. Jimmy's jaw drops. His father has rendered him speechless. "Relax, James! I'm kidding! You never need to knock here."

"Sorry if this is offensive, but I don't think I can say the same to you." Jimmy composes himself before throwing his retort.

Henry just lets that comment slide with just a small smirk. "You took quite a while to drop stuff off. How did it go?"

"It went great. We actually just bought a couch and table!"

"Awesome! Where did you go?"

"Feindman's." Jimmy says nonchalantly. Henry sits up a bit. That obviously caught his attention.

"You really went to Feindman's? Did they have some good stuff on clearance?"

Jimmy scoffs in his father's direction.

"I wouldn't know, Dad. I never checked. We got the stuff full-price." Now, Henry's eyes are wide.

"You paid full-price for a couch *and* table?"

"Sure did!"

"Wow! You really *do* have savings, don't you?"

"Well, duh! That wasn't something that I said just to get Mom to shut up. Although, it did work! I was being honest."

"I'm glad that you'll be okay on your own. I'm proud of you. You know that, right?"

*I can tell that this is a private moment that I should not be in the middle of. Jimmy looks like he might cry. No matter whatever he says or does, he will always want his parents' approval deep down.*

"Yeah, I know, Dad. Thanks...too bad Mom doesn't feel the same way lately."

"She does too! Why would you say something like that?"

Henry moves his feet so that Jimmy can take a seat on the couch beside him. I take this opportunity to duck out of the living room and into the kitchen. I'll just grab some water and get out of their hair for a few minutes.

I grab a glass down from the cabinet before turning the water on. I let it run for a few moments to cool down while I zone out. I hear footsteps behind me and jump, startled. I fill the glass and turn the water off finally. I take a large gulp as I turn to face Maryann.

"Oh, I didn't know that you guys were here." She offers me a weak smile like she is just trying to be polite. Just as I am about to take another drink, Maryann's jaw drops. "He actually did it? You're actually engaged?" She is shouting and the acoustics of the kitchen seem to amplify it even more.

"Uh...yeah, we are. Sorry. That's actually what we came over to tell you. Jimmy and Henry were talking, so I came in here."

"Oh my God! Henry! James! Get in here!" Maryann yells toward the living room. She sounds genuinely excited.

The men walk into the room with twin looks of confusion. They glance at both of us and then around the kitchen like they are expecting to find blood or some sort of rodent.

"What? Is everything okay?" Worried, Henry touches Maryann's arm. She nods with a large, toothy smile.

"Everything is great! Did James tell you?"

"About the couch and table? Yeah."

"Furniture? Did you really think I called you in here to discuss their *furniture*, Henry?" She looks totally dumbfounded. It's as if this is the dumbest thing she has ever heard come out of her husband's mouth.

"Well, that's all we've discussed since they just walked in the door less than five minutes ago."

*Woah, snarky Henry! That's a first!*

"James! I can't believe that you didn't say something right off the bat!" Maryann thankfully seems full of happy thoughts.

Henry glances from his wife to his son. Maryann is beaming and Jimmy looks super confused. He looks to me searching for some sort of hint to what she is going on about. I just tap my finger against the glass in my hand. The metal of the ring makes a small clinking noise on the glass. Henry eyes my ring and then rushes over to me. He wraps me into a tight, fatherly embrace causing me to spill what is left of my water onto the kitchen rug.

"Congratulations! Welcome to the family, Genevieve! You know, *officially*!" He gives me an intense kiss on the cheek with an audible smooch. "Son! Why didn't you say something?" He gives me another big squeeze before releasing me and wrapping his son in his huge hug.

"Well, I thought we were going to tell you two *together*!" Jimmy shoots me a look that screams *What the hell!* over his father's shoulder.

"Sorry! Genevieve didn't tell me! I noticed the ring." Maryann is quick to make sure that nothing messes up this moment. "It looks beautiful on you, by the way! I knew it would!"

"It really does, doesn't it?" Jimmy smiles at me and eyes the ring dreamily.

"Soooo, details! I want to know everything. How did it happen?" Maryann is acting like a schoolgirl talking about the hallway gossip.

"Well, honestly, I kind of messed it up." Jimmy shakes his head. "Not sort of...*completely*." He looks down at the ground and he is tracing the flooring seam with his foot.

"You couldn't have messed up too badly! She still said yes!" Henry injects, beaming brightly.

"That's only because she is understanding and too sweet to tell me no." He is insecurely biting his bottom lip.

"So not true! It was perfect!" I want to give him a hug and reassure him, but his parents are awkwardly in the way of me getting to him.

"I want to know it all! Why do you think you screwed everything up?" Maryann is sitting at the table and pushes out the chair nearest to her for me.

"It was private and so honest."

*I might cry telling her about it. The way that he looked at me and asked like it was the easiest question in the world is embossed in my brain.*

"Aww. That is so nice. Where were you? What were you doing?" She is being very inquisitive.

"We were at Paper & Joe actually."

*I am not going to give Jimmy another moment to feel like he ruined our moment. It was wonderful. I don't need some huge romantic gesture. All I need is him. That is enough for me.*

"It was just us and he said that he wanted to ask me something. I didn't think he was being for real at first. It was as if he couldn't stand to wait any longer. Honestly, he never even needed to ask. My answer always has been and always will be yes." Now, I *am* crying and so is Maryann.

"That doesn't sound like you did anything to mess it up." Henry gives Jimmy a sideways glance and then backhands his bicep.

"Yes, I did! I didn't even get on one knee for God's sake! I also didn't get to tell her all of the things that I wanted to. I just looked at her and knew that I needed to ask right then."

"That sounds like it was wonderful actually." Henry smiles with pride at his son.

## Jimmy

*We did it. We told my parents. It makes this whole thing seem more official. Thank God my mom didn't freak out again! Seeing my dad give Gen such a huge hug made me realize how much he misses Sadie. His hugs were always one of Sadie's favorite comforts. If she had a bad day or wasn't feeling well, Dad would pull her into a tight hug and hold her for a while. By the time he let go, she was always happier.*

As I sit here staring at Gen, I catch myself being enticed by the way that her neck is arched. All I can think about is how badly I want to press my mouth to that spot. She is chatting with my mom about the stuff we bought for the apartment today. This truly happy smile hasn't left her face this entire time. Gen catches me staring at her and scrunches her nose at me.

"What? Is there something on me?" She is turning self-conscious now. She has her hand up, covering the spot on her neck where I had just been staring.

"No. Nothing. I was just looking at you."

"Stop it! You're freaking me out!" She is filled with nervous laughter.

"I'm not going to stop. Sorry." I shrug at her and give her a lopsided smile. I scoot past my dad to get to where she is sitting with my mom. I lean down and kiss her.

*One kiss isn't enough. I'm starting to lose my control. My lips seem to have their own agenda.*

Mom clears her throat twice.

"I am so happy for you guys, but I'm still getting used to seeing you two kiss. Can you please not do it directly in my face?" Mom laughs. She is trying to let us know that she is okay with all of this, but I can tell that we should take this as our cue to exit before anything goes awry.

"Sorry!" We apologize in unison and laugh.

"Does Darcy know yet?" Dad takes a seat next to Mom.

"Not yet. We are going there next." I keep eying Gen's mouth. Her lips are red. The bottom lip is naturally pouting because it's plump.

*Her mouth is just begging to be kissed.*

"Actually, um, we should probably head there." Gen takes my hand and stands up.

We say goodbye to my parents as I quickly guide Gen out of the front door. As soon as we get onto the front step, I plant an insistent kiss on her lips. I press her back against the closed front door. There is a small thud as she makes contact with the door. She lets out a small moan that drives me crazy.

*I am so tempted to go back inside and take this to my room. If I don't tell myself no, I will probably end up causing another fight with my mom.*

"Come on. Let's go tell your mom."

We pull into the driveway and there is an unfamiliar black car parked in it. We both look at it and then back at each other. She shrugs her shoulders.

*They never have company. Well, no one other than Sadie and I anyway.*

As we enter the house, we see a man's peacoat slung over the back of the couch. A pair of black men's dress shoes are on the mat by the door. We can hear laughter coming from the kitchen. Gen raises her eyebrows at me. I shrug and follow her to the kitchen. She stops dead in her tracks. Sitting at the table with Darcy is Detective Ramsey.

"Is everything okay?" Gen's voice is full of concern.

"Oh, yes honey! Nothing to worry about! You know Blake." She gestures at the detective beside her.

"*Blake*?"

"I'm off duty at the moment." This version of him has a very nice smile.

"What are you up to?" I raise an eyebrow at my future mother-in-law.

"I, uh, took your advice and invited Blake over for a cup of coffee. What about the two of you?"

"Well. that's awesome. I wanted to talk to you about something, but it can wait." Gen is smiling but I can hear the disappointment in her voice. She was really excited to tell Darcy about the engagement.

"Don't let me intrude! I can leave if you have something you need to discuss." Ramsey can sense it, too. He is great at reading people. That is probably why he makes a good detective.

"No. You don't have to do that. Sorry that we interrupted. We will just be upstairs." Gen gives a small wave and heads to go upstairs. She is completely up the stairs before I even turn to leave the kitchen.

"Jimmy, can you tell her that I will come find her when Blake leaves?"

"For sure." I nod at Darcy and leave to join Gen.

Gen is sitting on her bed with her legs criss crossed. She is holding back tears. Her eyes are glazed and wet. I shut the door behind me softly and join her on the bed.

"Are you okay?" She nods silently and bites her bottom lip. "What's wrong? Are you upset that Blake is here?"

"I'm not upset that he is here, but I'm irritated with the timing. I wanted time for just us and Mom."

"She told me to let you know that she is going to come find you when he leaves."

"Okay..." She parts her lips like she wants to say something but then she closes it again. She is picking at the seam of her pants. "Actually, you know what, part of this *is* because of him. It feels weird seeing Mom with someone other than Dad."

"Gen, don't hate me for saying this...but, it was your idea."

"I know...I *do* want Mom to date and be happy. She deserves it. Plus, she is going to be living on her own soon. I want her to have someone of her own. I just can't help but to feel like we are betraying Dad a little bit."

"You aren't betraying him. He loved you both very much and would want your mom to be happy. Plus, it's not like he has only been gone for a few months...it's been what? Like six years?"

"I guess you're right...it's just weird."

"Well, I totally get it...picturing either of my parents in a different relationship is totally strange to me. As for timing, I'm a little bummed too because I wanted to tell her our news too, but we will be here all weekend."

"I'm afraid that she will notice the ring before I get a chance to tell her myself."

"If you're worried about it, take it off until after you talk to her. I still have the box. You can use that to keep it safe." She looks down at the ring and straightens the stone on her finger.

"I don't want to take it off...I just don't want her to think that I'm hiding it from her or something."

"I'm sure she won't think that at all." I can hear laughter from downstairs.

*I am truly happy for Darcy. I want Gen to accept Blake if this is what Darcy wants.*

"Why don't we go down and try to get to know him?"

"It just feels wrong for me to do that right now with Sadie's case going on."

"I think you should at least go speak to him a little bit. You know, on a non-professional level." She might get mad at me, but I feel like this is an important step for her to take. "Come on. I'll be right here with you the whole time."

She looks up at me like she is annoyed with me but knows that I am right. She takes a deep breath and exhales through her mouth. Gen pushes herself up off of the mattress. She opens the door and listens to the voices floating up the stairs. Although I can't hear their words, I can hear the happiness in their voices. Gen reluctantly walks to the steps, dragging her feet and slowly descends.

"Hey...um, again. Is there any more coffee made?"

*Is that really the excuse she is planning to go with?*

"I think there might be a partial cup left, but feel free to make more." Darcy shrugs and turns her attention back to Blake. She definitely looks happy.

*Hopefully, Blake leaves soon though. I can see how much this is bothering Gen. Why can't she see it?*

"So, uh, Blake. What are your intentions with Mrs. Porter?" I deepen my voice and puff my chest out jokingly. I try to give him my sternest look.

None of them can take me seriously. We all start laughing at me. I think I successfully broke the ice. The tension seems to be easing up in the kitchen.

"Well, right now, my intentions are to get to know her and hopefully rope her into going on an actual date with me sometime soon." He drums his fingers against the side of his coffee mug.

*He is obviously nervous.*

"Rope me into it? Are you kidding? I would absolutely love to go on a real date with you, not just coffee in my kitchen." Darcy is grinning and her eyes are twinkling a bit. She seems more alive right now than I think I have ever seen her. Don't get me wrong, she is normally feisty but this is different.

"Blake, I already know what you do for a living, obviously. Do you have any kids?" Gen is drinking her coffee and staring at him.

*I'm glad that she is at least trying to make an effort.*

"Oh, uh, no I don't. I've never really had the chance. I love kids though."

*I can tell by the look on Blake's face that she definitely caught him off guard with that one. She pulled the big one out first, for sure.*

"Are you from here?"

"Um, not right here *exactly*. I grew up about an hour and a half away from here in Langton. My parents still live there actually."

*This experienced detective is actually nervous. Genevieve, the kindest girl around, is making him sweat with her interrogation.*

"Langton is pretty. Was my mom a nervous wreck asking you out? She didn't think she would know how to anymore." Now, Darcy is blushing.

"She was nervous? Really? Why would you be nervous to ask me?"

*He is shocked!*

"You're the first one to capture her attention since my dad, apparently." Gen shrugs her shoulders as she drinks more of her coffee. At this, Darcy turns her full attention to her daughter for the first time since we entered the kitchen.

"Gen! *Hush!*" Darcy is smiling and shushing her. Her face is the shade of a lobster. She glances at Gen's hand. *She definitely notices the new addition to her hand!* She shoots her a serious look before doing the same to me. "I will be talking to the two of you later!"

*She sounds like a stern, strict parent which is pretty rare for her. Shit! She must be furious! I have never heard Darcy use that tone with Gen, and definitely never with me!*

I make eye contact with my fiancee. She is grinning smugly. *Is she enjoying this? Seriously?*

"Well on that *tense* note, I should probably head home. Can I call you tomorrow?" Blake stands up from the table and Darcy follows him to the door. Gen is purposely ignoring everything, but a part of me can't help but to be nosy. I watch as he gives Darcy a hug, whispers something into her ear, kisses her cheek and then leaves.

"Look at you, Little Miss I-Haven't-Been-On-A-Date-In-Forever! He kisses your cheek and asks to call you tomorrow after one cup of coffee? You caught him for sure." I smile at Darcy trying to keep the mood light.

"Shut it, Thompson!" *Darcy never calls me that! What the hell?* "We are done discussing Blake for the moment. I want to discuss why you guys didn't tell me about your engagement?"

"We were going to, but you had *company*." Gen is pouting.

"That isn't something you wait to tell! You should have said something when you walked through the door!"

"I wanted it to just be the three of us." I am afraid that Gen might crumble right before our eyes.

"Ugh, okay...I guess I can't be mad then." Darcy gives us each a small smile. "So, what grand gesture happened when you proposed?"

"Unfortunately there wasn't one...I just kind of asked conversationally." I glance at the floor, ashamed.

*I know that Gen says she doesn't care that it wasn't all roses and oozing romance, but I can't help this inadequate feeling in my gut. This is the girl that I have been dreaming of marrying my entire life. I can't believe that I didn't make it as amazing as it should have been.*

"Knowing you, it was probably still romantic without you even trying. How did it happen?"

*Darcy is being way too nice. I'm afraid that she has me on some imaginary pedestal that I am going to fall off of at any moment now.*

"Ehh, I wouldn't be so sure! We were just sitting at P&J waiting for our coffee and I just said, '*Hey, will you marry me?*' I didn't get to tell her all of the important stuff that I had planned on saying or anything. I wasn't even on one knee, so I'm not even sure if that counts as a proposal."

I can't make eye contact with Gen right now. I know that there will be an air of disappointment in her eyes, even if she says that she isn't disappointed.

"Was it just the two of you?"

"Yeah. Rhea was making our coffee, but she had no idea."

"Then, I would still count that as romantic! Did you plan it out?"

"Well, I actually almost asked her twice this morning, but neither one of them worked out. So when I finally asked her, the words just kind of spilled out of me. I didn't *want* to wait anymore."

"Plus, I probably pressured him into it. I told Gray that we were engaged when we weren't."

*I can't believe Gen is actually telling her mom about the fiasco with Grayson this morning.*

"You did *not* pressure me in any shape or form!" I say this at the same time that Darcy exclaims her daughter's name in shock.

"I'm sure it *did* put pressure on your brain subconsciously!"

"The two times that I was going to do it were before then, remember?"

"Maybe not then...I don't know...I still feel really bad about the whole thing though."

"Gen, what were you thinking when you lied to him? That's not some tiny, white lie. That is a huge whopping lie."

"Darcy, don't get on to her about it. Seriously, it wasn't a big deal. I wanted it to be true, so badly. Plus, Copeland was being a total dick."

"You aren't upset that she lied about your relationship like that?" Darcy looks really confused.

"Not at all. I wasn't even mad about it when it happened. I was just in shock more than anything. It sounded so natural coming out of her mouth that it felt true." I can't stop smiling.

"I'm going to change. I'll be right back." Gen rushes past both of us and up to her room.

Something deep inside of me thinks that she is just running from this conversation, instead of changing. Darcy looks up the stairs with concern creasing her brows.

*I know that Gen doesn't want her mom to know about the cutting incident, but she didn't say anything about today's panic attack.*

"What was up with that? Is she okay?" Darcy is staring at me.

I run my hands through my hair and exhale a sigh. "She is having a rough day. There has been a lot happening."

"How rough of a day?" Darcy's concern on her face has increased trifold.

"Uh, well...*man*, she is going to kill me for saying anything...she had an attack at my parent's today."

"What kind of attack?" She is whispering loudly at me.

"She shut herself in my parents' bathroom. I never should have taken her there, especially not after the breakdown this morning."

"Are you sure that she is okay? She broke down this morning and then had a panic attack *too*?"

"She did. I had to pull over and talk to her earlier because I could tell that something was on her mind. I think that she is *trying* to be okay, but I'm not completely convinced that she is truly there. She wants to go back on medicine."

"Should I be worried?"

*She is asking* me *if she should be worried? I have no clue.* She *is her mom. Shouldn't she know the answer?*

"I think for now I can keep it under control until she gets back on medicine. I am making sure that there are no razor blades around anymore and I'm keeping myself around her as much as possible. If I think it's getting too bad, I'll let you know. First things first though! I am keeping her away from my parents' house and my mother for a while."

Darcy's forehead crinkles in concern. "Did something else happen today?"

"Oh shit! I forgot that Gen hasn't gotten a chance to talk to you yet. We found some drugs in Sadie's room and then there was a pretty dramatic fight with my parents. That's when Gen shut herself in the bathroom."

"Drugs? Seriously? What was the fight about?"

"Um...Gen and I."

"She is still pissed off about you two?"

"Not *exactly*. The fight was about our sex life. She is happy about us being a couple now, but she wanted us to wait until we got married." I involuntarily roll my eyes.

"Really? How did that subject even come up?"

"You know, I'm not really sure. I walked into the kitchen and heard Mom say '*being intimate*'. Then, it seemed to spiral. She was asking really personal questions too."

"Like, *how* personal?"

"She asked if we were using protection or not. Can you believe that? How the hell is that any of her business?"

"Maybe it was just curiosity?"

"It *definitely* wasn't. She was trying to scold us."

"So you're not, are you?" Darcy just looks at me while she waits for a response. My face must be giving away my irritation at the moment. "Sorry, I'm not wanting to know so that I can scold you. I am just genuinely curious!"

I give in. "No, we're not. You might as well know since I'm sure Mom will find a way to work that into the conversation at Thanksgiving."

Darcy bursts out laughing. "She wouldn't really do that, would she?"

"Have you met this new insane version of my mother? She definitely will. She tried to give us a sex talk during dinner the other night too."

Darcy is laughing again. She looks like she may cry from laughter soon.

"Stop it!" Darcy is gasping for breath between laughs and holding her ribcage.

"Seriously! She was *so mad* earlier when she found out. It's not like we did it on purpose! Well...the sex was *definitely* on purpose." I'm laughing now too and I can't keep this dumb smile off my face. "I mean the whole no condom thing. It was just a heat of the moment thing...and then it happened *again.* At this point, it doesn't really make sense to start now."

"Are you guys ready to have kids? Have you talked about it?"

"We have discussed how we would feel if we got pregnant and that we definitely want kids. I haven't discussed the specifics, like how many or anything like that. I think maturity wise we would be okay. Emotionally, I would be fine. I worry about Gen though."

"I think those are some things you should discuss before it's too late. I'm not going to tell you guys to start using protection because it's not my place, but I will give you that advice. Talk to her about all of the little details of having a kid. Would you both still work? Who would watch the baby? How many kids do you want? Do you want them close in age or spread out? Who would wake up in the middle of the night with the crying baby? Things like that are important to put on the table."

"Why are you so much cooler than my mom? Not just about this stuff, but like in general?"

Looking at Darcy right now, I can see the resemblance to Gen. They have the same eye shape and high cheekbones. Darcy's nose is longer and more pointed than Gen's. Gen definitely has her father's nose and smile.

"Thanks." Darcy is laughing and I can tell that she is a little embarrassed that I called her cool. "I think part of it is because I was in a very similar situation with Gen's grandmother. Clark's mom was totally against us being together and she was so upset when she found out about Gen. She stomped all over our happiness and excitement of having a kid. She *really* hated me. She always acted like I wasn't good enough for Clark. I remember how horrible she made me feel all the time. I don't want either of you to ever feel like that."

"God, I love you Darcy! I don't know how anyone could ever hate you."

"She felt like I was stealing her baby boy away from her." Darcy rolls her eyes and curls her top lip like she is still disgusted by the whole thing. She shares so many of her daughter's mannerisms. "It didn't matter to her that Clark had obviously *chosen* me."

"That is so ridiculous. I'm so sorry that she did that."

"It's alright. It's been two decades. I'm over it." She smiles halfheartedly at me. "Where's Gen? It seems like she is taking a while to change."

"I was just thinking the same thing. I'm going to go check on her." I jog up the steps and knock on her door. "Gen?" No answer.

I turn the door handle and open it up. Gen is sleeping on her bed. I can tell by her body language that she was crying when she fell asleep. Her hands are up to her face like she had been wiping at her eyes or trying to stifle sobs. Her body is curled into the fetal position and facing the wall. I climb into bed beside her and wrap my arm around her. Her body seems still and rigid with tension.

*I knew she was about to have another attack when she ran out of the room like that. I want to make it all better for her. I wish I had the ability to fix it all: her anxiety and depression, Sadie, Grayson and* especially *my mom.*

As I start drifting out of consciousness, I feel Gen's breathing pick up pace and I can hear her whimpering a bit. I open my eyes to check on her. She must be having a nightmare. I close my eyes again and try to fall back asleep. I fade into darkness after a few minutes. I'm jolted awake by Gen letting out a small, but terrified scream. I sit up and look at her. She is still asleep but she is visibly upset.

"Gen, hey, wake up. It's just a bad dream." I lightly jostle her by the shoulder to snap her out of it. She flails about a little on the bed beside me like she is fighting to get free of something. "Gen. Gen. *Genevieve*!" Her eyes pop open. She has a deep sadness in her eyes cohabiting with pure terror. "Hey, it's okay. It was just a dream. You're okay. I'm right here."

"Don't leave me."

She sounds like she is going to start crying at any moment.

"I won't. I'm right here."

"No. I mean, don't *leave* me."

She is definitely holding back tears.

"You know I'm never leaving you. If you ever question that, look down at your hand. That ring is your proof that I'm yours." I place a small kiss on her mouth. "What were you dreaming about? Are you okay?"

"Um, no...I'm *not* okay." Tears are silently streaming down her face now.

"What's wrong? What were you dreaming about?"

"It doesn't matter. It was just horrible."

"Talking about it might help."

"We had a huge fight...you broke up with me and then, I got suicidal again. I was strapped to a bed in the hospital." She is sobbing with her head in her hands.

"First of all, that is never going to happen! I could never get angry enough with you to leave you. Also, I will do everything in my power to keep you out of the hospital. What were we fighting about?"

"I don't know. All I remember is you yelling that you were done and slamming the door behind you. You never came back. You wouldn't speak to me or even text me. I had no you *and* no Sadie. I couldn't deal with any of it. I totally shut down and wanted to end my pain. I took a bottle of pills and then everything went dark. When the light came back, I was restrained with an IV in my arm."

"Gen, you're never going to have to worry about that. I promise." I kiss her forehead. "Is that why you don't want to use medicine ever? Are you afraid that you might be tempted?"

"Honestly? A little bit."

"I didn't even think about that. I'm so sorry." I pull her into me and hold onto her. "Gen, I want to tell you something too before your mom does. You're probably going to be mad at me."

"Um, okay...what happened?"

She sounds a little scared at what I'm about to tell her.

"I kind of told your mom about today." She glances up at me with confusion on her face. "I told her about your panic attack. So then she asked about what triggered it and I had to tell her about the whole thing with my mom."

"*All* of it?"

"Uh, yeah...I told her that Mom was mad about us not waiting until marriage and that she was being all pissy about protection."

Her eyes pop open wide with shock. "*Wait*...you told my mom that we aren't using anything?" I just nod in response. I am totally prepared for her to be totally pissed at me. "How did she react? Was she furious?" She sounds scared.

"Nah, she was normal Darcy. She joked around with me and then gave me some really good advice actually. She is pretty amazing."

"Advice? Like what?" She is running her hand along my arm now in rhythmic waves.

"She just gave me a list of some things that we should probably discuss before we have kids. Things that are important, but we can discuss them whenever. We don't have to do it now."

"Are you tired?" She sounds wide awake now.

"Not really. Why?"

"Come downstairs with me. Let's get some popcorn and Coke. We can snack and talk." Before I can answer, she is headed down the stairs. I see the kitchen light click on. I check my phone and have a text from Jack.

Fuck, man! The cops?
Seriously? Do you realize how
angry David is going to be?
You better watch your back.

I'll text him back once the sun is up. My phone says that it's one thirty. Once I smell the popcorn, I head down to sit with Gen. She is lying with her stomach on the living room floor and her feet kicking in the air behind her. She throws some popcorn in her mouth and smiles up at me.

I sit down across from her with the bowl of popcorn between us. Grabbing a handful, I tip my head back and drop it into my mouth.

"Ramsey must have reached out to Jack. He texted me about it."

One eyebrow quirks up at this information.

"Was he pissed?"

"Seems to be more nervous than anything." I give a small, one-armed shrug.

"Well that makes sense. So what did Mom tell you to talk to me about?"

Gen is mindlessly munching on popcorn as we fall into the comfortable rhythm of conversation.

"Well, a lot of different things. Uh...the first one I can think of is: how many kids do we want to have? Do we want to be one and done, or do we want to have a few? What do *you* want?"

"I would love to have one of each, but we could stop at one *or* have a few. I think my limit would be five. What about you?"

"I'd like at least two. That way they have siblings and aren't stuck being only children."

"Hey! Watch what you say about only children! I am one, you know!" Gen smiles and throws a piece of popcorn at me playfully.

"You know what I mean...I would like our kids to have the opportunity to have what Sadie and I had."

"Me too. That would be really nice." She starts twirling a piece of her hair around her finger. "What else did Mom think was important?"

"Hmm, let's see..." My mind has gone blank.

*What else did Darcy say?*

"Oh, I've got it! So, whenever we end up having kids, are we both going to keep working or are we going to drop to one income?"

"I think I would like to work part-time still, just to have some time out of the house. I would love to be able to stay home with the baby and be the best mom I could, but I think for my sanity I would need some time out of the house."

"Sounds good to me!" I lean across the popcorn bowl to kiss her lightly. Her lips taste like salt and butter deliciousness. "There are so many tiny things we should probably work out before that time eventually comes. Let's play Ask Me Anything."

"Hmm, I am trying to think of what I don't know about you!" She is nibbling on her lip as she thinks. "What's your dream vacation?"

I answer without even a moment of hesitation. "Iceland, hands down!"

"Really? Why?"

"It's beautiful there and you can see the Northern Lights. I think you would really like it there. What about you?"

"Vancouver. The music scene there is fantastic. It's always overcast. It's like my perfect getaway. What kind of pet would you want?"

"A cat and a dog. I like aspects of both. I wouldn't want to choose just one. Do you want a pet?"

"I've been thinking about it. Are we allowed to have an animal at the apartment? Did it mention it in the lease?"

"It didn't say that we *couldn't*. I can check with Gregory to be sure." She nods while she chews a mouthful of popcorn. "What kind of wedding do you want?"

"Something small. Just us, our families, Rhea, Janet and maybe some of the guys. I don't want it to be all huge and stressful."

"I want you to get your dream dress then. If we aren't going to go crazy for the whole thing, you should go all out for your dress. Who is that designer Sadie always talked about? Panini Something?" This gets a huge laugh out of her.

"Pnina Tornai! *Panini!* That's hilarious!" She has her head tipped back in laughter. I've missed this version of Gen: the happy and carefree one. "Her dresses are insanely expensive! There is no way that I would ever get one of those. They are gorgeous, but *come on*!"

"What kind of dress do you want?"

"Something flowy. Tulle maybe. I've never tried on a wedding dress though so I'm not really sure. I would have to go look."

"I bet Mom would love to help you. Obviously, Darcy would too."

"When do you want to get married? Do you want a long engagement? I'm fine with either."

## Genevieve

*Even though it's the middle of the night, it feels like it's early evening. We are hanging out in the living room and having fun. I've missed this. Jimmy is concentrating really hard while thinking about the answer to my question. I think he is afraid that if he says that he wants a long engagement I'll be offended. I truly don't care though. I already know that I'm marrying him so I'm not concerned with when it becomes official.*

"You know, I don't really think that I want to have a long engagement. I would honestly take you to the courthouse first thing Monday morning and marry you if that was what you wanted. Do you want a church wedding or do you have a location in mind?"

*Hmm, where would I want to get married? It would need to be somewhere that I feel comfortable.*

"Honestly, the library would be awesome. Plus, we could probably get a killer deal." I smile and wink at Jimmy.

He seems confused or at least caught off guard. "Why the library?"

"I feel comfortable and safe there. I love books. It makes me think of you. It's also gorgeous."

"Okay, so library it is! Should I start looking at availability when I go to work again on Monday?"

"Sure! Look at something after the holidays! Then, I'll have enough time to get a dress and invitations."

"We're really doing this? We are going to get married in January or February?"

"Absolutely. It will give me something to look forward to and keep my mind busy."

"Okay! Sweet! I can't wait to tell Darcy and Mom! Dad is going to be stoked."

I lean over the popcorn bowl to kiss Jimmy and the kiss turns deeper. I try to pull myself into Jimmy, but I knock over the bowl and our sodas. Popcorn and unpopped kernels are scattered across the floor. The soda is soaking into the area rug that Mom keeps in the living room.

*This is going to stain. Damn it!*

"Shit!" I jump up and rush to grab a towel to clean up the soda. Jimmy is collecting all of the popcorn up from the ground and laughing quietly to himself. I run back into the living room to start soaking up the mess I made and I trip over the edge of the rug. My body skids across the floor like a baseball player coming into home plate.

"Woahhhh, calm yourself *Slugger*!" Jimmy laughs at me. "Are you okay?"

"I'm totally fine. Just seriously lacking in the coordination department." I'm laughing at myself now. My forearms are going to have rug burn now, but oh well.

"It's okay. It gives me chances to save you! Plus, you make up for it in other departments." Jimmy grabs my hand and helps me to my feet before pulling me into him. He plants a heavy kiss on my mouth. My mind flashes back to when Jimmy caught me in their driveway.

"You're always saving me. Do you remember when you saved me on Sadie's birthday?"

"You mean when you almost smashed your face on the pavement? Yeah, I remember." He flashes a jovial smile at me.

"Sometimes I replay that moment in my head, but at the end we kiss. I used to do that a lot actually."

*I can tell that I'm starting to blush. I don't know why I'm embarrassed by this fact. He is my future husband, after all. It's okay that I have dreamed about kissing him for pretty much my whole life. Well, my entire life with his presence anyway.*

"Finally it gets a happy ending! I almost kissed you that day...*actually*, I almost kissed you *a lot* of days. I always chickened out at the last minute or someone would walk in the room...or car."

"In the car?" I can feel my face crinkling in confusion.

*When would he have possibly kissed me in the car?*

"Sadie was always with us. Plus, I was always in the backseat. How would you have kissed me?"

"Well, the two occasions that you were in my front seat. The one was at that party where I saved you *once again*, but then Sadie jumped into the car. The other one was the night that you two fought. That night, I just completely chickened out. I didn't want you to think that I was trying to take advantage of your vulnerability. I still wish I would have, both times."

I push onto my tiptoes and kiss him gently. His lips are salty from the popcorn. I pull away and smile.

Jimmy's hair is tousled and messy from being asleep just a little bit ago. His eye is still healing. The bruise is turning yellow mostly, except for a deep purple spot where the blood had pooled beneath the skin. I lightly run my thumb over his bruise.

"Does it still hurt?"

*I'm not sure why I'm whispering.*

"A little, but it's way better. I would do it all over again if I needed to. It felt like it was my last chance to protect her."

"Well, it kind of was." His eyes are looking down at something in the limited space between us. He blinks slowly a few times before moving his glance up to meet mine. The way he looks right in this very moment is the most similar to Sadie that I think I have ever seen him look. It's like he is channeling her very soul into his body right now. "You look a lot like her, you know."

"Not really, I look so much more like Dad than she did."

"There are still things about you though that are totally Sadie."

"You might want to keep that on the D.L. unless you want people to think that the lesbian lover stories are true. I'm sure some of the people around here would say that you only got with me when she was gone because I look so much like her." He starts laughing lightly.

"Oh stop it!" I give his shoulder a playful shove.

"You're telling me that you don't think Gray would take that and run with it?"

"I know he would! You know that is so untrue though."

"Right, because I look nothing like Sadie!" He is smirking at me, thinking he won that argument.

"I find you extremely sexy *in spite* of how much you *do* look like her!" I kiss him gently and bite his bottom lip a tiny bit before pulling away. "I've *always* had a weak spot for you."

"You have, huh?" He smiles and gives me a flirtatious kiss. "We should probably ask some more questions before I take you up to your room and test out that weak spot." I raise my eyebrows at him.

"Hmm, what should I ask you? Um, ooh I know! When do you actually want to start trying?"

"Trying?" His brow wrinkles in confusion. "To get pregnant?" I just nod in confirmation. "I don't know, in like twenty minutes?" He gives me a huge smile.

"For real? You want to actively start trying today?"

"Well…I mean, what's the difference between '*actively trying*' and what we've already been doing? We aren't doing anything to prevent it, right?"

"I guess you're right." I kiss him with a nervous laugh. "So, does that mean that we *are* trying?"

"If it happens, it happens! I don't think we should stress about it right now."

*He has always had the ability to be laid back and just go with the flow. Unfortunately, I was not graced with that trait.*

"Okay…no stress! I will try that! I'm not very good at the whole *not worrying* thing." I inhale deeply like I am about to do yoga.

*Namaste, Gen!*

He smiles at me and brushes my hair out of my face. I absolutely love that he looks at me like that. I bite my lip a little bit. I feel something similar to anxiety rising in the pit of my stomach. All of a sudden, I feel like I am meeting Jimmy for the first time.

*This is so ridiculous. Why the hell am I nervous? What do I have to be afraid of?*

"Jimmy, what do you even see in me? I feel like you deserve so much better."

"Ugh, see? This is why I should have done my speech when I asked you to marry me! Then you would know!"

"Well, you could tell me now."

"It's not romantic enough right now. I have a plan that I'm actually going to stick with this time. I can *show* you right now if you come upstairs with me." He kisses me playfully and winks. "Well, only if you want to of course."

"Are you already done with Ask Me Anything?"

"Maybe not…this could be *fun*. Where is your favorite place to be kissed?"

"Hmm, my room."

"Haha, very funny! You knew what I meant, Gen."

I feel a sudden urge to be overly flirtatious with him. "Maybe you should just do an experiment and figure it out hands on."

"That sounds like an incredibly fun challenge!"

Out of nowhere, we are pulled from our private little world by a shattering of glass and then a loud scream of agony. We exchange a wide-eyed look. He whispers for me to stay here. Jimmy runs up the stairs to check on my mom. I'm shaking from fear and crippling anxiety. I can't move.

*The only two people that I have are upstairs right now facing God knows what. If I lost them both, there would be no hope for me. I would literally have no reason to live.*

Jimmy yells down the stairs for me to call 911 and ask for an ambulance.

*Oh God! Why do we need an ambulance?*

"911. What's your emergency?"

"There has been an accident. We need an ambulance."

"What happened?"

"I don't know. There is something wrong with my mom."

"How old is she?"

"Forty-three."

"What's your address?"

"925 Sycamore."

"Help is on its way."

The dispatcher disconnects and leaves me in a flurry of panic. Less than three minutes later the front door flies open and there is Blake. His eyes are as wild and panicked as mine feel.

"Where's Darcy? What's wrong? I heard your address on the scanner requesting an ambulance for your mom."

"I think she is up in her room. I don't know what happened. We heard glass break and Mom scream. Then Jimmy went to check on her and yelled for me to get help." Blake dashes up the stairs taking them two at a time gracefully like an athlete. He glances at the four doors in the hall at the top of the stairs. "It's the one at the end on your left." I yell up, offering guidance. I want to follow but I should stay here to guide the paramedics when they arrive.

A couple of minutes later, I hear the sirens wailing as the ambulance pulls into our driveway. I meet them outside and lead them to my mom's room. I see the cause of the commotion for the first time. My mom is laying on her bed with blood everywhere. I can't tell where she is bleeding from. Her bedroom is freezing though from the wind whipping through the broken window. Blake is in the corner of the room on his phone. It is definitely a business call. The tone of his voice is a dead giveaway.

Jimmy moves out of the way for the paramedics to get to my mom. He looks over at me and I can tell that he is flashing back to Sadie. The paramedics are asking Mom if she remembers anything or knows what happened. The room is chaotic and I start going into a sensory overload. I shrink backwards into the hallway.

*I need silence.* I lock myself into my bathroom. *Another anxiety attack is on its way. I can feel it clawing its way through me.*

There is a small rap of knuckles on the other side of the door followed by Jimmy's soothing voice, "Gen, babe, they need to take your mom to the hospital for some imaging and maybe stitches."

After trying to compose myself, I step into the hall where the paramedics are helping Mom down the staircase. There is blood all over her face and shirt.

"What happened?" I turn to Jimmy trying to fight back the tears coming to my eyes.

"Someone threw a large rock through her window. It hit her in the head. Ramsey is making calls. There was a note attached to the rock."

"A note?"

"Um, yeah...we think it may have been David."

"What did it say?"

"Um...Blake wouldn't tell me. He is having more cops coming over though."

*It's almost three in the morning. I guess I won't be sleeping at all tonight.*

I take a deep breath and try to exorcize my tearfulness. My mother is going to the hospital because of something that was my fault.

*How am I going to live with myself if she gets hurt even worse because of me?*

This is already ripping my heart from my chest. I can't even imagine what is going through Jimmy's mind.

"Are you okay? I'm sorry that you had to deal with this, especially so soon after Sadie."

"Am *I* okay?! I'm more worried about *you*, babe. How are you?"

"I'm stressed…really, *really* stressed."

"It's okay. I'm here. I am not going anywhere, Gen."

Jimmy runs his hand repeatedly over my upper back to console me. Having his hands on me helps me feel at least a little better.

A few uniformed officers let themselves into my house and make their way to my mom's room upstairs. They start taking photos of the scene, especially of the broken glass and blood. Blake joins me in the hallway, shutting my mom's door behind him.

"Genevieve, can we go downstairs and talk?" He gestures toward the stairs.

"Um, sure…" We walk down the stairs to the kitchen. Ramsey sits back into his seat that he was at not too long ago while enjoying coffee with my mother.

"Do you have anywhere else that you can go?"

I can feel my body starting to seize up with panic.

"Um…why?"

"I don't think it's safe for you to stay here, not until we have David anyway."

"What about Mom?"

"I'll stay here and watch the house. I can keep an eye on her for you. Do you think you can go somewhere for a few days at least?"

"We can go to our apartment." Jimmy interjects, entering the kitchen.

"Okay, does anyone know where it is that might tell David?"

"No, we just got the keys today."

"Go there as soon as possible and *stay* there. I can contact your employers if you need to call in. Oh, and another thing Mr. Thompson. Can you promise me that you won't leave Genevieve alone?"

"I can absolutely promise you that without a doubt. We will go to the apartment first thing in the morning." Jimmy holds my hand.

*Hopefully Mom is going to be alright.*

"Is there any way that you could find out how Mom is? She doesn't have her phone."

"I'll make a call. Why don't you try to get some rest? I'll be here for the rest of the night keeping an eye on you."

"Thank you. Please let me know what you find out."

Back in my room, my chest feels like it may implode at any moment. Jimmy joins me in my bed. As soon as I feel his body holding mine, I snuggle in close and the tear dam breaks. I sob hard.

"Gen, babe, it's going to be okay. Try to get some sleep. I'm right here and Ramsey is here too, helping to keep you safe." He holds me firmly against him as I fade into sleep.

I wake up to bright sunlight drenching my room. Jimmy isn't in bed beside me though. I get up and I can smell coffee wafting up from the kitchen. I walk downstairs and see Ramsey sitting at the table with my mom. Her head is wrapped in bandages like a mummy in a B-rated movie. Bruising creeps down her face. She looks tired and fragile. I don't like seeing Mom like this. It makes me think of when Dad was sick. Jimmy is leaning against the counter, drinking his morning coffee. He looks so at home here. It makes my insides all warm and fuzzy.

"Hey, Mom. How are you feeling? Are you okay?" I rush over to wrap her up in a tight hug. I was so worried about her.

"It hurts, but I'm okay. I wasn't the intended target. He just had a tragic aim. I'm worried about *you. You* are the one he was looking for."

"Why me? Jimmy went to the cops first."

At this, Jimmy shoots me a look that screams '*Gee, thanks!*'

"We don't know yet why he is targeting you and not Jimmy. He may be trying to use you as punishment for Jimmy."

"Sadie wasn't punishment enough? He feels the need to hurt Gen, too? What did I ever do to him? We used to be something close to friends." Jimmy sounds concerned and bewildered.

"I think that he may see the relationship between you two as the greater threat. Perhaps because you two have what Sadie and him never could." Ramsey is making a lot of sense. "I am serious when I say that I want you two to go lock yourselves in somewhere for a few days. Jimmy, don't let her too far out of your sight either."

"I won't! I'm going to forewarn you that if he comes near her, I will probably end up with assault charges."

"They would be dropped because they would be counted as self-defense. I'm going to be staying here with Darcy to make sure that he doesn't come by. You two get your things together and get to your apartment."

*He is going to be staying here with Mom? Why do I get the feeling that he isn't having the most professional of intentions? Who knows? Maybe Mom will get some this weekend!*

## Jimmy

Detective Blake Ramsey is sitting at the Porter ladies' table with Darcy. His face looks exhausted, but the rest of his body isn't showing it. Blake's strong hand is resting on Darcy's forearm. He is making both of the ladies feel more secure. I hope that I can manage to have that effect on Gen. This whole mess with David is going to be terrible on her mental health. She tossed and turned beside me all night long. She kept whimpering like she was having a nightmare. I will do anything in my power to make sure that she stays safe and happy. Gen looks unbelievably nervous.

"Gen, I'll grab some stuff for you to bring with us. Spend some time with your mom." I head up to her room to grab a few of her last belongings that we didn't take over yesterday. Then it hits me that we don't have a bed there yet. Hopefully Dad can move mine today. Otherwise, we will be camping out on the floor.

As I look around Gen's lifelong safe haven, I can't help but to be overwhelmed with emotion. This room is where a large amount of her memories with Sadie were made. Leaving it must be so hard for her. Tears start falling as I continue thinking about Sadie. I open Gen's closet to double check that we didn't leave behind anything of importance. I move Gen's prom dress over to the other side of her closet to make sure nothing has fallen behind it. There, in black marker on the white wall, is a heart containing bubble letters spelling out James + Genevieve 4ever with red marker (or maybe lipstick?) off to the side saying XOXO, Sadie.

*I wish there was a way that I could take this with us.*

Once I have composed myself again and am certain that tears aren't lingering on my cheeks, I walk downstairs. The two ladies with the same vivacious laugh are housing carefree smiles on their faces. Blake is telling them some story about a guy that tried to run up the downward escalator during a chase at the local mall. Even though Darcy's face is bandaged and bruised, she is still just as beautiful as always.

*Genevieve is going to be just as beautiful as her mother when she is her age. A vision of a middle-aged Gen laughing beside me on the couch passes through my mind. I want more than anything to be the one making her laugh, now and forever.*

"I think everything is all set for us to leave whenever you're ready, babe."

Darcy does a little happy dance in her seat hearing me refer to Gen in that way. She is definitely our biggest fan. Gen's eyes are welling with tears. She nods with flared nostrils. I can tell that she swallowed hard to hold down an audible sob.

"Oh, honey! It's okay! You're not going to be separated from me forever. I'll see you again once this all settles down. Blake is going to be here to protect me. Please don't worry about me." Darcy hugs her daughter tightly.

"What if he isn't caught soon? What about Thanksgiving?"

"Genevieve, I promise that I will personally escort your mother to Thanksgiving to keep her from missing a holiday with you." Ramsey better be able to keep that promise or Gen will be completely crushed. I just wonder if he will be escorting her as her date or as her security detail.

"Bye, Mom. I love you. Please stay safe." Gen's eyes are beginning to water. Her voice is about to crack under the pressure of impending tears.

"I love you, baby girl. I'll call you later tonight." Darcy kisses Gen on the cheek before turning to me. "Jimmy, please take care of our girl. Neither of us will be able to handle it if something happens to her."

"You know that I will. Gen isn't going to leave my side." I lean down and give Darcy a small hug. "Come on, Gen. Our humble abode awaits." I hold my hand out for my gorgeous fiancee to hold onto.

After a nearly silent ride to our apartment, we go inside and look around. There is so much to be done. Maybe we will be able to keep our minds occupied with all of the unpacking and settling that we need to do. I lock the doors behind us and sit at the kitchen bar.

"Jimmy...what happens if they can't catch David?"

"They will find him. He is bound to trip himself up eventually."

"What if he hurts Mom again? Or one of your parents?"

"You heard Ramsey. He didn't mean to hurt your mom this time. He was just planning on scaring us."

"It definitely worked." Gen looks overwhelmed.

*Is it just everything with David bothering her or is it the apartment too?*

I want her to be as happy as possible right now. I pull her into a tight hug.

"No matter what happens, we will get through it together. I promise."

I kiss her on the top of her head. Her hair smells so strongly of her shampoo. That scent is enough to send my mind on a pheromone-fueled spiral. I touch my lips to hers and my tongue slips into her mouth. I'm already getting hard in my jeans from just this one kiss.

*Jesus, I need to calm down!*

I pull away from her quickly and immediately busy myself with unpacking a box of toiletries. I load my arms up and head to the bathroom to put them in the proper place. Once I empty my arms, I readjust myself within my jeans to make them fit better.

*Pull yourself together, Jimmy!*

I go back out to the main living space to find Gen laying flat on the floor, staring up at the ceiling. "Hey, crazy. What are you doing?"

"I can't wait until we have furniture in here. I'm trying to figure out how we should place the couch. Here would create a separate space from the dining area, but over there would open it up and make it look huge in here. Plus, this floor is super uncomfortable." Gen's hair is scattered out across the floor, around her head. Her fingers with their chipped polish are tapping a beat of some sort against her hip bone.

"We need to get a t.v. in here too. I can't wait for our bed to be here and ready for use!"

*Shit! Did that just really slip out of my mouth?*

"James Anthony! You're insinuating something, aren't you?" She narrows her eyes at me playfully. I wink at her.

"Well, I *am*...but, we don't need a bed to do that." I lower myself onto the floor beside this gorgeous girl. I wrap her hand in mine. She closes her eyes and scoots closer to me. I deeply inhale her scent again. It's such a comfort having her beside me. "Gen, I love you. I know that this isn't how we pictured this weekend, but if I have to be stuck in a house nonstop, I'm so glad that it's with you." She rolls onto her side, facing me and kisses me lightly. I close my eyes and smile.

"Can you find out if your dad can bring over the bed at least? Or maybe even an air mattress? Ooh and a laptop with movies?"

*We need to find out about getting wifi hooked up. Ugh there is so much to do, but I have zero motivation to actually do it.*

"Yeah, I am going to call him in our room."

"*We* have a room!"

She excitedly squeals and giggles. I'm glad she is able to find some positives. I beam at her and go to our new bedroom to call my dad. I close the door behind me while the phone rings.

"Hey, bud! What's going on?"

"Hey...um, so David threw a rock through Darcy's window in the middle of the night and it hit her in the head. She had to go to the hospital. Detective Ramsey ordered Gen and I to stay bunkered down at our apartment for at least a few more days. Can you bring us some stuff?"

"*What*? Is Darcy okay? Why didn't you tell me earlier?"

"She's bandaged up and stuff but she is okay. It happened in the middle of the night. I didn't want to wake you. But anyway, can you bring stuff over?"

"You could have woken me! Thank God she is okay! How is Gen?"

"She's trying to be okay...Dad, *focus*! Can you bring stuff over?"

"Sorry! Yes, of course! What do you need?"

"A bed of some sort...maybe a new tv...if I put in a pick-up order at Target, can you grab it for me?"

"Absolutely! Just let me know when it will be ready."

"Thank you so much! I'll see you later today."

After ordering enough stuff from Target to fill my dad's car, I find Gen sitting at the bar scrolling through her phone. Tendrils of hair are falling along her cheeks. Her sweet voice is humming some tune that I vaguely recognize. She is so beautiful.

"He is going to bring stuff over a little bit later." I stand behind her and glance at her phone screen. My eyes grow wide when I see what she is browsing. Her screen is covered with women in various skimpy lingerie. "What are you doing? Looking at porn?" I laugh lightly.

"No! I was just thinking about how I don't have anything sexy to wear for you ever. Now that we are in our own place, I'd like to have something. What kind do you like?"

"What kind do *I* like? How am I supposed to know? It's not like I have experience in that department. I already think that you are incredibly sexy." I kiss her gently on her neck.

"Hmm...you're telling me that you have never fantasized about a girl seducing you in lace or silk or even leather?"

"*Leather*, huh?" I raise an eyebrow at her with a sideways smile.

"So is that a yes? You want me in leather?"

"No. I didn't say that...I just thought it was interesting that you listed that option."

Gen gives me a skeptical look. "You've never had a fantasy about *any* girl seducing you?"

"I've fantasized about *you*...but, you were never in anything long enough for me to notice." I am now blushing very hard.

*Although she is mine now, it is still so new. I feel like I shouldn't be telling her this yet.*

She laughs gently.

"Take a look at these and see if you like anything in particular." She hands me her phone.

"You're asking me to look at pictures of other women half-naked?"

"Yeah. Why not?"

"You're okay with that? Some of those don't seem to leave much to the imagination."

"I don't care. It's not like they are people you know and could possibly touch and leave me for." I chuckle lightly.

*Nice logic, Genevieve.*

"There is no one that could ever make me leave you. You would make any of those look hot. Get whatever you want."

"I love you, James."

♪♪

Dad finally brought over my order from Target. I ordered food for us to eat for the next few days, a new television and DVD player, paper plates and disposable silverware. Once we have completely unloaded his vehicle, he pulls me into a tight hug.

"Jimmy, listen. Your mom and I are really worried about you and Gen. If David hurt Sadie like we think, what is stopping him from hurting either of you?" Dad's voice is shaking.

"Well, for one thing, he doesn't know where we live now. Ramsey has units doing drive-bys once an hour, just in case."

"Do me a favor. Use this time to spend with Gen and get some much needed one-on-one time. You won't often get days in a row where you get to just stay home and enjoy one another's company."

"I will, Dad. I promise. Please call me if anything weird happens at home."

"You know we will, son. Go inside and keep her safe. Love you, Jimmy." Dad swipes at his eyes as he gets back into his driver's seat.

It takes me a few trips to get everything inside from the front step. Once I triple check that the door is secured, I go looking for Gen. I begin to panic when I can't find her.

*Where the hell could she have gone? There are only four rooms here.*

When I enter our new bedroom, I don't see her at first. Then, I hear a tiny grunt from her. I follow the sound to the closet. Gen is perched on her tiptoes trying to set a duffle bag onto a shelf about a foot over her head.

"Gen, babe, what are you doing in here?" I smile as I slide up behind her, wrapping her into my arms. "Dad brought us over a ton of stuff."

As I help her finish placing the bag on the shelf, she leans her head back against me. After a large sigh, she turns around to face me. "I was just trying to feel like I was being productive. I am already going stir crazy and we just got here. How long do you think we are going to be stuck here?"

"I wish I knew the answer for you, Gen. I'd like for David to be picked up by Ramsey in the next ten minutes, but we both know that probably won't be happening. We will just bunker down for the long haul. I bought us some movies and a television. Plus, if your mind starts getting to you at all, I am here to distract you." I press my lips to the curve of her neck. "Come on, babe. Let's go unpack the stuff Dad brought over."

I watch as Gen stacks all of the movies in the corner. She seems to be concentrating really hard on that stack. There are only seven movies. They cannot possibly be *that* interesting to organize. I slowly walk up behind her and as I touch her on the shoulder, she jumps about a foot into the air and shrieks.

"Woah, Gen! *Chill*! I didn't mean to scare you. I was just making sure that you're okay. You seem a little out of it right now." She shrugs one shoulder half-heartedly and then pauses momentarily before she begins to sob. I pull her into my arms to attempt comforting her. "Genevieve, I'm right here. I promise. I know that everything is a mess right now, but I'm not going anywhere."

Instead of fixing her mood like I hoped, it seems that I made things worse. Her sobs turn into frantic wheezes. I do the only thing I can think of at the moment: squeeze her tighter. After what seems like an eternity, her sobs quiet down as her breathing slows and her body grows heavy in my arms.

Petting her hair with one hand, I use the other to lower myself onto the floor against the wall and pull her gently into my lap. Gen rests her head against the curve of my neck and closes her eyes. Soon, the quivering stops and her breathing becomes shallow. I place a gentle kiss to her forehead once I know that she is asleep. Leaning my head back against the wall, I close my eyes and drift off to sleep while I have my whole world asleep in my arms.

## Genevieve

I woke up from an incredible nap in Jimmy's arms. After crying my eyes out, that nap with the guy I'm crazy about is exactly what I needed.

*There is this horrible emptiness inside my chest. It feels as if someone opened me up, removed a large amount of my organs, and sealed me back up again. I am almost certain that if someone yelled into the void within my torso, their voice would echo back tenfold. How am I ever supposed to feel whole again?*

*We have gotten everything that Henry brought over pretty much placed in the proper homes. Jimmy has now mentioned us eating at least four times in the past two hours. I just keep shrugging or ignoring it altogether. The truth is that even the thought of food is turning my stomach instantly to bile. Between stressing about everything with Mom and my depression over losing Sadie, I can't think straight. My entire body feels like it is made of lead. I want to sink into a big blanket and stay there for days.*

*This apartment is starting to look more like a home, but it isn't feeling quite like home yet. I don't know if I will be able to fully embrace our new space until all of this David stuff is behind us. I really hate that guy. Why did Sadie have to fall for him? He was never deserving of someone as amazing as Sadie June Thompson.*

*Whenever I close my eyes, I see this angelic little face of a newborn looking up at me. It has bright, beautiful eyes just like Sadie's and a toothless smile. I wish I could have met Sadie's little baby. Jimmy and I would have loved that baby as if it was our own. The fact that she kept that tiny little human from me keeps coming back into my mind and stabbing me directly in the heart. We told each other everything for so long. How could I not have sensed that she was hiding so much from me? Damn it! I'm crying again already. This is going to be a very long day if I keep this up.*

I glance out the window and notice that the sun is just starting to descend for the evening. I turn toward Jimmy and try to hide my face as I quickly rush by him. Slamming the door behind me, I shut myself into the bathroom. I can feel one of my panic attacks coming on. I don't want Jimmy to see me this way any more. Locking the door to keep him out, I start the shower and undress. I sink into a ball on the icy tile floor and let the water beat down on me. I can feel the sobs coming and my chest tightening, but I don't fight it. Instead, I give in and allow it to consume me.

I lose track of how long I stay huddled on the floor, but it is long enough for my fingers to turn pruny. After I drag myself to my feet, I turn the water off and take a deep breath to equalize my emotions. The tears that had streamed down my face flawlessly blended with the shower water. No one would be any the wiser unless they looked at my eyes. If it were anyone else, I could simply explain away the red-rimmed and bloodshot eyes by blaming my shampoo. Jimmy, however, knows better. The shower offered me some much needed privacy.

As much as I am going to love living with Jimmy, there is one downfall that I can already sense. He is going to be on my emotions like white on rice for the foreseeable future. I brush my teeth and quickly drag a comb through my wet hair before leaving the bathroom to find some clothes. I shriek opening the bathroom door thanks to Jimmy standing in the dimly lit hall. I was not expecting him to be right outside the door.

"Are you alright? You were in there for almost an hour. I didn't want to bother you, but I kept getting worried." He reaches out, grabbing my wrists. He gently rotates each arm, inspecting it carefully. "Okay, there's no blood on your arms. That's good. Let me see your legs." He begins to bend down toward my ankles.

I am suddenly very aware of how utterly naked I am beneath this towel. I quickly grow self-conscious and pull away from his touch. The confidence that I had earlier with him left along with my positive attitude. When my mental health took a nosedive this afternoon, so did my bold attitude. I can see the hurt in his eyes that I pulled away from him. "I'm sorry, Gen. I was just so worried about what was happening in there and why you ran off on me. I freaked out even more since you ran off."

I cannot bear to meet his eyes. I stare at a small moth hole in his tee. "I'm sorry that I ran off like that. I just got really overwhelmed and needed a bit of time by myself to calm down." My voice is barely a whisper.

"Your mom called to check on you while you were in there. I told her the truth. I'm worried about you, like *really* worried. You had two crying episodes back-to-back, followed by locking yourself in the bathroom; not to mention that you haven't eaten anything. You need to eat. It will be too easy to fall into bad habits if you start skipping meals."

*I know that he's right. I don't want anyone to see how bad I still get sometimes. If I don't take it easy, I will end in a very bad place. I need to fight this, for Sadie and her baby. Hell, I need to fight this for Jimmy and I! We deserve to finally be happy together.*

I lightly kiss him and then go to our new bedroom to get dressed.

# Chapter Ten

## Jimmy

♪♫♪

*It has been three days since we moved into our apartment. It has also been three days since I have seen Gen smile or heard her melodic laugh. Darcy calls at least twice a day to check in on Gen. As much as I hate making her worry, I can't bring myself to cover for Gen's depression. I am too terrified of what might happen if I brush it off. Making it out to be less than it is could prove detrimental to Genevieve's health and well-being; if not, fatal.*

*Blake has had a whole lot of nothing turn up in the case. I would love to know how David freaking Jerome got so good at evading police officers. He has never been overly intelligent. Blake told us that he had a patrol car going past my parents' house every hour. They had a few sightings that they think may have been David, but he didn't appear menacing so they could not do anything. My mother has been radio silent since I moved out. She has not even attempted to contact me. Dad is, of course, being very helpful in this situation and giving me whatever sort of assistance I ask for.*

*Last night, Gen woke up screaming from a bad dream. Apparently she dreamed that David broke into our apartment and was trying to hurt her. She said he was leaving me alone. He wanted me to watch whatever he had planned for her. As soon as he started walking her way, she screamed and woke up drenched in sweat.*

*The furniture should be here this evening. I cannot wait to have real furniture instead of makeshift beds out of blankets on the hard floor. Gen cannot seem to even get up in the mornings. I have been watching her for four hours now and she has barely moved an inch. I am going to try and get her in sooner with the doctor. She needs help sooner rather than later. Depression has its hooks deep within her soul. There is no way that she can wait as long as they wanted her to. Waiting until after Thanksgiving for depression in someone who has previously been suicidal is ridiculous! Even if I have to take her to the emergency room, I will be getting her help long before that appointment.*

*When she thinks that I am asleep, she gets up and goes into the bathroom to cry. Each morning, I check her all over for cuts. I feel like an obsessive creep, checking her body for imperfections, but I need to know for certain that she isn't cutting again. I just lost Sadie. I will not lose Genevieve too. I am even keeping track of her eating habits. She has been eating barely a cup of food at each meal. I even had some of her favorite snack foods delivered, hoping to entice her with the junk food. Unfortunately, they had no such effect on her.*

*I feel so bad for Genevieve. She keeps complaining of a headache and being nauseous. She also says that she feels numb. How am I supposed to fix emotional numbing? I wish Sadie was here to help with this. She was always so good at getting Gen back to smiling. Even Gen's kisses seem depressed. Her lips are still like soft pillows, but over the last few days they always seem to hold a slight quiver as if she is going to cry at any moment. I wish I could fix her depression and make all of this go away for her.*

"Gen, do you want anything? I can put an order in for delivery."

She swallows hard before answering me, as if she is choking on her sadness. "Honestly, what I want can't be delivered."

"What's that?"

"Mom being able to come over...or Sadie back."

"Babe, I want those things too. I'm sorry that I can't give you those. Is there anything else I can get you?" I put her in a tight hug and press my lips gently to her collarbone.

"I could go for some Paper & Joe. Rhea's special, *Sade la 'vieve*...but, we don't have delivery." I cannot help but to chuckle. I have always loved that drink's play on words. It was the first drink that Rhea made where Sadie and Gen both actually loved it on the first try.

"Listen, if you really want one, I will go get one for you. You need to promise me that you're going to keep the door locked and you're not going to do anything dangerous while I'm gone."

*I promised Ramsey and Darcy that I wouldn't let her out of my sight, but I also want to give her what she wants. I would do anything to make her happier.*

Batting her lashes at me with a small smile, she promises that she will do what I asked. She also reminds me that David has no idea where we are. I am hoping that all of this will settle down soon. I miss being able to take Gen places to keep her mind off of

Sadie. I also miss the sense of ease that overcomes her when we are around Darcy. I give her a deep kiss before I leave our apartment.

Out front of Paper & Joe, I feel eyes on me. An unsettling crawl glides across my skin as I walk through the door. The chime signaling my entrance notifies Rhea that a customer is in her midst. She spins around and her face lights up when she notices me.

"Hey there, Jimmy! Where is our girl?" She looks out around me as if I could be hiding Gen behind me somehow.

"She is at home...um, at our apartment. She has requested a *Sade la 'vieve*." I lean against the counter as Rhea grabs a cup and draws a smiley face on the side with a permanent marker.

"Anything for Genevieve Thompson!" Rhea winks at me as she throws her black braid over her shoulder. A huge grin is taking over my face at the mention of that gorgeous girl taking my last name.

"How have things been here? Sorry that I had to steal Gen away again when she had just come back."

"Detective Sweet Thing stopped by to fill me in and see if I knew anything else."

"You mean Ramsey? He's dating Darcy! Did you know that?"

"What? No way! That lucky broad!" Rhea cackles as she concocts her java masterpiece. "Things are okay here though. I've got everything under control until she can come back." Once Rhea is done putting on the finishing touch of white chocolate shavings on top, she hands me the cup and refuses my money. "Just take that to our pretty lady for me. I don't want your money."

Walking back out to the car, I feel like I am being watched again. I glance around the surrounding area, but I don't see anyone. I shake it off and head back to the apartment. I park outside of our place and go to the front door. I am glad to find the front door still locked. I turn my key in the lock and call Gen's name. She must be either in the bathroom or our room because I don't see her right away. When I don't get a response after three times of calling her name, I go to our room to find her. She is laying on the bed, seemingly asleep.

"Genevieve, I have your drink." I kiss her lips lightly. She slowly stretches before opening her eyes. "Rhea says hi. She misses you." I hand her the cup.

She takes her first sip and lets out a satisfied moan. Hearing that awakens something inside of me.

*I have been pushing my desire for her down for the last few days. I do not want to act on my desires when she is feeling terrible. I love her so much. I just want her to get back to my normal Gen.*

I squeeze her hand and kiss her once between her sipping her drink.

"Thank you for getting this for me. It feels like I'm drinking a liquid version of home. I love you, Jimmy."

"I love you too. I will always get you anything you want." I sit beside her on the bed and get comfortable.

There is a knock at the door. Gen and I exchange a confused look.

*No one knows where we live now, so having an unannounced visitor is really odd.*

I shake my shoulders out like a boxer preparing for a round before going to the front door.

When I open the front door, I am face to face with none other than David Jerome.

"What the *hell* do *you* want, David?" I cannot contain my disdain for him. My voice practically comes out as a snarl.

"We need to talk. You should never have gone to the police."

"You *cannot* come in."

"Listen, we *need* to talk. Seriously." Just as I am about to slam the door in his face, I hear Gen's voice from behind me.

"Let him in. *He* wants to talk and *I* want answers."

Her arms are crossed and she looks pissed. I want to argue with her because this goes against all of my better judgment, but I cannot go against her wishes, not when she has had such a shitty week. I move aside and allow this asshole into our house.

Gen leads him to the barstools. He takes a seat beside her and I have to fight my muscles' urge to punch him.

*This must be why so many wild animals fight to the death defending their mate. This primal territorial urge to keep him away from her is so intense that it is almost mind-numbing.*

## Genevieve

"Alright, *dickweed.* Let me ask some questions before you say what you came to say. First of all, how the hell could you not want her baby? She was a fucking phenomenal soul."

*I am not going to take it easy on this asshole. He is in my territory now and I am on the offensive.*

He groans. "It wasn't that I didn't want to have *her* baby. I didn't want her to be stuck with *my* baby. Believe me, I know how amazing she was. I've *always* known. You probably won't think I mean it, but I love her." David is running his hands frantically over his face.

"You *love* her? *Really*? Then why the hell did you *kill* her?"

*Keep your voice down, Genevieve. Do not start yelling.*

"I didn't kill her! That is why you shouldn't have gone to the police. You opened a huge can of worms that you have no idea about."

"What the hell are you talking about? If you didn't kill her, how did you know where she died and why did you apologize afterwards?"

The father of Sadie's child has the audacity to start tearing up.

*This drug-dealing, rock-throwing asshole is really trying to make me feel sorry for him? Are you fucking kidding me right now?*

"Okay, listen...this is going to take a while..." Jimmy sits beside me, preparing for whatever we are about to find out. He runs his hand along my thigh to help ground me. "I've been dealing for a long time...a *really* long time, actually. The guy that used to be my supplier got sent to jail. His business was taken over by some guys from out of state. They demanded that I up my prices and said that it was going to be better quality shit..." David sighs heavily. His leg is bouncing frantically like a jackhammer. "Jack used to buy off me all the time, but occasionally he couldn't meet up when I was available. Those are the times that he would send Sade. We hit it off again immediately." He sniffles and wipes at his nose. "She kissed me first. As soon as our mouths touched though, it was like a dam let loose. I couldn't help it, Jimmy. She was...*ugh*, she was something special." A breathy sigh passes his lips as he remembers her.

"*We* know that she was special. You don't need to tell us that." Jimmy butts in, sounding like an obstinate child.

David holds his hands up in surrender. "Sorry, I know...anyway, we hooked up a couple of times when she was still messing with Jack. After they finished, I thought I had seen the last of her...that is when I got the call from her that she wanted stuff for herself. I didn't think that she used anything...the first couple times, she bought only weed. We would smoke a few bowls together and then she'd take the rest with her." His eyes are glazed over as he is reminiscing.

"One night, we were in bed together when she asked me if I could get her some pills. I was honestly shocked...she wanted stimulants and opioids. When I gave her the first baggie, she popped all of them in her mouth at once and dry-swallowed them...I couldn't believe it!" David's head is shaking in disbelief involuntarily. "She was...*crazy* when she was on the pills. She was intense and *oh God*, so fucking horny. She was insatiable." He glances at Jimmy and blushes a bit. Jimmy's expression is as hard and cold as stone. He is not impressed by these comments about his little sister.

"Sorry man...I know that's your sister...*anyway*, she kept that up for a few weeks and then she started asking for stuff to shoot up...I didn't want to give her any. I was worried about her. She told me that if I didn't give her some, she would turn me in to the police...so I gave her some. She shot up in front of me twice. Both times were some of the scariest moments of my life. Her head lolled back and she was limp like a ragdoll. She'd murmur something and then blindly grab for me. I hated seeing her like that. I told her I was done and wouldn't give her anymore...that was right around when she told me she was knocked up. Can you imagine that poor baby going through withdrawals from heroin? Even *dealers* have souls and some sort of boundaries. I told her that I thought she should get rid of it, but she didn't want to do that. She wanted to get married and have a family. Oh yeah, the strung-out barista and her dealer boyfriend would make for great parenting material." He shakes his head and looks at his feet to avoid eye contact. My brain is having a hard time computing this seemingly drug-obsessed version of Sadie June.

I wait a few moments for him to go on. "You still haven't explained how you knew where she died..." I mumble. He clears his throat and starts back up.

"We fought and fought about it. She kept getting pissed and pushing me. She was also withdrawing from the heroin and I refused to give her more poison while she was pregnant...we made up and we decided that we were going to keep the baby. We had decided to try and clean up our act...or so I thought." I'm holding my breath at this point. David draws in a shaky breath through his teeth. "I fell asleep after sex and when I woke up, she was gone...so were three vials of extra-concentrated heroin that was also laced with fentanyl. As soon as I noticed they were gone, I reached out to her but she wouldn't answer. I was so afraid that she had used it and overdosed somewhere. That was Sunday night. She ignored me all day long on Monday. I was so scared. On Tuesday, I texted her to meet in the woods and then I waited for her to show up.

When I got to our spot, she was already high. She was sitting on the log and had her sleeve rolled up. There was a drip of blood coming from her track mark still. She looked up at me and smiled as if she hadn't just done something horrible. Then, she smoked a small joint while we talked. We were talking about the baby and then I noticed everything about her started to change. She was growing agitated and stuttering. Her words were starting to slur.

I asked her if she used what she had stolen from me. She wouldn't answer...I was just *so frustrated* that I grabbed her by the shoulders and started to shake her like that would knock some sense into her or something. She stood up to try and push me away..."

He stifles a sob. His voice is shaking when he resumes. "She tried to push me, but started to slip by herself. I caught her, but her head snapped backwards and then she started seizing and fell to the ground. She smashed her head on the rock and then I panicked...she wouldn't answer me and there was *so much* blood. I didn't want her to get in trouble for the drugs, so I gathered everything illegal and ran like hell. I had no clue that she was dying. I would have tried to help her."

"You drugged her and left her to die?" Jimmy's voice is very loud in my ear.

*There is a rough edge to it that I am not used to hearing out of him. It's actually a bit frightening. I can hear a desire for violence in his voice. It sends a cold shiver down my spine.*

"*I* didn't drug her. She took the drugs herself. I didn't even *sell* it to her. She *stole* it, which is a *large* problem. The supplier was expecting those vials. The distributor of that stuff delivered it to me as a middle man. They were supposed to take what I had and split it into non-lethal doses. Those three vials were worth well over ten thousand dollars. Now they are going to be after me...especially when they find out the cops are involved." David's eyes are wild. I can see his frantic pulse in his neck. He is terrified.

"You may not have been the one who shot the poison into her veins, but she only had access to it because of you. It is still *your* fault, David." Jimmy's volume is still raised. "She was bleeding and seizing and you *left* her there. How the fuck can you claim that you loved her?"

David is crying. He honestly seems remorseful and grieving.

"It's the absolute worst thing I have ever done in my entire life. I cannot stop beating myself up about it. I am a piece of shit human being. I swear to you, I truly loved your sister. I still do. I miss her. I was actually really excited to give our relationship a real chance."

I am trembling and feel lightheaded. Something is really bothering me. "David, I have some questions..." He looks up at me and wipes his tears from his face. When I know that I have his undivided attention, I continue. "You said that Sadie asked you for pills and she swallowed them dry...Did she do that often?"

"She was taking random mixtures of pills every couple of hours or so this spring. The way she was acting though, it seemed like she did this before quite a bit. I don't really know when she started that or who else she was getting shit from." He shrugs and stares down at his hands.

"Sadie actually shot up in front of you? You physically saw her use the drugs?"

"Yeah, Genevieve. I did. I get that you're confused. I was too. I really still am. Sadie was so *vibrant*. She didn't need to do drugs. When she first asked me for the stuff, I thought she was just looking for a reason to keep seeing me. I wasn't expecting her to actually use it." He stares at the ground again for a few long moments of uncomfortable silence. Then, he looks up at us and looks very serious. "I want you both to know that I am really, really sorry. I didn't mean for this to happen. I would never have chosen to hurt her."

"Maybe not, but what about my mother?" A sudden surge of anger comes out of me with these words. He looks extremely confused.

"Your mom? I didn't touch her. I don't think I've ever even met her."

"That rock you threw into her window last night smashed her in the head, asshole. She had to go to the hospital last night. First, you turn my best friend into a drug-addicted bitch. Then, you kill her. Now you attack my mother. Well, guess what, *fuckhead*! I am not afraid of you nor do I feel sorry for you. I have so many things I want to say to you before I turn you into the police, so you're going to sit right there and fucking listen to *all* of it. You try to move and I will lay you out myself. If you think I'm kidding, go ahead and fucking try me."

David and Jimmy are both looking at me with horrified shock. I walk to our room quickly and get out a stack of photos from my suitcase. Returning to the men, I shove the pictures violently into David's hand.

"Go ahead and take a look at these pictures. That beautiful girl in those photos loved *you*, of all people, for some fucked up reason. She was happy, intelligent and hilarious. Sadie was all of the best parts of me. Now that I don't have her because of your idiocy, I am *no one*. I am a shell of the person that I used to be. I don't even know where to begin with living my life now that she is gone." Angry tears are streaming silently down my face. "She was *pregnant* with your child. She would have been the absolute best mother. Why the fuck did she decide to start keeping secrets from me after so many years? You never deserved her, you asshole. *Fuck*, I don't even know what she ever saw in you."

A smug look overtakes David's face as he thinks about his time with Sadie. He has the audacity to lick his lips at the memories. "She thought I was sexy and mysterious." He mumbles.

Before I realize what I am doing, I slap David across the face hard enough that the sound reverberates.

"What the fuck, bitch?" His volume is raised in an attempt to intimidate me. He starts to stand up and Jimmy is between us in the blink of an eye.

"Jerome, back the fuck up *now*!" Jimmy's voice has extra bass in it when he is being protective. "First, you fucking follow me and now you're considering putting your hands on Genevieve? You have obviously lost your motherfucking mind! You can go right ahead and explain to the police about what happened. Maybe they will let you off easily. If you put your hands on my wife though, I will fucking murder you myself. *Right. Now*." With each sentence, Jimmy is walking closer and closer to David until he is backed against the wall. "Gen, call Ramsey."

Not wanting to remove my eyes from where David is, I blindly grab my phone and dial my mother's number. She answers the phone and sounds winded. *Weird...*

"Is Detective Ramsey right there?"

"Um...yeah. B-b-blake, Gen is on the phone for you."

"Genevieve, is everything okay?"

"He's here at our apartment."

"I will be right there!" Ramsey sounds frantic and...*equally winded?*

*Oh my God! Were they...? No! No, definitely not! Right...?*

"He's on his way." Then, my brain finally processes what Jimmy just said. "Wait, did you just call me your *wife*?"

Jimmy's anger disappears for a moment and is replaced by a joyful grin that puts a twinkle into his green eyes. "Yes. Yes, I did." I flash him a small grin before he turns to look at David again. "You hear that, dickwad? The detective investigating Sadie's death is on his way here to haul your ass into the police station."

"He has no reason to take me in. I didn't kill her."

"Maybe not, but you left her there bleeding and didn't get her help. Plus, you are the reason she had access to the drugs."

"You don't seem to get it, Jimmy. I am going to be killed over this. It won't matter if I'm in jail or not. Nowhere is safe for me now. The product that Sadie stole was worth more than my life is to them." David runs his hands over his face. "Actually, you know what? Let him come and take me. Maybe I can delay my own death for a while." He leans back in his seat. He glances around the apartment, taking in his surroundings. "This is a cute little place. It's a bit...*empty*."

"We haven't really gotten a chance to move our stuff in yet since we were forced into hiding by *someone*." I shoot David a dirty look. "It will be really nice once we can actually get our stuff all together. God, I cannot *wait* for Ramsey to haul your ass in. Then I can get out of these godforsaken walls again!"

"Can I use your bathroom? You know before he gets here?"

I glance in the direction of the bathroom and then back at Jimmy. He shrugs half heartedly. "Let him. I don't want him to piss himself."

As David is finishing up in the bathroom with Jimmy standing guard, there is a knock at our front door. I take a deep breath before opening the door. Ramsey comes flying into our apartment.

"Where is he? By the way, your mother is beyond sick with worry." He appears rather disheveled.

"He's in the bathroom...Jimmy is making sure that he isn't trying to run. Detective, were you and my mom...fooling around?"

He doesn't answer me with his words, but his face turns a flaming shade of scarlet. Ramsey rushes down the hall to the bathroom. He practically pushes Jimmy aside and flings the bathroom door wide open. David lets out a shout and quickly zips his pants up.

"Mr. Jerome! You are a difficult man to track down. You're coming with me now though. First, we are going to have a discussion about Miss Thompson. Then, depending on how well that goes and how much cooperation I get from you, we will discuss what charges you'll be getting."

"Charges? You're arresting me?" *David actually seems surprised. How dumb is he?*

"At the very least you are going to be arrested on assault charges, harassment charges and dealing."

"You have nothing on me."

"Nothing? I have personally seen the rock and note you threw last night that injured Darcy Porter. I have also run the phone records from when you called Genevieve. I have an inkling that I can get you on stalking as well since you showed up here."

Ramsey manhandles David out of our apartment to his car. All I can do is stare behind him with my entire body trembling from the adrenaline rushing through my bloodstream. After several long moments, I sink to the floor. I feel numb all over.

"Do you think this is over? Do you think we'll get the truth from him?" I murmur to Jimmy.

"I hope so, but honestly I have no idea." His voice sounds smaller than usual. Almost like he is closing in on himself. I turn my head to look at him. He hasn't moved since Ramsey walked David out.

"Jimmy, babe, are you okay? Talk to me." I reach out for him. He looks like he is in a trance.

"Um...I don't really know. I am feeling...*a lot* right now."

I close the distance between us and wrap my arms around his waist and rest my cheek against his chest. "Me too." I start to get a little choked up. "I am glad that Ramsey has him, but I'm scared that they won't be able to make anything stick. I am also happy that David seems to have actually known how wrong he was for Sadie, but I keep thinking about that poor little baby."

"I feel...relieved, but still apprehensive. I just want justice for Sadie June."

We stand, holding one another like this, for another five or ten silent minutes. I break the silence by letting out a breathy chuckle. "Um...did you happen to get a good look at Ramsey while he was here?"

"He looked like he had just gotten out of bed. His hair and clothes were all messy. That seems so odd for him. Doesn't it?"

I laugh louder and longer this time. "Well...I'm pretty sure he was a little...*preoccupied* with my mom when I called him."

Jimmy's face slowly transforms from confusion to grinning like the cat that got the canary. He bursts out in gleeful laughter. "Good for him! Hell! Good for her, too!"

I join in the laughter. It feels really nice to laugh. Laughing makes life seem a little more normal. Suddenly, a wall of exhaustion hits me. I let out an exaggerated yawn.

"Gen, let's go lay down."

I let Jimmy guide me to our room. I may be able to actually sleep now that I know David is in Ramsey's hands.

## Jimmy

♪♪

After David being dragged out of our house, Gen and I went to bed. We ended up soundly sleeping all through the night. I wake feeling refreshed. Easing myself out from bed beside Gen, I head to the kitchen where my phone is charging. A message from Dad is blinking in my notifications.

I listen to the voicemail that he left me. According to my phone, he left the message at two in the morning.

"Jimmy, great news! Detective Ramsey called us. David has been arrested on trespassing, harassment and intent to distribute. He said some more charges are in the works, but you two are safe now. He can't get to you. Also, he said that when they were questioning him, they found out some more information on Sadie. Call us sometime tomorrow to check in. We love you, James. *Both* of you."

*Once Gen gets up, I am taking her out on a date. I am taking her anywhere she wants to go. Even if I have to drive for hours, I will get her where she needs to be to feel happy.*

♪♪

*Gen woke up with a new sense of comfort and ease in our new life together. After slowly making love, we took a relaxing shower together with a lot of wandering hands. Those wandering hands led to more time in bed together before leaving for our date.*

*We got coffee, walked at the park with quite a few kissing stops, and decided to drive out of town for a late lunch. The highway was pretty fast-moving today. After driving for two hours, we found a nice little restaurant tucked away in a cove of evergreens that had wonderful food and a homey atmosphere. We managed to get through our entire meal without a single mention of Sadie or David. The pulsing energy that has always been between us is heavily noticeable today. It feels like we are coming out on the other side of this ordeal with our bond stronger than ever. I cannot wait to see what the future has in store for us.*

♪♪

We are almost back to our apartment from going on our mini-road trip. The only light coming into the vehicle is the sporadic street lights and occasional headlights of a passing car. Gen is resting her head back with her eyes closed. The dashboard light is barely cascading over her face, but it's enough for me to admire her features. Right now, she looks peaceful. There is no crinkling in her brow or a grimace on her lips. She seems content.

After parking at our place, I snap a quick photo of her in this melancholy state before I lightly shake her shoulder to wake her up. Rubbing her eyes, she lets out a yawn and then does a small and very uncoordinated stretch of her arms above her head. Forgetting she is in my car, she smacks her hands on the ceiling.

She whines, "*Owwww*", in the most pitiful slumber-drunk voice. I can't stop a small chuckle from escaping my lips.

"Gen, come on. Let's get you inside and into bed." Climbing out of the vehicle, I head to her side of the car and help her up to the front door. She leans on me the whole way and stumbles a couple of times, half-asleep. Inside the apartment, she flops herself onto our bed and is back asleep almost instantly.

*This is great. She needs some quality sleep.*

I climb into bed beside her and scroll through photos on my phone. I come across quite a few of Gen and Sadie together.

*The good news is that tonight I don't get the sharp pain of someone stabbing me in the chest each time that I see my sister's face. The bad news though is that now I am looking at these photos from a different perspective, knowing everything that I learned from David.*

*The photos from the last year or so show off the changes in Sadie that we managed to miss. Her hair looks more brittle and frizzy in the more recent photos. Her skin is much greasier in them, too. There are bags that progressively got worse. Long sleeves were worn a lot more frequently, too. How did we manage to miss all of this? It all seems so obvious now.*

"Sadie June, who were you *really*? I never thought I would ever say that I didn't know the real you, but now? I'm not so sure that I truly knew you at all."

*Look at me, sitting here talking to my dead sister...I must be going nuts. I need to stop that nonsense before people start believing it.*

I keep scrolling through the photos until my eyelids begin to grow heavy. Gen is curled up beside me like a warm invitation to snuggle.

*I will gladly take her up on that offer.*

# Epilogue

## Genevieve

*Our apartment smells heavenly with the scents of Thanksgiving dinner wafting about. Our parents will be arriving soon to eat and celebrate the holiday as one large family.*

*Since David has been arrested, we have gotten ourselves settled into our little home. We are working daily to make it have the feeling that we want with our personal touches. Jimmy surprised me two days ago with a shadow box that is now hanging in our living room. It has a piece of my closet wall from Mom's house inside of it. He carefully, with Mom's permission, cut out the part where Sadie wrote our names in lipstick. Also, there is the photo inside of the shadow box from the movie theater on our very last night together as a trio. That is hands down my favorite piece of decor gracing our apartment.*

There is a knock at the door. I giddily glide over to the front door. Swinging it open with a huge smile on my face, I greet all of our guests at the door. The Thompsons come in carrying their contributions to today's feast. They are smiling, but it is subdued. There is no doubt that today is hard on all of us without Sadie, but I am going to try and keep my head up.

Directly behind Jimmy's parents, my mother walks in and hands her desserts to Blake before hugging me tightly. "Genevieve, I love you so much. Happy Thanksgiving!" She nearly squeals with delight.

Once we are all sitting around the table, loading up our plates, Blake fills us in on the situation with David. "We have him in custody on numerous charges with more that are likely to be added once more evidence is collected. He has fully taken responsibility for all of it so far. He is pleading guilty to all of it. He also asked me to pass along his apologies for all of the turmoil he caused. Losing Sadie was the beginning of his punishment. David told me that anything else we deal out to him now will be extremely easy to get through."

This was all very welcome news. Sadie is getting some sort of justice and it seems that David did truly love her. Once all of the plates are loaded up with food, we take turns stating what we are grateful for this Thanksgiving.

Maryann is grateful for the love and support she has received throughout her grief so far. She is also grateful that Jimmy and I are making one another happy.

Henry thanks all of the stars above for the health of his remaining family and for David Jerome's cozy holding cell. He gave a special shout out to his lovely wife which made her tear up.

Blake's thankful for his acceptance into our family. He used his turn as an opportunity to announce that he and Mom are moving in together.

"Yes, we know it is really fast, but if you know, you know." He shrugs with a lopsided grin and squeezes Mom's hand adoringly.

My mother is blushing like a schoolgirl when she states that she is thankful to have finally found a man that makes her miss Dad a lot less. She never thought that she would let another man into her bed, but Ramsey changed all of that. She can actually picture herself getting remarried someday to her *"hunk of a detective"*, as she nauseatingly calls him.

Jimmy looks as though he may start bursting at the seams when it is his turn to speak. He is grateful for all of us around this table, the house that we share and the fact that he finally is able to call me *his*. To finish his speech, he beams at all of our guests. "Also, we have officially set the date for our wedding! We will be getting married on January 15th in the atrium of the library."

Suddenly, the parents break out into happy chatter discussing how happy they are that we set a date and all of the things that we need to do before the wedding. There is so much joyous conversation that my turn is almost skipped. I clear my throat to get their attention. They all look over at me.

"Um, I didn't get to go yet." They stammer out some apologies. I smile sheepishly. "I am thankful for all of you and for Jimmy. Without any of you, I wouldn't be able to live without Sadie by my side. As you know, I have struggled with my mental health in the past and throughout this whole ordeal." There are some polite nods being offered around the table. "I wasn't supposed to see my doctor to get on medication again until next week sometime, but her colleague had a last minute cancellation yesterday. I went in and was able to address my concerns. I am so incredibly thankful for that."

My mouth is really dry now, so I pause to sip at my water. I hold my finger up while I drink to let them know that I'm not done yet. I swallow and shakily set my glass down. "So, anyway, she let me open up to her about a lot of the thoughts that have been running through my mind since Sadie passed. The main one has been *'Sadie June, who were you?'*. I have been asking myself this constantly since the entire David thing came to light. Did I truly know her? Was she just really good at keeping secrets? Yesterday, I finally got my answer." The whole table is staring at me with a sense of wonder and seem to be on the edge of their seats waiting to hear what that answer really is.

"Sadie June was my best friend and best half of myself. Whether she hid things from me towards the end or not, nothing will ever change the fact that we were kindred souls. She was and always will be a huge part of my life. Sadie June is now gone, but she will forever be in my heart. She is also a mother *and* an aunt."

Every jaw at the table drops open, including Jimmy's. This is the first time that I've mentioned it at all to him. There are five pairs of eyes beginning to water up with the news that we will be adding a new Thompson to the family. All I can do is beam happily.

*Did you hear that, Sadie? We are officially family for life, just like you always wanted us to be!*

# Bonus Chapter

## Jimmy

**January 15th**

*It is so hard to believe that today is finally the day that I will make Genevieve my wife. In a way, it feels like this has been in the works for such a long time; however, it also seems like the holidays flew by after the announcement at Thanksgiving dinner.*

Standing in the library's ornate atrium surrounded by our loved ones, I am stuck in limbo between feeling like I am about to fly away like I am in a Red Bull commercial and like I am about to pass out from the anticipation.

Janet comes giddily around the corner and steals a quick hug from me before whispering in my ear, "Your wife is stunning!"

A moment later, Darcy walks down the makeshift aisle toward me. She is sniffling and wiping at the tears in her eyes delicately. She flashes me a huge smile and then takes her place beside Ramsey.

A soothing instrumental version of *You'll Be In My Heart* starts quietly filling the atrium's vaulted ceiling. My eyes are trained directly on the hall where Gen will be entering. I can't even blink in fear that I might miss even a moment of her approaching me at the altar.

Gen rounds the corner wearing a white floor length satin sheath dress with a scoop neckline. She is carrying a single burgundy chrysanthemum in her hands. Her hair is hanging in loose curls around her face which is shimmering from makeup. The lips that I adore kissing are coated in a plum lipstick.

As soon as I see her, my chest tightens up and my eyes start to burn with tears. She is so damn beautiful. Once she is almost to me, she finally glances up from the floor and makes eye contact with me. The air in my lungs wooshes out of me as our eyes meet. I am beaming at her. When she gets a little closer to me, she lifts the hem of her dress a bit so that I can see which shoes she is wearing. Underneath her wedding gown, she is rocking her Chuck Taylors that are adorned with my sister's handwriting all over them. We covered the handwriting in epoxy so that they won't get washed away.

Once our vows are finished, I get to finally kiss her. I lace one hand through her hair at the base of her skull and the other I place lovingly on her newly formed teensy baby bump as I pull her into a deeply meaningful and passionate kiss. To most people, they wouldn't be able to tell if it's a pregnancy or if she just ate too much food at lunch with how small it is at the moment. Her mother and I, however, know her too well to mistake it for a food baby. Her dress is a bit snug in that area, so it is showcased a bit more. Our loved ones clap and cheer for us as our lips intertwine. Instead of walking back down the makeshift aisle to exit, we walk away from our guests and toward the side study that is used as an event space. The guests follow us to begin our reception.

Our wedding guest list is a very intimate one. The only people in attendance are my parents, Darcy, Blake, Janet and Rhea. The hall is still decorated from Christmas with large prelit garland strung around the ceiling and from the ornate fireplace mantles. We have a small buffet set up for everyone to eat and we are all seated at one long wooden table that runs the length of the room. Low instrumental music is playing in the background as we eat and mingle.

Each guest takes a turn giving a speech after Janet clinks her knife lightly against her glass of sparkling cider. Janet stands at her seat and chooses to go first. Turning a sweet smile and twinkling eyes toward us, she places her hand on her chest before beginning to gush about us.

"Jimmy Thompson, the boy who interned once and never left, has become one of my favorite people not only at this library but also in the world. I spent *years* in his company listening to him spill his heart out about his little sister's beautiful best friend." I blush as she chuckles at my embarrassment. "After all of that pining finally brought something to fruition, I couldn't hold back my glee for this wonderful union between these two souls. Genevieve, you are the *entire* world to this man and don't you ever forget that! He will move mountains for you if you ask him to. If the two of you ever need anything at all, I am here for you no matter what. I love you both and I love your *love*. Congratulations to you both and that amazing little bundle of joy that you're growing."

Everyone claps as she takes her seat. Rhea stands next. She has to clear her throat and wipe away tears before she can speak. "Wow, Gen. What the hell can I say that will wrap all of my thoughts and feelings for you both up into a pretty bow?" A small laugh is followed by a huge exhale and shaking out her body. "You and Sade will *always* be my favorite duo. *But*, my second favorite is definitely you and Jimmy. Something about a Porter and Thompson combination just hits different! *Speaking of a Porter and Thompson collaboration*, have I mentioned how damn *stoked* I am about your baby? I absolutely cannot wait to spoil the shit out of that little one and I am very serious that I want you to bring the baby to work with you anytime that you want to. Congratu-freaking-lations, Mr. & Mrs. Thompson!"

Once the clapping is done and she is seated, Blake stands up to do his talk. "I know that I'm the latecomer to this amazing group, but I have never been so honored or touched to be included. We all know that I absolutely hate the turmoil that led to our introductions, but I am forever going to be thankful that I now have you all in my life. Genny Girl, I know that I will never be a replacement for your dad and I would never want to do that anyway; however, I am so in love with the way that you have openly embraced me as a new man in your mother's life. You have made me feel like I am truly welcome." This is making Gen tear up. "Thank you so much for including me today and every day. Congratulations to you both."

As Blake sits down smiling, he kisses Darcy who is blubbering too hard to talk next. My dad stands up and is beaming from ear to ear. "Today is one of my proudest moments as a father. James is officially married to an amazing woman that was personally handpicked for him by our Sadie June. She has been helping bring this marriage into being for so many years. I am so happy that he has found his *person*. Genevieve, you know that you've been my second daughter for many years, but now that you are truly a Thompson, I couldn't be happier. Welcome home, bonus daughter!" He comes over and plants a kiss to the top of Gen's head. She is silently crying while never breaking her smile.

Mom blows her nose and then stands up while crying. "I am a basket case which unfortunately seems to be my normal now. Genevieve, you are the absolute best match that I could ever imagine for James. I have loved watching you grow from that eleven year-old who giggled all the time with Sadie to the beautiful and courageous woman that you have turned into. I cannot wait to watch you transition into your wife and mother era. I love you both so much. Congratulations on your wonderful new adventure together."

Darcy lets out a soggy laugh as she stands up. "Sorry. I guess I'm the only one left, huh? I will try to stop crying long enough to get through this. I have spent so many hours listening to Gen say so many amazing things about Jimmy over the years. She has been head-over-heels for him for so long that this day has felt inevitable. Gen, your father would have adored Jimmy. They have so much in common, but most of all, their unending love for *you*. Jimmy, I can never thank you enough for how happy you make our girl and how determined you are to keep her safe. That baby is going to be the luckiest kid in the world to have such a united team for parents. I am so proud of you both. I love you so much."

Gen squeezes my hand as she stands up. "Thank you all so much for coming and supporting us in this. I am so happy to be Mrs. James Thompson now, but my heart is moments from crumbling. I cannot stop thinking about how Sadie should be here laughing with us. She should have done my makeup for today and been my maid of honor. Today has been such a hard day for both of us. We miss her so much. Jimmy, I will love you for the rest of my days and this amazing little one."

Gen places both of her hands framing her adorable bump and smiles down at me. I pull her into me and kiss her tenderly. She eases herself into her seat beside me. I stand up to address these wonderful humans that have graced us with their blessings.

"I have been dreaming of the day when I would finally be able to call Genevieve *mine* for years and years. The fact that she is my *wife* is something that I will never stop being incredibly grateful for. We love you all so much and are so lucky to have all of you. My beautiful little sister brought her best friend into our home and simultaneously into my life. Unbeknownst to all of us, she was setting the wheels of fate into motion." I am starting to tear up, so I look up to the ceiling as I blink away those tears. Keeping my eyes to the sky, I say, "Sadie June, thank you so very much for the absolute best gift that you ever gave to me. Keep watching over us until the end of our days."

As I take my seat, I close my eyes and have the vivid image of Sadie giving me a small wave on her way into the woods on that very last morning. I smile to myself and let the tears fall.

# Acknowledgements

Thank you to all of those who have supported my writing. Without your encouragement, I would probably never feel confident enough to put my work out into the world.

Taylor Ashely

# About The Author

Taylor Ashely is a lover of everything related to books. Words are her comfort zone. She is a married mom of five crazy children. While writing is one of her favorite things, so is autumn and Christmas. Romance is her go-to when she is writing, but she has been known to dabble in poetry, journalism and more.

Check out her Lawton Crew series on KindleUnlimited and Amazon, too!

www.ingramcontent.com/pod-product-compliance
Lightning Source LLC
LaVergne TN
LVHW010629110826
845149LV00014B/2814

* 9 7 9 8 9 9 5 4 5 3 8 0 2 *